AS CLOSE TO US
AS BREATHING

This Large Print Book carries the
Seal of Approval of N.A.V.H.

As Close to Us As Breathing

Elizabeth Poliner

THORNDIKE PRESS
A part of Gale, Cengage Learning

GALE
CENGAGE Learning·

Farmington Hills, Mich • San Francisco • New York • Waterville, Maine
Meriden, Conn • Mason, Ohio • Chicago

GALE
CENGAGE Learning®

LIBRARY OF CONGRESS CATALOGING-IN-PUBLICATION DATA

Names: Poliner, Elizabeth, author.
Title: As close to us as breathing / by Elizabeth Poliner.
Description: Large print edition. | Waterville, Maine : Thorndike Press, 2016. |
    © 2016 | Series: Thorndike Press large print reviewers' choice
Identifiers: LCCN 2016013153| ISBN 9781410490773 (hardcover) | ISBN 1410490777 (hardcover)
Subjects: LCSH: Sisters—Fiction. | Jewish women—Fiction. | Life change
    events—Fiction. | Large type books.
Classification: LCC PS3616.O5673 A9 2016 | DDC 813/.6—dc23
LC record available at http://lccn.loc.gov/2016013153

Published in 2016 by arrangement with Little, Brown and Company, a division of Hachette Book Group, Inc.

Printed in Mexico
1 2 3 4 5 6 7 20 19 18 17 16

For my parents

and for the family,
Madnick, Matzkin, Pashalinsky, Poliner

You are as close to us as breathing, yet
You are farther than the farthermost star.
> — *Gates of Prayer:*
> *The New Union Prayer Book*

PART ONE

1
An Inheritance of *Here*

The summer of 1948 my brother Davy was killed in an accident with a man who would have given his own life rather than have it happen. The man was Italian, and for my mother, Ada Leibritsky, that was explanation enough for why he was a killer. Had he been Irish, she would have said the same. Had he been Polish, or Greek, or even some kind of Protestant, she'd have likewise put the blame on that. Back then it was common enough to think this way, to be suspicious, even hateful, of outsiders, and the Negroes and Jews got the worst of it. So had the man been Jewish, like us, I've often wondered if in her mad grief my mother would have attributed the killing to that. *Kike,* she would have called him in her rage, not noticing that in so doing she'd have missed entirely that it was us, her family, a whole body of Jews, who were more to blame than anyone else.

■ ■ ■ ■

The summer began typically enough. We arrived at our beach cottage in Woodmont, Connecticut, and my mother flew from the car, determined as always to be the first inside, leaving the rest of us — her three children, her older sister, and her only niece — behind. She rushed up the porch steps, unlocked the door, and strode into the living room. The place was dim, with shades drawn and lights off, and the air was stuffy from three seasons of windows locked shut. Still, from the way she breathed, gulping in the unstirred air as if it were fresh from the shore, you'd think she'd been starved for the stuff. From the living room she looked behind her, at me, on the porch, reluctant to follow her lead until at least one window had been cracked. "Oh, Molly," she said in a voice that was almost scolding. "We're here. *Here.* What in the world are you waiting for?"

We'd almost not gotten there, at least that week, the first one in July, for my father had been sick with a cold over the weekend and couldn't drive us to Woodmont from our home in Middletown. On Monday he'd felt better but had to go to work. Monday night, after a glum dinner — my mother, two brothers, and I sighing dolorously and effectively throughout — my father had suggested that my older brother, Howard, just graduated from high school, could drive us the next day, Tuesday, as long as he came back on Friday to pick up my father and our uncle Leo for the weekend.

From Middletown we'd be two families in the car: ours and my mother's sister Vivie's. But neither woman could drive. Neither could their other sister, Bec, who was to meet us there, traveling from New Haven.

Howard, then, was our only hope. He promised my father that he'd come back on Friday early, in time to join the morning minyan.

My father was a serious man; everyone knew that. But Howard's words made him beam with joy. Still, he leaned forward, peered over his glasses, and warned, "Howard, sometimes all a man has is his word."

"Here's mine," Howard said, his voice confident, his tone sincere. The two shook hands. Then the whole family, especially Howard, cheered.

But upon our arrival at Woodmont, Howard was less genial, more himself. As he stood by my father's old Dodge station wagon, unloading suitcases, he yelled, even to our mother, "Hey, nitwits, get your fat fannies over here and *help.*"

My mother didn't budge. At forty years old she was still the family beauty, her mass of mahogany hair, pinned up, only just beginning to sprout the occasional gray. A middle child, she was the most forceful of the three Syrkin sisters, and the most opinionated, which had something to do with her beauty, the extra confidence it gave her. She was the certain one, the one who told us that Bess Truman's idea about her daughter, or any daughter, was right: she should most definitely not become president. And in our world of interethnic hatred, she was the one, spewing forth slurs, who could hate right back. But at that moment, even though from the living room she'd heard Howard well enough — a rudeness he'd never dare in front of our father — she was silent and statuesque, her big black pocketbook, a near appendage of weathered patent leather, dangling from the crook of her bent elbow, her back straight, her head raised, her eyes once again closed, her whole being seemingly intoxicated by the cottage's oppressive air.

A moment later, though, she came to and charged through the front doorway. She'd just returned to the porch and had opened her mouth to address Howard — *apologize, I hoped she'd say* — when her eye caught the mezuzah nailed to the doorframe, its pewter casing glinting from the sun. At the sight of it she closed her mouth, was silenced.

Even though he was a religious man, my grandfather Maks Syrkin had waited to nail the mezuzah there until he'd paid off the cottage's mortgage in June of 1939. *For value received, we the undersigned, Maksim and Risel Syrkin, hereby agree to pay to the order of The Bank of New Haven $3,600. . . .* The mortgage papers were dated 1915, which put him at twenty-four years in violation of Jewish law: *and you shall inscribe these words upon the doorposts of your house and upon your gates.* Yet for all those years my grandfather, who never missed a mortgage payment, didn't consider the cottage his home. Like his house in Middletown, the Woodmont cottage was not a home until every last cent of it had been paid for, he'd told his family again and again, and then he'd told the Woodmont neighbors — Jews all of them — and then, once we were born, he told us, his grandchildren, though we were too young then to understand the rules of Judaism much less the rules of real estate.

I remember my grandfather Maks as a strange old man.

Howard, still by the Dodge, continued his rant. "Is this Egypt? Is that sand out there the desert?" he called. I was still on the porch, by my mother's side, and from there I watched Howard point ahead, toward the beach and Long Island Sound. "What am I," he continued, "your goddamned slave?"

Our cousin Nina, then fifteen, was the one to yell back to him, "You're the one treating *us* like slaves!"

Howard wasn't the only one startled by Nina's remark. I was too, for Nina had been virtually silent the entire road trip from Middletown to Woodmont, paging through Darwin's *On the Origin of Species* the whole hour. "Is it good?" I'd interrupted once to ask. I also liked to read, but mostly about twelve-year-old girls, like myself. Nina's answer was quick. "Fantastic," she'd said, her face, heart-shaped and pretty, tense with concentration. But until she rebuked Howard she'd not said a word since.

Following her remark, Nina simply stopped, halfway between the car and the cottage. Like her mother, she was short, and her hair, the same thick and unruly brown mane of all the women in the family, was pulled back with a ribbon. She wore shorts and an unusually tight summer jersey. You could see that she already had a marvelous figure, even at fifteen. But from everything I knew about Nina I was certain the jersey wasn't tight for effect; Nina was just too absorbed with the likes of Darwin to notice. My mother had a saying about Nina: "She's too smart for her own good."

It was Howard who couldn't take his eyes off the tight shirt. "Hey Nina, can you and your bazooms hike it over here?" he said next.

"That's brilliant, Howard. You're a genius, aren't you?" Nina snapped back. She strode over, arched her neck, and even though she blushed, she looked him straight in the eyes.

Everyone knew Howard's grades didn't compare to Nina's.

"Ouch, ouch," he teased, reaching behind her as if threatening to snap her bra strap.

"Don't be an ass," she told him, then slapped Howard's arm down.

For a moment it looked as if a fight, as much physical as verbal, would break out between them. But the tension eased when my aunt Vivie rushed off the porch to step between the two, who were often enough at odds with each other. The problem, or so it seemed, was generational: everyone knew my mother had stolen my father from Vivie, and though the sisters no longer fought with each other, their respective firstborns — like biblical characters, born into their animosity — seemed unable not to.

"Don't be mean," Vivie told Howard calmly, her hand on his shoulder. "We just got out of the car. Give us a minute, won't you, to stretch our legs?"

My mother still wasn't paying attention to the goings-on by the Dodge. Rather, transfixed by the sight of the mezuzah, she reached up and touched the pewter casing. Then she brought her hand to her lips and kissed the fingers that had reached for the words of God. But she wasn't religious, I knew, only nostalgic. She would have preferred just then to have touched the skin of her father rather than the metal of the mezuzah's casing, but Maks had died six months after that last mortgage payment in 1939. My mother, Ada, was thirty-two years old then and heavily pregnant with my younger brother Davy, her third child. Maks was seventy-four.

A Friday morning, cloudy, the last week of June 1939, and Maks held the mezuzah in one hand, a hammer in the other. In his shirt pocket were any number of slim nails, and in his left pants pocket were eight more

encased mezuzot, enough for all the door-
ways inside and the back door. Risel, his
wife, the woman to whom he'd been
matched all those years ago in his birth
town of Balta, the woman whom he'd
returned to Balta to fetch some five years
after his start in America, a woman transformed by her journey across the world
from a confident Russian girl to a bewildered and dependent American wife, a
woman whom Maks loved endlessly nonetheless, was to have the privilege of holding
the first mezuzah, to be nailed to the front
entrance. We had all gathered on the cottage porch: Maks and Risel, my mother and
Vivie and Bec, and the grandchildren then
born — Howard, Nina, and a three-year-
old me. Though it was only eleven in the
morning, Risel already wore her best Shabbos dress, along with seamed stockings and
heels, and Maks had on a necktie, which
flapped as the ever-present breezes of early
summer crossed the porch. My mother and
her sisters wore bathing suits as always,
though out of respect for the occasion they
had covered them with day dresses, belted
and short sleeved. Only we kids showed up
in our usual Woodmont wear of swimsuits
with sandy bare feet. The fathers, working
still in Middletown, would hear about the

event — the clothes, the breeze, the lifting clouds, the unborn child kicking for the first time in my mother's stomach, the tears welling in Risel's eyes — when they joined us later for our Shabbos meal. The ceremony began: *Baruch atah Adonai, Eloheinu melech haolam,* Maks began chanting, and when he finished the blessing, Risel turned, pressed the mezuzah to the doorway, angled the thing just so, and my grandfather placed and then hit the first nail.

Vivie repeated her request to Howard. "Can you give us a minute?" This time she squeezed his shoulder and added, "Honey. Please."

"Honey?" Nina muttered incredulously, causing Vivie to raise an index finger to Nina's lips.

"Sorry," Howard said to Vivie, the rising blush on his face matching Nina's fading one. Vivie, calm as ever, could do this: soften Howard's hardness. She then leaned into the back of the Dodge and pulled out a bag of groceries. Nina, too, reached for a bag. Howard remained standing amidst the suitcases he'd already unloaded, staring at them as if deciding which to carry in first. But just then he spotted Davy — who up until that moment had been standing unnoticed beside him — lugging up the porch steps a suitcase almost as large as his eight-year-old frame.

"Squirt!" Howard called, running to him. He reached for the suitcase.

"I can do it," Davy protested.

"I know you can," Howard said as he tugged at the suitcase. "I just want to help."

Davy was small but strong, a baseball star in the making, our father hoped. When Howard, with a good ten years on Davy, pulled at the suitcase, Davy pulled back. "I can do it," he said again, sure of himself. But when Howard tugged harder, the suitcase flew from Davy's grip.

Suddenly off balance, Davy fell backward. He rolled from the middle step of the porch to its first, and then to the ground.

"See?" Nina called. "See what you did, Howard? *Genius.*"

I ran off the porch to help Davy, but by the time I got there Howard had him by one arm and Nina by the other. His left knee was scraped but not bleeding. He had another scrape on his left elbow.

"You okay?" we all asked. My mother, still at the front doorway, called the loudest.

You never knew. That was my grandfather Maks's sense of things and the reason he'd waited so long to hang the mezuzah. You never knew. After all, so many times during

Maks's youth in Russia the family had been driven from their home in the middle of the night. Balta was home, then it wasn't, then it was again. But you never knew, after that first exile, how long any home would last. And then Maks's father had died just outside of Balta, the man and the horse he was astride frozen while riding home with firewood one blizzard-ridden February night. Maks was nine then, and because his mother had asked him to go out searching he had found the man himself, had touched the horse's icy lips, then his father's boots, lodged forever in stirrups, then his equally unmovable hands, frozen to the reins, before his own screaming set in.

"You okay?" I asked Davy again. As I inspected his scraped elbow Davy jerked it away.

"I can do it," Davy told me, just like he'd told Howard a moment ago, though this time, hands empty, he wasn't making sense. Still, because he clearly wanted to be left alone, I returned to my mother's side.

"He's all right?" she asked me, and I nodded, turning Davy's way to be sure.

Below us, at the bottom of the porch steps, Nina glanced over Davy's head, which put her, chin raised, eye to eye with Howard. "See what you did?" she said again.

■ ■ ■ ■

If it was predictable that my mother would be the one to open the cottage, to be the first to grab at that cottage air, however intolerable it actually was, then what came next was equally predictable. My mother and my aunt Vivie stood beside each other in the living room, Vivie's arms full with two bags of groceries, my mother's arms empty except for her dangling pocketbook. They looked at each other, then at the couch, a sofa bed that Nina and I would share all summer. Lifting the corner of a sheet that covered it, Ada patted the worn brown plaid then nodded Vivie's way. In the same manner, and without thinking yet to relieve Vivie of even one bag of groceries, Ada turned to the two armchairs in the front corners of the room, also covered by sheets. To watch my mother nod at the chairs, though, you'd think she could see right through the white cloth. An uncovered, dusty side table held a ceramic-tiled ashtray, and when Ada lifted the cheap thing, she and Vivie both sighed then said, in near unison, "Daddy's Sunday cigars." There was the photo hanging on the wall over the sofa bed to acknowledge too. Approaching it,

Vivie finally set the groceries down. I stood in the doorway and watched.

Framed and fading, the shot was of their parents, in late June 1939, before their deaths within the next year — Maks of a heart attack, Risel, six months later, of heartache — two stocky souls in the bulky bathing attire of the past, sitting side by side on beach chairs, Maks Syrkin clutching Risel's hand as if prescient of the separation death would soon bring.

Davy, by then inside, was the first to grow impatient with just looking. Turning from the photo, he raced, fully recovered from his earlier spill, past the radio console, almost knocking it over, until he came to the glass doors on the far side of the room. He opened them in time for Ada and Vivie to step through and into the sunporch, a room that contained a folding cot and dresser, along with a wicker chair and side table. This was the room of their younger sister, Bec, and because of its identification with her I knew my mother and Vivie wouldn't step into it again for the rest of the summer. But just then they glanced about it, sighed some more, then cranked its many windows open.

From the sunporch the women made their way back through the living room and into the dining room, its oak dining table covered by yet another sheet, which the sisters expertly yanked off then dropped to the floor in a heap. We children, all of us silently following the mothers from room to room — as if this annual rite of examining the place was intrinsically about our well-being rather than about their past — knew that in the next hour we'd have to shake out that sheet and all the others before folding them and tucking them away. The dining room also contained a china cabinet for the best dishes, used only for Shabbos, and a sideboard stuffed with serving platters, pitchers, tablecloths, napkins, and the like. All of it came from Maks and Risel and was included in the sisters' shared inheritance of the cottage. The dining room's only other furnishings were a small table holding a telephone, and a simple chair set beside it.

My mother lifted the phone's receiver, having promised my father that she'd call when we arrived. By this time, just past one in the afternoon, my father, Mort, in Middletown, would have returned from his after-lunch walk up and back Main Street. Satisfied with the morning's business — ten customers, six sales — he'd be standing in the doorway of his store, staring out the front window. Everyone who passed Leibritsky's Department Store would know him and wave, and he would wave back, solemnly. Nelson, his bachelor brother and the store's co-owner, would be downstairs in the basement, placing a needle on the new recording of Benny Goodman that he planned to listen to while on his post-lunch break. Leo Cohen, my father's brother-in-law and Vivie's husband, would be alone in the back office, nibbling a bologna sandwich as he read, slowly, about Darwin's meticulous studies of mold, an early work. For years already Leo had passed his best reads on to Nina and in so doing had recently gotten his daughter hooked on this particular and, in Uncle Leo's words, "uncannily patient" man.

My mother knew all this, could no doubt picture it in her mind. Phone to her ear, she listened to the buzz of the dial tone as if it were a voice on the summer party line. Then, without dialing, she put the receiver down.

The kitchen was our next stop, but outside its doorway another photograph called for attention, one my father had hung there. Taken in 1942, it showed Davy atop Mort's shoulders as my father, along with a crowd of Woodmont Jews, walked the length of

Woodmont to protest the imprisonment of European Jews — five thousand or so, we thought then — a way of showing the world, however much of it would take note, that they knew what was going on; yes, the Jews of Woodmont knew. In the photo my father, wrapped like the other men in his sacred tallis, was his usual serious self, but Davy had thought the event a festival. Davy pointed. "Me," he said, smiling just as he was in the photograph. "Us," my mother answered. She took his hand and moved it across the scene in a sweeping motion that seemed to include the six million that by 1948 we understood to be not merely imprisoned but killed. "Us," she said again.

We entered the kitchen, then, the way my father wanted us to: reminded of our luck. And there it was, in the speckled linoleum floors and counters, and in the table, a white porcelain enamel top with steel legs, but most especially in the automatic washer, recently purchased from Sears, Roebuck, without a wringer on top. Moving upstairs, the six of us stopped first at the master bedroom, the largest bedroom, at the cottage's front, which, because my mother had married first and had the most children, she felt entitled to claim. Moving along, we paraded down the hall, past the cottage's only full bathroom, where an old tub with high sides and clawed feet was the center-piece. A bit ludicrously, in a way that made us laugh, everyone leaned in to wave at the beloved thing. At the far end of the hallway was a second bedroom, plain enough, shared by Vivie and Leo. Finally we landed at the snug third bedroom midway between the two others, which Davy shared with Howard. Of the twin beds almost touching, Davy's was the one on the left, and after running a few steps, he managed a flying leap from the doorway onto it. Then he righted himself and began jumping. Before my mother could order him to stop he'd already bounced on the mattress several times, declaring with each airborne lift, "I'm free! I'm free!"

Yes, we were *here,* as my mother had first noted. *Here:* this cottage, the one she and her sisters had grown up spending their summers in, the one her father — a handy-man who developed a knack for distinctive cabinetry — had bought and was able to hold on to, even throughout the Depression.

The cottage was itself part of a small complex of cottages, all of them crowding in on each other, set at times three deep between the road and the beach, and not in an orderly line but rather a haphazard clustering. Before ours, but not entirely blocking the view of the Sound, was the Isaacsons'. Beside us lived the Radnicks. Next to them came the Weinsteins. And on and on it went, one family after another, one cottage after the next. And this too, this familiar and messy collection of cottages, is what my mother meant by *here.*

Here: the shore, that small piece of it unofficially called Bagel Beach, which was our beach, the Jews'. We were among the many Jewish families throughout Connecticut (and a few from Massachusetts and New York as well) who funneled down to this spot where some of us owned cottages, some rented, and others stayed in seaside hotels, but all of us kept close, crowded, because in 1948 there were so many places Jews still couldn't go, so many covenants, formal and informal, restricting us from neighborhoods, resorts, clubs — you name it. The genocide in Europe had yet to change that. But *here,* in this hamlet, we could be. Near the intersection of Merwin and Hillside avenues were Jewish bakers and butchers, and even a one-room Orthodox synagogue — the Woodmont Hebrew Congregation — a building of white clapboard, in the New England way. But its door had recently been painted bright blue, which was hardly a Yankee touch. Rather, it gave the place the vibrant colors of Israel. "Aren't you adorable," Howard had said that past May, when, at the news of Israel's independence, I'd compared Bagel Beach, a small and sandy place that offered solace to the Jews of Connecticut, to Israel, another small and sandy place that would offer solace to the beleaguered Jews of the world. Recently we'd learned that we had a cousin there, Reuben Leibritsky, from Poland, a survivor of the camps, and my father and his brother Nelson sent him money each month.

Technically Bagel Beach was outside the bounds of Woodmont, or at least past the little sign at Woodmont's western edge that read *Leaving Woodmont on the Sound.* So was the synagogue and so was the place across from it, Sloppy Joe's, the hamburger shop all the high school kids gravitated toward in the evenings. But all of it — that world inside the bounds of the sign and that small, particularly Jewish stretch beyond it — was what we knew of and meant by Woodmont.

The coastline's natural shale formations, often huge and jagged piles of rocks, created boundaries that formed Woodmont's several and distinct beaches, the popular Anchor Beach, for example, which bordered Crescent Beach then Long Beach. Some rock formations had names, like Lazy Rock, Potato Rock, and Signal Rock, identifiable off the shore of Anchor Beach by its flagpole. Our beach was separated from the others not only by rocks, though, but also by a seawall, too high to climb over, which meant we needed to walk on the roads, rather than along the shore, to get to the others.

Bagel Beach was just a slice of Woodmont, and Woodmont, too, was just a slice — a small mile-and-a-half stretch — of the city of Milford's coastline. Connecticut's abundant Irish came there as well, though in our area of Woodmont their homes were set back from the water, in the hills past the Jewish world. And there were "Yankees" there too, my father's word for Protestants. But of course we didn't mix. Nor did we mix with the people living in the neighboring shoreline boroughs, as dominated by gentiles as Bagel Beach was by Jews, places like Bayview Beach and Pond Point, populated for the most part by Italians, or Morningside, which was a Protestant place, and as closed to us — or so I'd heard — as if surrounded by a fence.

Yes, we were here, engaging like everybody

else in a kind of segregated ethnic tribalism that for us was part necessity, part comfort. But my mother didn't mean only that when she said, her voice confident, her chest filling with air, *Here.* She had her own sense of the place, which had to do with the past, with the summers she spent at Woodmont before her marriage. Though my father and Uncle Leo paid the yearly taxes and provided funds for upgrades, for Ada the men's contributions never changed the fundamental fact of the sisters' inheritance: the cottage was theirs. They'd grown up in it, they knew it best, they spent more days in it. They could look at the living room radio console and recall countless gatherings beside it to listen to the soap operas of their youth: *The Carters of Elm Street, Lorenzo Jones, As the World Turns.* They could open the dining room's sideboard and point at the dishes, knowing which set was for milchidik, which for fleishadik. A given stain on a tablecloth was to them a particular shared memory that the men, the husbands of the weekend, knew nothing about.

It hadn't changed. To grasp that constancy was the point of roaming, room by room, through the cottage. And once we'd been assured of that indelible sameness, the unpacking could begin. Off went the remaining white sheets covering beds and dressers. Out came the vacuum to gather three seasons' worth of dust. There was the front porch to be swept clean and the kitchen table and counters to be wiped down. Soon enough, Davy had his second helpless jump on his summer bed, which with the cottage walls so thin he didn't get away with for more than a few leaps. "Out!" my mother called, and she waited at the bottom of the stairs until Davy reluctantly trudged down them and made his way through the front door, onto our open front porch.

The sisters had yet to change out of their Middletown dresses, their hose, their almost identical brown shoes with practical one-inch heels, when they decided to walk down to the water. The Long Island Sound, too, needed to be seen and felt again. They needed to say hello to it and to hear, in the gentle, unending lapping of waves, a kind of voice they'd heard a million times before.

As I watched them make their way around the Isaacsons' cottage and onto Bagel Beach I thought how ridiculous they looked, all dressed up like that, their good town shoes sinking into the sand and no doubt filling with it. Standing on our porch as they ambled forth, Davy — then and forever eight years old — was beside me. Howard had already gone off to meet his best Woodmont pal, Mark Fishbaum — the person I'd eventually marry and then divorce, though in 1948 all that was inconceivable. Nina was inside reading. As I stared ahead I noticed Mrs. Isaacson peeking through a back bedroom window that looked out on us. When I waved, she waved back. "Nice to see you, Molly," she called, not at all uncomfortable with being found out. When Davy then said, "I'm going to build a new sand castle every single day," I silently nodded. Glancing at the groupings of people on the beach, mothers and children in proper swim attire, many of them waving at the sisters as they made their entrance onto the summer scene, I was embarrassed for them. I was even more so when my mother bent over, grabbed a shoe, then stood straight as she tipped the shoe over, giving it a shake. "I'm going to build forts, too, and maybe I'll let you hide in one," Davy added. When I looked his way I noticed Mr. Weinstein two cottages over, one of the old radios he liked to fix set before him on a table on his porch. "And I'm going swimming, even in bad weather." As Davy continued, my mother returned her shoe to her foot. Then she and

Vivie marched on, determinedly, toward the water, though with a space of about two feet or so always between them.

The space made me wonder where my aunt Bec was, why she still hadn't arrived yet. It was as if with that open air between them Ada and Vivie were holding a place for her, a niche Bec would fill perfectly, if only she were there.

Davy continued talking. My mother and aunt continued walking toward the water's edge. Mr. Weinstein leaned over and twisted a knob on his radio.

Recently, this present year of 1999, my aunt Bec bequeathed to me her house. I'll move in fully after the New Year; it seems right to make such a change at the start of a new millennium. But for now, this fall, I'm only making visits, getting to know the place anew, without Bec there. And the process — looking through Bec's rooms, opening the trickle of mail that still arrives for her, beginning to sort through the contents of certain closets and drawers — has triggered another one, of trying to put the pieces of the summer of 1948 together as best I can. What, exactly, happened to that twelve-year-old girl so confident in her judgments that first day in Woodmont as she stood on the porch, watching? What happened to Davy, tragic as it is, is at least clear. But what happened to the rest of us — the ways our worlds collapsed, the ways we made sure they did — remains for me the mystery.

This morning I wandered through Bec's home, modeled so much after the cottage, and decorated just as modestly but for a rather fancy Victorian desk, the kind with little drawers and vertical compartments. The desk stands in a corner of the living room. Opening its drawers I felt a pang of guilt, for clearly this was a private spot of Bec's, the corner nook, the window, and the lovely old desk, its drawers filled with letters, sketchbooks, scraps of paper, some with addresses on them, others with more of Bec's sketches. In a bottom drawer the sketchbooks were older, the pages more yellowed. In one I found a page dated January 7, 1950, with some writing on it rather than drawing. This was a time, I recalled, when Bec was living with us, after Davy's death. Singlehandedly, it seemed, she saved our family, pulled us through. In the sketchbook Bec's handwriting was especially tiny, but I could see it clearly enough. *I could die,* she'd written. *No, no, am already dead.*

When Bec finally did arrive at the cottage

that Tuesday in 1948, close to dinnertime and in high spirits, it was the roar of her boss's Buick Roadmaster, the only sound all afternoon louder than the background drone of waves, that first signaled to us that she was near. After Vivie and Ada had returned from the beach and finally changed their clothes, and after the cleaning and unpacking, and after my mother had at last called my father to let him know all was well, we'd gathered on the front porch where, for the most part, we were simply taking in the air. Only Howard was absent.

The Roadmaster was a gleaming red and white sedan, so much fancier than our faded green Dodge with its many rust spots. The year before, Bec's boss, Tyler McMannus, had also dropped her off, but not in as glorious a vehicle. This day he parked the Roadmaster beside our Dodge and honked a greeting. Then he got out and tipped his hat to us, calling, though not particularly loudly, "Hello, ladies," to Ada and Vivie as he did. Slowly, because of his slight limp — the remains of a war injury that had brought him home earlier than anticipated from Europe — he walked around the car. Bec sat inside it, waiting, familiar with the routine. We'd seen it before too. When Tyler reached her, he opened the car door and then held Bec's arm as she stepped out. For a second, he held her gaze.

Bec looked elegant in a short-sleeved red dress, belted in white, with a coordinating white collar and white trim around each sleeve. Oddly, her colors matched the Roadmaster's perfectly. After turning from Tyler she raced up the porch steps, singing out our names. As she spun around, spewing hellos, her skirt twirled with her. That she'd made the dress was a certainty, for Bec was a master seamstress. In New Haven she worked in Tyler McMannus's dress shop, and by all accounts its upper-crust clientele were especially fond of the garments Bec designed and sold there. She was so good, in fact, that Tyler gave her eight weeks each summer at the beach with her sisters — whatever it took to keep his most valuable employee happy, he'd explained to us on more than one occasion.

As Bec greeted everyone, Tyler remained by the car and watched. He seemed genuinely pleased for Bec, smiling throughout the welcoming period. Once things quieted down on the porch Tyler joined us and soon stood beside Bec, his fedora in his hands, his suit jacket unbuttoned, the limp that you couldn't help but notice as he climbed the porch steps no longer so apparent, his near-black hair and gray eyes glinting as a ray of late-afternoon sun landed on him. "Quite a day, yes?" he said as he thrust his hand out to shake Ada's, then Vivie's.

When Bec stepped closer to him, she too was caught in the sun's light and there they stood, two exceptionally well-tailored individuals whose smiles, when they looked at each other the next moment, were almost as bright as the sunshine they momentarily basked in. It would be decades before I understood the extent to which they were in love with each other that summer. In fact by that day Tyler, though still married, had proposed that he and Bec start a life together in New York City, but even as I watched them on the porch, in all the ignorance of twelve years old, it seemed to me that one could only wish to be just like them, so well put together, so well matched.

Though on vacation, Bec still had a little sewing to do while she was at the beach, and on several Fridays she'd have to go back to New Haven for any fittings that couldn't be delayed until early fall. Because of this she'd brought her Singer, which Tyler awkwardly lugged up the porch steps then carried to Bec's sunporch. He quietly hummed as he hauled in next her suitcases and her large sewing basket. Tyler granted

Davy the privilege of carrying in Bec's mannequin — Eleanor Roosevelt, we proudly called her — that she couldn't work without.

Minutes before Tyler left — without fanfare, the only sign of anything between him and Bec his left arm dangling out the car window, extending back — Bec was the one to shoot down the porch steps and whisk from the car one last item. From a hanger flowed a dress, pale yellow with small white flowers on it, covered by a short jacket of the same material.

Once she'd carried it to the porch she held it out to Nina. "Strapless," Bec explained, pushing the jacket back, revealing the dress. "Made it for you," she said, excited for Nina. As she thrust it at Nina, Bec added, eyebrows raised, "Could change your life. Dresses do that, you know. They really do."

By dinnertime the sisters were wearing nearly identical outfits: floppy cotton housedresses. Even Bec. Yes, I saw, dresses *could* change your life, and so much for the better.

And with the return of their casualness we were most definitely *here.*

The next day, Wednesday, the sisters rose early for a quick dunk in the Sound then spent the rest of the morning around the kitchen table talking to Mrs. Isaacson, who came by with a freshly baked coffee cake and ten months' worth of news. She'd brought along her granddaughter Judy, too, who was in her second year of a failing marriage and needing a break from it. Everyone knew it was Mrs. Isaacson's great hope that Judy would eventually have as loving a marriage as she and Mr. Isaacson had had — "Fifty-two years and still French-kissing," as she put it — but we could all see that even though Judy was pregnant, there was no real joy in her life. She passed on the cake, endlessly stirred her black coffee, said nothing.

When Mrs. Isaacson was finally through talking, the sisters set off for a walk, starting along the roads between Bagel and Anchor Beach. Even when they turned off the road and scrambled over the rocks that abutted the shoreline at Anchor Beach, slowing to a crawl to do so, they acted like they didn't know that Davy and I were right behind them, having our own walk, collecting shells and gull feathers and the occasional starfish along the way.

During the afternoon, after lunch and a smoke on her sunporch, Bec began to sew, a party dress, she said, for a Mrs. Arthur Coventry of New Haven. She was the wife of a retired law professor from Yale. A little hoity-toity, like so many of those Yale wives, Bec noted, but nice. Though we couldn't know it then, as she sat at the Singer that afternoon Bec was contemplating, as she'd been since Tyler had voiced it a week before, his proposal. ("We could be happy in New York. I know that. I believe that, Bec," he'd said.) The proposal wasn't for marriage — he was Catholic and couldn't find it in himself to divorce — but she knew it was for a lifelong commitment all the same.

That day Nina stayed on the porch, reading Darwin. The hefty book was clearly an endless read and summer would be gone, I worried, before she'd come to the beach with me. I was hoping she and I would be close, like we'd been the summers before, and like the sisters were that morning, their eyes flashing signals to each other about the silent Judy as Mrs. Isaacson yakked on, and later, their heads bent toward each other while they chatted during their walk; and even like Howard and his pal Mark Fishbaum, an only child always eager for company, who showed up that first full day for both breakfast and lunch. In the morning Howard sailed with Mark, who had a twelve-foot Sailfish to launch, but after lunch the two parted and Howard set off for Treat's produce stand on the outskirts of Wood-mont where he hoped to get a part-time job. "Noon to four thirty," he proudly announced that evening as we gathered outside on the porch for supper.

Davy followed Howard's news with some of his own. Over the summer he'd be working too, he told us. But he didn't sound as happy as Howard. What he meant was that he expected mail soon from Lucinda Rossetti, who that past year had been in his second-grade class in Middletown. Their teacher had assigned the students a summer project: they would pair up and share in drawing a picture. One of them would draw a portion of it then pass it to the other, and so forth. "She broke the rules," he complained about his teacher, a woman who, until that moment, it seemed he'd simply adored. "There's no homework in summer. Everybody knows that."

"Buddy, there'll come a day when you actually *like* that girls send you things," Howard told him with an assurance born of the fact that Howard rarely went without a girlfriend, though just then he was single.

Nonplussed, Davy had no answer to that.

The next day our first piece of mail in fact arrived, a white envelope that hailed, ominously for Davy, from Middletown. We kids were in the kitchen eating lunch when Bec wandered in, holding the thing.

To Davy's relief Bec handed the envelope to Nina, who promptly tore it open and read out loud her father's words: *There are so many mysteries to life, Nina. Darwin looked hard, and looked for a long time, and in the end, it seems to me, he figured out one of the biggest of them all. I look forward to talking with you about him — soon enough.* "Nice," she said, folding Leo's note and tucking it, like a second bookmark, into the thick pages of *On the Origin.* She nodded before repeating, "Nice."

"See? Mail's fun," she then told Davy. "Ever get any? Just for you?"

"I've never gotten a letter," Davy acknowledged.

Later that afternoon Davy, Nina, and I ran into Sal Baby, known to adults as Sal Luccino, the local Good Humor man — the person who, come Friday of the third week of August, would run his truck over Davy. As we walked on Hillside Avenue toward Sal and his wares we could see that Sal was breaking up a tussle between the Weinstein twins. One of them, Jimmy Weinstein, already had an ice cream bar in hand and despite the tears running down his face had just taken a first bite. The other boy, Arthur

44

Weinstein, had a bloody nose. "If you can stay out of trouble for the next week I'll give you a free one," Sal was telling Arthur as he mopped up the blood with a paper napkin. He did this while holding a lit cigar in his left hand. Once we'd arrived at his truck, Sal glanced our way, winked hello, puffed at the cigar, and then resumed his negotiations with Arthur Weinstein. Ten minutes and five bloodied napkins later we at last got our Good Humor bars.

By late Thursday afternoon, after Howard had come home from Treat's, clouds gathered and my mother stood on the beach, admonishing Howard and Mark, and then begging them, not to go sailing. "Can't you two play cards?" she asked almost desperately. "Or help Mr. Weinstein over there with his radio?" But sail they did, out past Bagel Beach, over toward Anchor Beach, where they slid past Signal Rock, then past Crescent Beach then Long Beach, and finally they were beyond Woodmont altogether, sailing through the border of West Haven, which for them was uncharted territory, a place of friendly enough coastal waters but unknown depths.

In the photo of Maks and Risel of June 1939 they were sitting at the beach, hand in hand, looking more toward each other than the camera. Earlier that day, following the affixing of mezuzot throughout the cottage, the two had celebrated paying off the mortgage in yet another way. Risel, this time, had the idea. Heavyset and prone to napping, she nevertheless scuttled, breasts and belly jiggling, down to the shore. She was still in her Shabbos dress and her seamed stockings, though she'd taken off her heeled shoes even before the last mezuzah was hung. In her hand were the mortgage papers, rolled and jammed into an empty Coca-Cola bottle, its cap secured with adhesive tape. The tide was out. My grandfather, delighting in the cool but bearable touch of the shallow waters of low tide, the soft ridges of wet sand under his feet, the renewed energy of his typically sedentary wife, followed Risel as she waded out to where the waters were knee-deep. There she stopped, her hem drenched, her stockings ruined, her waist twisted, and with the expertise of a discus thrower she heaved the bottle into the sea. Then she whooped with joy and splashed her husband. But Maks only stood there quietly, a yard or so from Risel, watching the bottle bob as it drifted from them. At last, the bottle gone from sight, he stepped closer to Risel and grabbed the hand that had done the hurling. For some time they stood there, staring at the hazy and distant line of the horizon. Above them gulls flew, as always, and by their legs a jellyfish floated past, barely noticeable as it swayed with the sea's mixed currents. Time was a strange thing, Maks muttered to Risel, pulling her close. And by that he meant that it seemed impossible they'd been married forty-four years.

Friday morning was a simple enough matter. Howard, who'd been up carousing with Mark Fishbaum the night before, was late taking off to join the morning minyan in Middletown. When he finally pulled the Dodge onto Hillside Avenue to begin his drive to Middletown he thought he was still dreaming, for there was Davy, yawning as he stood roadside at the mailboxes, waiting hours too early for the day's mail to arrive.

On his hand he wore his favorite puppet, Samson, the boy in a family of puppets we'd named after our beach. Lenny Bagel. Esther Bagel. Linda Bagel. Samson Bagel. Brilliant, we'd thought, to name them so aptly: the Bagels of Bagel Beach.

2
BREATHING

By 1948 Sal Luccino had been smoking cigars for the dozen years that he'd been a Good Humor man. A Milford native who'd been trained by his father in the art of plumbing, Sal had split from the family business, Giuseppe Luccino & Sons, in 1936, when he was forty and had socked away enough money for the down payment, seventeen hundred dollars, for his own Good Humor franchise and a truck. The first cigar, smoked the day he signed the papers for the franchise, was a means of celebrating his independence, as was the second, smoked at ten in the evening when he finally parked his truck in front of his home after his first day of making rounds. He'd begun the day promptly at nine that morning. Independence, he discovered right away, came with a price — those daunting hours — but he was determined to make a go of it, and after that first day the cigars were smoked because they made him feel less alone inside his cab, like his father and brothers were right there beside him, just as they were when they fixed the pipes of the buildings in downtown Milford. Quickly, then, the cigars became a habit, and soon enough, for old times' sake, he even called them "pipes." "Not fixing the pipes anymore," he told his wife, Marie, and all five of their children on a Sunday morning in July of 1936, one month after he'd begun his new work. In four weeks he'd cleared eighty-seven dollars, more than he'd ever made before. He held his cigar proudly for them to see. It being Sunday, he'd gone to mass then taken the rest of the morning off. "No, not fixing pipes. Just smoking 'em now," he'd said. The work of the ice cream franchise ran from late April through mid-September, and in fact he returned to fixing pipes during the other months, when the families remaining off-season in the shoreline boroughs of Milford didn't want to rush outdoors for something even colder than the weather. But once he'd adjusted to being a Good Humor man — driving and maintaining his truck, meticulously dressing each morning in pressed whites, ringing those luring bells, and chatting it up with his customers, the world's children — his months as Sal Baby, as he'd come to be called, were by far the better part of the year.

He'd been the one who'd first offered himself to others as Sal Baby. August of 1937, a second summer of the new franchise almost gone, and a group of six kids — all from the Monroe family of Morningside — had begged him to "whistle it more, please," as the youngest, a child of four, had put it. At the time Sal hadn't even realized he was whistling. But that's how whistling was for him — like breathing, he simply found himself at it. He'd even learned the hard way, through the cries and complaints of his own children to keep it down at night or he'd keep them up. But here in the streets of the Milford shoreline, the ocean gleaming in the distance, the open sky above, he'd belted it out for all six sandy-haired Monroes to hear. While he did, the children's faces were transfixed, so much so that three out of the six didn't even notice the melted chocolate dripping onto their hands. Even when he finished his song the children's expressions of joyful wonderment didn't change. "Sal Baby thanks you," he told them with a wink. They repeated the phrase, "Sal Baby," and while doing so each had laughed. So he tried out another phrase.

"Bye-bye, apple pie," he said, and without a moment's hesitation they repeated that too.

Something settled over Sal that day, a sense of well-being, of knowing that this idea of his, the small business of selling treats, was the work he didn't even know he was made for. The realization hit him first as he watched Mrs. Monroe, concerned that her children hadn't returned home yet, come fetch them and urge them off, which did nothing to dissipate the cloud of sweetness surrounding them. The next January, 1938, while frantically fixing the pipes of a downtown apartment building after an unusually deep freeze had caused a riot of bursting, Sal, once again of Giuseppe Luccino & Sons, sat back on his heels, the bones of his arms and shoulders aching, his throat dry, his breathing shallow from bending at the waist as he worked. An image came to mind of the youngest Monroe child, Tommy, the one who'd said, "Whistle it more, please," who, later, his mother clasping one of his messy hands, had strained to keep his head turned toward Sal long after his mother pulled him away. For a moment Sal was there, on the shoreline street, the sun blazing above, the child so impressed Sal could have told him he was the one to have invented ice cream and the kid would have believed him.

He put his wrench down. He looked around at the dim cave of the basement where he'd spent the better part of the morning. The place was unheated. On his hands were woolen gloves, clipped so his fingers were free. Three more months, he told himself, and then he'd be back at it. Outside. Breathing deeply. Whistling whenever the spirit moved him to. And, when it did, letting it rip.

That Friday of our family's first week in Woodmont Sal was doing just that, letting it rip, as he drove to New Haven to restock, and that's when he passed Davy, waiting for the mail, wearing shorts, a puppet, and a pajama shirt that in his sleepiness he didn't realize was inside out. And, as if I were Sal that day, I can see Davy, all these years later, so very clearly. I can even hear him call "Sal Baby!" — his voice still the chirp of a child, his words a little rushed. And there we — the family members — were those early days of summer, swirling around him, each of us bathed in a light of innocence we didn't even know was there. Davy's innocence, the fact of his still being a child, wasn't the light's source. I talk of a grander innocence. Unlike my grandfather Maks during his days in Russia, in America we'd been lucky so far. Even the recent war, in all its anguish, hadn't broken our spirit, and in fact that summer, 1948, we were particularly hopeful, given Israel and all. "I'm free!" Davy cried while jumping on his bed, the words nearly his first upon our arrival at Woodmont that summer. And as I sit here now, once again at Bec's desk, staring for a second day in a row at that fraught note she wrote so long ago, after that innocence faded, here's what I sense: that at the summer's start Davy's words were true for each of us, though not for the same reason, and that all of this — the different ways we found and grabbed at our freedom — had so much to do, ultimately, with this boy's death.

But when the going is good, when the day is light and sunny, how can you not grab at freedom?

Take my mother, for example, who, in ways not so different from her nemesis-to-come, Sal Luccino, didn't even know she had.

"This is where I feel I can breathe," my mother always said of Woodmont — always showed as well — and it was there, in the cottage with her sisters each summer, that I would watch the usual knot of her brow unwind, the taut vein lines in her neck slacken, the apron strings, inevitably wound round her waist in our Middletown kitchen, fall by the wayside. Wearing her daily house-dress, one of her many shapeless cotton shifts, her mass of hair pinned haphazardly behind her head, and her beloved wedge sandals, oddly stylish given the rest, she could look almost comic. Yet she was con-tent, even happy. For in Woodmont she gained a kind of autonomy over her life, something she lacked in Middletown. For one thing, as co-inheritor of the cottage, she was on her own turf. And she loved that ownership, loved taking stock of the place at the beginning of each summer, scouring the building — as my father did in our Mid-dletown home — for any needed repairs, any further upgrades. She even loved the smaller acts of day-to-day maintenance such as sweeping the cottage's ever-sandy front porch. On many a morning I would find her there, humming. When she finished, she'd lean the broom against a wall, sit herself down on one of the porch's chairs, and hum — as she never did while doing housework in Middletown — even louder.

Then again, at Woodmont the daily work of cooking, cleaning, shopping, and watching over us was shared. That was another feature of summer so different from life in Middletown. Our cottage was a kind of commune, and if my mother ever had any ambitions outside the home, the live-in help she had at Woodmont in the form of her sisters could have allowed her the time for it. She could have taken up painting water-colors, for example, or studied shorebirds. Like Nina, she could have read an extremely long book. But Ada had no such ambitions. Years ago, when she'd used her keenest wiles to steal my father from Vivie, she re-alized all the ambition she'd ever had. She'd got her man. Her life, she knew then, despite the eighteen years of it already lived, was about to begin.

Odd, then, how during those childhood summers the five weekdays when the men weren't there were the most relaxed of her adult life. I remember the sound of her wak-ing each morning, early, not long after daybreak, along with Vivie and Bec. That Friday morning of our first week was no different. I was still snuggled under the cotton blanket on the sofa bed I shared with Nina, my eyes heavy with sleep, when I heard the creaking upstairs begin. Even before there was any movement in the boys' room it was clear that at the front of the house Ada had risen. At the other end of the upstairs hall Vivie had too. In the sun-porch beyond the living room Bec was rising, and the glass doors separating her room from Nina's and mine squeaked as she opened them to make her way to the toilet near the back door. Soon she returned, and in what I imagined as perfect synchrony the three sisters then stepped into their identical bathing suits, black one-piece suits with skirts that covered the tops of their thighs. These were their morning suits, to be replaced later by lighter-colored ones, or even floral-printed ones, suits that they would wear in lieu of underwear under their inevitable housedresses. But the black suits were what they stepped into each morning for what they referred to as their daily dunk.

For all their years at the beach their parents had dunked, first thing in the morning, walking hand in hand from the cottage porch, around the Isaacsons' cottage in front of them, to the sands of Bagel Beach, and finally to the water's edge. When Maks and Risel died, they bequeathed to their daughters not just the cottage and its contents but also so many years of Woodmont-only traditions: the cottage cheese and fresh fruit salads Risel favored for lunch, the Saturday evening rounds of rummy, the early-morning dunk.

The stairs, creaky as the cottage's floors, squeaked as my mother and Vivie descended, towels and bathing caps in hand. My eyes still heavy, I didn't have to actually see them to know what was under way. At the base of the stairs Vivie and Ada stopped, leaning over the banister to check on Nina and me. At the same time, Bec, also carrying a towel and cap, emerged once again from her porch. The sisters paused briefly in the dining room to greet each other, whispering a hushed but audible "morning" before they scurried out the back door and began making their way, their legs and arms, chests and backs exposed, as they strutted forth in their bathing suits, which, at this time of day and this time of day only, went uncovered. If you were to stare out a window you could see that they were nearly the same height, though Bec was a little taller than the others, and that Vivie had noticeably wider hips, and that my mother's waist was the trimmest, despite her having borne the most children. You would see each of them holding her head high, her posture straight, her near-black mane still braided from the night before and falling past her bare shoulders onto the skin of her upper back. You would see they were lovely, the three of them, as they walked silently through the misty grayness of the early morning air.

But at six thirty a.m. who was up to see? Thus the exposed swimwear and skin, the goose bumps rising on their arms, the determined pace. For this was business, this dunking, this daily reminder of Maks and Risel, this morning prayer — a form of Kaddish, really, except the practice, silent, was wholly physical — and a moment later the sisters dropped their towels, tipped their heads, and began the synchronized stuffing of those thick manes of hair inside their snug rubber caps.

But that synchronicity — a kind of peace — wasn't always the case. My mother was seventeen when she betrayed Vivie, who then didn't speak to her for the next five years. The undoing began when Vivie, who was twenty at the time, was laid low with the flu. This was during the winter of 1926, and Vivie was incapacitated for a good three weeks. Bec, too, was sick. But my mother had a hardiness to her and never took ill. Instead, she acted as house nurse, a role she enjoyed, carrying pitchers of juice and water to her sisters' bedside tables, taking their temperature, buttering their slices of toast, rushing to answer their throaty calls.

Her mother, Risel, couldn't have been more grateful for this invincible girl, her darling Ada, the middle child who happened to also have the most charming face and a lively, headstrong personality. During those long weeks Risel's thankful adoration was a kind of pampering, as steady as the pampering Ada offered her sisters. The approval bolstered what was already in Ada, due to those striking looks and that outgoing disposition: a healthy dose of self-confidence. And so my mother was grander than usual, as well as more purposeful than usual in her role as nurse. High school, which she'd been missing those weeks while her sisters needed her, already seemed a thing of the past, despite the four months of it still looming. But with the business at home Ada began to see beyond her school days, when she'd be expected to take a job, a caring job, much like the house nurse position she'd stumbled into, and then, soon enough, find a husband and start a family — which, as everyone knew, was any woman's real job, her future permanent position. Vivie, who upon graduating from high school had taken a part-time post at Leibritsky's, in downtown Middletown, was certainly on the same path, just a bit ahead of Ada. And every other young woman Ada knew, or knew of, also trekked that very path. It was at Leibritsky's that Vivie had met Mort, the owner's eldest son, who worked there with his father. For the last three months, on Saturday nights following Shabbos, Mort had come by to court Vivie. Twice they'd sat completely alone, just the two of them, in the Syrkin living room, quietly conversing. Once they'd gone out to see a picture show.

In three days, Vivie told Ada one evening, it would be Mort's birthday. He would be twenty-four. She'd hoped to bake him a cake, to surprise him with it. They were to have a little party there at the store, Vivie, Mort, and the old man, Mr. Leibritsky.

"I had it all planned," Vivie complained. She pulled her blankets over her face, despairing, and then pushed them down again, waist high. She was still flushed with fever and sweating. Ada urged her to drink more water, which she'd iced to help battle the fever.

Vivie sipped while Ada held the glass. Sated for the moment, Vivie dropped her head back onto her pillows. "It was going to be a yellow cake with chocolate frosting," she said, her voice almost a whimper.

Ada nodded. Everyone loved a yellow cake

with chocolate frosting. The choice was sensible enough, but maybe a little predictable, a little bland.

"Oh, Lord, Ada. Do you think this will ever end?" Vivie asked. Upon seeing her sister swipe her brow, Ada offered Vivie a hanky to mop up the moisture. Ada wasn't sure if Vivie was speaking of her fever or of the courtship with Mort. "I think I need to sleep," Vivie added, her voice falling. In the next minute she dropped off.

Ada brought Mort the cake. She baked it, on Vivie's behalf, Risel encouraging Ada when she thought to make a chocolate cake with butter cream frosting rather than Vivie's yellow cake. "Yes, yes. Bring him a *good* cake, at least," Risel said. And *good*, Ada knew, was Risel's best word for marvelous.

A *good* cake — the batter light, the frosting thick — is exactly what my mother brought him, on a platter, covered with wax paper. She donned her boots, coat, gloves, and scarf, and as she carried the cake to Leibritsky's on Main Street, a mile-long walk, she trod carefully to avoid slipping on patches of winter ice.

"It's for you," she announced upon her arrival at the store, the tinkling bells as she walked through the doorway startling her.

Mort stood before her, thin and not particularly tall, a dimple in his chin, waves of hair crossing his forehead, a warm smile marking his face. In his own way he was handsome, she thought, more so in the store than on those evenings in their home when she caught glimpses of him as she passed by the living room where he and Vivie sat. There he was stiff, in both posture and facial expression, but here he was so much more himself: smiling, self-assured, welcoming. She said, "Vivie couldn't deliver it herself; she's still so sick. But I know she wanted you to have this."

"How is she?" he asked, taking the cake from Ada then pointing to a chair.

"Coming along."

Mort insisted that Ada sit. "This is an awful lot of trouble," he told her. He eyed the cake as he brought her a cup of coffee.

"It really *is,*" she answered.

When he widened his eyes in response, she laughed, a quick hoot.

She spun around to take in the store before seating herself in one of the leather armchairs that were more or less at the store's center. She'd been there before, many times over the years, but never by herself. The place looked different, somehow, from the vantage point of her first journey there alone. More interesting. The green-rimmed dishes to her left were rather pretty, she thought. On a shelf across from them the men's ties were as colorful as a rainbow. Just as always, there seemed to be no plan to the inventory at Leibritsky's, but for the first time the disarray was less confusing than appealing.

"Can I interest you in anything?" Mort asked. A moment ago she'd heard him ask the same thing of a customer, an older man, who was now talking to Mort's father.

"Cake?" she answered, smiling.

Soon they all had some: Ada, Mort, old man Leibritsky, and the customer. She amused them with talk of another cake she almost baked but didn't. "Not quite *enough*," she said of Vivie's yellow cake. "But you have to understand. My sister's sick with fever and not thinking at her best. When she comes back just tell her how you loved her cake, how the chocolate frosting was irresistible." She lifted a forkful of the butter cream icing to her mouth and winked.

And that was the last Vivie was spoken of that afternoon.

"You're a live one," Mr. Leibritsky remarked with a laugh.

There was talk then of cakes: a favorite

coconut cake that the customer, a man introduced as Thomas Tucelli, described with nearly obsessive detail. Mr. Leibritsky's favorite was his mother's babka, from the old country, baked with cinnamon, raisins, and nuts.

"Good God, child," he told her, warming to her as he ate, and soon enough taking a second helping. "But do you know how good that cake is?" She wasn't sure if he meant her cake or the babka of his youth. Still, she nodded. She began to feel an increasing comfort there at the center of the three men.

During this time Mort said little about cakes or anything else, but he never took his eyes off Ada. She knew it and liked it. Wriggling back into her coat, readying to leave, she realized that between the verbal attentions of the father and the nonverbal attentions of the son she'd had one of the most pleasant afternoons of her life.

Would she think of coming back soon? the elder Leibritsky asked as she stood in the doorway to leave. Mort was still staring at her, glancing over his father's shoulder to do so. Even the customer Thomas Tucelli seemed to want her to return.

She directed her gaze at Mort and nodded. When she opened the door to leave, the tinkling of the bells caught her by surprise again.

"Did he like the cake?" Vivie asked. She struggled to rise from the bed. She sat on its edge, her bare feet dangling. Ada told Vivie they'd both liked the cake, Mort and his father.

"Mr. Leibritsky too?"

"Yes, Mr. Leibritsky too. He was very dear. Very animated."

"Mr. Leibritsky? You sure?"

"Yes. The old man himself. He told me to come back soon."

"He didn't!"

"Sure he did. Why so surprised?"

"He never really talks to me, is all," Vivie said.

"That's because you're too nice, Vivie. Too bland. He likes a little spit in his face. You've got to give it to him. That's what wakes him up."

"Lord, Ada. I'm sure you gave it to him. I'm sure you did." Vivie shook her head. "So, tell me about Mort," she continued. "What did *he* say?"

But before Ada could answer — a bunch of lies she'd practiced on the way home — Vivie had dropped back into sleep.

The next time Ada visited the store, three days later, she brought a jar of herring. Perhaps the men would want some with crackers for lunch, she figured. Upon her arrival, the old man threw his hands in the air. "What's that? Babka?" he asked, smiling. His delight didn't decrease when he saw she'd in fact brought fish.

Mort was with a customer, but when he finished, the three took to the seats at the store's center as they had the last visit. The men enjoyed the herring and ate it, as she suggested, with crackers. When they'd finished, Mr. Leibritsky mentioned a new shipment of women's shoes. "Special," he said. "Ladies' dress shoes. From *New York.*" He winked as he pronounced *New York* slowly, as if it were as exotic as Buenos Aires or Hong Kong.

They walked to a wall lined with shoe boxes. The pair Mort pulled out to show her, made of shiny black leather, had a bit of a heel and an ankle buckle. "Oh," Ada whispered, surprised to see such quality.

"Try them," Mr. Leibritsky urged. "Come on, what the hell." He gave Mort a look, then shook his head. "Help the girl," he finally directed.

A couple then entered the store. Mort rose but his father told him he'd handle them.

While Mr. Leibritsky shambled away, obviously tired, Ada returned to her chair and sighed. She felt a little tired too, or perhaps a little impatient. Mort remained standing as he pulled one of the shoes from the box, and then he knelt before Ada, shoe in hand. When she offered him her right foot, pointing her toe as she held the foot aloft in front of him, she noticed he was blushing. Her face, she had to admit, felt warm, was perhaps flushed as well. Suddenly she no longer felt tired or impatient. As he reached for her left foot she held her breath.

"Pretty," Mort said once the shoe was on. He was staring at her foot, not at her, and still blushing.

She nodded, and soon he'd placed her right foot in the other shoe. She waited contentedly while Mort managed the ankle buckles on both shoes. As she rose from the chair Mort offered her his hand. She was glad to grab it and held on a moment past the point of rising. Her face once again felt warm. His was an even deeper shade of red.

When they glanced at each other she

wondered if she looked as shocked as he did.

"Go for a spin," Mr. Leibritsky called from across the floor. He pointed to the store's entranceway, and as she walked she sensed the rapt attention of the two men on her, along with the customers', an attention that made her feel even more important than she did at home, despite the recent elevation of her status there. In the next moment she grasped in a way that was more certain than ever before the meaning of her beauty, its power. As she moved forward she stopped blushing like a child, instead held her head high. She turned at the entranceway, tugged at her sweater and skirt, and then proceeded, proudly. Reaching Mort, she stopped, stood before him, turned in a quick circle, then dropped into the chair.

"That's a good-looking shoe," Mr. Leibritsky called. "A very nice shoe, hey, Mort?"

Mort nodded. She stared at him until she caught his eye, then she smiled.

She reached to unbuckle the shoes. In an instant Mort dropped to his knees, lifting a shoe from each foot, holding her ankles as he did. "There's no way you're going to get me to buy a pair of shoes," she said. "Who's got money these days? But that was sure fun."

"That's just it," Mr. Leibritsky said as he neared them. He was looking at Mort when he added, his voice almost grave, "Everyone needs a little fun."

"Did he say anything?" Vivie asked.

"Who?"

"What do you mean, who? *Mort.* Did he ask about me, Ada?"

"He asked. Sure he asked. 'How's Vivie,' he said. 'Is she well?' "

"And? What did you tell him?"

"I told him you were sick. I told him you were weak as a limp pickle."

"But I'm walking now. I walked yesterday and today. I'm no limp pickle, Ada, please."

"Vivie, you are. You're not well. Now lie down and take a load off." She fluffed her sister's pillows and wiped her still sweating brow. "A limp pickle," she added, "is exactly what you are."

Just a week later, Vivie, by then well enough to amble about the house, caught them holding hands outside the front door. Mort had accompanied Ada home after another visit to the store. She'd nearly slipped on ice and he'd taken her arm, to steady her, and then held her hand. They'd walked that way, hand in hand, without talking, the last half mile. Just as Vivie opened the door to take in the mail, the lovers-to-be were standing, facing each other, hands still entwined.

"Oh!" said Vivie. She was wearing her bathrobe and slippers. Her hair was ready for nighttime, braided and down.

Ada stepped inside. Mort tried to speak but Vivie dismissed him with an unusually forceful "Go." Then she slammed the door. In the front hallway, the two sisters faced each other. Ada began to unbutton her coat when her sister's words, a rain of Yiddish, struck her. *"Vaksn zolstu vi a tsibele, mitn kop in dr'erd!"* You should grow like an onion, with your head in the ground!

I first heard these words some twenty-one years later, January of 1947, when Nina and I, aged fourteen and eleven respectively, were talking one late afternoon, a Friday, in the kitchen of my home. Nina had come over for a rare winter sleepover. We were helping my mother prepare the Shabbos dinner, and I was elated by Nina's company.

My mother had asked me to chop an onion, and Nina another one, and the saying, just as we'd commenced peeling the onions, flew from Nina's mouth.

"You should grow like an onion, with your head in the ground!"

She meant it only as light humor, and indeed, the oddness of the expression had me and Nina instantly laughing.

But my mother froze. A moment before she'd been crouched before the oven, checking the baking challah loaves. But hearing Nina's words, she shot up.

For what seemed a whole minute she didn't speak or move. During this time she might have been thinking, I knew, about us, her children, about whether we were bathed on schedule, or had finished our homework, or, the night before, had gone to bed on time, or, more generally, whether we were on the *right track,* as she often called it. Then again, she might have been thinking of my father, of whether she'd sufficiently cleaned and ironed his clothes, or had sent him off that morning with a decent enough breakfast and a happy enough wave, or whether she could muster the energy to sufficiently welcome him home that night. Tradition advises, my father once explained, that on Shabbos a husband make love to his wife, and this desire, too, was something to consider. In the totality of Friday she had to dust, sweep, and otherwise tidy the house; get us children washed; knead, braid, and bake the loaves of challah bread; set the table, prepare the meat, peel the potatoes, and rinse and chop the vegetables; wash herself, present the dinner, clear the table, put the food away, and wash the dishes. She had to do all this, and then she had to go upstairs to make ready for, as she once put it to me, *the you know what.* She didn't think this custom was sanctioned by God, but rather was godforsaken, clearly man-made. So many Shabbos nights, trudging up the stairs to her bedroom, my mother was certain of it. There was all this — which on a yearly basis included the extra cleaning and cooking for the Jewish calendar, not only the weekly Shabbos meal but also the feasts for the New Year and Passover, and so many other holidays too, even minor festivals like Purim and Chanukah — and somewhere along the way this prize she'd felt propelled to rush toward and claim, marrying Mort Leibritsky and having his children, had become something to both love and hate. Confused, tired, my mother might have, in her pausing, been thinking about that.

Finally she said to Nina, "That's an awful expression. A *curse.* Don't let me ever hear you say that to anyone." Her expression stricken, she looked Nina in the eyes and then me. We hadn't yet had a chance to ask her what she meant when she reached in front of us, grabbed one of the still uncut onions, and, as if it had spontaneously rotted, threw it away.

"Can't you tell?" She wiped her hands on her apron. "Molly. Nina. I'm cursed."

But the curse lifted during those cherished weeks at Woodmont, where, despite the trajectories of their adult lives, my mother was convinced there were no longer any differences of significance between her and Vivie, no one was luckier, better married, prettier, more vivacious, and all she'd ever done to Vivie, however badly she'd broken her sister's heart (the shock, the crying, the anger, the nearly five years of silent treatment that followed), however hard were those next years of uncertainty (Would Vivie ever marry? Was it time to take up nursing yet?), it no longer mattered, and they were who they were before — before what? For my mother there were no words for what had driven her in a blind walk toward what had nearly destroyed them.

That first Friday morning at the beach, once Ada, Vivie, and Bec had stuffed their long manes into their caps, the three sisters strolled, more gingerly than before, toward the water. Arriving at its edge, Bec was the one to plunge right in, no hesitation, then to come up from under with a yelp and a smile. Ada and Vivie watched, ankle deep. They glanced at each other. *If you go, I'll go,* Ada thought. They were only little more than knee deep but they held their arms out as if the water already rose to their waists. They laughed. They whooped. Vivie bent down and splashed water onto her belly and shoulders. Ada watched, then followed her older sister's actions in a way that was as automatic as when she was a child. Oh, how she'd loved being a child! They had never fought then, in those days of early innocence, when Vivie, older, doing everything Ada wanted to do but doing it better, more easily, was only to be imitated, worshiped, chased, revered. Here at the beach, each morning when they dunked, all that goodness they were born into, all that they had ever been to each other, was restored. The salty air, cool with breezes, an air wholly other than that in Middletown, had to be responsible, she reasoned. How else could you explain this transformation in their relationship? *If you go, I'll go,* her eyes told her sister once again. And at that Vivie raised her arms over her head, hands together, and dove forward, and Ada raised her arms over her head, hands together, and followed her sister into the cool waters of the Long Island Sound.

The three floated on their backs, kicking occasionally, their arms sculling beside them to keep them afloat. This was happiness, my mother knew, this early-morning chill they so willingly endured. She raised her head briefly, enough to look shoreward, in the direction of their cottage and of Hillside Avenue running behind it. Later in the day they'd confront a whole body of men: the peddlers driving past — the iceman, the fish man, the milkman, the produce man, the ice cream man — and, later still, their husbands would return for a Shabbos meal they had yet to even think about making. But for now she was here, buoyant on her back in the waters of her childhood, her sisters by her side, and not a single one of those many men had the power to change that fact. They were here, doing just what they wanted. She took a deep breath. How glorious, she thought, simply to breathe.

3
OF MINYANS AND BASEBALL

That same Friday my father, Mort, alone in his bed in Middletown, woke in the morning from a marvelous dream. My father had had this dream before, but not in a long while. In it he was already at shul, praying at the morning service. The other men of the usual minyan were there too — Jerome Kaminsky, Nathan Novak, Abe Leiberman, Stanley Levine, Harold Sokull, Marvin Abkin, Sid Pasternack, Freddy Horowitz, Mort's brother Nelson Leibritsky, and his brother-in-law, that sorry-ass (as my father typically put it) Leo Cohen — but special to the service was the presence of my father's father, standing right next to him, Zelik Leibritsky's body wrapped in his old tallis, its white fabric as aged as the man's beard but its gold embroidery still bold and shiny. More than the others, my grandfather Zelik prayed especially fervently, as in life he always had, bowing and rocking, mumbling and sometimes singing the Hebrew words. Nevertheless, because the laws of dreams were not the laws of life, the two men — father and son — were simultaneously talking.

"How's business?" Zelik asked.

"Good, good," Mort answered, relieved to say as much. He explained to his father how the war had broken the relentless economic depression. And with the war over, along with its rationing, sales were so much better. In the past year — the time since their last dream-talk — Mort had felt secure enough to get the store's floor professionally polished and its walls painted. "Business has not only picked up, but it's gotten *that* good," he said, relieved once again.

His father nodded. "And how's the family?" he asked. "How's the lovely Ada?"

"No one's sick," Mort began.

Again, his father nodded.

"And we found our cousin," Mort told Zelik. "Reuben Leibritsky, from Poland to Palestine to Israel. A survivor."

"Survivor," Zelik echoed. After a pause he said quietly, "Good, good."

"And the kids, my kids, do well, or well enough, at school," Mort said.

Not surprisingly, Zelik raised his eyebrows; the subject of the kids, my father knew, was always a good one for the old man. He had died when Davy was two.

Mort continued. "Molly's a good girl. And Davy, you never know, he just might be the baseball player I never was. Shortstop. Shortstop," Mort repeated, and unknowingly repeated again, the words quickly falling into the rhythm of the prayer that the men of the minyan surrounding him uttered.

"And Howard," he added, blinking. "Turns out Howard shows some talent in business. We had him three days after school the whole year, and while the kid may not make straight A's, he can sure make a sale."

Zelik raised his eyebrows even higher. He also whistled, a note that quickly rose and fell in time with the rocking of his praying body.

About then Mort woke, and though the dream faded, he nevertheless heard his father's response as well as a strange knock at the synagogue's door.

"That might be Howard right now," Zelik suggested, nodding. "And about that talent," the man added, "he got that from me."

Mort sat up in bed, fully awakened. "Maybe so," he told his father, smiling, glad to have pleased him.

Breakfast was an easy enough matter for

my father to prepare, even without my mother to do it. A cup of Nescafé, some toast, two boiled eggs. How nice, Mort thought, that fourth morning without us, the *Hartford Courant* splayed before him, and beside him his toast buttered, his eggs peeled, his coffee stirred. As on the three days before, it astonished my father this morning how much peacefulness there was to family life, minus the family.

As he sipped his coffee he began to page through the *Courant*'s sports section, searching, as he'd been doing recently, for any updates on Babe Ruth, who two weeks ago had appeared at Yankee Stadium for its twenty-fifth anniversary celebration. He could do this, page through the sports section first thing, because he'd already taken in the latest news of Israel the night before, on the radio. At the moment, after months of battles that came on the heels of Israel's independence, truce was where matters in the Middle East stood. And so there was hope, my father concluded. He'd emphasize that hope to his cousin Reuben, still struggling to get settled there, in his next correspondence. But for Babe Ruth, photographed at Yankee Stadium leaning on a bat as if it were a cane, hope wasn't so obvious a matter. Hero that he was, he was sick as a dog, couldn't possibly have many days left. *You know how bad my voice sounds,* Ruth was quoted as saying to the crowd that day. *Well, it feels just as bad.*

Mort looked up from the paper. "You heard about the Babe?" Once again he was talking to Zelik, who he knew was still there, lingering, as eager as Mort was for coffee and news. His father had been the first in the family — the first Leibritsky in America — to fall in love with baseball. Thoroughly — because he missed his father, because he'd always loved talking sports with the old man — Mort told him everything he knew about Babe Ruth's illness.

In fact Zelik had also succumbed to the kind of internal rot that was ruining Babe Ruth, and perhaps because of that connection, when Mort got to the part about Ruth's recent words at Yankee Stadium, he heard them that second time around in the voice of his father. *You know how bad my voice sounds,* the old man, by way of Babe Ruth, repeated sadly. *Well, it feels just as bad.*

Mort was going to respond to his father, tell him to hang in there and that God would surely answer his prayers, but just then his brother Nelson honked his car horn. Mort shot up, grabbed his hat, and rushed toward the back door, leaving the Nescafé half-drunk and the opened sports section strewn across the table. Then he turned around. He placed the coffee cup and other dishes in the sink, and neatly, section by section, just as his father used to do, he folded the paper.

He and Nelson were approaching the synagogue when Mort recalled Howard's promise to drive that morning from Woodmont to Middletown in time to join the minyan. Then he recalled that knocking in his dream. His father had been right, he realized. It probably was Howard.

As he and Nelson closed their car doors, Mort looked up and down Broad Street, scanning the cars parked along the curb for his Dodge. When he didn't see it he looked in both directions again, this time searching not for his car but for Howard. He didn't see him either. The person he saw instead, opening the synagogue's side door, was his brother-in-law Leo Cohen, a man so frail it seemed for a moment that the simple feat of pulling the door wide enough to slip inside would be too much for him.

Mort turned from the sight of Leo to that of Nelson. "Any minute now," he told Nelson about Howard's arrival, patting his brother's ample back as the two headed toward the synagogue door, which by then had already closed. Mort realized, too, that Howard might in fact already be there, having parked the car behind the synagogue, where they wouldn't have been able to see it from the road. Yes, any minute now, he sang to himself.

Mort surged ahead of Nelson, his eagerness to get to it motivating him as always. His outpacing Nelson also had to do with Nelson's being fat; his younger brother always lagged behind. Still, once at the door Mort waited for Nelson, holding it open for him. Standing there, hand clenched on the metal handle, one foot on the sidewalk outside the building, the other foot a step inside, he could almost taste it, the sweetness of entering the shul, the satisfaction he'd feel just a moment later, after closing the doors behind him to that whirlwind of American society, that melting pot of everybody from everywhere. For a few minutes each day, behind the synagogue's shut door, my father could pretend it was just them: the Jews. They were in a little shtetl somewhere in eastern Europe, doing what Jews always did, and they weren't getting blown to pieces. Or, he sometimes imagined of late, they were in Israel, the Israel that could be once the current truce matured into a lasting peace.

As he and Nelson ambled toward the utility room used for the morning minyan — no reason to muddy the upstairs sanctuary for such a routine occasion — Mort could hear the mutterings, the hellos and how-you-doings, of his fellow minyan brothers. For a moment he thought he might sidestep Nelson, who in the hallway blocked his way and stalled him. But soon enough he was standing inside the utility room, a bare place with nothing but white walls, a wooden floor, and a flood of fluorescence pouring from the ceiling. Because the minyan would stand the whole time, the metal folding chairs that might have served the group remained pushed against the walls. For a few years already theirs had been a Conservative synagogue, not Orthodox as in Woodmont, which meant that the women could stand right there with them, but, truth was, the women had other things going on in the morning; they never showed for the service.

So there he stood amidst his friends, the same pious group as in his dream. He glanced at Jerome Kaminsky, who stood by Nathan Novak, chatting. Then he joined Abe Leiberman, Stanley Levine, and Harold Sokull, who weren't talking but waiting, and in doing so formed a kind of row.

But where was Howard? he wondered, glancing from face to face.

In the next instant, as if the minyan had been waiting for him and Nelson, the service began, a chorus of Hebrew muttering. Perhaps because his brother-in-law Leo Cohen was standing just outside the clump of men, the group soon enough considered Leo their minyan leader, and within minutes Mort heard Leo's Hebrew mumbles rise above the mumbles of the others and sharpen into defined words every so often, enough to keep the pack praying at the same pace. Good for nothing was the way Mort thought of Leo at the store where he employed him, despite how frail and sick he was, because he owed Vivie that much. He knew he did. But right then, surprisingly enough, Leo Cohen was good for something. The rabbi, as was often enough the case for morning minyan, was nowhere in sight. Mort was glad, for he liked it better this way, a minyan of equals, men perfectly able to get the job done, without supervision. God was with them, after all, and that was all the supervision they needed.

The prayers began, the Bar'chu, the Sh'ma, and they were racing already toward the second Kaddish, not a mourner's Kaddish, just a regular Kaddish, a kind of marker, five sections of the service, five Kaddishes. That's how it went. My father could almost glide through them, saying each Kaddish without even knowing he was saying them. In fact, if he didn't snap himself out of it he could get through the entire morning service that way, waking up at the end as if from a nap. He'd done that on so many occasions he felt ashamed; come Yom Kippur he always had much to atone for. That was a hazard, yes, but there were so many days that were otherwise; there was that point, and perhaps they were nearing it just then, when he'd become immersed in prayer, when the sound of the Hebrew mumblings around him, and the sound of Hebrew issuing from his own lips, and the sound of Hebrew swimming through his mind, transported him and he felt that the language and he were one, that the prayers and he were one, that God and he were one. This phenomenon, he understood, was the transcendence of prayer, a kind of freedom he'd experienced now and again as a kid but more and more as an adult, and the older he got the more frequently he found himself in that place — foreign, unmapped, lost — a wonderful, ethereal place conjured forth by the beauty of the ancient words, and his soul would nearly burst with the gratitude he felt for them, and his heart ached with joy. It's true, your heart can literally hurt with joy, my father said to us on more than one occasion, though when he did we had no idea he was speaking of prayer. It can really be a pain you feel, he continued, a terrible, wonderful pain. I always assumed he was talking about fatherhood.

At shul that Friday morning Mort hoped that he was nearing that moment when he was to achieve that blessing of transcendence, hoped it was just around the corner, following the second Kaddish, swooping in at the start of the next prayer, the Amidah, and, like the others, he took three steps back then three steps forward to ready himself for the presence of God that he would meet, if he were steady and focused, in prayer, in this most serious prayer, this prayer so big, so central, one of its many names, his father had once taught him, was simply *The Prayer*. But just then, three steps backward, three forward, a quieter Hebrew muttering began, a mentioning of the ancestors, God of Abraham, God of Isaac, God of Jacob, and another relation came to mind, an extant one, his son Howard, who had promised to arrive that day from Woodmont in time for morning minyan but clearly wasn't going to come through.

God of Abraham, God of Jacob, God of Isaac, *God forgive me,* Mort continued, ad-libbing, which was not allowed, which was another thing for which he'd ultimately have to atone, God forgive me, but you grant a son a wish, help him and the family get to the beach, a summer of all play and no work, a summer of paradise and sunshine and endless bowls of fruit salad, a summer unimaginable to me and my father, and what does that son do but take it all for granted. God forgive me, he told himself, but I expected more from Howard, never would I have broken my word to my father, ignored my father, God rest his soul, God hope the old soul's not really hurting, God help him if he is, and then Mort was back to the written text, back to God, busy and industrious — so very unlike Howard — sustaining the living with loving-kindness, resurrecting the dead with great mercy, supporting the falling, healing the sick, releasing the bound, and fulfilling his word to those who sleep in the dust.

He'd once slept in the dust, Mort realized, his heart seized by the word, and by dust he meant ignorance, and by ignorance he meant himself, before his awakening, for which he had his father, Zelik, to thank. At the time he'd been a few years younger than Howard was now, just twelve, his bar mitzvah nearing, but he was far more in love with baseball then than with Judaism. Games and practices were on Saturdays and he'd appealed to his father for permission to forgo the rules of Shabbos for the freedom of playing Saturday games. His team wanted him, a natural as a shortstop, and he wanted them. But Zelik had shaken his head; the law was the law, he'd said, not without sympathy for Mort's request. After all, baseball was certainly a worthy concern. But, his father had remarked, you couldn't compare the pursuit of baseball with the rules of Judaism, the teachings of Torah, the love of God, and — here Zelik cleared his throat for dramatic effect — the fate of the Jewish people. There was talk then of the old life before America: of expulsion from Moscow, of life within the Pale, of dire poverty, robbings, even killings, of every law designed to keep you down. This was what the family, because of their Judaism, had suffered. But hadn't Mort heard all this a thousand times before? He looked to his father. "We have to remember the Sabbath," the man concluded. "We can't choose not to. That's the same thing as choosing not to be a Jew."

"Then I choose not to."

"You don't know what you're saying."

Zelik had stepped back, as if wounded, and they'd walked away from each other for the afternoon. Later, as my father had come down the stairs for dinner, Zelik met him at the landing. His words, heated earlier, were now calm, even kind.

"Listen," he told Mort. The unusual sweetness of his father's voice captivated Mort and he did listen. "What this is," Zelik said, "is a responsibility. This is how you were born: Jewish. This is the family you were born into: of Abraham, Isaac, and Jacob. You can't change that, and this is how it comes: with responsibilities. We have to meet them, or —"

Zelik looked at him and the words, which at first came so easily, and had sounded almost like music, were now seemingly beyond his grasp. "Don't you see?" he added, shaking his head as if to clear his mind. "Responsibilities," he repeated quietly.

This moment was the first time his father had talked to him like that, like Mort actually did have a choice, to meet or refuse to meet his responsibilities. In a few months the bar mitzvah would mark him a man, at least in religious terms, and with that his full participation in adult Jewish life could begin, but it was this moment that my father always thought of as the one that truly began his adulthood. He did have responsibilities, he realized, blinking his eyes, as if to push past the dust of sleepy denial. He just hadn't seen his life that way before. He didn't know he had the will to do it, but in the end he did: he made his choice, and it was against baseball.

The words of the Amidah continued, and as Mort rocked forward and backward, his eyes focused again on his prayer book, his mind working to find that center point, that place that stilled his increasingly bewildered thoughts — Where's Howard? Where is he? — he let the Hebrew ground him: "Restore our judges as in former times," he prayed, "and our counselors as of yore; remove from us sorrow and sighing, and reign over us, You alone, O Lord, with kindness and compassion, with righteousness and justice." He read and he davened and still he heard Howard telling him, convincing him, "I'll come back early, in time for morning minyan." In his prayer book he read, "Blessed are You, Lord, who crushes enemies and subdues the wicked," and in his mind he was wagging his finger at Howard, telling him that the thing about Judaism was that either you were in or you were out. The chosen people. Well, it didn't work to be chosen unless you chose right back. And he had. Mort was in. He was there. He was present. *But where the hell are you?* he asked Howard.

He shook his head, attempting to clear it, bowed deeply, and began again.

"Look with favor, Lord our God, on Your people Israel and pay heed to their prayer," Mort prayed, though at the same time he heard his father say, speaking of Howard, "He gets that from me." Mort read, "You are the Beneficent One, for Your mercies never cease," while the words forming in his mind were *goddamnit, goddamnit, goddamnit.* The prayer was coming to a close. "May the words of my mouth and the meditation of my heart be acceptable before You, Lord," Mort intoned while inwardly he said, strangely enough, *shortstop, shortstop.* Then, suddenly speaking of Davy and his talent with the glove and ball, he turned to his phantom father and said, gloating: *He gets that from me.*

That was not the prayer, the Amidah, Mort had anticipated. Rather than transcendence he felt in its wake disgrace. His prayer book, usually weightless to the touch, might as well have been made of stones. Even his body, filled by that lightness of spirit he'd gained upon entering the shul, felt deadened by his failure, wobbly, weak. His face, he soon realized, was damp with sweat.

When he looked around he noticed the men had gathered near him, and Nathan Novak, leaning closest, soon wrapped an arm around his shoulders. Jerome Kaminsky pulled a chair from against a wall and unfolded it, then pointed at Mort, then at the chair.

You know how bad my voice sounds. Well, it feels just as bad, he almost began to explain to them, his knees quivering just like Babe Ruth's reportedly had at Yankee Stadium.

Internal rot. Surely, he reasoned, considering the rancor of his prayer, he had it as bad as Ruth, as bad as his dead father. He wondered: Was he going to die of it too? Was the morning's visitation of spirit — his father's and Babe Ruth's — a kind of premonition? Was that knocking in his dream the knocking not of Howard but of the other world? He then thought of something else, even worse: Did he not know how to be a father?

For a moment all prayer ceased and the men gathered even more tightly around him. Harold Sokull urged him to sit; he was tired, Harold told him, he didn't look so good, maybe he needed a rest. It had to be hard, Freddy Horowitz suggested, what with the family gone and all. Abe Leiberman and Stanley Levine pointed at a chair; Jerome Kaminsky was patting his back.

As Mort eased himself into the chair, Nathan Novak wouldn't let him go, had his arm in a grip. Once seated, Jerome Kaminsky stepped forward, loosened Mort's tie. His brother-in-law Leo Cohen then stood before him, holding a glass of water he'd seemed to conjure forth. For an instant my father stared at Leo in disbelief: all those years in the store he'd never seen Leo move so swiftly. But soon his attention shifted. Marvin Abkin was speaking to him, his voice as gentle as he'd ever heard it. "Drink up, big boy. Drink up."

Not one man continued to pray without him.

Finally, Marvin Abkin said, his voice hushed, "Heart? Heart bothering you?"

Mort shook his head. "Not a heart problem," he said quietly. "God, no. Just a touch of worry. That's all."

He looked up at the concerned men surrounding him. How glad he was to know them, he thought, scanning the familiar faces. How lucky each morning to be right there with them. Indeed the minyan's love at that moment was as palpable and clear as any my father had known, even Ada's, he realized, even his kids'. He sat in the chair and the cluster of men moved in one motion, like an amoeba might move, a shifting blob of life and energy, inches closer toward the chair, toward him. Jerome Kaminsky began fanning him, while his brother Nelson and Nathan Novak gripped him, one man to each of his shoulders. As Mort observed the men's attention he was reminded of his wedding day, when he'd been lifted in a chair by a group of men not unlike this group, lifted high in the air in this very synagogue, this very room, which that day was decorated with flowers and had tables of food set out that were overflowing. He felt just that way again, like they'd gathered around him and in doing so had lifted him up. With gratitude he looked once again from one man, one friend, one prayer brother to the next. Howard, he would tell his son when he saw him, gently and wisely teaching him, just as his father had once taught him: This Jewishness is no game. It's nothing to toy with. It's your essence, he'd say, simply enough. It's your very soul.

Now that he'd recovered the men returned to their prayer, for they could pray and they could keep an eye on him and they could shift like an amoebic blob when necessary and all the while they never missed a beat of the service. The last of the Kaddishes now approached and this would be a mourner's Kaddish, Mort knew. As he struggled to stand and then, feet planted, to steady himself, the group turned to him, and looking out he saw many pairs of eyes questioning his rising at all, much less his rising to mourn.

"Babe Ruth," he said, by way of explanation. All the rest was just too complicated. "I've been anxious, lately, for the Babe."

But that was all the explanation needed.

Suddenly, with Ruth recalled, they were all mourners, though the great man — not a Jew but close enough — hadn't fallen just yet. Nevertheless, they bowed their heads, began the Kaddish, and, together, the men prayed.

When he left the shul moments later my father felt as he always did: cleansed and clearheaded. He shook hands with his minyan brothers, smacked their backs, and watched them scatter.

When you got right down to it, he understood anew, trailing Nelson at this point as they made their way back to the car, life was pretty simple. Just one rule, above all others. He looked up to the sky, a flawless, bright blue, and then at the houses and buildings on Middletown's Broad Street, the rows of cars parked neatly along each side. Everything was God, he told himself, nodding.

Then he inhaled deeply.

For every breath was Him.

Howard snored. That's how I knew he was going to be late that Friday morning, by the sounds emanating from the thin walls of the cottage well past seven a.m., when he should have risen. Freedom can be a complicated thing, and even at the very start of summer Howard had grabbed a little too much, too soon.

When he did wake it was already twenty past, and the sisters, who had left some time ago for their dunk, weren't back yet. The cottage was quiet. Howard changed that with a thud, then a worried "Oh, shit. *Shit.*" Soon enough he was making his way down the cottage's creaky and by then quite sandy stairs, then tiptoeing around Nina and me lying in the sofa bed, as he looked for the car keys he'd last dropped into a living room ashtray. A moment later he walked past us again, into the dining room, where he rummaged through the mound of unfolded laundry covering the large oak table, and then he went into the kitchen, where I could hear him open the fridge. I could have told him that I, at least, was already awake, that the sisters, who had left for their dunk, had woken me up. I could have. But to take in Howard struggling, at least in the days before we lost Davy, was one of the best kinds of fun.

Well over an hour later Howard pulled into Middletown and parked the Dodge on Broad Street, slamming its door as he raced toward the synagogue. But he'd taken only a few steps when he spotted them: Mort and Nelson. Their yarmulkes, which covered their bald spots perfectly, were already off their heads and stuffed in their pockets.

Nervously, my brother called to them. When they looked his way he waved, and they in turn waved back, Mort's hand lingering in the air.

"So you made it," Mort said, sounding strangely matter-of-fact, a tone that worked to relieve Howard of some of the worry he'd been shouldering as he drove.

"Sorry," Howard said. "Got going a little late."

As Mort observed him — the wrinkled khakis, the partially untucked shirt, the loafers worn without socks, the chin stubble (Howard realized, scratching at it) — Howard shifted on his feet. While he tucked in the shirt, Mort's expression, which at first had almost seemed friendly, shifted in increments until it was decidedly grim.

"Don't tell *me*," he finally said. "Tell God." He walked past Howard and waited beside the Dodge. "Throw me the keys," he said, and Howard did.

When Mort started the car Howard gave him a questioning glance. Howard was standing yards away, beside Nelson. He didn't know if he was expected to get in the car or not.

"I'll see you at the store," Mort said, his tone still matter-of-fact but his gaze removed from Howard and focused on the road ahead of him. In the next moment he pulled away from the curb.

"It's going to be a long day," Howard told Nelson. As Howard watched Mort drive off, his stomach dropped from the middle of his body to his feet, a sensation he'd experienced before, and always in connection with his father. *A long day,* he repeated to himself.

Just then Nelson threw his arm around his nephew's shoulders. "Tell you what," Nelson said, patting his back. "Stick with me."

Leibritsky's Department Store on Middletown's Main Street was where the men all worked: Mort, Nelson, Leo, and sometimes Howard. I often thought of my brother's time there during his high school years as a male rite of passage, as if the bar mitzvah alone hadn't been enough of an ordeal to transform him from boy to man. But some regularly logged hours at Leibritsky's Department Store would do it. Years ago the store had been a snug sell-anything kind of place located at the north end of Main Street — at least that's the legend we children had always been told — but all throughout our childhood it was the spacious five-section (men's apparel, women's apparel, children's apparel, shoes, and housewares) department store located toward the south end that my brother, from his time there, came to know as intimately as our home. First thing that morning, to Mrs. Rossetti, mother of the same Lucinda Rossetti who had yet to mail the beginnings of a picture to Davy, Howard promptly sold the latest Sunbeam Mixmaster.

"It'll make your life easier. You deserve that," he told Mrs. Rossetti, who looked at him with surprise and then agreed.

On a good day, a normal day, a substantial sale like that would be cause for Mort to proudly slap Howard's back, but that morning when Nelson clapped his hands, calling attention to the sale, and then said with deliberate volume, "Nice one, Howard, nice one," Mort, though standing only yards away, pretended not to hear. Once again Howard's stomach dropped to the floor and for some time after that his head hung low. He could have made another sale, or at least have tried to, but he didn't feel like approaching anyone. Instead he closeted himself in the back area of the store, unnecessarily folding and refolding children's play clothes.

Later that morning, close to noon, Nelson found Howard and asked him out to lunch, just the two of them. Howard explained that though he hadn't had much of a breakfast, and was maybe a little hungry, he nevertheless didn't feel like eating.

"Come on. Do you some good. What do you say?" Nelson asked again.

This time Howard nodded. Nelson had always been good to him. Howard didn't remember this, exactly, but he'd been told at least a hundred times how he'd taken to Nelson right away, even as a baby. When he'd cried, touched at times by colic, Nelson's ample arms were a reliable comfort and Howard would quiet right down, even sleep. And when Howard was still a small boy Nelson would come by to take him for walks, often to the local playground, where Nelson would gently push Howard's back as he sat on a swing. In the years following that, Nelson had taken Howard to the Saturday movie matinee at the Palace Theater on Middletown's Main Street. Just him. Together they'd seen *The Adventures of Robin Hood, Mr. Smith Goes to Washington,* and *The Wizard of Oz.* There was even a couple of years, 1942 and 1943, when Howard was twelve and thirteen, when he and Nelson had gone to the movies together once every month during the school year. They'd watch the show and Nelson, always armed with bite-sized Tootsie Rolls, would pass Howard candy throughout the story's progression. That was all in the past — high school had come along, and with that a natural enough orientation more toward friends than uncles, however kind — but even so Howard had continued to feel good in Nelson's company, important, and Nelson, in turn, unfailingly lit up simply at the sight of him.

They ate together that Friday at Regina's, a tiny restaurant, four tables total, in the living room of the home of Regina Scantelli. They might have eaten at Angelina's, in Angelina Tucci's living room–turned–restaurant, but Nelson preferred Regina's. Only one other customer was there, Judge Luigo, of the Middlesex County municipal court. As Nelson took his seat he nodded, and the judge nodded back. "What'll it be?" Regina then asked Nelson and Howard, and by that she meant either the spaghetti and meat sauce or the chicken parmesan. That was what she'd cooked up that day, so far.

Since there was such a good chance of chicken that night for the Shabbos meal in Woodmont — roast chicken, not chicken parmesan, but chicken all the same — Howard ordered the spaghetti. Besides, the chicken parmesan, combining meat with cheese, wasn't kosher, even in the relatively loose way his family defined that term. But Nelson, who wouldn't be coming with them to Woodmont for the weekend, who was single and who had once told Howard that he ate bologna sandwiches for dinner most nights, ordered — without hesitating, and apparently without worrying about the rules of kashruth — the chicken parmesan for lunch.

They didn't talk while they ate, but over coffee Nelson said, "You can't see it now, but you made your father happy this morning with that sale and all. He'll forget about the rest. It was just one minyan out of a million."

"I didn't mean to be late," Howard said, the memory of Mort pulling away from the curb and driving past him revived in his mind.

"No one said you meant it," Nelson offered. Quietly, he tapped his fork on the edge of the table.

Howard paused, watched his uncle play with his fork, and then glanced at Nelson's face. "He might as well have meant it. You saw it. The way he drove off."

Nelson nodded. He lifted his fork then placed it on his empty plate. Glancing toward the kitchen, he looked as if he wanted something else, but then he turned back to Howard. "It can be hard to be a son," he pronounced at last. "I know what I'm saying."

A look of deep sadness overcame Nelson. Howard waited for him to say more — being a son was indeed a difficult business, the most difficult of his life — but Nelson wouldn't. Instead he flagged Regina over to the table. "You got any dessert?" he asked, suddenly agitated. "A little for me, a little for him. We'll split whatever you've got."

When Regina brought them two bowls of fruit cocktail, Nelson dug right in. Howard, who hadn't been able to finish his meal, had no appetite for it. He slid his bowl toward Nelson.

"I'll tell you about it sometime," Nelson offered at last, his voice calmer, the two bowls of fruit cocktail eaten clean. "It's not about your father, it's about my father," he added, and that was at least something.

Howard nodded.

At three o'clock that afternoon Mort and Leo grabbed their weekend suitcases, stuck in a corner of the back office at the store, and, along with Howard, headed off, out of Middletown and toward Woodmont. Because Leo was prone to car sickness, he sat in the front seat beside Howard, who drove. Leo was reading a book by Charles Darwin, *The Formation of Vegetable Mould, Through the Action of Worms.* With a title like that, Howard didn't even want to begin to ask about the book. Behind Howard, Mort sat compliantly enough in the backseat, though for Howard the sight of Mort in the rearview mirror, serious as ever as he gazed out the window, and even as he nodded off napping, was more than a little daunting.

At four o'clock Howard pulled the Dodge into the parking lot at the Savin Rock amusement park in West Haven. His father was still napping, but this detour was expected, Howard knew, and so with only Leo's consent, but not Mort's, he drove toward that part of the parking area abutting Jimmies hot dog stand. They would each get a hot dog at Jimmies, known for its split dogs, perfectly fried. The stop was a secret from the women at Woodmont. The men knew that the women would scold them for ruining their appetite, but because dinner wouldn't be served until at least half-past seven, the fortification was indeed helpful, and besides, "there comes a point," Mort had said the first of the two previous times Howard had joined them, "when a man has to take a little time out from the family." As they sauntered moments later toward Jimmies, Howard trailing his newly awakened father, he noted to himself how odd a rationale that was, for the men had already taken time out — at the morning service, for example, not to mention during the whole week at the store. But Howard didn't dare question it: the men, Leo as much as Mort, were religious about their pre-Shabbos hot dogs. Apparently they needed the stop, couldn't quite make the transition from Middletown to Woodmont without it. And today was not the day to start even a friendly argument with his father.

Their hot dogs paid for, the men settled themselves at a nearby picnic table. Off in the distance was the famous Savin Rock roller coaster. Closer by, at their feet, was a veritable sea of littered napkins. The place was seedy, Howard always thought. But the hot dogs sure were good. For a few minutes the men ate in silence. Howard glanced several times Mort's way, but his father was steadfastly gazing out toward Long Island Sound. Leo's gaze was similarly seaward. Then Leo spoke.

"Your father frightened us at minyan." He turned to Howard. "He looked like he might pass out."

"It was nothing," Mort said, glancing at Leo then back to the water.

"Maybe a little more than nothing," Leo insisted. Again he looked Howard's way. "His face was pale. His heart was pounding."

"You don't know that," Mort told Leo firmly but not unkindly. "My heart was fine the whole time. I just grew weary suddenly. Needed to sit."

"I don't know," Leo said. "Seems bigger to me. Pull it out of him, Howard."

But Howard didn't say anything. Clearly, Mort didn't want him involved. In fact he was deliberately ignoring him, Howard understood, staring out at the ocean as he was, his back to Howard even when Leo addressed him.

Howard turned toward the ocean, which looked friendly enough, then toward Mort's icy back. The summer before, a Friday in July, everything had been different, more convivial. Mort had been driving that day. When they'd pulled in to Savin Rock and Howard had asked what was up, Mort began laughing. "Something for us," he'd finally said. Then they'd risen from the car and as they walked toward Jimmies, the smells of fried foods increasingly wafting their way, Mort had slapped Howard's back over and over. "Us, us, us," he'd eagerly repeated. Then he'd added, winking, "Don't tell."

Howard had gone with the men to Jimmies again, later that summer. Once more Mort welcomed Howard's joining them. He was even proud of Howard, who had come back to Middletown for a week to help with the store's summer inventory. "Eat up," Mort had told him then, adding a moment later, "What the hell, have two if you like."

But this day Mort merely said, "Ready?" exclusively to Leo, who nodded.

At five o'clock they arrived at the cottage.

Walking into a spotlessly clean kitchen, then past a dining room table perfectly set with flower-patterned china, wineglasses, and candlesticks, and then into a living room with the sofa bed folded up and no signs at all of two girls spending their nights there, Howard called, "Whoa, what happened *here*?"

Mort stood behind him, and Howard turned in time to see him remove his hat and place it, for one of the women to pick up, on the little telephone table in the dining room.

Mort looked around, nodded his approval.

"At least some people have respect," he said, finally staring at Howard, but only for the purpose of directing the implied criticism his way. He then turned from Howard and toward the dining table, where he focused his gaze on the unlit candles at the table's center.

When he spoke next, Mort was still staring at the candles as if mesmerized by a flame they didn't yet emit.

"Lovely, lovely," he said.

4
WHAT THEY TELL US WE ARE

There was something about Davy's personality — a touch of silliness, a whole lot of energy, an easy likability — that allowed us to see in him what we wanted to. My father saw that part of himself, the boy so very good at being a shortstop, that was never allowed to be. Howard, in contrast, very often saw someone to protect, perhaps against the father to whom he felt at times so vulnerable. In the same breath, however, Davy could be a way for Howard to buffer himself against Mort. That's why, perhaps, upon arriving at Woodmont that Friday evening, Howard grabbed Davy, threw him over his shoulder, and carried him, kicking and squealing, outside for a quick pre-dinner game of catch. The baseball gloves and ball were lying in a protected corner of the front porch, always ready for such an occasion. Without even stopping to take off his tie and shoes, Howard grabbed the mitts and ball and led Davy to the beach, where we could see them throwing the ball back and forth, and we could hear the distinctive thump of the hardball hitting the mitt's leather, and we could even hear Howard's gentle coaching of Davy — *good one, run, get it* — whose favorite part of the game was to chase a fly ball, the highest Howard could throw. Had he lived to play the game beyond his childhood, there's no doubt in my mind that Davy was destined to be an outfielder and not the shortstop of my father's projected dreams. But such is the way of family: we are what they tell us we are, and part of life's great struggle, it's always seemed to me, is to know oneself despite that imposing collective definition.

That effort was perhaps my great task that summer, other than trying to hang out as much as possible with Nina, and to do this I found myself that first week in Woodmont drawn at times to the claw-footed tub in the upstairs bathroom, which I'd recently discovered was a good place to think. The tub dry, my clothes still on, I hurdled the high rim and sank down, just as if I were soaking, but in silence rather than water. And something about that silence, along with the confinement of the tub, got me into a particular frame of mind, one in which it became more than evident that this was uncanny — this life, this existence at all — and what I meant by that was that it seemed so very strange to be me, just me, this silent inner self whom only I actually knew. The outer self, whom the family knew quite well, was but a shell, a quaint cover story, and that week I had only just begun to understand that no amount of living with them, cramped cottage and all, would ever change that fact. She didn't even have a name, this essence of myself, this non-Molly whom I quickly took to, rather liked, and that Friday, after Howard had taken off with Davy, and in the time we still had before we'd begin our Shabbos meal, squirreled away in the upstairs bathroom with the locked door and the womb-like walls of the tub surrounding me, I managed in just a few quiet minutes to do it, to woo her from the cave of my soul. *Hello,* I whispered to my near stranger of a self. *Hello.*

Moments before, upon the men's arrival that evening, after my father had loosened his tie, my mother, already dressed in a proper skirt and blouse for Shabbos, emerged from the kitchen to bring him a glass of water and told him to "Sit, sit," to which he answered, "I've been sitting already, too much sitting," and then she, as if she hadn't heard him, walked back into the kitchen, and he, as if he hadn't heard himself, sat, in the corner chair in the living room. And that's how my parents behaved toward each other then, courteous but cool, aware of each other but imperturbably so, as if they inhabited separate spheres and saw each other only from a distance. From what I observed it was hard to imagine them ever being passionate toward each other, hard to imagine that time when Ada was eighteen and Mort was twenty-four, and the attraction they felt for each other was so strong that Vivie was thrown, easily enough, by the wayside.

For Vivie the ordeal — something in hindsight she called her slow march toward freedom, toward a self she never knew she had — began like this.

A week after she'd spotted Ada and Mort hand in hand outside her front door, Vivie had to endure the fact that when Mort finally apologized to her, coming to her home just to do so, he didn't even hint at the possibility of their resuming their old courtship. It was real, then, she knew: the hand-in-hand business wasn't just an accident as Ada had tried so hard to convince her, describing over and over again the spill she'd taken just seconds before on their front walkway.

"He was pulling me up," Ada had insisted. "That's all. That's it. I was so embarrassed to fall like that — on my tuches! — but he acted like he didn't even see."

But with Mort's apology Vivie came to know better, came to know that her younger sister was capable of making a lie sound not only convincing but even sweet.

Then Vivie had to endure that first time, several weeks later, when she watched from her bedroom window as Mort approached her front door, rang the bell, and asked — albeit timidly — for Ada. Vivie crept from her bedroom to the top of the stairs where she could hear everything but not be seen. She gasped as Mort and Ada laughed upon meeting again. The laughter was quiet, meant not to be heard, but it was laughter — joy — all the same. And that's when my aunt decided that her survival, her dignity, depended on her moving out.

She knew of an extra room down the street in the Bloomberg home, where she'd babysat Lorna Bloomberg for so many years. The family was more than happy to offer it and to her relief accepted only the most nominal of pay. "We think of you as family," Mrs. Bloomberg told her, surprisingly enough. She thought of them as simply the Bloombergs, a couple who'd had a pest of a child late in life, people she didn't really know.

That first night at the Bloombergs', late February of 1926, was the first time in my aunt's life that she'd spent even a night on her own. The Bloombergs' extra room was a small one on the third floor, a former nanny's quarters, furnished, though barely so. When she'd arrived there, a Sunday night, she placed her suitcase down at the doorway then took a few steps inside the room and finally sat on its twin bed. For over an hour she stayed there, her coat still on, her hat in her hands, her mind determined to ignore Lorna Bloomberg, then fourteen, who kept peeking in on her, asking her if she needed this or that. More water? An extra blanket? Something to read? To all this Vivie shook her head, and she continued to sit still, frozen, even as she heard Mrs. Bloomberg scold Lorna, telling her to leave "poor Vivie" alone.

"Poor Vivie." The words resonated with how she felt about herself, a single woman in a room with a single bed, a single pillow, a single dresser, and a single window to glance out of. There was a small night table beside the bed, and on it was a glass filled with water and a dusty vase containing a single artificial red rose. It, too, was dusty.

She'd arrived at the Bloombergs' at seven. At nine or so the radiators began to clank loudly. At nine thirty the bulb in the lamp beside the bed flickered. Vivie thought the light would go out but it didn't. She wouldn't have minded if it had, blacking out the present scene and brightening the one in her mind of a different room, the one she was to have had as Mrs. Morton Leibritsky, a woman who might just work for a time at the store, she'd long figured, but only until the first child came, and then she'd be caught up in the whirlwind of responsibility that was motherhood. Her bedroom, the one she would share for a lifetime with Mort, was to look, with its full-sized bed, its several dressers, its lovely draped curtains and colorful bedding, nothing like the room she now inhabited. At ten o'clock she reached for the extra blanket at the foot of the bed and threw it over her lap. She was still in her coat but, strangely, she was shivering. By eleven, though, she rose to take off her coat and shoes, then she leaned back, placed her head on the pillow, and eventually wiped her eyes dry, flicked off the unsteady lamp, and fell asleep.

■ ■ ■ ■

Because she was on her own, just a half
block from her family but in this new room
feeling miles and miles away, and because
she'd never returned to Leibritsky's Department Store once she'd spotted Ada and
Mort together that day, Vivie needed a new
job. This she acquired promptly through a
suggestion from Mr. Bloomberg. She should
visit his doctor, he told her, who was out a
secretary, and within the week she began
working for Dr. Walter Shapiro, one of Middletown's two Jewish general practitioners.

The job gave her the money to keep going, to board, and it offered something to
do. Often those first weeks on her own she
reminded herself that the job was a step up
from the sales work — just a whole lot of
talking — that she'd been doing before.
She'd remind herself of that and then she'd
remind herself again, because in fact it was
so very quiet in Dr. Shapiro's somber waiting room, with its windows covered by
faded blue drapes, its worn carpeting, the
few pictures on the walls of foreign land-
scapes, and the patients who walked in, typically tired and anxious.

Still, the work gave shape to what otherwise would have been entirely unwieldy days, without purpose, with too much time to think. "Poor Vivie," Mrs. Bloomberg still called her weeks after she'd moved in, and who knew how many others thought of her in the same way, as forlorn as a patient waiting for Dr. Shapiro, as weakened at the core.

Spinster. The very idea of it made her shudder.

The job gave her a different title — Secretary, Gal Friday, Dr. Shapiro's Trusty Viv. Arriving by nine each morning, she'd get through those early hours by greeting patients and making appointments. In the afternoons she'd pull out the billing. But at some point she'd be interrupted by Tillie Hirschfield, Dr. Shapiro's nurse, who, just weeks into Vivie's tenure, couldn't resist the daily urge to drop her bottom right on Vivie's desktop and talk, not so much to her as at her. In this way Vivie invariably knew what Tillie Hirschfield would have for dinner that night, was thinking of doing over the weekend, and, most interestingly, what she'd gone through when she suffered both of her divorces. That the patients could hear Tillie as easily as Vivie could didn't seem to affect her oration. It might even have been the point, Vivie soon concluded. At five she'd leave the office and amble back to the

Bloombergs'. "Poor Vivie," Mrs. Bloomberg would be sure to say, without even realizing it, upon seeing her. "How was work?" she'd then ask, sadly. The phone, with her mother, Risel, calling her, might or might not then ring, and if so, another married woman would say "poor Vivie" at least once. This scenario wasn't much to come home to, and Vivie walked toward it slowly, breathing deeply as she did, at times gulping in the evening air as if whatever winds and fragrances and warmth or coolness that combined to form it were a prescription from Dr. Shapiro, medicinal, healing.

After some months she began to feel a bit better. It was April then and she trekked toward the Bloombergs' more slowly than ever, though not because she dreaded being there but because the evening air had become like a friend: fragrant, comfortable, comforting. Once she was midway to the Bloombergs' when, lost to the wonders of the spring air, she nearly bumped into a young couple, a man with his arm draped over the shoulder of a woman, who in turn had her arm wrapped around the man's back.

"Excuse me," the man said.

"Oh," Vivie muttered, not because of the near collision but because it pained her instantly to see these lovers. Rather than their faces, she focused on their shoes, his and hers. Then, because even that was too much, she focused on something else, the empty porch of the house they were in front of, its mailbox, nailed beside the front door, overflowing.

"Yes, I'm sorry too," she said, her face still turned from them. Then she dashed away, suddenly racing toward the Bloomberg home, which had never before seemed so much like a haven. After dinner she spent the evening in her room, lying on her back, soothing herself with heavy sighs. She had promised Lorna Bloomberg she'd play cards with her, but when Lorna knocked on her closed door Vivie told her she wasn't well, she had a stomachache, that tomorrow she'd play with her any game she wanted: rummy, hearts, Old Maid.

Tillie Hirschfield's remarkable two divorces didn't mean she was done with men. On the contrary, she was on the prowl, as she put it, searching for Mr. Right. "Two Mr. Wrongs don't make a Mr. Right," she quipped one afternoon. Then she added, "After what I've been through I deserve my Mr. Right." This time she was sitting beside Vivie's desk, not on it, and her voice was lowered, demonstrating a need for discretion that surprised Vivie. It was late spring and the flowery scent of Tillie's perfume reminded Vivie of the lilacs in bloom along her walk to and from the office.

"Maybe you and me could go out some night," Tillie proposed to Vivie. "You know, we'd be two ladies having dinner, maybe even having a drink or two." When Tillie winked, Vivie noticed the beginnings of lines around her eyes. "You never know what might happen. We just might run into a pair of handsome men."

Tillie nodded and smiled cajolingly.

"I spend my weekends with my sisters," Vivie lied. "It's my only time with them." In fact she spent some of each weekend at home, visiting her parents and one of her sisters, but the other one, who dated Mort Leibritsky, she still couldn't be around.

"Well, just think about it. You're not getting any younger." Tillie rose and broke into a yawn. "God, I'm bushed," she muttered, as she retreated to the examination area.

Such talk about men and age and, implicitly, about failure — those two divorces that kept Tillie Hirschfield on the prowl — unsettled Vivie. Sadly, she sighed and then scanned the waiting room. Two people were there, a mother, a young woman about

Vivie's age, and her small son, who was pale and couldn't sit still. The mother struggled to keep the boy seated. She talked to him, read to him, patted his back to calm him. She scolded once or twice. She looked exhausted. Watching them, and still thinking about Tillie, who was soon to turn thirty-five, she'd recently confessed to Vivie in a voice that sounded frightened and grave, a tone, Vivie understood, connected to her increasingly improbable search for Mr. Right, Vivie felt the stirrings of a new insight, something about the hardships of adult life, its awful loneliness, which hit you whether you were married or not; something about marriage itself not being the haven or even the prize she'd always thought. She rose and handed the boy a pad and pencil. "Want to draw a picture?" she asked, kneeling on the floor before him. When he grabbed the items, she patted his head. His mother said to him, "What do you say?" But before the child could thank Vivie she told the mother, "It's nothing. The least I could do. Doctor should see you in a minute."

That moment was a turning point for Vivie, who felt more free from then on to rise from her chair behind the reception desk, walk out to the sitting area in the waiting room, and engage a needy patient. Sometimes she brought a person a glass of water. Sometimes a better, more recent magazine. Sometimes she sat there and listened as patients complained about their aches and pains. Often they told her they didn't know what they'd do without Dr. Shapiro.

He was an unusual physician, she gradually understood, someone who frequently took in patients with unsolvable problems, people other doctors had given up on or considered overly sensitive, the kind who only imagined themselves to be sick. But in Dr. Shapiro's office, under his uniquely generous care, she watched those weakened souls gain hope, even much-needed color in their cheeks. Soon, a number of them would gain weight on their bones and energy in their step. Not everybody in this category of patients got better, but enough improved that Vivie began to wonder if Dr. Shapiro had a magic formula he passed out behind the closed doors of his examination rooms. She wouldn't mind seeing him herself, she often thought. But when Tillie Hirschfield told her that when all else failed Dr. Shapiro ordered the daily ingestion of cod liver oil along with more broccoli than you'd ever think to eat, Vivie's desire for Dr. Shapiro's special treatment, however helpful it apparently was, quickly waned.

One night in early summer, following a quiet day at the office — like everybody else even the sick were on vacation, Dr. Shapiro had joked — Vivie walked up Main Street to stop at a pharmacy before heading to the Bloombergs'. Because Leibritsky's Department Store was also at the street's north end, she'd not taken a step in that direction for months. But the pharmacy wouldn't take her nearly that far, she reasoned. She passed any number of businesses before she got to the pharmacy, and as she walked she took an interest in them, staring into the window displays of a florist's shop, a shoe store, a beauty parlor, an Italian food market. She was just passing a five-and-dime store when she spotted a couple sitting on stools at the closed lunch counter. The woman, wearing a blue sleeveless dress, held her arms outstretched toward the man beside her, who had shifted on his stool so that he faced her and not the counter. Whatever he was saying made her laugh. He leaned forward then, into her arms, and kissed the woman.

Vivie slowed her steps, fascinated. At some point, just like the woman through the window, Vivie raised an arm, though only to clutch at her chest. Then she stumbled forward. By the time she arrived at the pharmacy she was blinking back tears, embarrassed when the pharmacist called to her asking if he could help. She was fine, she told him, though as she raced home that night, and for many nights and days to come, she felt the deep pain of it: her love-less life, her dull routine, her bleak future, the one without Mort, the man she'd counted on, had seen that future in, the man who suddenly cropped up in her mind — despite everything, despite how far she thought she'd come — again and again.

Mid-July, while her parents and Bec, along with Ada and Mort, were away at Wood-mont, and while Vivie stayed behind in Middletown to hold down the fort, as she put it, at Dr. Shapiro's, she decided she would go out to dinner one night with Tillie Hirschfield. Why not? She'd saved her money, could afford a little extravagance. They ate at Angelina's, one of Middletown's many Italian kitchens. Tillie wore a string of fake pearls around her neck. Vivie wore an old charm bracelet. They talked about this and that, mostly their childhoods. Tillie was from West Hartford. "It's pretty there," she said wistfully, as if the place no longer existed.

They didn't meet any single men. The three other tables were filled by families. "Oh, well," Tillie had said, early into the evening. "Might as well eat up then."

And they did. They were delighted with the veal Angelina brought them, along with side bowls of pasta and marinara sauce. Their bellies full, they took a walk afterward, down Main Street, arms linked.

"I bet you're some sister," Tillie told her, leaning her head toward Vivie.

"I'm not so sure about that," Vivie answered, matter-of-fact. But when Tillie began laughing for no reason — the wine at dinner probably gone to her head — Vivie laughed too, because even without the aid of so much alcohol she felt strangely carefree. She'd have to buy herself more meals, and maybe some new stockings, maybe even a new dress. That's what a working woman could do, she suddenly knew. And that thought made her laugh again, louder.

Early that fall, even before her mother told her about Mort and Ada's engagement — arriving at Mrs. Bloomberg's doorstep to do so, sitting with the woman at her kitchen table, the two of them across from "poor Vivie," as they'd said in unison — she'd heard about it already. A patient of Dr. Shapiro's had told her by way of congratulating her, assuming she already knew.

What surprised her upon hearing the news was that it didn't knock her over. She did open her eyes wide. She also gasped, but almost silently. Then she resumed her work. Seated in the waiting room was that same tired mother she'd helped before, a person she now called Frances, and her son, Thomas, and soon Vivie rose, moving away from the patient who had told her the news and toward Frances and Thomas, both of whom obviously wanted her company, the mother for comfort, the child for some kind of new game to play, some kind of treat.

In November there would be a family dinner celebrating the engagement, and Vivie was to come. "You can't avoid them forever," her father, Maks, had said firmly, her mother and Bec nodding behind him.

"I'll come," Vivie said, simply enough.

The night of the family dinner Vivie was seated at the far end of the table, away from Mort and Ada, even away from Mort's parents. For starters soup was served but her appetite wasn't hearty. A light patter of conversation ensued, but Vivie remained silent, listening. Brisket, potatoes, and green beans came next, and while the meal was being eaten she didn't even attempt to engage in small talk with Bec, who, seated beside her, kept turning Vivie's way, a caring and constant vigil Vivie knew the whole family assumed was needed.

By dessert the talk focused on the impending wedding and it was Ada who then dominated, telling them what food she'd like at the reception, how the tables at the synagogue were to be arranged, whom she'd like to invite, which tailor she'd already visited to get fitted for a dress. She barely paused between sentences. Her excitement and sense of importance were on grand display, and there was Vivie, quiet at the other end of the table, comprehending what the moment meant to Ada while simultaneously thinking about the upcoming week at work, which patients would be coming on which days, Frances and Thomas again on Monday, a wheezing but lovable Mable Stump on Tuesday, a new patient, a fellow named Leo Cohen, with some kind of chronic cough, on Thursday. She thought of Tillie, too, her sad desperation, and a sense of tenderness for everybody she knew through her work with Dr. Shapiro, the world's wounded, filled her heart. Ada was blabbing on and on but to Vivie all that talk didn't really matter.

Until suddenly it did. "You're not always going to feel this big," she told Ada, abruptly interrupting her sister's eager monologue. These were the first words she'd directed Ada's way since the betrayal and they came out in a voice Vivie didn't know she had: confident and clear.

The talk in the room stopped.

"What? What did you say?" Ada asked, obviously surprised to hear Vivie address her.

"You're not always going to feel so big," Vivie repeated, her voice still full with the truth of her words. She was well aware that everyone was staring at her and that no one looked particularly happy to be doing so.

"What's that supposed to mean?" Ada asked. She held her hand at her collar bone and she tipped back slightly, as if knocked off-kilter by Vivie's words.

"Now's the time to be happy," Vivie answered. "Ada, enjoy your happiness while you have it. That's all I'm saying. Be happy, Ada. Be happy right now."

Around her the staring faces looked confused, as did Ada's. Then Ada nodded, said, "Thanks, I am happy. Very happy," and in the next moment the monologue of the bride-to-be resumed. Vivie sighed.

Six months after Davy's death, my aunt recalled her words to my mother that evening so long ago. Back then she'd meant to upset her, to pull her down a peg or two. "Enjoy your happiness while you have it," she'd told her younger sister, which wasn't so bad a thing to say, really, but was just bad enough, enough to cause Ada's flushed face to blanch. As the years progressed, and Vivie married a man she adored, it was obvious to Vivie that Ada's happiness had in fact shrunk, long before Davy's death, and her long-ago warning had come to seem like a bit of prescience rather than the bit of hate it really was. By then Vivie no longer felt such hatred, only compassion as she saw Ada's confused dissatisfaction take root. Ada obviously felt stuck in a rut but was cursed, Vivie could see, with the inability to fully understand it much less pull herself out of it. But after Davy's death, the idea that she had wanted Ada to suffer — even back then, when such a desire was understandable — haunted Vivie. She wondered if she'd really released all that early hate. "I'm so sad for you," she told her sister over and over again.

"What's that?" Ada once responded when Vivie called to say the words yet one more time. "Who's this?" she then asked, the bewilderment in her voice part and parcel of the tailspin, Vivie knew, of such a severe, unacceptable loss.

"It's Vivie," Vivie told her, saying her name slowly, as if it were a foreign word.

"Oh. Vivie," Ada said, her voice flat.

"Yes, yes, it's me. I'm so sad for you, Ada. Do you know that I'm sad? Truly and deeply sad?"

"Not as sad as me," Ada whispered.

"No. Of course not. No one could be as sad as you," Vivie finally said.

At Mort and Ada's wedding, a month after the engagement dinner, Vivie kept to herself, standing in a corner where she told herself she could fall quietly if in fact she were to faint, but to her surprise her legs never gave way and her head never felt at all woozy. In another corner an elderly aunt of Mort's — a woman she'd met once before at the store, a woman now clearly losing her wits — was sitting by herself in a chair, and Vivie dragged over another one to seat herself beside the old woman.

"Let me get you some food," Vivie told the woman, who nodded.

She brought back herring and a bagel, and some slices of tomato. On another plate she brought the good stuff: wedding cake, rugelach, and grapes.

When it appeared that the woman couldn't hold a fork steady in her hand, Vivie took the fork and gently fed her. While she did, a relative of the woman walked over, identified the woman as "Old Rose," patted her head, and walked away. Vivie continued to feed the woman, talking to her as she did, calling her by her name. "Eat up, Rose," she urged, "we're at a party." She wiped her mouth, and, the meal done, held Rose's hand. All the while, Rose stared ahead, vacantly. But then her mood shifted, something focused, and she turned to Vivie, her eyes comprehending.

"I know you," Rose told Vivie, and the limp hand inside Vivie's came alive and gave her hand a squeeze.

Smiling, Vivie said, "I know you too, Rose." Then she and Rose continued silently watching. By this time Mort and Ada were being lifted in chairs. A crowd danced around them, clapping. Yet louder than their clamor was Ada's voice, screeching with delight. In her corner with Rose, Vivie nodded her head in time with the music. She noticed that Rose did the same.

"Care to dance?" Vivie asked the woman jokingly.

"Not today," Rose answered. "Come back tomorrow, won't you?" Vivie looked her way as Rose continued, confused, "Maybe I'll buy something from you tomorrow. Yes, I'll have the money tomorrow . . ."

In this way Vivie survived her younger sister's wedding. She was still not speaking to Ada, still stunned by her sister's old lies. But at least Vivie could move back home now that Ada had moved out.

Bec was still there, finishing high school, that and dating her classmate Milton Goldberg. For some time once Vivie moved back home the days passed uneventfully. She was relieved to be there, though a certain amount of pressure was being put on her, by way of her father, to consider a long-term career. There was always teaching, Maks said. And then there was nursing.

"I'm happy with Dr. Shapiro," she told her father, her voice once again filled with that confidence that she didn't quite know how she'd acquired.

At work Frances no longer needed to bring Thomas in. But by then Vivie had made other friends. In particular, she was always eager to see a young woman named

Ruth Brintler, who had begun to see Dr. Shapiro for the treatment of significant fatigue. Dr. Shapiro, Vivie learned, was having trouble finding the root cause of her symptom, as were the other doctors Ruth had seen, but Dr. Shapiro insisted she not despair. Yet Ruth was alone in the world, unmarried, without relatives nearby, supporting herself by working in a library, and she was finding that work unbearable under the weight of her exhaustion. Despair was the hardest thing not to feel, she told Vivie once. That's when Vivie began to cook for Ruth once a week and bring the meal to her home. Ruth lived in an apartment above the Italian grocery on Middletown's Main Street, and it was there that the two woman dined together each Tuesday evening, not talking so much as listening to the various sounds issuing from the store below. Soon enough Thursdays became another regular night out as Mrs. Bloomberg and Lorna missed Vivie and insisted she come at least once weekly to dine with them. They wanted to know everything, they told her, as if when she left their home Vivie's life had taken on an adventurous edge they could only imagine. Mrs. Bloomberg dropped the "poor" and now simply greeted her as "Vivie."

A year passed this way, with work, her

regular Tuesday and Thursday evening engagements, a few nights out with Tillie Hirschfield, and several awkward Shabbos meals at home with the newlyweds there, Ada still puffed up with the self-importance of being a new bride. The first Passover seder was no different — there was Ada, glowing and gabbing, which by this time only made Vivie feel tired. But the second seder redeemed the first. Vivie was invited that year to Dr. Shapiro's house, along with Tillie, and there, seated at Dr. Shapiro's dining table, interested to see him wearing a suit and yarmulke rather than his white doctor's coat, delighted to see him feign shyness when his wife, Penny, complimented his recent haircut, thrilled when he began the service not by lighting candles but by acknowledging her and Tillie as his second family, Vivie found herself stirred more deeply than usual by Dr. Shapiro's warmth and glad to have broadened her life such that it now was touched by what she thought of as the special grace of his.

The day that Bec announced her engagement to Milton Goldberg, in March of 1928, Vivie might have thought her own life was as past as winter. She might have thought that, the newfound fullness contracting in an instant, but the evening before she'd had an encounter that left her feeling more hopeful than she'd been in a long time. Work finished, she'd gone once again up Main Street to the pharmacy. She was about to turn in to it when she saw ahead of her a young couple walking hand in hand. They weren't talking but wore contented looks. Minutes later, while staring at bars of soap, Vivie realized that nothing about seeing the couple had caused her to trip or lose her breath. For all she knew, she'd been walking past couples for some time and not even noticing them. And so the next day, with Bec's news, she was determined not to lose the ground she'd apparently gained. "I'm happy for you," she told her sister, her tone matter-of-fact. Dutifully, she leaned toward Bec to embrace her. But a moment later she pulled her sister close. "I'm so happy for you," she repeated. "Really, Bec, I am."

In the fall of 1928, some six months after Bec's engagement, Vivie began to take an interest in Leo Cohen, a thin, already balding fellow, one of the patients with chronic problems. A touch of headache, a bit of a cough, weakness in the knees — these were the ailments, always a little vague, of Leo Cohen. He seemed embarrassed to see her whenever he came in, once every other month or so, never speaking to her but merely nodding her way then quickly seating himself in the farthest corner of the waiting room, where a lamp set there made for especially good reading of the book he invariably came in with.

It seemed important reading, she quickly noticed. She'd caught a title once, *The Interpretation of Dreams.* Her own dreams were a messy business — trains rushing past her, angry dogs chasing at her heels, one in which her perfectly buttoned dress inexplicably fell off her shoulders — dreams so uncomfortable she'd thought only to forget them rather than record them for interpretation. She'd not heard of the book's author but she assumed from the solemn look on Leo Cohen's face as he read it that the author was of some note. And she assumed, too, because Leo Cohen always came in with a book as seriously titled as that, that he was a deeply thoughtful man, perhaps even a professor, someone with an office in one of those imposing brownstones that marked the Wesleyan University campus on High Street.

As much as Vivie noticed Leo Cohen he seemed determined to slip in and out unseen. Finally, one day in March of 1929

— Vivie was twenty-five by then — she was able to strike up a conversation with him. A flu had hit the community and the waiting room was unusually full; Leo had to sit by her desk rather than in the far corner. And, oddly, he'd not brought a book.

"Here," Vivie told him, offering him the *National Geographic.*

Once he'd finished, handing the magazine back, she questioned him about what he'd just found so interesting. Seville, Spain, he said. He described the elaborate processions he'd just read about during Seville's spring-time Holy Week and the equally elaborate fairs held in the weeks after. He suggested she look at a photograph of women dressed in the flamenco style, leaning Vivie's way for the first time to do so. Then she asked him a few more questions, not about Seville but about him. No, he said, he didn't work at Wesleyan, though he'd heard of the place; no, he had no wife and kids; and no, he was not originally from Middletown.

"Born and raised in Bridgeport," he said, rising for his examination.

They didn't converse the next few times he came to the office but he did make a point of saying hello to her when he arrived and good-bye to her when he left. "Good-bye, Mr. Cohen," she'd respond. "You have a good day now. And feel well."

June 1929 and Leo Cohen walked in the office on a Friday without an appointment. He had a small bouquet of daisies in one hand and no book.

"Mr. Cohen?" Vivie asked, confused. "Did I forget to put you on my schedule?" She flipped a few pages of her appointment book.

He cleared his throat. "I didn't come for that." Then he offered her the daisies. "I came to ask you to dinner," he whispered. Just as tentatively, he suggested the next Saturday night.

And so she had a date. Just like that: out of the blue. And with such a thoughtful man, she mused, though he was awfully quiet. On her way home she stopped by the Bloombergs' to run the whole thing past Mrs. Bloomberg. Later she'd tell her mother and Bec. Over tea, Mrs. Bloomberg and Lorna leaned in for the details. The fact that Leo Cohen could hardly get the words out was the best part of all, even better than the daisies.

"I wouldn't tell Tillie," Mrs. Bloomberg advised Vivie as she rose to go.

"Poor Tillie," Vivie said.

"Poor Tillie," Mrs. Bloomberg, nodding, agreed.

■ ■ ■ ■

Over the next months, during which Leo
Cohen stopped by Dr. Shapiro's office
toward the day's end with increasing fre-
quency, offering to walk Vivie home, occasionally taking her out to dinner, Vivie
gradually learned that she was wrong about
everything. Leo Cohen wasn't even close to
being a professor; he was a baker's assistant,
rising at four thirty each morning to get the
dough started. And not only did Leo Cohen
lack a college education, he even lacked a
high school one. He'd been pulled out of
school at fourteen, he explained, the poverty
in his family requiring him to work. This
he'd done at an arms factory near Bridgeport, and because of the lead involved, his
health had been off ever since. Dr. Shapiro
charged him next to nothing, he added, to
which Vivie responded with that assurance
that seemed to bubble up more and more,
"He does that a lot. Don't you feel bad
about anything."

This information took a long time to pull
from Leo Cohen, who, just when Vivie
thought things were steady between them,
would sometimes stop coming by to walk
her home; weeks would pass without a

word, and then Vivie would confront a mountain of self-doubt. Had she made the whole thing up? Was she *that* desperate? And if so, how come she didn't even know this much about herself. But then he'd return, shy as ever, and she'd get the sense that his fear was even greater than her own. She'd have to crack his shell all over again. Questions about whatever book he was reading could get him going, even animate him, but he remained reticent on the subject of himself. "Not much to tell," he told her on more than one occasion. But by the time he said this Vivie knew enough to find his story a moving one; she felt sorry for the child wild with curiosity who couldn't finish his schooling and inspired by the personal drive he showed to overcome that limitation. The books all came from the public library, which he visited weekly, as he'd been doing since he was a kid. Crushed to have been pulled from school, he'd heeded his father's advice to use the library, where books were both bountiful and free. "That was my father's best idea," Leo said, his face brightening with the memory.

He proposed to her on one knee, the traditional way, on a drizzly evening in May. They'd gone walking after a dinner out, and were standing outside her home, under an oak tree at the yard's edge. When he rose from kneeling, a wet patch marked the knee of one pant leg, something she could see even in the dimness of the fading evening light. He was thin as ever, and a street lamp gleamed on his balding head. The truth was, he didn't look so good. But she'd said yes and he was smiling as she'd never seen him smile before.

"Are you sure?" Maks asked her later that night after Leo had gone, after the news had been delivered to her parents and Bec. "He just doesn't seem like, you know, much of anything," to which Vivie answered, firmly, swiftly, "He seems like a whole lot to me."

At twenty-six, then, Vivie was finally married, the second Syrkin sister to do so. Bec had been engaged the whole time during Vivie's courtship with Leo, but Bec was waiting for Milton Goldberg to finish college. And so Vivie left a sister behind at home when she moved with her husband into a tiny apartment over a fabric store on Middletown's Washington Street, an apartment the same size as Ruth Brintler's. Ruth had passed away the year before, a loss that broke Vivie's heart more deeply than she'd anticipated. Still, that first year of marriage started well enough with Mort offering Leo a better job right off the bat at Leibritsky's

Department Store, but sometimes Leo felt good and sometimes he didn't, which meant Vivie would cook up a soup, feed him dinner in bed. And because of Leo's fragile health she kept her job with Dr. Shapiro, unlike Ada, who stayed home while Mort worked. Sometimes, too, Leo complained about the job, particularly about Mort's younger brother Nelson, who had an enviable higher education. "Why do the goods always go to the undeserving?" Leo would say about Nelson, whom he faulted for not honoring the value of his schooling by reading even one additional book. And it was lonely, too, Leo griped on occasion, all day on that Leibritsky's sales floor, a reader among nonreaders. Could make a person feel invisible since no one ever talked to you about the things on your mind, the things that mattered most. But none of Leo's complaints, physical or emotional, bothered Vivie, as she came into the arrangement well aware that marriage wasn't a picnic. She knew, too, that it wasn't a wall protecting you from life's more difficult blows. Marriage wasn't anything, really, she reasoned contentedly enough, just a way to live, a way to love someone else. And most folks find that out, sooner or later. Yes, my aunt concluded early on, even someone like her sister Ada, whom she could still hear screeching with unabashed delight on her wedding day, and who'd carried an unthinking air of superiority since the whole thing happened, and who by then had topped matters off with a first child — a boy, no less — would eventually know that.

But that was lifetimes ago. Early July of 1948, our first weekend in Woodmont, two days of clouds, humidity, winds, but no rain; of the ocean swelling and retracting with more force than usual; of intense games of rummy played on the porch (that would be Bec, Vivie, Ada, Davy, and me); of Leo and Nina reading side by side on the sands of Bagel Beach under a large but, because of the clouds, mostly unnecessary beach umbrella (but at least Nina was actually *at* the beach, I thought); and of Howard dragging himself about while our father continued to punish him for breaking his word about joining the morning minyan by ignoring him and favoring Davy, choosing him as his fishing partner when the clouds finally broke early Sunday afternoon. The sisters were mostly in tending mode — to husbands, meals, children — and whatever echoes Vivie once heard of a younger, screeching Ada had long ago ceased. Time had passed.

You could see that most clearly in the way that, once the men packed the car and drove off Sunday evening, my mother, dropping her waving hand, turning from Hillside Avenue back toward the cottage, did so with a look of unbridled, albeit unknowing, relief.

Howard, too, was relieved. But the weekend had affected him, and even after the men left, Howard continued to drag about. Rather than head off for a Sunday evening with his pal Mark Fishbaum he stayed home with us. He was tired, he said, when he phoned Mark. He added that he ought not to have stayed up so late with Mark the previous Thursday evening; the next morning he'd overslept. He might as well have murdered someone, he complained.

The men had been gone for less than an hour when Howard and Nina had their first real fight of the summer. It began with my asking Nina if I could try on the dress Bec had sewn for her. Nina and I were in her parents' room, which was where we hung whatever summer clothes we needed to hang.

"Come on," I urged Nina. "Won't you even try it?" I leaned into the closet, unable to take my eyes from the dress, despite the fact that I'd peeked at it every day that week. The yellow fabric was a soothing pale shade, the cream-colored flowers running across it summery and delicate. The jacket had sleeves that went just past the elbow, an obvious and perfect length. It seemed incredible that after a whole week Nina still hadn't tried on the dress.

"I can't see myself in it," Nina said, not without remorse. "It's not me."

"Then *I'm* going to wear it," I told her, whisking the dress from the closet.

"It's too big," she argued. "You're a twig."

"Can't I try it? I just want to see." I dangled the dress, still on its hanger, before her.

"All right, Molly. Don't beg. It's just a stupid dress," she said.

I wriggled out of my shorts and top. Seeing me in my bra, which was new and barely needed, Nina smiled, a small turnup of the mouth, the very same smile, more plaintive than cheerful, that my mother had offered when she'd taken me just months before to get fitted.

The dress on, I asked Nina to zip the back. But even the secured zipper didn't prevent the dress from sliding down my frame, its top section settling in waves at my waist.

"Told you. Too big," Nina said, though she didn't laugh. She simply took me in, her neutrality a kind of indifference.

"Hey," Howard then said, surprising us. He stood in the doorway. I grabbed the dress, yanked it high, and clutched it like a towel.

"Where'd you come from?" I asked, embarrassed.

"I was just in my room," he answered. "I'm not trying to sneak up on you." He glanced behind him as if to prove he'd been nearby.

"Don't you know to knock?" I shrieked.

"Don't blame me," Howard said, pointing at the room's open door. "Besides, Molly," he continued, leaning my way, "there's not really much to see." He took a few steps toward me.

"Don't you dare," I said, leaping back and landing beside Nina, on her parents' bed. Howard, I knew, might pull at the dress. In the right mood, he was just that kind of brother.

"Hey, squirt," Howard said, seemingly surprised by my reaction, "you know I wouldn't do that." Despite his words, when he took another step forward Nina and I sat up straighter, even more on guard.

"Relax," Howard said, staring at us. "Molly, I'm not going to touch that stupid dress."

"Not *stupid,*" Nina remarked, though in fact she'd said the same thing just a moment ago.

She and I glanced at each other with suspicion as Howard repeated, "I'm not going to pull it off."

He lunged forward then, onto the bed. We screamed.

"You dumb girls," he muttered as he settled himself behind us where he could lie prone. "You dumb girls have it so easy."

The weekend with our father ignoring him had clearly taken its toll, as did, I figured, Howard's business as the eldest son, the child required to bear the most responsibilities.

That may have been what he was referring to, but that's not how he'd put things.

"Dumb? Easy?" Nina twisted at the waist to confront him. "Honestly, Howard, sometimes I think you don't know anything. Or see anything. Or hear anything. What's easy, Howard, is that *you're* dumb."

Howard wasn't trying to anger us, I could see, but rather attempting with this visit to soothe himself. But his words were poorly chosen and just his presence set Nina on edge. Though I'd witnessed their wrangling before, the rancor between Howard and Nina, a visceral thing, always surprised me

148

when it flared. As Nina challenged Howard she crossed her arms over her chest as if the dress exposed her rather than me, as if Howard were still pointing at her as he had the day of our arrival and commenting on her "bazooms."

Howard rose, rolled past us, and took to the floor. "I know something, Nina," he said, standing before us. He nodded at me in the dress then thrust his chest out, clearly implying breasts. Holding that posture, he strutted about the room. "Too big," he teased again and again.

"You're disgusting," Nina yelled. "Stop it." When he didn't she added, alluding to his many past romances, "I can't believe you've ever had a girlfriend."

Howard sighed, almost happily. "Ah, you know I don't mean it," he told Nina a moment later, with particular kindness. And there it was: the charm that generated the girlfriends. In this instance it worked again, even on Nina in all her anxiety.

She was just about to relax her folded arms when Howard, pursing his lips, made a series of loud smacking noises.

"Disgusting!" she said.

"Think I don't know anything?" Howard continued. "Well here's something everyone knows: Nina's never been kissed!"

Seeing the depth of the blush spreading on Nina's face and neck, Howard pushed further. He pursed his lips again and the ugly smacking sounds followed. He finished his performance saying, "Kissing's fun, Nina. *Fun.* Don't you wish you knew about *that*?"

Then he left, slamming his bedroom door once he reached it. Through the wall we heard him complain, as he had before, "You dumb girls have it easy!"

Moaning, Nina fell back on the bed. As I stepped out of the dress and rehung it I could see she was thinking something, not speaking but sporadically kicking her feet, still upset.

Once I'd changed into my own clothes I joined her on the bed, laying my head on a pillow beside hers. "I guess it's too big," I said of the dress, sighing with resignation.

"What'd you think?" Nina said, irked suddenly with me.

"I thought maybe it would fit," I answered.

"And then what? I'd let you wear it? Just like that?"

"I don't know. I thought it might be fun to wear."

"Well now you know it isn't," Nina concluded. After another bout of kicking her feet, she added, "Besides, Molly, what do you know of *fun*?"

That evening we ate dinner in near silence, the sisters seated in the chairs on the porch, we kids spread out on the steps. Howard ate at one end, Nina the other. Davy, who'd been fishing all afternoon with our father, was exhausted and irritable, not quite liking the egg salad, or the half-sour pickles. When my mother asked if he'd rather have chicken salad, he squawked senselessly in response, a weak imitation of gulls, which caused my mother to roll her eyes then sit herself down beside him, pulling him close. "Eat," she urged, but Davy stopped eating to rest his head in her lap. "Howard, could you carry him upstairs?" Ada then asked.

Later, I heard her talking to Howard. They were back on the porch steps, where Howard had returned after dinner. Over the water, the sun, sinking lower, neared the horizon line.

"It's my fault," she told him. "I should have given you a curfew. I shouldn't have left you boys to your own devices. Live and learn." She wrapped an arm over his shoulder.

"It's not your fault," Howard answered. "I'm eighteen, for God's sake."

"Eighteen," Ada repeated. "Lord knows I

made one hell of a decision when I was eighteen. And that's how come, soon enough, I got *you.*" She laughed, which caused Howard to nod then finally smile.

While Howard and my mother talked on the porch steps, Vivie sat in silence at the table with Nina. The two sipped tea. "Walk with me?" I heard Vivie cautiously ask Nina.

They left the cottage and headed toward Hillside Avenue. I rose from the living room couch to watch them go. Nina walked with her arms crossed over her chest, as coiled as when Howard had come into the bedroom. But with a tug, Vivie linked arms with Nina. They headed east, toward Sloppy Joe's and the Villa Rosa, and past that, toward the evening crowd at Anchor Beach. Minutes later, I knew, they'd turn onto Beach Avenue and arrive at the Anchor, where, arms still linked, standing before Sal's Good Humor truck, they'd confer, mother to daughter, daughter to mother, as they decided which treat to share.

Later, Howard, Ada, Nina, and Vivie found themselves by chance in our cottage's kitchen. By then a kind of truce had descended between Howard and Nina, each of them having been successfully consoled by their respective mothers, who, backs against the new washer, seemed pleased to be standing beside each other. But for that curious space, a body's width, between them, you'd think that all was truly and finally well.

5

FAIRIES AND
GENETIC MUTATIONS

Twelve years old — my age when I lost Davy — is an interesting time of life. You're still a kid at twelve but at the same time you're on your way toward physical and emotional maturity. At home you grasp things, invisible things that used to pass you by: that your parents aren't as perfectly happy as you'd always assumed; that your beautiful cousin isn't comfortable in her beautiful skin; that you were born in Middletown, Connecticut, and spend the summers in Woodmont, Connecticut, but that all this might have been otherwise. There's such chanciness to the business of life, you suddenly know at twelve. For example, you might have been born to other parents, in other states, maybe even other parts of the world. You're Jewish, but you just as easily could have been born Catholic or Congregationalist or even Buddhist. Or you could have been born in another time, all those years back, like your grandparents were, in Russia. Or, easily enough, you might never have been born at all. At twelve you know the facts: one egg, one sperm, one life. But what are the chances of its being *your* life, right then, right there? The probability of you is so rare, in fact, that you're nothing short of a miracle. And so you silently tell yourself, *I'm a miracle. I'm a miracle.* Which isn't bragging. At twelve you understand this miracle for what it is: just another plain fact of life.

Another plain fact that summer, when I was twelve, was that in addition to my growing awareness that Nina was uncomfortable in her skin and consequently vulnerable to Howard's worst insults — the ones about the female mind and body — she was also preoccupied and wouldn't be making much time for me. She was reading and reading and reading. She'd read a lot the summers before, but this summer she was particularly unstoppable. Whatever Darwin was trying to tell her, I assumed, must have been just as she'd originally said — "fantastic" — because she couldn't, or wouldn't, pull herself away.

My life, then, during those early days of that summer, had a surprising solitariness to it, despite the crowdedness of the cottage and despite the fact that I knew any number of kids in the surrounding cottages. Yet even more than friends in the neighborhood I wanted a friend right there, at home, just like my mother had in her sisters. Like my mother, I wanted to wake up humming rather than yearning. But over a week into it and Woodmont, so far, hadn't worked this transformation on me. The sister I wanted in the form of Nina was still elusive.

Looking back, I'm surprised to realize how often during those days Davy filled the hole I was hoping Nina would fill. But after breakfast, when Nina took to one of the metal chairs on the porch to start in with her reading, and I would sit on the porch steps, waiting, as if this day, unlike the day before or the day before that, she'd actually put the book down and join me for a walk or a chat or a swim, Davy would invariably land beside me, with Samson Bagel on his left hand.

Nina, Davy, and I had made the Bagels three summers before, when Bec arrived from New Haven with a set of four cotton mittens, the puppet equivalent of bare bodies, and a bag full of fabric scraps, buttons, sequins, and yarn. Davy's Samson, like the Bible's, had a good head of hair and was exceedingly strong. Though the men in our family hadn't fought the war's battles — one too old, another too fat, another too sick — the heroic exploits of Samson Bagel could make up for all that. Moreover, the Germans would never have imprisoned Samson Bagel, Davy insisted. This was just when we'd learned of our cousin Reuben from Poland, who in fact had been imprisoned but was just then in a displaced persons' camp, homeless but free. Davy was also the maker of Lenny Bagel, the father, who, like our father, ran a small department store. "Good God, another day," was one of Lenny's habitual sayings. Nina was the one to create Esther Bagel, the mother, and though Nina gave Esther characteristics a bit different from our mothers' — Esther was a part-time journalist who, whether at home or on the job, wore pants — Esther was nevertheless as fussy about household matters as the real mothers in our lives. My puppet was a girl, Linda Bagel, obedient and content. What I knew about Linda I knew about myself: she'd grow up, get married, have children, be even more satisfied. I was nine when I invented her and I loved her like crazy. When I was ten and eleven I felt pretty much the same. By twelve, though, I'd stopped thinking about Linda Bagel.

Yet there was little else to do, those first lonely mornings at Woodmont, but to pull her out and join Davy in his antics. Sometimes Davy simply donned one of the puppets and waved the thing around, senselessly, and I'd don Linda and wave her senselessly back. Other times he'd rope me into enacting a scene: the Bagel family drives to Woodmont (Samson and Linda secretly kicking each other in the backseat), the Bagel family takes a swim (Mama Esther runs from Papa Lenny, who insists on splashing), the Bagel family lights the Sabbath candles (Mama Esther inexplicably forgets the words of the Hebrew blessing and cracks up in giggles). The most fun, though, was when I served simply as Davy's audience, listening as he picked up one or another of the puppets and began a spontaneous monologue. "What did I ever do to deserve such horrible kids?" Lenny Bagel grumbled one morning, and even Nina put her book down and laughed. It was obvious where Davy got some of his material — Mr. Weinstein had howled those very words the day before when his son Arthur had gotten into yet another fight — but often I never knew. And I didn't care. I'd assumed all that play was but a substitute for the real stuff that would surely come when Nina finished her book. But then, weeks later, we lost Davy. And I suddenly grasped that all that time with the puppets *was* real stuff, for without Davy I was more alone than ever before.

Throughout this fall about once weekly I've stopped by Bec's house to continue exploring it, piecing the past together as I do as if it were here, in the walls and floors, notebooks and photograph albums, of this youngest Syrkin daughter. I've come here alone because I am alone, more than ever before, and I mean that this time quite literally. Bec was the last to go of her generation. Of my generation only Nina is alive, and she long ago left New England for California. I've been divorced for more years than I want to admit from Howard's best friend, Mark Fishbaum, and we never had a child. I've not remarried.

September came and went, and now it's mid-October, the leaves mostly fallen, the air cool. Still, each visit I take some time on the front porch, sitting, thinking. Bec kept two rockers on the porch, and though I don't recall ever seeing her sitting out there, I've nevertheless felt something like her presence beside me during my time here. She'd set flower boxes on the porch as well, which, all blooms gone, I've emptied, and as I've stared at the boxes I've begun to imagine them filled once again come spring, perhaps with impatiens, perhaps petunias. The place, I've told Bec in my thoughts, will bloom again.

This morning it drizzled but that didn't keep me off the porch. I had my sit, waved to a neighbor whom I've yet to officially meet, a middle-aged woman like myself lifting groceries from her car and rushing them inside, and then I came inside too to warm up. Bec's kitchen table is actually a booth, just like in a restaurant, wooden benches padded for comfort, a wooden table set between them, and all of it tucked against a wall. There's a window there too, with a view of a Japanese maple tree outside, something Bec planted to remind her of a particular Japanese maple she loved to walk past in Woodmont. As I sipped hot tea I also browsed through an old photo album, something I pulled from a shelf in the front study. The album began with a photo of Bec, my mother, and Vivie, taken when the sisters were still young, still wearing identical bathing suits and identical braids. In the shot they're at the beach, the water glistening behind them. Vivie, eleven, and then still the tallest, poses with her arms crossed over

her chest, her body erect, as if dutifully waiting for Maks to snap the picture. But Ada,
eight, has stepped past her, closer to the
camera. Already the prettiest of the three,
she smiles exuberantly, though the fullness
of her grin is partially obscured by the slight
turn of her head toward the big sister
behind her. Bec, six years old and crouch-
ing, stares not at the camera but at the
formation of sand her hands are sunk into.
She looks relaxed and, unlike her sisters,
genuinely happy. She must have been dig-
ging, or building something, a maker in the
making, I thought, as I stared at the photo.

It seemed to me she was born to be the
dressmaker she became, that the seeds of
the endeavor, or the temperament for the
work, were there all along. And I believe
she'd agree with that sense. In fact she told
me once that we disregard our authenticity
at our own peril. But that's not how she put
it. Her words were simpler. "Molly, you
have to be yourself," she said. "You *have* to.
Or something in you dies."

Years before she'd written: *I could die. No,
no, am already dead.*

She'd stopped sewing then, stopped designing those dresses that only she could
make.

Go on, I told the spirited girl in the photo.

Go on and dig in the sand and create whatever you want. I didn't say this as if I could remake history, erase those awful words on the note I'd found. I said it because it was impossible to look at her in her youth, messy, happy, confident — not so different from the way I once looked — and not cheer her on.

The dress Bec was sewing in July 1948 for Mrs. Arthur Coventry of New Haven was made of a stiff burgundy taffeta, a fabric that Bec had not used much before and found unyielding, trying. But its surface had a lovely sheen, which made it the perfect choice for the fiftieth-anniversary party with which Mrs. Coventry was planning to surprise her husband, the retired Yale law professor. He was a man of great dignity, Bec had been told by Mrs. Arthur Coventry. Many of his students had gone on to judge-ships all over the country. Others were in distinguished practices. He had been a good husband, too. Very devoted, very kind, Mrs. Coventry had said. For example, he'd been sure to take her to Paris every third year, in June, for two weeks. There they would walk the banks of the river Seine and hold hands, as if they were still courting, as if time had never passed. Each afternoon they'd stop at the same patisserie to eat sweet Napoleons and sip coffee. Theirs was a marriage of simple joys, of uncomplicated compatibility. Mrs. Coventry had raised four children, but that was a long time ago, she informed Bec. Fifty years of marriage. She sighed wearily. She'd always hated Napoleons, she finally confessed.

The dress was somehow to live up to that accomplishment, that mass of time, and to reflect the dignity (or was it the costs, Bec wondered) of a life lived by the side of that professor, and to capture the repeated trips to Paris, their joys and limitations, and even to hint at the trial of raising those four kids, of keeping them quiet each evening so the professor could read. The dress was to be more than a dress. Somehow it had to reflect the complexity of a lifetime as surely as the lines on Mrs. Coventry's seventy-two-year-old face did.

But that fabric — the stiff taffeta — was making it especially hard to shape.

That second week in Woodmont we could hear more than the occasional sigh of frustration as Bec sat at her Singer, her feet pumping its treadle, her hands splayed over the taffeta as she worked the fabric forward, running yet another seam. The portable radio that my father used on the weekends to listen to his baseball games while sitting outside was now on the dresser in Bec's sunporch, and when the going got too tough for Bec, she'd stop with the Singer, face the ocean, and, ears pricked for Doris Day or Bing Crosby, she'd hum along for a while, the dress seemingly forgotten on her lap. Then we'd hear a resigned sigh, signaling that she'd turned away from the ocean and back to her Singer, where she resumed her struggle with the dress.

The air was especially good out there on her screened sunporch, or so Bec insisted no matter how hard the sewing project at hand was for her, and so it became a particularly cherished moment to be invited to join her there, which, on Wednesday of that second week at Woodmont, Nina and I did. We knew, like our mothers, not to enter the sunporch absent an invitation. We knew too that this was a working visit, no interruptions of Bec's sewing allowed, and Nina, who was still reading *On the Origin of Species,* wisely brought the book with her. She plunked herself down on Bec's cot, curled her legs underneath her, and soon enough the pages began to slowly flip.

I took the other end of the cot, curled my legs, and began to doodle on an empty notepad I'd brought along. I drew a starfish, then a seagull, then a whole bunch of seagulls picking at something on the beach, then a series of the wild rose bushes we saw throughout Woodmont, scrappy seaside shrubs offering the occasional scarlet bloom. As I drew, Nina's pages continued to turn and the frenzied needle of Bec's Singer continued to mount its attack on the stiff taffeta. But that afternoon things seemed to be going well for Bec. She'd finish a seam then triumphantly burst into a tune, something she must have been recalling from the radio, which that day, so Nina could better concentrate, Bec had turned off. As she worked, several times Bec turned in her chair to hold up a sleeve or a piece of collar for us to see. Other times she'd turn our way just to acknowledge the sea air. "The air's nice here, don't you think?" she asked us more than once. Each time she took a deep breath, not unlike the breaths my mother habitually took at Woodmont, though in Bec's case I knew the fresh air she referred to was specific to her sunporch. Following her remarks, the three of us settled back into our respective occupations: the book, the doodles, the fiftieth-anniversary party dress.

That Wednesday was not particularly hot, but when the breezes swept past, they were as delightful a sensation as ever and seemed to carry with them all the good feeling that came with this quiet and industrious camaraderie. In this way the air circulating throughout Bec's sunporch *was* good, uniquely so. Several times that afternoon my mother and Vivie walked through the living room, past the double doors leading to Bec's sunporch, and they'd glance at us from the doorway with curiosity, even a longing, or so it seemed to me, to join us. But they'd made different life choices: they had no Singer, no vocation to speak of, no need for a bedroom that was as much a studio as a place to sleep. What would they do out there, even if we made the room to let them in? That afternoon it seemed clear to me that Bec's sunporch was a world apart from Vivie's and Ada's, a world of our own, and though I wasn't the intellectual that Nina so clearly already was, nor the master seamstress Bec was, I had a feeling that day that I was something, *something,* mere doodles and all, that even my own mother couldn't understand.

If the dresses Bec designed were for her a kind of freedom, a way to be herself, then Bec's journey toward making them, like Vivie's journey toward Leo, was circuitous and chancy. I use the word *choice* to distinguish Bec's less conventional life from that of her sisters, but though I didn't know it that summer of 1948, in reality Bec stumbled into that life of making dresses, landing upon it only after being loosed from the planned life, the far more typical one that during her long engagement to Milton Goldberg she'd assumed was her destiny.

He loved her, he said that last time they spoke. He still loved her, he always would, but he couldn't marry her. He had just graduated from Amherst College. They'd been engaged the entire four years of his education there. During that time she'd waited for him, at home, taking in mending from around town and occasionally sewing a dress or skirt to order. By Milt's senior year Bec had made an outfit for each member of her family. Though Milt was tall enough when he left — a commanding guard on Middletown High's basketball team — he seemed even taller after college, as if his education had added inches to his frame. Late May of 1932 and they were standing outside Bec's back door where he could kiss her without anyone seeing. That's what they always did first thing when he came home. They'd stand out there, no matter the weather. But this time he started talking. His voice, she noticed right away, was deeper, more authoritative. What he planned to do next was to shoot for business school, he told her in that new voice. He explained that Middletown's banks and businesses were faring better than in so many other places, that it was pure disaster most everywhere else. He shook his head. He wanted to help. He certainly wasn't thinking this way when he'd first gone off, he noted. "If I only knew then what I know now," he repeated as he turned toward her, and then away, never once taking her hand or bending to kiss her.

He was looking over her head, as if at the house next door, when he said that what he also didn't know when he'd left those years ago was a girl named Audrey, someone he'd met at one of those many mixed socials between his college and the girls' college next door, Smith. And in coming to know her — really it had been just that past semester — he'd come to know that he preferred being with someone who was like him.

"Like you?" Bec couldn't imagine what he meant. She and Milt had grown up together, had had the same teachers, played on the same playgrounds as kids, knew each other's friends and family. They may have only begun dating their senior year in high school, but in fact they'd known everything about each other for a long, long time. How were they not alike?

"Educated," Milt answered. "I prefer the educated kind."

If ever there was a time for sisters, Bec's sudden breakup with Milton Goldberg was it. And how mightily Vivie and Ada had rushed, despite their ongoing tensions, to Bec's aid. In an instant she'd gone from being the sister so admired, about to make what was clearly the most advantageous marriage of the three — Milt's fine education had in fact set him apart — to the sister most wronged, jilted more severely after four long years of engagement than even Vivie.

"The snob," Ada exclaimed. They were in the Syrkin kitchen, around the dining table, where all important conversations between the sisters had always taken place. Vivie was married to Leo by then, but until that moment — the as yet unrecognized start of a slow reconciliation — she still preferred to avoid Ada's company.

"The stinking lowlife," Vivie added, surprising the others with what was for her an uncommon insult. "I mean it. You don't forget where you come from. He's a fool, that Milton Goldberg is. A terrible fool." She paused. "And besides," she said, her face broadening with a mischievous smile, "the guy couldn't eat a meal without spilling half of it on his pants."

Bec looked at Vivie across the dining table, bewildered.

"That's right," Ada said, suddenly hopping in her seat. "And he couldn't talk without so many 'ums' you'd, um, want, um, to finally, um, kill him!"

"And for all his schooling," Vivie added, "the guy never showed up here except with his shirt untucked, his face unclean."

"That's just not so," Bec said. But even she began to smile.

"The klutz," Ada noted, slapping her hands on the tabletop. "Besides a basketball, what could that man hold on to without dropping it? Wait a minute; wasn't he constantly dropping that basketball? Lucky for him it bounced back. You marry someone like that, you'd never have a full set of dishes. God knows, should he ever whisk you off your feet, he'd likely drop *you.*"

"And did he ever tell a truly *funny* joke?" Vivie asked, throwing up her arms.

Outside, a pair of cardinals landed on a nearby branch and the sisters, without thinking, paused at the sight. Dusk, late May, and they had the window open.

"Snob," Ada argued more seriously, turning from the window. "Who marries a girl just because she goes to Smith College? Who does this? *Who?*" She paused, thinking, and then she raised her right hand, jabbing her index finger pugnaciously forward. "Episcopalians!" she said, spitting the word out, sure of it. The birds flew off. "That's who."

"Ada, you know that's not so," Bec said, but gently, letting the way Ada boiled a whole people down to one bad thing stand essentially unchallenged. For a minute Ada rattled on, about snobby Episcopalians then idiotic Congregationalists then uppity Catholics then, more specifically, uppity and rotten Irish Catholics then uppity and rotten Italian Catholics. For some reason her mind then looped to the Negroes, who, for no reason in particular, were worst of all.

Bec didn't even try to follow her thinking.

"He did write me the dullest letters," Bec finally said, interrupting Ada.

"You see?" both sisters cried in unison.

"And he did sometimes snort like a pig when he laughed." This news out, Bec began to chuckle, at least momentarily, and her sisters joined in.

"Life goes on, sweetheart," Vivie told her in all seriousness once they'd calmed down. "You have to trust me on that."

The cardinals returned.

"And you're still young," Ada added. "Look, take it from me, what's the rush anyway?"

That summer while at Woodmont, Bec was simply marking time, feeling wounded and low. Even during the weeks of her sisters' visits — Ada and Mort in late June, and Vivie and Leo in early July — Bec slept late. She took long walks alone. She wandered the length of Beach Avenue, coming at last to a grassy park at the east end of the street where a Japanese maple tree's quirky and grand burgundy foliage called out to her, soothed her for the time she took to stare at it. Except for that tree she was angry at everything, even sunshine, even billowing white clouds.

Midsummer, Bec went with her parents into New Haven for the day. For her birthday, Risel wouldn't accept anything less than her favorite pizza pie at Pepe's. After the meal, Bec had linked arms with her mother and was strolling down nearby George Street when Risel spotted a woman posting a sign in a dress shop window.

Seamstress wanted. Apply within. "Look!" Risel told Bec.

Bec was as startled as her mother. That someone was hiring was indeed a miracle. But Risel meant something else.

"Me?" Bec shook her head.

"You," Risel said, and then she threw her shoulders back and posed for Bec, right there on George Street's sidewalk. In fact Bec had designed and made the dress Risel was wearing, a navy-and-white-polka-dotted cotton. A birthday gift. For a couple of lonely weeks, something to do. Her mother had a thick waist, a narrow bottom, and a large bosom, and still the dress fit her like a glove. Bec, taking that in, wasn't sure how she'd done it.

"What is it?" Maks then asked. He'd been trailing behind the women, indulging in a cigar.

Risel pointed at the sign in the store window. Across the glass the name *McMannus* was printed in large black letters.

"A pipe dream," Bec said. "Come on."

Pipe dream or not, the next morning Maks returned to the McMannus shop, Risel's dress folded in a paper bag that he carried as carefully as he'd once held the dress's maker when she was but a child, the baby of the family. Hours earlier, while Maks and Risel walked to the ocean for their dunk, they had agreed: if it would get Bec that job, Maks was to show the McMannus people Risel's dress as an example of Bec's work. Risel loved the dress, and had worn it just that once to Pepe's, but she could part with it for a day or so, she said.

Upon Maks's arrival he was told that Mr. McMannus was out, home with a backache. The woman he spoke to, Pearl Delaney, served as Mr. McMannus's assistant seamstress. "I'm temporarily in charge," she told Maks, her voice firm, her Irish accent strong. Her face was craggy, worn, just like the shale of Woodmont, just like his own face, Maks noted, but oddly her hair had barely aged, was still a crow's black. Of the occasion for the hiring, Pearl explained the recent retirement of the shop's only other seamstress. "Eighty and sewing blind," she said.

Maks explained about Bec, "the family seamstress," he called her proudly, and then he pulled the dress from the paper bag, sorry as he did that he hadn't packaged it in something more special. He watched as Pearl Delaney grabbed what she didn't know was Risel's gift then turned the dress inside out only to tug at it as if determined to see it rip. For the next several minutes she examined each seam. "Dear God," she said once, shaking her head. When she finished she flung the dress, like a mere rag, over her right shoulder. Seeing it treated so, Maks was glad that Risel hadn't made this trip with him and that he'd kept it a secret from Bec.

Two more applicants, sewing samples in hand, entered the shop. Pearl Delaney told them to stand in line, and then she told Maks, "You'll have to wait for a reply from Mr. McMannus."

"You're going to keep the dress then?" he answered, confused.

A week later, the phone rang at the Woodmont cottage. "Shall I come get it?" Maks asked once he realized the woman he was speaking to was Pearl Delaney. He only hoped that no one else was on the party line, listening.

"On the contrary. We're interested. Mr. McMannus is right here, standing beside me. He asks me to tell you to have your daughter come in to talk to us." She told him they should come in the next Monday, at nine sharp. "Lateness will be your first mistake," she said.

It took some convincing to get Bec off to

New Haven that next Monday. Bec had cried each evening since Maks broke the news of her pending job interview.

"You don't want me," she told her parents. Their reassurances only made her weep more. "Milt didn't want me and now you don't," she countered stubbornly.

In the end, though, she let her father take her to New Haven. And after she'd met Tyler McMannus, after she'd heard him say to her father, "Your daughter has a pleasant way with fabric," she'd nodded and told Maks that she'd give it a try, at least for a week.

Pearl Delaney, who'd been silent, said, "A week?" Then she laughed.

"A week it'll be," Tyler said, turning to Bec. Smiling, he handed her Risel's dress.

"I'll take that," Maks said with noticeable relief.

A week wasn't much time, but from the start Bec took to the smell of the place: the sweetness of unworn clothes, a pureness that didn't exist in any closet. The look of the place, too, intrigued her with its simplicity: the racks of pressed clothes along the walls, the set of cushioned chairs lining the shop's back wall. And the work itself satisfied a need to do something, anything, beyond stewing about Milt. Mr. McMannus, as Bec called him then, could throw any project at her — a man's suit, a woman's gown — and from the start Bec could tailor it well enough, and sometimes, it seemed to her, almost to perfection. All those years of taking in mending while she stayed home, waiting for Milt, were at least coming to something, she figured during the long days of that first week. Or so it seemed until she was told otherwise by Pearl Delaney, who, she soon discovered, had been working at the shop before it even was a shop. Pearl had been hired by Tyler's father, a tailor, when she was only fifteen. She'd come to America from County Cork with her two sisters the year before. She was desperate for work when Tyler's father took her in. Tyler had been only a baby then.

"No," Pearl told Bec more than once those first days. "Your work isn't adequate." Her stitches weren't even, she'd remark sharply, and then she'd insist Bec rip apart hand-sewn seams and try again.

Tyler wasn't with them in the back room when Pearl spoke to her this way, but when he was there his comments weren't like hers. "Good job," he'd say, simply enough. Or, as on their first meeting, "You have a pleasant way with fabric." But Tyler spent most of his time on the sales floor, pushing as hard as he could the shop's inventory of men's suits and women's dresses. If she had a pleasant way with fabric, then he had a pleasant way with people, Bec grasped soon enough. The actual tailoring he left largely up to Pearl, and now to Bec, too. But Bec was second in line, someone, according to Pearl Delaney, who had yet to prove her worth, and by ordering so much of Bec's work to be redone, Pearl made sure Bec knew it.

So there were things about this new life she was instantly drawn to — the smell of the shop, Tyler's infrequent but sincere admiration for her skill — and things she could readily do without, especially Pearl Delaney, all five feet of her. But Tyler seemed to adore Pearl, would bend low to kiss her cheek each evening before she left the shop and wish her good night, and Bec understood that no amount of willing Pearl Delaney away was going to do the trick. She was a fixture there, much like the clothes racks and the chairs lining the back wall. And there was a history between Pearl and Tyler that Bec could only imagine. Something about Tyler's good night kiss made the hardness in the woman soften, and after a day full of complaints Pearl would invariably leave work with a girl's shy smile and often a giggle.

"Come on, tell me something," Tyler once said to Bec. It was evening, mid-March, close to closing time. She'd been working there eight months. Even more incredible than that was the fact that she lived on her own, three blocks away on Howe Street, in an apartment her father hadn't wanted her to take. "I didn't mean the work to be what you did for forever," Maks had said back in August when he'd helped Bec move in. "What did you think? I'd just quit on him?" she responded incredulously. As she spoke, she clutched a sketchbook to her chest. In the last month she'd begun drawing, which was something like dreaming. There were dresses, dresses, and more dresses. Now she sat in a chair against the store's back wall, hemming a dress. Tyler sat beside her, forgetful, as he often was, of the measuring tape draped around his neck. Pearl Delaney had already received her kiss and left. "Tell me just one thing about yourself," Tyler said.

"I'm not the educated kind." After a pause she added, "And I really couldn't care less."

"Well, then. That's firm. I won't attempt to educate you."

She stopped sewing. She looked at Tyler briefly. He was glancing at her with an amused expression. "Anything else I shouldn't do?" he asked.

She laughed, then nodded. "Could you finally tell me what *that* means?" She pointed to the wall above his head. Hanging there, framed, was an embroidery with the words *The Fairies Are Always Passing.* Pearl had stitched her name at the bottom. She'd stitched in the date as well, *1921.*

Tyler pulled the tape measure from his neck, stood, and grabbed his coat from a nearby hook. "Come on," he said. "Day's done. I'll tell you on the way out."

What he told her, as they walked a block, and then another, was that "the fairies are always passing" was a saying of Pearl's. It had to do with the old tale of Paddy Corcoran's wife, Kitty, bedridden for seven years, who was finally visited by a fairy who told her that her children were throwing her dirty water out back, just when the fairies passed. A little adjustment, the fairy suggested, and with that change — dirty water out the side window, please — Kitty's health came right back.

"It's an Irish tale. I guess she figures if you're aware that the fairies are always passing, you'll be mindful of your ways," Tyler explained. They'd come to a corner. Bec's apartment was one way and Tyler's home another. The March air was cool but not cold. Still, they both wore their winter coats. A street lamp cast a glow over Tyler's face. He wasn't smiling, but he was content, she could see, to be standing there, talking.

"Mindful of your ways? She figures *that*?"

"We may not always be who we want to be, but we can always aspire," Tyler said, and it relieved Bec to hear in his words an understanding that Pearl was harsh.

"The fairies are always passing," she said, her voice more agreeable than before. She looked around.

Tyler, too, began to search, and when he apparently didn't see any fairies in the streets, he turned his face upward and Bec followed. They stared at the nearby street lamp.

"See any?" he asked.

"Maybe one or two," she said blinking at the light.

Every Saturday night she received three long-distance phone calls, from her mother and her sisters. And once monthly her father came to get her and she'd spend a weekend back home. "You don't have to stay here," Maks told her each time he returned her to Howe Street. "We've got room for you at home. Just like always."

Her response was to point to the windows

of her two rooms. "I like it," she said, surprising even herself. This was a year into what she referred to as "the new life."

Two and a half years into it, and countless Irish folktales later, Tyler gave Bec more space in the back room, a worktable of her own along with a new Singer sewing machine, a splurge he insisted he could afford and was certain would pay off. He gave her time to design as well. Since her start at the shop she'd made several dresses special order, much like the one for her mother, and the women were pleased. Friends of those women then came in, asking for a dress from Bec. As the circle of clients widened — a godsend in such times, Tyler remarked — it seemed only right that Bec be given room for the design work. He bought more sketchbooks, a pile of them. The homemade dresses added something special to the inventory, he said nodding. Priced modestly, they could very well save the place, keep it afloat until the world began to spin again. She stared at the floor. The news was good but somehow embarrassing.

Pearl Delaney was incensed at the development and in the weeks following the new setup Pearl's comments to Bec became personal. "You don't look so good," she told her on more than one occasion. "Old," she explained. "Beyond your years. And that's what happens to a working girl who never marries."

"Is that what happened to you?" Bec once dared to ask.

Pearl cackled. "I had my Billy," she said. "I wasn't an old maid, just unlucky in the children category. But until Billy passed I had a man in my bed every night." She laughed some more and turned to Bec. "That's right. Every night."

The remarks did their work; they hurt Bec, reminding her of the obvious: that nobody shared her bed. Perhaps because of the reminder there soon followed nights when she fell asleep dreaming of Tyler. She'd wake ashamed then tell herself that's what a certain kind of loneliness did to a person. It made you hungry. It left you helpless, feeding off whatever was in front of you. She dreamed of Tyler, married as he was, because she knew of no one else to dream about.

She saw his wife now and again, a pretty woman, her face always made up with just the right touch of rouge, her attire something sharp from the store. She stopped by infrequently but when she did, all work ceased. They were being visited, as if by the

queen. And as befitted a royal visit, everyone, even Pearl, was on the best of behavior.
Though morning was Mrs. McMannus's
typical visiting time, she came to the shop
once in the late afternoon, a fall day. Tyler
took his wife's arm, sat her down, brewed
her tea. Bec and Pearl were asked to join
them. From previous visits Bec knew that
Tyler's wife liked to talk, and it seemed to
Bec that she was even starved to do so. At
least she asked her usual unstoppable questions. How was business? What were they
each working on now? Who would they be
voting for in the upcoming election? She
thought Tyler should run for something local, she said. He had the personality, the
way with people, Mrs. McMannus argued.
He could do more, make a name for himself. The suggestion prompted Tyler to rise
from his chair. He pointed to the black letters on the store window. "Don't you see?"
he asked his wife after some silence. "I have
a name," he told her firmly. "And I like it
here."

In December of '37 — Bec was five years
into the job by then — Pearl Delaney took
sick. She was out a week, and then another.
When she didn't come back the third week,
Tyler took to stopping by her place on his

way home with some food in hand. At first he brought her sandwiches from the coffee shop across the street, and then he brought her whole bags of groceries. Toward the end of the third week Tyler asked Bec if she could help him prepare some meals for Pearl. She was bedridden by then, he explained. She couldn't make a thing, and he wasn't much help. They'd go together to her apartment that night, a Thursday, he suggested with some urgency, if Bec didn't mind.

When they entered Pearl's apartment that evening the lights were off, and Tyler left them off for a few minutes, even after he'd taken the groceries he and Bec had carried in and placed them on a counter.

"She's asleep," he whispered upon returning from Pearl's bedroom.

The lights finally on, Bec began to simmer a soup stock. In a separate pot she boiled potatoes. Pearl's kitchen was narrow and equipped with just the basics. Bec had counted the pots hanging over the stove — three — to make sure she could manage what she'd planned to make. Soup, potatoes, peas.

When they finally took the food to Pearl, Bec saw that the room adjacent to the kitchen, a sitting room — two upholstered

chairs and a coffee table between them —
was as tiny as the kitchen. But the bedroom
beyond that finally had some space to it. A
person could walk several paces between
the bed and the dresser and the single chair
in a corner, and something about that space
— all the room in the world that belonged
to Pearl — brought a new understanding to
Bec. Pearl Delaney, she said to herself, now
I see what it means for you to have come to
America at only fourteen.

The sight of Pearl herself was cause for
worry. In just three weeks she'd shrunk
dramatically. Her eyes bulged from her face.
Her dark hair was finally streaked with gray.
She was silent as she ate, but she was alert,
nodding as Tyler calmly reported the day's
news, the weather, who had come into the
shop.

The next week Tyler asked Bec to accompany him again, though this time it was
a Monday, and she had a feeling he'd ask
her again on Tuesday, and then on Wednesday as well. Mrs. McMannus, she was told,
wasn't fond of Pearl and didn't feel comfortable in her home. Well, then, Bec said to
herself. What choice was there? "Is there
any hope?" she asked.

"Hope, yes. But just now she can't make
a meal. Won't you come?"

And Bec nodded.

She cooked that Monday, and then Tuesday, and then again on Wednesday, just as she'd suspected she would. It was on Thursday, after Bec had prepared for them all a simple meal of eggs and toast, and after Tyler had talked through the day's business with Pearl, that Pearl asked Bec if she wouldn't mind helping her scrub up. Bec nodded and rose.

In the tub Pearl shivered despite the heat pouring from the room's clanking radiator. When Bec asked, Pearl turned her face to the ceiling so Bec could soap and rinse her hair. When Bec signaled, Pearl lifted an arm so Bec could reach the armpit. Bec didn't know this new Pearl: subservient, silent, fragile. Toweling her off, Bec wrapped her arms around the woman and held her as if willing the old Pearl, feisty and bullish and mean, back to life.

And Pearl did seem to revive in the hour or so after that bath. The three of them were in Pearl's bedroom, where they'd spent so many nights, but this time Pearl sat up readily, her hair still dripping, a touch of color at long last on her cheeks.

"You know," Pearl said to Bec, "I was always worried about him." She pointed at Tyler.

Bec leaned forward and fluffed Pearl's pillows behind her head, then adjusted the towel on her shoulders. She suddenly liked being there, actually wanted to do for Pearl. In this way the bath had cleansed Bec, too. She threw another towel behind Pearl's head. "You were saying?" Bec asked.

"I was saying I was always worried about him. Yes, about you, Tyler. Not your brother. Not your sister. But you were different from them. A little quiet, maybe. A little something. I told your father many a time to watch out for you, but he'd just shake his head. But I did worry. I didn't think you could hold your own."

Pearl stopped for a sip of tea, which inspired Bec to do the same. Tyler, sitting on the other side of Pearl's bed, left his cup on the table beside him. He stared at Pearl, nodding as she recalled the days of his boyhood.

"No, no. I didn't think you had it in you to hold your own, but then one night while I was minding you, that bully in the neighborhood came to taunt. All you kids were outside, the boys playing stickball, the girls watching on the sides, talking, and the bully — Jerry McAndrews, I think — was bothering one of you and then the next. You were twelve at the time, Tyler, and Jerry, maybe

188

thirteen, went all the way down the line of the boys. A bad word for each and every one of you. And then he began with the girls — unable to stop himself, a mad rush of naughtiness. He called your sister 'the ugliest on the street.' Right in front of everyone. And that did it."

Bec looked from Pearl to Tyler, who at this point seemed to be hearing the story, as she was, for the first time.

"Yes, that did it," Pearl continued. "Insulting Margaret. That's when you stepped forward, told Jerry McAndrews to shut his fat trap. Enough, you said. But you said it like a king, and that made all the difference. *Enough!*" Peal beamed, her eyes bulging all the more. "After that," she continued, glancing at Tyler, "I knew you'd be okay."

Tyler laughed quietly then turned to Bec. "Truth is, Jerry McAndrews would have killed me if *she* hadn't come out right then." Tyler held Pearl's hand as he continued talking. He glanced from time to time at Bec. "She was minding us that night but still working, as she always was, for my father, and she burst from our house with her shears in one hand and a tape measure in the other. That's what stopped him cold. Not me, but the sight of *her!*"

Pearl lifted her free hand, as if to gesture,

but it fell limp beside her.

"What she was going to do with that tape measure," Tyler continued, "I'll never know."

"If I couldn't stab him I was going to measure him to death," Pearl answered, nodding.

Tyler grinned, then sat back. His gaze was distant, as if he was recalling that day so long ago. Bec looked from him to Pearl. Pearl, too, seemed to be in a private world. Soon enough, Pearl fell asleep. Tyler didn't move. The room felt vast, Bec noticed, without a story to fill it.

"You're great old friends. I see that better than ever," Bec said at long last. The comment saddened Tyler, who looked down as he nodded. "Come on," Bec told him, helping him rise from his chair and then turning off the lamp beside Pearl's bed. "Don't worry. I promise. She'll be here tomorrow."

What Pearl said the next night surprised Bec even more than the story from the evening before. "I always knew your work was excellent. I just couldn't say so."

"That's all in the past now," Bec said.

"All in the past. Probably so," Pearl said sadly.

"Pearl, you'll pick up one of these days,"

Tyler said, almost pleading. "You just need rest."

Pearl closed her eyes and nodded. "Rest, yes," she whispered.

An hour later, when Bec and Tyler rose to go, Pearl opened her eyes, surprising them. "Don't forget to throw the water out the side window," she managed to say.

Pearl died three weeks later, her body rapidly wasting away. Each night of those three weeks Bec and Tyler were at Pearl's side. Bec made them food, and Tyler sat by Pearl's bed, never leaving her, always holding her hand, telling her what news he could, recalling for her the old stories, and occasionally singing her tunes from her youth, long ballads with simple melodies. Pearl, whose eyes were closed more often than not, nodded when the music began. Then she'd sigh when it ended. She said almost nothing except to beseech them just as they were leaving, in all seriousness, not to forget to throw the water out the side window.

"We have, Pearl," Tyler whispered each time she mentioned it. Then he'd add, reaching for Bec's hand, clutching it, "You're sure to be well soon."

A profound quiet descended on the shop

after Pearl's death. Tyler was in deep mourning, Bec could see, and she held back, tried not to bother him with unnecessary remarks or questions. To replace Pearl, they hired a young woman named Irene, who knew a thing or two about working with a Singer but was still clumsy with the hand stitching that was so much a part of their work, especially since the special orders for Bec's designs kept coming in. Once Bec told Irene to start over again, and in doing so she wondered if Pearl's admonitions all those years ago were less personal than Pearl had finally admitted them to be. Still, whenever Tyler asked about Irene, Bec lied, telling him that Irene was competent as anything, was just what they needed. "Good, good," he'd respond, though absentmindedly, his gaze unfocused. In his distress he always seemed to be looking for something he couldn't find. More than once Bec wanted to step in front of him, tell him, "I'm right here. Right here for the taking." Something had happened during those weeks of caring for Pearl. Bee had come to care for Tyler as well. She'd heard the stories, shared the cooking, and walked him home, because he was in no shape to get there alone, again and again.

And maybe something had happened to

Tyler, too, she thought, because he began staying with her late at work. They'd sit long after the shop had closed, the two of them, in a pair of chairs along the back wall. They didn't talk much. She would invariably be stitching, a hem or a sleeve, and he would simply sit beside her, sometimes humming softly. Other times he'd recollect a moment from the past, one he'd shared with Pearl Delaney. But the lingering had to do with more, she knew, than his ongoing grief. If she glanced his way he would often give her a helpless shrug. Begin to say something, then stop. Sometimes he'd cough and then look away. Once he said, "I'm trying to think of another story. I can't help but notice how your work improves with a story." She replied, simply enough, "It really does."

They continued in this way, night after night, and in time she likened them to two people in a sailboat on a sea of heaving waves. The hours they spent together at the day's end were the sailboat; all the other hours of the day, not to mention all the other people in their world, were the heaving waves — Mrs. McMannus, as well as Ada and Vivie, who could never know of her growing feelings. She kept those to herself then, determined not to spoil the ride, to flip the boat and sink it. "What do you think?" she often asked Tyler during those intimate hours in the evenings, but the question was always about a sleeve or a skirt, a neckline or a new sketch.

"I think it's lovely" is what he'd most often say.

Six weeks after Pearl's death a cousin of Vivie's old boss, Dr. Shapiro, came to court Bec.

"Dr. Shapiro's done you a great favor," Vivie said on the phone the evening she told Bec the news about Richard Shapiro, who was studying medicine at Yale. "Bec, look, play your cards right and there's a way out of this at last."

This.

Spinsterhood was what Vivie meant, Bec figured, and she wanted to argue back that *this* wasn't some kind of void; it was her work, the orders for her dresses keeping her plenty busy, and it was Tyler, and it was the startling and dear friendship that had broken out in the end between her and Pearl, and it was teaching Irene, and it was New Haven and the few streets of it she walked back and forth, back and forth, between her apartment and Tyler's shop.

This, she wanted to tell Vivie, this was everything.

"But you know how it'll turn out," Bec
answered instead. "He's a Yale boy. And I'm
not the educated kind."

"Give the poor slug a shot," Vivie urged.
"I hear he's a good man."

As it turned out, Richard Shapiro was
hardly a poor slug. Bec was shocked to see
as much when he stopped by the store a
week later and introduced himself. He'd just
happened by, he said, though Bec knew that
wasn't so. For a while he took stock of the
men's suits. "I could use one. I'll come back
and have you fit me," he finally told Tyler in
a tone that suggested, in a way that irked
Bec, that in needing a suit rather than making one he was the better man. Still, because
she'd promised Vivie she'd give him a go,
when he asked her to dinner she nodded.

Ushering her out the shop door, he said
to Tyler, as if Tyler now played a paternal
role, "I'll take good care of her."

"You'd better," Tyler answered, his words
emphatic but his back turned to them.

The dinner was delicious but endless.
They were served an appetizer, then a salad,
then the main course, and then dessert and
coffee. She thought she'd never eaten so
much, even on Passover, but Richard Sha-

piro seemed unfazed by the feast. When he drove her home he told her he'd like to come for her at the same time, the same day, next week.

"All right," Bec said tentatively, sadly, her mind on Tyler, on that emphatic tone he'd taken about her care. Did *he* care? Is that what his intonation was saying? She wished he'd intervened in that imperial voice she'd learned about from Pearl. "Enough!" she could almost hear Tyler tell Richard Shapiro. But Tyler was married. And how could she not give this good a prospect a chance? What would her family say?

And so she consented to being taken to dinner again the next week. She consented as well when Richard Shapiro reached for her hand across the table, and then she nodded when he told her how lovely she looked. In his car, after the meal, she braced herself for a parting kiss. In this way, she would consent to it. But to her relief, he merely took her hand, told her she was good company. He suggested another meal the following week, but something lighter, pizza perhaps. "Pepe's?" he asked. Just naming the place brought out a boyish smile she hadn't yet seen. She laughed as she nodded, glad to be going to a place she knew. "Nice time," he said to her the next week at

Pepe's, and Bec had to concede that this third outing was better than the first two. When Richard Shapiro kissed her that night, briefly, she found she could bear it. All right, she told herself once she was home, inside her apartment, the door locked behind her as soon as she'd stepped across the threshold as if he were right there behind her, following her, about to step over the threshold himself. All right. This is how it will be, then.

"Are you going to leave me?" Tyler asked her, bluntly enough, after a month and a half of weekly dinners with Richard Shapiro. They settled on pizza each time since that first go at it. Something about the pizza and the familiar restaurant put her at ease. By the time Tyler spoke to Bec she could almost imagine it: life with Richard Shapiro. He was to be a surgeon and she was to be his wife. And perhaps, if she were lucky, she'd be a mother too.

"Are you going to leave me?" Tyler repeated.

She faced him. All day they'd been rushing to finish an evening gown. Bec had worked the last-minute adjustments, Irene had done the multiple pressings, and Tyler had managed the talking — "Just a few minutes more," he kept saying each time he phoned the client. They'd been working and laughing and dashing about. Now he looked serious. But then he made a joke. "You know, leave me for married bliss?"

As he spoke, her heart had risen, fallen, and finally landed somewhere close to the floor. But it rose again when he clasped her hand. As usual they were in adjacent chairs at the shop's back wall. She was ripping out a seam, one of Irene's, and he was simply there, beside her.

"What do you mean, leave you?" she asked, pulling her hand back, wanting him to reach for it again.

"Are you going to marry that fellow? Is that the plan?"

"No plan," she told him. "I gave up plans a long time ago." Then she told him the story of Milt Goldberg, of that good-for-nothing four-year plan.

"Now that's a fool if I ever heard of one," Tyler declared once her story was concluded.

"Doesn't matter," Bec said. "Things have a way of working out."

They looked at each other for some time until Tyler, perplexed, turned away.

"The thing about Richard Shapiro," she told him next, choosing her words carefully, slowly, "is that he just doesn't have a way with fabric. It's not at all interesting to him."

Tyler turned her way, his eyes clearly questioning her reasoning. He began fiddling with the tape measure around his neck, pulling it off and rolling it into a tight ball.

"And he thinks a shop is just a place to buy things, not a place to make a life."

"But he'll soon feel for the hospital what we feel for the shop," Tyler countered, his words just as cautious as hers.

"And he doesn't know a single Irish tale. Not a single one." Bec almost stamped her foot to emphasize the deficiency, silly as it was.

"The man was born into the wrong set of stories. That's all." Tyler's words, more assured than before, were kind, even generous. He tugged at the tape measure, lengthening it. "You can't blame a fellow for the accidents of nature."

"Tyler," Bec said. This time she did stamp her foot, the left one. "I'm trying to tell you something."

He reached for her hand again. "You shouldn't let me get in your way," he said, rubbing her hand, then briefly lifting it to his lips. "You ought to marry him. He'll provide for you marvelously. That's what you ought to do."

They were silent for a time, and then Bec gathered her work, resumed her sewing. When she finished, she rose and said, "Well, then," before she grabbed her coat.

"Are you leaving me?" Tyler asked again just before she opened the shop door, not a hint of joking anymore in his voice.

"Of course I'm leaving you. But only for the night." She left but didn't walk home. Instead, she found herself at the center of New Haven, at its green, and from there she ambled along any number of streets before she was back where she started, at the shop, which was closed now, locked, the lights off. Still, she didn't go home but went to the coffee shop across the street and sat there at a table by the front window sipping bitter coffee, the night's last brew, and staring well past the dinner hour at the home away from home that was her workplace.

It was a week later when Tyler told her that he'd moved out, that he and his wife, who weren't suited, Bec knew well by then, had finally separated. "I can't offer you much," he said. "Only my word. You understand?"

In an instant the possibilities inherent in a life shared with Richard Shapiro — the very normalcy of it all, which was its main attraction — vanished. Instead, there was *this,* a small, admittedly abnormal, but deeply cherished life with Tyler. Over the years everything she'd ever wanted, ever thought she wanted, had apparently, without her even knowing it, changed.

"I understand," she said.

To Richard Shapiro, who took her to dinner the next night, she said, as kindly as possible, "Enough."

Seven years into the job — she was twenty-nine by then — her parents died, and only months apart, and that's when Tyler told her to go on, to be with her sisters at the beach the whole summer if she wanted. "Take all the time you need," he said, then added, "Just come back to me."

"Where else would I go?" she answered.

And so their patterns fell into place — the summers apart, the other seasons essentially though secretly together. Throughout it all they maintained the appearance of separateness. Until Maks and Risel died Bec still went home one weekend a month, and toward the end of her mother's life it was every weekend. Tyler still celebrated Christmas as though married, by agreement accompanying his wife to church and to holiday visits with her family. By the summer of 1948 Bec and Tyler's love for each other, and the accommodations they had made to keep it alive, hadn't waned. And throughout those years of their togetherness, even the year he spent away at war, even those dizzying months when he returned, his leg wounded, his thoughts as scattered as they'd been during those weeks following Pearl's death, she had the sense, as true as any she'd known, that he and she were meant to be. In all the time he was away, not once did she think he wouldn't come back to her. And so she was shocked by his limp, shocked by the new understanding that what they had, as with any love, was fragile.

Our second week in Woodmont, and as Bec neared the finish of the party dress she was making for Mrs. Arthur Coventry she was just as much in love with Tyler as she'd been the first night she'd finally slept with him, just hours after he'd announced his separation and had offered Bec his word. Their love had lasted, deepened, and by 1948 Tyler wanted it to deepen more. During those working hours on the sunporch Bec flipped the idea of Tyler's proposal, to move with him to New York, over and over, searching for a way that choosing him wouldn't also mean coming out with it all and therefore breaking with her sisters, who she knew would never approve of a common law marriage to a Catholic married man.

And so she was with us, and yet with her secrets and worries she was alone, too. More than ever before.

But what did we know? To us she seemed happy enough, busy, filled with the special air of her sunporch. We didn't suspect a thing, and just kept on with it — our summer's business.

On Wednesday of that second week Davy received his first correspondence from Lucinda Rossetti, an event that pleased him no end. The envelope was a large one, which he ripped open in a second, and he pulled from it an even larger sheet of paper that Lucinda had folded into quarters to mail. Unfolding it, staring at the start of the picture he was to draw with Lucinda, Davy had no idea what it was. He told us that he'd expected some blue on top, for a sky, maybe some green on the bottom, for grass. "That's how I start them," he said of his own rare drawings. But Lucinda Rossetti had drawn several inches of red at the bottom, which went from one edge almost to the other. At different points along the top of the red space other colors emerged, a line of brown, a line of gray, and a line of blue.

For a long time Davy sat on the steps to the cottage porch with the picture in his lap. At one point he placed the picture beside him, stood up, and looked down on it, as if the new angle would bring to light Lucinda's obscure intentions. When Bec asked him if he needed help, he only complained as he'd done at the summer's start that it wasn't fair to get homework during summer vacation. At that Bec stopped working the treadle of the Singer, walked from her sunporch to the front porch, and pulled him onto her lap. If anyone else tried this, even our mother, Davy would have wriggled free in an instant, but perhaps because Bec was present in our lives only during the summer, her lap was still to be cherished. Davy eased farther into it and from their contented looks it was clear the two would sit like that, as they did every so often, for some time.

The summer's business, simple enough.

That same week, at Treat's produce stand, Howard had begun noticing a certain girl who handled checkout, but he didn't know her name or where she came from. In fact he didn't recognize her at all from summers past. She was quick with numbers; he would often catch her adding up a load of them, her mouth puckered as she worked the equation, her round face freckled and topped by a frizzy mass of strawberry-blond hair. As he bagged tomatoes and cucumbers and endless ears of corn he'd glance her way, watch as she smiled at the customer before her, another Mrs. So-and-So, then drop her head in concentration as she added up the total, quick as anything. Megan, he finally learned on the same Wednesday afternoon that Davy stared stupefied at the start of Lucinda Rossetti's picture. The girl at Treat's checkout counter was named Megan O'Donnell.

Nearing the end of that second week, Nina finally finished *On the Origin of Species*. And she agreed, at last, to accompany me to the beach. As we lay side by side on matching towels, Nina explained to me as best she could how Darwin's evolutionary theory rested on a process called natural selection. Over time, lots of time, she noted, random genetic mutations passed from one generation to the next and, if beneficial, helped in the ordeal of survival. Though I listened closely enough, there was much I couldn't follow. But I didn't care what Nina said as long as she was speaking to me. Our mothers and Mrs. Isaacson sat behind us and they were talking too, as always, the this-and-that of their lives a source of quiet but constant conversation. Mrs. Isaacson's granddaughter Judy, for example, was still sullen, and that couldn't be good for her unborn child, we heard. Though my tan was already so much darker than Nina's, I still had this idea that we were as close in looks as the sisters jabbering behind us, their voices as familiar and comforting as the susurration at the shore's edge of endless unwinding waves. Gradually, as Nina's words sank in, I began to wonder if Ada and Vivie had passed enough beneficial and random genetic mutations down to us so that Nina and I were even closer than cousins, were more like sisters. A summer afternoon like this and such an evolution for a girl like me, wedged between two brothers, gave me hope for the ordeal of my own personal survival. I just didn't have the words to explain the desire or the process. But, thanks to Darwin, Nina now did.

Friday once again arrived, and unlike in the previous week, Bec took a break from the family. She was feeling a little claustrophobic, she insisted, what with so many of us packed into such a tight space and all. But we knew better. Shabbos was soon to arrive, which meant the men would be returning, and the sisters, so entwined with each other during the week, would unravel and split, like branches on a tree. Two would find their energies rushing toward their husbands, while Bec would once again be alone. Come a given Friday she needed time to herself then, to readjust her expectations, to get to know herself once again as the solitary person that each weekend in Wood-mont revealed her to be. For years already everybody knew that, figured as much, though no one ever said so out loud. But any Friday afternoon she wanted it, we gave her, gladly, all the space she suddenly needed.

"Going for a walk" was how she put it that Friday when she headed out shortly after lunch. "Need some air! Sure do!"

But ten minutes later, at the corner of Merwin and New Haven avenues, when she saw a familiar red and white Roadmaster parked in a nearby lot, she stopped all that business with fresh air and walking and instantly — because she couldn't help it — broke into a run.

6
A STRANGER AT SHABBOS

The companionship I had enjoyed that Friday afternoon at the beach with Nina didn't last. When her father arrived for the weekend he'd come with another book for her, a biography of Abraham Lincoln, almost as thick as the book she'd just read by Darwin. Oh God, I thought, she'll be gone for at least another whole week. Switching gears from science to history didn't seem to bother her. Her ease in this matter had much to do with the note her father wrote her, a note for each book, which worked to pique her curiosity, no matter the subject. Of the Lincoln biography Leo had written: *Nina, This is my third Lincoln biography in ten years and still he retains what I call a mystery of character.* Nina didn't read this one out loud as she had the last. But once when she wasn't looking I glanced at the message tucked into the biography's pages. Finishing it, I rather wished for a note like that from my father, but he wasn't a reader like Leo. He didn't write notes.

And so the third week of our stay in Woodmont came, July inched onward, and Nina was back to her metal chair on the front porch, reading. She'd still not even tried on the dress and jacket that Bec had sewn for her. She barely had a tan either. We could have been in the middle of New Haven, or back in Middletown, for all the interest Nina took in going to the beach. She remained porch-bound, always wearing shorts and a jersey, though since Howard had teased her, never one as tight as on that first day. The sisters were beginning to wonder what was up with all this ducking of sunshine, sand, and water. "Honey, you're hiding," I heard Vivie say to her the Monday morning of that third week. Nina's answer was firm. "Go away," she said, waving her hand and returning to the words on the page.

That same Monday Howard began to tease Nina again. "Whatcha reading, Nina?" he said, though he knew perfectly well what she was now on to, and as he waited for her answer — a predictable bark at him to leave — he began to sprinkle sand over her book and to drip water onto its pages from his wet hair. Mark Fishbaum was with him, as he typically was in the late afternoon after they were through with their sail on Mark's boat. That day, as was their custom, Howard and Mark had lugged the Sailfish ashore then rushed back into the water for a quick swim before supper. The two had whooped loudly as they leaped into the sea, and then, dripping in their bathing trunks, revved from their sail and swim, they'd climbed up the beach and onto our front porch, where Howard started in with nagging Nina.

Mark was nicer, though, polite, mild-mannered, and he didn't join Howard, whose teasing lasted only seconds, just enough to get a rise out of Nina, which allowed Howard to then throw his arms up over his head and yell a victorious, if not ludicrous, "Touchdown!"

"Are you through?" Nina retorted, wiping the sand and drops from the pages and glancing up for only the briefest instant.

The next day Howard and Mark sailed again, swam again, and climbed onto our cottage porch, dripping wet, again. This time, though, Howard dropped himself into a chair, said nothing, and simply began to towel off. To Nina's surprise, it was Mark who said, "Whatcha reading, Nina?"

"You too?" she exclaimed. She almost

jumped from her chair. Her body tensed and she looked ready to punch him.

"No, I mean it. What is it?" His tone of voice was calm, sincere, not undulating with sarcasm. After Mark repeated the question, he walked behind Nina, glanced over her shoulder and down at the biography on her lap.

When she looked up she was beginning to blush. "Just a book," she answered. "On Lincoln."

"Good?" Mark asked.

"Reasonably," she said, and then she snapped it shut, shot up, and almost bumped into Mark as she opened the screen door and ran inside, both annoyed and flustered, away from him.

Though Davy had no idea what Lucinda Rossetti was getting at with that thick border of red at the bottom of the picture she'd begun, he finally responded by adding an inch of blue to the top of the page. He'd make a sky, no matter that the picture's foreground didn't resemble anything like grass. He sent it back, and on Wednesday of that third week, when Bec came in at lunch with the mail, she sang, "Letter for Davy Leibritsky!" in a voice just like the bellboy's in the radio commercial who cried, "Call for Philip Morris!" At that Davy leaped from his chair. He tore open the new envelope, unfolded the picture, and then stood in the middle of the kitchen as befuddled as the week before. This time Lucinda Rossetti had added an inch of color to each of the three stripes — brown, gray, and blue — that she'd placed on top of the red border at the bottom. Grabbing the drawing from Davy, my mother gave voice to Davy's silent confusion. "What the hell?" she said. After a moment's more scrutiny she added, her voice charged, "Is it something Catholic? Is that what it is?"

"Don't respond right away," Vivie advised, stepping toward Ada and yanking the picture from her, stopping her before she had any more thoughts about Catholics or anybody else. "Give it some time," Vivie told Davy. "Something about it might come to you."

Davy, nodding, returned the picture to the envelope and placed it on the little table in the dining room on which the telephone sat. Resuming his lunch, he said, "I just don't get her." One elbow was on the table and his chin rested in the palm of his hand. "Elbows off," Ada said. "Off."

Because Nina was so preoccupied, I began to hang out at the beach with some other girls I knew, girls my age who liked to sunbathe as much as I did, and swim and play hopscotch in the sand, and chat long after lunch in someone or another's cool kitchen, and who liked to collect shells and, especially, sea glass. Melissa Bornstein was one friend and Anna Weiss another. But I still longed for Nina, the person of summers past with whom I'd tanned, taken walks, and even sat beside while reading; the person with whom I gladly shared the sofa bed even though she tended to kick the blanket off at night; the person I'd tell everything to, if only she wanted to hear, and who I hoped would tell everything to me. But Nina wasn't talking much that summer. Whatever her thoughts were, more and more she seemed to keep them inside. By that third week her mind was a hive of hidden secrets. As we approached the week's end I began to say to myself of Nina, just as Davy had said of Lucinda Rossetti, "I don't get her."

Thursday of that week began with a cloudy morning, and for something to do inside Davy pulled the Bagel family out and he and I began to toy with them. Later that day he tried once again to make sense of the picture Lucinda Rossetti had sent, but once again the brown, gray, and blue stripes were indecipherable. Davy sat with the picture awhile, along with a box of crayons, then pushed them aside. By the time we met Sal for our Good Humor treat, Davy had traded in Lucinda's drawing for Esther Bagel.

"Hello, Esther," Sal said as Davy stood before him, holding Esther out. "What kind of day you having today, Esther?"

"Okay," Davy, as Esther, said. "Ho hum." Esther then scratched her head as if she didn't quite believe her own words. "I'm here for a pick-me-up, Sal," she said more forcefully. "You got anything for me?"

"Is it the regular?" Sal asked, concerned.

"Yeah, Sal," said Esther. "It's the regular." The regular was vanilla ice cream coated with chocolate, on a stick, just like the picture on the truck's side.

"The regular for you too, Molly?" Sal asked, and I nodded. A moment later he handed me a toasted almond bar.

"All picked up?" Sal asked before we left.

"And then some," Davy answered, still in Esther's voice.

"That's what I like to hear, Esther." Sal winked. "Bye-bye, apple pie," he called, and as he climbed aboard his truck we heard him whistle, sharp as a bird's song, a remarkable sound that caused Davy and me to turn back for a better listen, then to jog beside the rolling Good Humor truck until Sal, spotting us, opened his eyes wide and frantically waved his hand with the cigar in it, motioning us to back off. "Oh, no," he hollered, his voice firm but still friendly. "No, no, no."

As the days of our third week in Woodmont passed, we could feel the end of July approaching. At Treat's produce stand the peaches of summer were at their juiciest and selling nicely. As were the tomatoes. The strawberries of June had come and gone but the raspberries of August were beginning to ripen. Megan O'Donnell was still adding columns of numbers those long, hot summer afternoons and Howard Leibritsky was still unloading and bagging merchandise: green beans, heads of lettuce, and zucchini; blueberries, plums, and peaches. Whenever he could he would glance over at Megan, who had begun, at last, to glance back at him. Whenever their eyes met he didn't smile and neither did she, and because of that shared seriousness Howard had a feeling that when he met Megan officially, when they finally talked, he'd find out what he already suspected: she was different from all those other girls he'd known, and not just because she wasn't Jewish.

On Friday of that third week Nina and I were told to borrow bikes from the Weinsteins and ride out to Treat's together to get tomatoes and several cantaloupes for the weekend. To my surprise, without a fuss Nina agreed, and off we went, flying on those borrowed bikes. When we got to Treat's, Howard waited on us, or rather on me, for Nina hung back, close to the checkout stand, unwilling, or so it seemed to me, to engage with Howard. Instead, she gradually struck up a conversation with Megan O'Donnell, who stood only feet from her. Soon, Nina was talking away, laughing at times, nodding at others. Megan was doing the same. As Howard handed me one melon, then another, I began to sink dejectedly under their weight. Howard, too, seemed sullen as he eyed the congenial scene at the checkout stand.

"Hey, Nina," Howard said to her coolly as he approached the checkout area carrying a bag filled with tomatoes. The phrase wasn't so much a greeting as it was a call to attention. But for once Nina felt free to ignore Howard, and as she continued talking with Megan O'Donnell — I heard them discussing Middletown, which Megan was saying she'd once been through — Nina turned her back to Howard.

"Hey, Nina," he repeated, this time with noticeable irritation. Finally he cut in to the conversation, speaking to Megan for the first time with a banality that had to be a letdown for him. "Three cantaloupes and a bag of tomatoes," he told her, dropping the bag on the counter. He backed off but not without muttering to Nina, "Leave her alone, already, why don't you?"

Megan was the one to answer his question. "It's okay," she said, smiling and nodding, which caused her frizzy bangs to fall into her eyes. "I'm really fast with numbers. I can always catch up."

She looked at me first, then Nina, then Howard, without changing her expression. Howard obviously found the neutrality disturbing. For a moment it seemed like he might say something else to Megan, something more substantial that would turn her eyes specifically his way, but he merely coughed and then gave up the effort, staring off in silence with an expression that was rare for him, anxious, even vulnerable. In his frustration he kicked an already soggy fallen tomato, causing the red juice to splatter over both his sneaker-clad feet.

Nina looked at the sullied sneakers then at Howard's perplexed face.

"Touchdown," she said.

■ ■ ■ ■

That afternoon Tyler McMannus came to the cottage — an official, legitimate visit — to pick up Bec and take her into New Haven. Mrs. Arthur Coventry would be coming to the shop for a fitting. In preparation for it, that morning Bec had asked my mother if she would try on the dress, now fully finished, which Ada was more than happy to do.

"Gorgeous," Vivie remarked from her seat in one of the corner armchairs in the living room. Though we'd been up for some time, the sofa bed was unmade, and Nina and I were still in it, Nina sipping tea, me just lying about. Because of that, the one corner chair Vivie sat in was the only seating available in the room. Bec stood in the doorway between the living room and her sunporch. Carefully, she handed the dress to Ada, who put it on and then posed in a different doorway, the one between the living room and dining room. The space was wide enough to allow her to hold her arms out, and when she did she also spun on her toes, the dress's skirt ballooning around her. Her dark hair was still braided from the night before, and it too flew out as she twirled.

"Hot dog," she said excitedly. "I feel seventeen again. How do I look?"

She was asking Bec, who was inspecting her, inch by inch.

"Hold still," Bec told her, smoothing out the skirt, slapping at it at times as if to tame it. A moment later she said, "Now turn. Slowly. *Slowly.*"

My mother complied. The dress was classically styled, with long sleeves, which we were told Mrs. Coventry had specifically requested, a low neckline with a collar, which Mrs. Coventry wasn't so sure about and had to be convinced of, and a belt at the waist, which Mrs. Coventry was sure would be a disaster but had nevertheless, with Bec's urging, consented to. From the waist down the taffeta took over and the dress flowed out. Though the fabric was stiff, it nevertheless hung in a way that seemed almost natural. The burgundy color against my mother's tanned olive complexion was its most striking feature.

"Oh, Ada," Bec finally said. "A bit big in the middle, but still, Vivie was right. It's that color. It's splendid on you."

For a moment my mother couldn't stop touching the dress, its sleeves, its collar, its stiff but flowing skirt. Though Bec sewed for us all she'd never made us anything this elegant. Even the enviable dress and jacket for Nina was a much simpler affair.

Ada shrugged. "Oh well," she said, dropping her arms, resigned to finally parting with it. "For a moment I felt like Cinderella, dressed up for the ball. Yes," she said, nodding. "I did."

When she laughed, plaintively, her sisters joined her.

"Those ladies from New Haven," Bec said, patting my mother's back as she turned her around one more time. "You wouldn't believe it. To them a dress like this is just any old day."

But that afternoon, once Bec and Tyler had arrived at the shop, Bec understood that she'd been wrong about Mrs. Coventry. The woman, anxious about the upcoming fiftieth-anniversary party she was planning for her husband, wasn't taking anything for granted. She'd invited the whole world, Mrs. Coventry complained upon entering the store. "What was I thinking?" she asked.

Rising to greet her, Bec gave Mrs. Coventry — dear in a way that Bec didn't recall from two months back, and a little rounded in the shoulders — a quick squeeze. Her white hair curled around her weathered face. She wore pearl earrings and a necklace with a large stone attached that Bec didn't recognize. "Garnet," Mrs. Coventry explained. "Native to Connecticut." She seemed tired, her voice dragging, and Bec offered her a chair. The woman dropped into it, sighing.

"Remind me never to throw another party," she told Bec, shaking her head and pulling a hanky from her purse, which she used to dab her brow. "I'm too old for this. That's what I've found out. That this was a very silly idea."

"Not silly. It's exciting, and very generous of you," Bec insisted. Something about the women's vulnerability, her fatigue, touched Bec. "Also very loving," she added.

"Very, very," Mrs. Coventry answered, waving the white hanky as if in surrender. "Oh, I guess you're right." She laughed, her spirits lifted, apparently, by Bec's remarks. "Now I have to see if I can get this old bag of a body into the dress." She stopped laughing. "I invited everyone," she added sadly.

Bec nodded.

"Foolish," Mrs. Coventry quipped. "Very, very."

As the women talked, Tyler approached them carrying the dress, which was the same color as Mrs. Coventry's garnet. Despite her hesitations in the planning process, especially about that belted waist, at the sight of the finished dress Mrs. Coventry quickly smiled. Her back straightened. It seemed to Bec she was holding in her already dainty tummy.

"Come on, let's get you into this," Bec urged. "Would you like me to stay?" she asked once they were in the fitting room, and the woman nodded, almost frantically.

"Someone to lean on," Mrs. Coventry said.

"Bec," Tyler called minutes later. "How's it going in there?"

She turned to Mrs. Coventry, who had yet to speak. "Well?" Bec asked. When designing the dress she'd worried that the style was too young for the woman, but she'd gone ahead with it anyway, as Mrs. Coventry had a trim figure that could in fact withstand the belted waist, and upon meeting her she'd noticed there was such energy and lightness in her spirit. She seemed youthful at heart, despite her years. Bec had spent considerable time the day of their initial appointment getting to know Mrs. Coventry, discussing style options while taking her measurements. Bec had spoken her usual "Trust me" at the end of the meeting, to which Mrs. Coventry had answered, "But I do. I do. That's why I'm here." The woman had touched Bec's cheek then, such a gentle, loving gesture that when Bec recalled it as she sat watching Mrs. Coventry stare at herself in the mirror, waiting for her response, she wanted to reach out and soothe the woman's worries in the same way.

"I don't know what to say," Mrs. Coventry blurted, finally turning to face Bec.

With Mrs. Coventry's assent, Bec pulled the curtain aside. Tyler's eyes widened instantly. From behind him, Irene, their junior seamstress, gave a loud and pleased gasp.

"Goodness," Tyler whispered to Mrs. Coventry, "but you look amazing."

"Mrs. Coventry?" Bec asked in almost the same hushed tone as Tyler's. "You haven't said anything. Do you like it at all?"

The woman took a step back. "Do I like it?" she repeated, fluffing the skirt of the dress, lifting it up then letting it fall. "Truth is, I never expected something like this. It makes me remember how it used to be. That's it. That's why I'm nearly speechless." She lifted the skirt once again then dropped it. "I adore this dress. I do!"

Bec clapped in delight. That Mrs. Coventry's words were so much like Ada's was as surprising as how much the woman had taken to the dress. Irene insisted on dashing out for some champagne.

When Irene returned, the four sat in the chairs at the rear of the store, sipping and chatting. Bec had the dress draped over her lap as she hemmed its sleeves — a touch too long — then rose for a quick pressing. Soon enough she'd finished, and Tyler wrapped and boxed the dress, then placed it at Mrs. Coventry's feet. When she was ready to leave, Mrs. Coventry turned to Bec.

"You may not understand this, but I see a lot of myself in you," she said, pulling Bec close. "I can't sew like you, of course, but I rather like making things. Like this damn party," she said, a hint of mischief in her voice. "It's quite the concoction. You see what I'm saying?" Mrs. Coventry tilted her champagne flute for a final sip. "I'd like you to come to the party," she said next with near urgency. "I really would. You and Tyler and Irene. I consider you friends. I'd be so honored."

Bec walked the woman to the door. Tyler was a step behind, carrying the box with the dress in it. "That's generous," Bec acknowledged. "But we can't. Not our place. You just come back and tell us all about it. Won't you?"

"I will. I'll tell you all about it," agreed Mrs. Coventry, raising her head to kiss both Bec and Tyler. "But I wish you'd reconsider. It *is* your place. Because it's *my* place," she said with an earnestness that made Bec think of the very store they stood in, a place she thought of by then as his and hers, not exactly a home, but something close to it, and wasn't that all right? The accommodation?

That same Friday afternoon in Middletown, after Mort and Leo had left for Woodmont, a new shipment of men's shirts arrived at Leibritsky's Department Store, short-sleeved, for summer. As Nelson pulled them from their box he was reminded suddenly of another box in the store's basement containing almost the same shirts. He'd forgotten about them, had never gotten them to the sales floor last year. Why the hell did the summer shirts always manage to arrive so late in the season? he wondered, frustrated. And given last year's blunder, why'd he go and order them again? He shrugged. He knew the answer well enough. He was lousy at business. The simple fact was undeniable. Nelson was glad then that Leibritsky's Department Store came with such a spacious basement, a place he often visited to take a moment to himself, a place large enough to hide his many mistakes in.

In certain respects he'd moved in down there, staking out a corner for himself and furnishing it with a rocking chair, along with a lamp and a two-drawer desk. The desk was covered by a phonograph and stacks of records — worn 78s for the most part, though over the past weeks he'd added a few 33 1/3 s, able to play for a whole forty minutes, a technology just out that summer. Benny Goodman was what he turned to when he needed a workday lift, the instantaneous rapture of "Sing, Sing, Sing" the tune he could count on to get his blood pumping as dramatically as the song's insistent drums. But that Friday, arriving at his basement nook, the one place in the universe of Leibritsky's where he was at home, where his breathing, despite the basement's dampness, came easy, he decided against "Sing, Sing, Sing" or anything else by Goodman. Instead he chose silence. He rocked in his chair for a time, ate one and then another penny Tootsie Roll, then turned toward the desk, opened its top drawer, and pulled from it an old framed photograph.

He wiped the glass over the picture. The face he looked at, female, was smiling and young as ever. Just twenty-one. Nelson was now forty-two. He'd been thinking about that smiling face since his lunch with Howard two weeks back. "It can be hard to be a son," he'd told Howard then, which was an indirect reference to his long-ago love affair with the girl in the photo, Mimmie Klein. His loss of her love was not unrelated to something his father, Howard's grandfather, had said. That day at lunch with Howard, had Nelson not stuffed his face with fruit cocktail, he might very well have talked about Mimmie, the girl of a thousand years ago and yet of only yesterday.

Two weeks later, and he still couldn't get her off his mind. He ate another Tootsie Roll. He didn't speak her name for fear that it would un-dam a grief he wouldn't be able to stop. "Lousy at love," he said to no one. "Lousy at summer shirts."

While Nelson sat in the basement staring at the photograph, and while Bec said goodbye for a second time to Mrs. Coventry, hugging her even more warmly, Mort and Leo stood at Jimmies hot dog stand at Savin Rock amusement park in West Haven having their weekly pre-Shabbos snack: two dogs and a Coca-Cola for each of them.

They'd listened to a ball game the whole ride up, the New York Giants versus the Dodgers, who were hot this season with that "blackie Jackie," as Mort called the Negro, Jackie Robinson. For some reason, Mort couldn't stop with it. "Blackie Jackie," he said again as he waited for his hot dog.

Leo raised his eyebrows.

"Ah, hell. Didn't mean anything by that," Mort said. "I'm not Ada, you know."

Leo only nodded.

At the same time my mother and Vivie were still at the beach, sitting in their folding chairs, wearing old housedresses over even older bathing suits, their feet soaking in the waters of the Long Island Sound, their hair in the same braids they'd worn to bed the night before. They hadn't picked up the house yet. Nor had they begun to marinate the chicken for dinner. The dining table had yet to be set, too.

Vivie yawned. Ada sighed.

"It's Friday, you know," Vivie reminded her sister.

Ada sighed again, but this time with just a hint of frustration. "For crying out loud, let's take ten more minutes," she urged. "What's the rush? You know?"

■ ■ ■ ■

So the cottage was a little messy when the men arrived later that afternoon, the dining table not yet set, the women still in their flowery housedresses, Davy, in bathing trunks, not yet showered. Mort, inspecting the place, inspecting the women, inspecting his youngest son, seemed momentarily alarmed. But the chicken was in the oven, along with baking potatoes, and the smells from the food were reassuring. There would be a Shabbos meal like every other Shabbos meal.

And there was, except for Bec's surprising absence. By the time we sat down at the table and readied ourselves for the pre-dinner blessings, Bec still hadn't returned from the fitting in New Haven for Mrs. Coventry. The sun was sinking, the breezes off the Sound had stilled, and Mort sat at the head of the table, his yarmulke in his hands, his prayer book opened, waiting. Gradually, we gathered around him and waited too.

"Where's Bec?" Mort finally asked after a long and cold silence. He was drumming a forefinger on the table's edge. Outside, over the ocean, the sun had dropped beneath the line of the horizon. My empty stomach was growling and I suspected other bellies were too. Davy hungrily eyed the mound of challah loaves.

No one answered. Ada turned to Vivie, a questioning look in her eyes, but Vivie only shrugged. "You know," Vivie then began, her voice quiet but earnest, "it can be uncomfortable for her on the weekends. I don't think she feels about Shabbos the way we feel." I assumed Vivie was speaking about Bec's Friday claustrophobia, her weekly need to take off in preparation for the weekend. "Let's just give her a bit more time," Vivie added.

Mort glanced toward the darkening sky with a disapproving eye. He checked his wristwatch. He sighed. "All right," he finally said.

But a moment later he nodded impatiently Ada's way, which was her cue to rise and light the Sabbath candles, then to circle her hands over the flames, as if conjuring the sacred light, cajoling it into being.

The Sabbath had begun, too, for Bec, though in a different way. The fitting over, the champagne drunk, the dress shop locked for the weekend, Bec and Tyler had said good-bye to Irene (Tyler crooning that old song "Goodnight Irene, goodnight, Irene, goodnight") and they'd headed back to the Buick Roadmaster. They were driving out of New Haven, toward West Haven and Woodmont, when, waiting at a stoplight, Tyler slapped his hands on the steering wheel in obvious frustration.

"Come on, stay with me longer," he said, turning Bec's way. "Let's have dinner somewhere. Bec, please."

His words surprised her. He'd never interfered with her family life before. And that was just it: as long as she kept her worlds separate — the independent and private life in New Haven, the family life in Woodmont — then she could have them both. But she couldn't bring them together; she knew that as well as she knew anything. She'd tried to visualize it many times, inviting Tyler to the cottage, not as her employer but as her love, the two of them sitting side by side at the Friday Shabbos meal. That was the image that shattered her heart. A stranger at Shabbos. A married Catholic man sitting at the sisters' beautifully laid table, not knowing what in the world was going on as they lit the candles, blessed the wine and bread, chanted the ancient Hebrew prayers. There was a sanctity to their ritual that an outside presence would simply violate. And Mort! Just thinking of Mort sharing a Shabbos table with Tyler made Bec shudder. She'd be destroying his Shabbos, which was their Shabbos, their world. A stranger at Shabbos and the family might as well be eating regular rather than challah bread. A gentile at the table and everyone would know the difference in an instant, would feel the dilution, the diminution of everything they valued. Indeed, what she was doing with Tyler was so far outside the bounds of acceptability that no one even suspected it, not even after all these years. Yes, to have everything she wanted with Tyler was to lose everything she had with her sisters. In this way Tyler's asking her to come with him to New York was really his asking her to make a choice that for all these years she'd been more than content to avoid.

"Bec, please," Tyler said again. The light changed and he drove forward then pulled the car to the curb. He looked at her, reached for her, and she said, in words she couldn't quite believe, "Okay, yes."

In West Haven they found a little Italian restaurant neither had been to before. Using the restaurant phone, she called the cottage to tell the family she'd be late, but they already knew that. She'd interrupted their meal. With an unsteady hand, she hung up the phone. How easy it was, she realized, as she stumbled back to Tyler, to be left behind. She and Tyler had been seated by a window. Their table was small, intimate, and covered by a white tablecloth. Already the sky outside was growing dark and a waiter came over even before they'd ordered their food to light a candle at the table's center. As Bec stared into the flame she felt a growing impulse to raise her arms and circle her hands over it just as she was sure her sister Ada had done over the two Sabbath candles at the center of the dining table in Woodmont. Soon their waiter brought them glasses of red wine and a basket of bread. They could have their own Shabbos, she realized. She explained to Tyler about the candles, the wine, and the bread. In the next moment he lifted both a chunk of bread and his glass of wine.

"Good Shabbos, Bec," he said, so sincerely that for a moment her eyes welled up.

Then she laughed. And he laughed. They clinked glasses, sipped wine, chewed the soft bread. Before long the waiter brought them two plates heaping with summer greens, carrots, and tomatoes. She was hungrier than she'd realized. Tyler kept talking throughout the meal, about the week that he'd spent at the dress shop without her. She nodded as she ate, cheese ravioli that were more delicious than any she'd ever had.

By the time they finished their meal the sky had completely darkened. Only two other couples had come in for dinner, and they sat at tables some distance from hers and Tyler's. She glanced out the window. There was water out there somewhere, the Long Island Sound, connecting this place with that other place, that cottage at Bagel Beach, but in the dark she couldn't see it. She turned back to Tyler, who sat with a look of contentment on his face. His gray eyes reflected the glow of the candle's flame. He was quieter now, having gotten the this-and-that of the week out of his system, but he wasn't quite ready to go yet, he said, and she agreed, quickly, that neither was she.

They kept sitting like that, serenely, not speaking but enjoying a kind of coupled solitude that made Bec feel as if this little restaurant were there solely to serve them. In the darkness outside the rest of the world had disappeared. Their waiter came by, asking them if they'd like coffee or dessert, and Bec was taken by the mellifluousness of his voice. He too seemed to be there solely for them. Whatever they wanted, he said. That was what was for dessert. Then he added, joking, but better to order tiramisu, or maybe, a little lighter, some sherbet.

They sat, they smiled, they sipped coffee, and for the first time in a public place, they reached for each other's hands. When had Shabbos ever been this lovely? Bec began to wonder.

When had she ever felt this much at the center of it, this loved, this well fed?

When had she, single and childless, ever been anything but a stranger, really — a guest, an extra — at the family Shabbos meal? And how strange not to have felt the weight of it, her years and years of Sabbath loneliness.

But she didn't even realize Shabbos *was* lonely until just then, when it suddenly wasn't anymore.

She began to shake her head, a measure of her bewilderment, then to nod over and over until Tyler understood from the insistent repetition the depth of what she was saying to him, that she would go to New York, begin that new life, and as he straightened in his chair and cleared his throat as if to speak, it soon became obvious he couldn't speak, could only do as she was doing: the nodding, the silent *yes,* over and over again.

7
NO MORE FRIDAY
CLAUSTROPHOBIA

Bec's house that I've inherited is in Middletown. Not New Haven. Nor New York. She lived in the house with my uncle, Nelson Leibritsky, not Tyler McMannus. That is to say, she became Mrs. Nelson Leibritsky — sister-in-law to her sister Ada — and never, even unofficially, Mrs. Tyler McMannus. But with Nelson's death occurring so many years before Bec's, I can hardly find a trace of him here.

The few belongings of Nelson's that Bec kept I found, aptly enough for a basement fan like Nelson, in this home's basement. Tonight is Halloween, and earlier in the day I decided to come to the house to put the lights on, as if to woo the parade of small costumed souls who will ring the doorbell in hopes of a treat if they see someone is at home. Bec was always well stocked for Halloween and I'd made sure to bring multiple bags of Tootsie Rolls, Nelson's favorite candy.

But in the basement, looking for holiday decorations, I found nothing beyond the predictable washer and dryer and furnace until I came to some boxes lined up against a wall and marked, plainly enough, *Nelson.* The contents, I saw, were Nelson's LPs from yesteryear: Frank Sinatra singing with the Tommy Dorsey band, Ella Fitzgerald singing with Chick Webb's group, a solo album of Rosemary Clooney and another of Dean Martin. But as I flipped through the stacks I saw that more than those solo artists, Nelson collected recordings of the big bands of his youth. There was Johnny Mercer and Glenn Miller, more Tommy Dorsey, and finally I came to a series of recordings by Benny Goodman.

Everybody knew that "Sing, Sing, Sing (with a Swing)" was Nelson's all-time favorite — many a time we must have heard the music, or at least its signature drumming, rising from the basement of Leibritsky's Department Store; Nelson, contrary perhaps to his own view of things, was hardly hiding down there — and finding a recording of it, lifting the old album from the box, felt almost like I was exhuming Nelson from the grave. The impulse to play it was irresistible, and so I climbed the stairs, laid the record on the turntable of the living room's antiquated music system, and dropped the needle. It began: that inimitable tom-tom beat of the drums, then the roar of trombones, then trumpets, and finally it was Goodman himself, wailing on his clarinet. But always the music returned to the drums, "the drumbeats of God," Nelson once said in a rare moment of speaking up at a family meal in Middletown. The genius of drummer Gene Krupa was just a contrivance, Nelson urged us to understand, a way for God to tell us all to wake up, to be sure we felt something of our own heart's beating.

"Who doesn't feel *that*?" I remember Davy asking Nelson, surprised, his hand pressed against his chest. And such a memory dates the occasion: a Sabbath meal in Middletown in the weeks before we left for Woodmont in 1948, Nelson then still a bachelor — always the bachelor, everyone assumed — and invited to our home for the evening, and Davy throughout the meal staring at Nelson's suit jacket as if by so doing he could bring forth the Tootsie Rolls Nelson was sure to be pocketing there.

"Everyone knows their hearts are beating," Davy insisted. He was smiling as he said the words, his hand still pressed to his chest.

But Nelson didn't grin back. He said, his face dour, his tone just the tiniest bit angry, "Not everyone, boy. Not everyone."

Upon saying those words Nelson reached into a suit pocket and, just as Davy had anticipated, he pulled out a Tootsie Roll, then ate the thing even though his plate was still full of my mother's roast chicken and potato kugel.

Davy watched in disbelief as Nelson unwrapped, chewed, and swallowed the candy. Davy even turned to our father, as if expecting him to scold Nelson just as he would one of us if we were to pop a chocolate into our mouth in the middle of a meal.

But Mort pretended not to see, and following his lead, neither did Ada or Howard. Even I looked away.

"Can I have one?" Davy finally said, turning Nelson's way.

"When you finish," my mother answered.

"But —" Davy began.

"No buts," Mort said.

"But —" Davy tried again.

Ada reached over, pointing her fork at Davy's plate.

Davy, confused, turned toward Nelson, then toward one parent, then the next. He was clearly dying to finish his sentence, to argue his case further. The inequities of the situation were glaring.

"Tell you what," Nelson told him. "You listen to 'Sing, Sing, Sing' sometime with me at the store and I'll give you two candies. And if it gets your heart going like it does mine, going so that you know for sure it's going, I'll give you three."

But we left for the summer before Davy got his chance at those three candies, his chance to listen to the music with Nelson, who was telling Davy, telling us, what it was to be depressed. You can't even feel your own heart beating. And that news, at least to my parents who pretended not to hear it, was shameful.

Instead, before he could ever take Nelson up on his offer, Davy's was the heart, young as it was, that literally stopped beating. And some time after that Nelson's figurative ticker began to revive, to beat once again such that he could feel it, though he was already middle-aged and had assumed, for so long, that he'd always exist in the numbness of his solitude. The night of that Shabbos meal Bec was in New Haven, living a life that included her secret love for Tyler McMannus. It was only after Davy died that she was present often enough in Middletown for Nelson to get to know her, then to find in her a companionship he deeply longed for, then to marry her and live with her in this house. In Bec's living room this afternoon my foot tapped to the drums of "Sing, Sing, Sing," and though I knew theirs was a union born of loss and marked by loss, somehow under the music's spell — the drums of God, yes, yes! — it seemed entirely possible that they did what people do, perfectly ordinary people, people all over the world and for all time: they became better acquainted, grew to like each other, and, redeeming years of loneliness and years of secrets and years of half-lived lives, they fell in love.

But that's not how it went. Rather, three years after Davy died Bec indeed married Nelson. It was enough love for Nelson — transforming love, in fact — but for Bec it was not love at all.

She loved, with all her heart, Tyler McMannus. But in the aftermath of the accident that would ultimately take Davy's life, while he was still alive and in the Milford hospital, while there was still reason for hope, she'd made a bargain with God: if Davy lived, she wouldn't see Tyler that upcoming Friday as they'd secretly planned.

And it worked. Davy did live, at least for the next week. So at the week's end she made another deal: if he continued to live, she wouldn't see Tyler again. She'd give him up entirely if that's what it took to keep Davy alive. She would, she implored God; really she would.

But Davy died at the start of the second week following the accident, on an otherwise fine Saturday morning. Bec's desperate prayers had done nothing to change that.

The funeral was set for Tuesday, and she was to go with the family that Saturday evening back to Middletown, where she would help Ada with the arrangements and with everything else. My mother could barely stand. "Everything else" was just that: rising, sitting, using the toilet, getting dressed, eating, walking, combing her hair. Bec would attend the funeral, of course, and though she wasn't required like us to sit shiva, she'd nevertheless stay for the formal mourning period of seven days.

"You understand, right?" she asked Tyler from the phone in our Middletown hallway.

"Take all the time you need," he said.

Two days after the funeral they decided Tyler would drive to Middletown and they'd meet on the Wesleyan University campus, which was within walking distance from our home. There they sat on the steps of an old and towering brownstone building. Before them the campus lawn sloped downhill in a shimmering sheet of newly mowed green. Though it was September already, the semester had yet to start and no one was out. She leaned her head on Tyler's shoulder as he wrapped his arm around her. They hadn't seen each other for three weeks, a fact that would normally have been cause for a relieved sense of reunion. But in the wake of the disaster they had almost nothing to say. She cried for the most part, quietly, lifting an embroidered hanky to her eyes every so often. After a while she closed her eyes as she continued to lean on his shoulder.

"I should be going," she said after a half hour or so had passed. She rose and faced the direction from which she had come. "Ada needs me."

After she'd begun to walk away from him, she turned back. Tyler was going in the other direction, his fedora in one hand, his limp more noticeable than she'd remembered.

"Careful!" she called. But he didn't hear her and continued on, almost staggering at times, it seemed to Bec, who hadn't budged, was still watching, and did so until he'd turned a corner and was no longer within her sight.

After the week of shiva, Bec returned to the cottage for a day and a night, with Ada and Mort this time. They were there to pack and close the place for the season. When they finished, Bec would be dropped off in New Haven to resume her life and my parents would go back to Middletown to resume theirs.

Though she'd come to Woodmont to work, Ada sat for the most part, in one of the chairs that surrounded the kitchen table. She stared dumbly before her, at the walls, the sink, the washing machine. Bec was the one to empty the cabinets and the refrigerator, and it was she who covered the dining table and chairs with one of the old sheets we'd tucked away at the summer's start. Upstairs, Bec pulled any remaining clothes from the boys' room, stripped the beds, and smoothed the matching navy bedcovers. In the bathroom she scrubbed the bathtub with the clawed feet, along with the sink and toilet. She left Vivie and Leo's room alone, as Vivie had said they'd drive out, despite Leo's aversion to driving distances, and take care of that themselves. She left Ada and Mort's bedroom alone, too, as they would sleep there that night, and it didn't seem right to her, going through their things while they were in the cottage with her.

While Bec worked, Mort took care of the outside of the place, sweeping the front porch and stacking the painted metal chairs. He folded and stored the umbrella clothesline. Inside again, he closed and locked the windows throughout the house, except for those of Bec's sunporch, which she'd crank shut in the morning, and a window in the master bedroom so he and Ada would have air while they slept.

But no one slept that night. Bec tossed and turned on her cot, and throughout the night she heard footsteps upstairs, someone pacing the hallway. When she rose in the morning she was surprised to see that Mort had not been upstairs but had bunked on the sofa bed in the living room.

When Bec reached Ada she winced to see her sister's eyes circled with dark bags and her thick hair, which she'd forgotten to braid the night before, in a tangle. It took Bec a long time to comb it through and pin it up. It took even more time to get Ada properly bathed and dressed. While the dressing ensued, Mort was downstairs, pacing from the kitchen to the dining room to the living room and back again. By the time the sisters were ready to go he was angry with them, impatient, worn out from the extra care his wife needed, which he, in fact, hadn't provided. Bec had done it all. And she could see from the coolness between them, an almost complete absence of communication, that should she stay on with them she'd continue to do it all, because Davy's death had caused something terrible to happen between Mort and Ada. He had grown angrier and angrier with her. That morning, as the three sat at the kitchen table, sipping coffee, he was barely able to look at her.

Who, Bec wondered, was going to nourish Ada in the days to come, provide a shoulder for her to lean on, get her up and dressed, help her make the family's meals? Certainly we children couldn't, and shouldn't, Bec knew. And in the wake of Davy's death Vivie had taken a step back from the extended family, into her own home, where she was busy consoling an almost inconsolable Nina.

By the time they arrived at Tyler's dress shop, Bec had made up her mind. She told Mort she'd be only a minute. Inside the shop she waved at Irene, then grabbed Tyler's arm and pulled him into his office.

"I have to go back to Middletown. Ada needs me. I'm the only one she has." She leaned toward him, straightened his tie, then held on to it.

He was nodding, quickly, insistently, just as he was that evening — not so long ago — at the little Italian restaurant in West Haven.

"Okay?" she asked. Then she added, "It's just until she gets on her feet again. Just a little while more."

Though still nodding, he said, "No, not okay at all."

They embraced and she told him, "You have no idea what this means to me."

"Go on," he said, releasing her from his arms. "I'll be here, waiting."

She offered a small smile of gratitude though she knew what she was doing to him, knew from those years of her long-ago engagement what a peculiar hell it was: waiting.

"Just until she's on her feet," she said again, and then she kissed his mouth, straightened his tie once more, turned, and left.

Thus in mid-September of 1948 Bec moved in with us, sleeping, though she refused to at first, in Davy's room, but capitulating to that arrangement, however awkward, after a week or so since it was the only vacant bedroom and she needed among the rooms of our Middletown home just a little space to herself. Nobody minded that she cleared out Davy's things; nobody minded because nobody knew what to do. Emptying the room of the things that signaled a life that was no longer in it seemed as good a way as any for us to start this new life, a kind of afterlife. She removed his clothes from the drawers of his dresser, his collection of baseball pennants — Yankees, Red Sox, Dodgers — his old stuffed teddy. The only thing she left was the picture, almost finished, that Davy and Lucinda Rossetti had drawn together over the summer. She had brought that back with her, in the envelope addressed to Davy at Woodmont. The envelope stayed in Davy's room, on top of his old dresser.

She'd left her Singer, her mannequin, and her sewing basket in her New Haven apartment. With the intention to do nothing for the time being but take care of her sister, and of us, she'd packed only her clothes. But my mother had a sewing basket too, and in no time Bec was roaming the house, looking for seams to adjust, buttons to tighten, or hems to let down. Not that she didn't have plenty to do; there was my mother, who, throughout that fall, as the leaves turned and fell from the trees, was still barely functioning. After nearly sleepless nights she would finally fall into a slumber in the early morning, which put her waking time at about noon. Bec, then, was the one to rise early, make breakfast, see us off. Howard had planned to start college that fall at Wesleyan in Middletown, but he'd taken a year's deferment, and he joined my father each morning at minyan and then spent the day with him at the store. I was off to eighth grade. When I'd return from school in the late afternoon it was Bec, not my mother, who greeted me, held me, and made me cups of hot, sweet tea. I would often find my mother sitting by herself in the living room, staring mindlessly out a window. Bec brought her cups of tea as well, and crackers. And she'd sit with her, as the late-afternoon light waned, and talk to her, though of nothing important. Finally Bec would rise and begin dinner preparations. When my father and Howard walked into the house each evening they were welcomed by the smells of roasting meats, and the tunes sounding from the kitchen radio, popular music Bec liked, and that I, her helper, was growing fond of too. Except for the woman sitting in the dark in the living room it was, at least on the surface, a nearly normal scene.

So Bec was busy, but she was restless, too, and the mending was one way to keep her hands active at her beloved trade, her mind occupied, her heart beating when so many times she must have felt like it was soon to give out.

And there were meetings with Tyler. In the mornings she could practically have had him over to the house, what with all of us gone and my mother sleeping, but she never even considered that, disrespectful as she thought it to be. Instead, she met him at a nearby corner of Hubbard Street, and they'd go from there to a diner on Route 66 on the outskirts of Middletown. The first time there they sat on the same side of a cozy booth, his arm never leaving her shoulders. She wasn't crying anymore but she still wasn't saying much. How could she put into words everything that had changed? She mentioned the cups of tea, the nibbles of crackers, the late-afternoon light fading in the living room. She listed the meals she'd made: meatloaf, pot roast, baked chicken, spaghetti and meatballs, stuffed cabbage, broiled steak, and on Sundays, always, because she was tired, because it was easy, and because Mort liked it that way, franks and beans.

"Mrs. Coventry came by to tell us about the party," Tyler reported. "It was a nice party," he said, squeezing Bec's shoulders and kissing her head. "That's what she told us. Her husband was very happy."

"Very, very," Bec replied, her voice but a whisper. "That's how she would have put it."

"Yes," Tyler said, his tone gentle but eager. "Exactly, Bec. That's just what she said."

They resumed their silence. He ordered egg salad for them both. When they'd finished their meal, she said, "Ada needs me," and though they hadn't had coffee yet, he promptly paid and took her home.

For the next month they saw each other every week for a meal at the same diner, where they sat until Bec declared, "Ada needs me." By mid-November, though, the pace of their meetings slackened and he began to drive to Middletown every other week, then every third week. During January of 1949 he hired another dressmaker, a woman named Mildred Butler, but he assured Bec that this was only until she was ready to return.

"I understand. You have to," she said, knowing the truth of it.

By February he stopped asking her when she was coming back. Why would he? she figured. Her answer, after all, was always the same: "Ada needs me." True as that was, there was another reason she kept away, one she couldn't tell him: that she didn't deserve him, that she didn't deserve happiness, that given what had happened she didn't deserve anything good at all.

In the last weeks of winter Ada began to rise earlier and to help make breakfast for the family. Soon she was doing some cleaning: a little washing, a little ironing. Once or twice as the earliest days of spring emerged she spontaneously sang along to a tune from the radio Bec played as she cooked. Ada especially liked Doris Day's "It's Magic" and Mel Tormé's "Blue Moon," just out. During those long sits she still took in the living room she began to flip on the light. "Thank you," she once said to Bec on a rainy evening, the third week of April. The two were seated on the living room couch, staring into an unlit fireplace. "I think you've saved my life." Bec shook her head, continued her staring. When Ada grabbed her hand to give it a squeeze, Bec didn't squeeze back.

As spring set in the crocuses bloomed, as did tulips and irises, all growing wild in a scattering around our Middletown home. My mother had never cultivated a garden but a former owner apparently had, the intrepid remains of which popped up, blooming that year with a conspicuous audacity, or so it seemed, given our heavy hearts. Howard was still living at home and working at the store. There was talk of us all going back to Woodmont for the summer, just like always. One day in late May I heard Bec on the phone with Vivie, discussing it.

"You have to come," she implored Vivie.

When I asked Bec what Vivie had said, she only shook her head. "Can't. That's what she said."

"Then what do we do?"

"We do what your mother wants," Bec answered. "It's her decision."

What Ada wanted turned out to be a return to the cottage. "Yes, I think so," she said feebly one dinnertime in early June.

"I can't be there, you know," Mort told her, sounding almost indifferent to what she did or didn't do.

"It never mattered before," Ada answered with the same indifference. "Why should it matter now?"

"Of course it mattered before," Mort snapped. He couldn't hide his contempt as he looked her way.

"Stop blaming her!" Bec urged, leaning toward Mort, almost grabbing at him. "It's not her fault. For God's sake, you have to stop with that." She turned to me. "Molly, don't listen," she ordered, as if such a thing were possible.

My father's head dropped to his chest. A long moment of silence passed. "Like I said. I can't be there." He seemed less angry than matter-of-fact. In the same detached tone he added, "Ada, I'm not blaming you."

But he'd thought it for so long that his words that night did little to melt the block of ice, solid and ever-widening, that lay between my parents. And two weeks later, when Mort drove us back to Woodmont, he said his good-byes only minutes after he'd dropped us off.

Howard hadn't come. He'd feel better, he said the night before, looking more toward Mort than anyone else, if he stayed in Middletown and kept working. And so it was only my mother, Bec, and I who moved into the cottage that summer of 1949. That year for the first time ever Bec was the one to open the door and step inside first, though her steps were timid, tentative ones, not the impatient, joyful strides of my mother in years past. Bec flicked on a light or two then went to her sunporch, where she cranked open the windows. She lifted the sheet from the dining room table and carried it out to the front porch to shake the dust free. My mother remained on the porch, letting the dust fall around her, holding her breath, seemingly afraid to go inside until Bec linked arms with her, tugged, and said gently, "It's no worse here than in Middletown. Ada, come on now. I'm here. Molly's here. It'll be all right."

That summer there was no more Friday claustrophobia for Bec, no more meetings, secret or otherwise, with Tyler McMannus. They hadn't seen each other since late February. Nor were there the weekend meetings of Ada and Mort Leibritsky. My father stayed away all summer, which meant we never had to get the house especially clean on Fridays, never had to prepare a big Shabbos meal. On Friday evenings we three still lit the candles, each of us circling our hands in unison close to the flames, each of us quietly murmuring the old prayers. We still took a piece of challah and chewed it, still drank a sip of wine. But then we'd take our plates — some reheated food from the week's cooking — out to the front porch of the cottage, where we'd sit in the painted metal chairs and eat off our laps. It was better out there, my mother thought, because of the possibility of a nice evening breeze.

That summer the dunking was the only thing that didn't change dramatically from summers past, other than the fact that it was me rather than Vivie who stood at the shore's edge with my mother, watching as Bec dove in first. Once my mother and I managed to get wet, we three would spend a moment floating on our backs, then we'd sink down again under the salty water before we'd rise from it, not so much refreshed as chilled, alert, aware that what faced us was yet another difficult but passable day.

Over the summer weeks, Mark Fishbaum became my friend. It was so odd, so very lonely, to be at the beach without Davy, and without Nina, Howard, Vivie, Leo, and my father. I didn't like sleeping in the double bed of what should have been Vivie and Leo's room. But sleeping on the sofa bed without Nina would have been worse, and to even think of sleeping in Howard and Davy's room was out of the question. During the days, besides following my mother and Bec about, I didn't quite know what to do with myself, and in the evenings, when the kids my age gathered at the beach or near Sloppy Joe's, I felt lost without Nina beside me. And so when Mark Fishbaum wandered over, looking for Howard and not finding him with us, but lingering at our cottage nonetheless, I began to linger with him. We were two lost souls, it seemed, but in each other's company just a little less so. I sighed often that summer, offering up to the winds of Long Island Sound any number of melancholy exhalations, and Mark Fishbaum responded to these inadvertent but steady bursts with the kindest nods and pats on the shoulder. "Is he your boyfriend?" Ada, come August, wanted to know. But that summer, with the nearly six years between us a veritable chasm, and with Mark's identity still as Howard's friend and mine only by default, there was no romance between us. But that he was increasingly important to me was clear enough. As the summer progressed the most common answer to my mother's invariable question "Molly, where you going?" was "Going to find Mark." And when I did find him, or when he found me, I felt a rush of relief. In an effort to make me smile he performed handstands in the sand, even walking at times with his long feet wriggling in the air. Soon I began to accompany him upside down, spinning cartwheels around him, transfixed as I did with the sight of the world turned topsy-turvy: a moving, shimmering silver sky and an earth, seemingly so fragile, of cerulean blue.

In this way, with help from Mark, the summer passed, and in late August we returned to Middletown. Only then did I understand how calming the summer had been for my mother, how, over its warm months, days spent sitting on the front porch and by the shore's edge, or walking the few streets from Bagel Beach to Anchor Beach and back again, a kind of useful resignation had set in for Ada that Davy was gone, that that was just the way it was. She'd returned with this resignation, which took the form of an inner stillness she hadn't shown since the first weeks of the summer before. She wasn't happy; that would have been too easy. But she was living again, rising early, taking an interest in managing her home, sometimes smiling sadly at my father, and occasionally — I saw this every once in a while — she'd take a moment to herself for something long ago and almost forgotten: a deep breath.

Bec was still living with us — as much because she had no place to go as because my mother still needed her help, functioned so much better with her sister around. That September, with my father's and Howard's assistance, Bec emptied her New Haven apartment, bringing her Singer and mannequin to her room in our house. What furniture she had in New Haven she stored in our basement. With Bec now settled in our home, and my mother on her feet again, a kind of routine set in. That fall, in the late afternoons before dinner, Bec and Ada took to playing cards, rounds of rummy that I sometimes joined in on as well. They'd play at the kitchen table with the radio close by so that as they arranged their cards and strategized their next move, they often did so humming quietly in unison.

Bec and Ada were each other's constant companions, and in her new role — this unwanted afterlife we'd all been thrust into — suddenly, oddly, Bec wasn't itching to get back to sewing. Though she had her Singer with her again, it sat idle beside the dresser in what we now thought of as her room as much as Davy's. The mannequin beside it, Eleanor Roosevelt, as Tyler had once in happier times christened her, remained relentlessly bare.

In November, as Veterans Day approached, Bec was surprised to read in the afternoon newspaper that Tyler McMannus, newly elected to the New Haven Board of Alders, was soon to receive an honorary service medal from the city. The award was part of the city's efforts to raise the profile of its aldermen. Bec read the article three times. She clipped it, finally, and stuck it inside the top drawer of Davy's old dresser, beside her stockings and brassieres. After that Tyler was on her mind again, though these were dangerous thoughts, she knew, stabbing her heart as they did. Unwittingly, she imagined herself sitting in the audience at the awards ceremony in New Haven, clapping loudly despite her properly gloved hands as they pinned a medal on his uniformed chest or handed him an officially sealed document or did whatever they were going to do to honor him. She imagined him standing on a stage, looking down, unwilling to take credit for anything that happened during that "pitiless project," as he'd always put it, of war.

"You were defending my people," she once told him, when, postwar, the news fully emerged of the death camps, with their starvation and gas.

"I didn't know what I was doing," he'd said. "None of us did. I just went where I was told to go, did what I was told to do. I'm only glad to know it wasn't all for nothing." And that's about as much as he'd ever said about his war experience, culminating in his injury during what became known as the Battle of the Bulge.

At the awards ceremony she envisioned him limping slightly as he set forth across the stage, down the steps, and resumed his seat, the one next to hers.

She couldn't bear it that she was only dreaming, that she wasn't actually going to be there.

On the day of the ceremony, Veterans Day, for the first time since she'd moved to Middletown she had that claustrophobic feeling again, the one she claimed to have had almost every Friday afternoon in Woodmont for all the years I could remember. Telling Ada she'd be right back, Bec left the house midday and went for a two-hour-long walk, past the Wesleyan campus on High Street, up Route 66, closing in on the diner where she'd last seen Tyler, where they'd shared what they didn't know would be their last meal together: a messy meatball grinder and a bottle of Coca-Cola.

Later that afternoon she didn't want to play rummy, though my mother and I were eager to. At school I was studying Asia, its geography, religions, and cultures, and uncharacteristically, Bec didn't want to hear anything about it. Instead she sat in the chair my mother used to spend her endless hours in, staring out the window, gazing into the distance as if she might find something she once lost, if only she stared hard and long enough.

"Teach me to drive," she asked Mort when he came home that evening. He hadn't taken the day off from work but instead held a "Veterans Day Sale" at the store, an idea that even Howard, always one to make a sale, found to be verging on disrespectful.

"Please," Bec said, lifting Mort's coat from his shoulders. "Please."

For the next six weeks Mort took her out regularly in that old Dodge we couldn't seem to part with. By mid-December she was ready for her driver's license test. The day, a Wednesday, was a windy one with a possibility of snow, and by the time my father picked Bec up at one o'clock and brought her to the Department of Motor Vehicles, a dimly lit brick building on Route 66, a light showering had begun.

Though Mort urged her not to, insisted he wouldn't mind coming back the next day or the next, she took the road test anyway, and passed.

In obtaining her driver's license Bec had a plan. She'd return to New Haven. She'd see Tyler again, repair the damage she'd done in staying away for so long. It didn't have to be all or nothing: all Ada, nothing for Bec. Her self-imposed sentence, she'd come to realize, especially those last months as Ada was more and more able to take care of herself, was simply too harsh. Bec had inflicted it on herself in the raw days of her mourning, when Davy's death was a catastrophe no one would ever recover from. But here they were, living on, their days difficult but bearable, and the idea of what she would do with the rest of her life became more and more pressing. She had smashed the old life. Now, could she put it back together again?

The day she chose to see Tyler, a week before Christmas, was cold but stunningly clear. Without any questions Mort had lent her the car, a generosity she considered while heading south on the Wilbur Cross Parkway. She'd never been alone in the Dodge before, and every once in a while she found herself speaking out loud, as if to Mort, who had taught her to drive with a patience she didn't know he had. All of it had been a kindness. He'd been aware of her all this time, his actions showed. "Thanks, Mort," she'd told him that morning as he handed her the car key. "You've no idea what you've done for me."

She drove to the center of New Haven, past the city's green, and then to Howe Street, where her apartment had been. She decided she'd rather walk the few blocks from there to the dress shop, to come upon it just as she always had. As she neared the shop, the awning over its entrance caught her eye first, and seeing the familiar green and white stripes, she stopped short. Feeling weak, she veered toward the coffee shop across the street where she sat at a table by the front window.

Strangely, there were lights strung across Tyler's storefront, for Christmas. He had never bothered with such decorations before, something she hadn't thought about until right then, when she wondered if he'd held back for her sake. Not that she would have minded. Feeling stronger already, she thought she'd go and tell Tyler that. She didn't mind a little festivity for the holidays, she'd say. Truly, she didn't. But upon standing, she felt her heart begin to race, and she dropped back into her seat, ordered coffee, sipped, and stared.

Inside the dress shop everything seemed still. The lights were blazing, however, so she knew they had to be there, Tyler and Irene and that new dressmaker, Mildred

Butler. Peering more determinedly, she wondered if she could see Irene that very moment, walking to a dress rack then away from it, but from the distance of the coffee shop she wasn't sure. A moment later she set down her cup, left some change, and rose.

Just as she opened the door of the coffee shop, the dress shop's door opened too, a surprise that caused Bec to jump back, scurry to the table she'd just left, resume sipping the remainder of her coffee. When she looked over again Bec saw Irene, her signature blond curls lifting in the wind as she held the shop door open, waiting for someone.

The woman who finally walked through the door was typical of the clientele Bec remembered: stylish, seemingly moneyed. Taking stock of her nicely tailored woolen suit and jacket, Bec wondered if the new dressmaker, Mildred Butler, had cooked that one up. The suit fit the woman well, Bec had to concede, though it was a conventional look. Surely, Bec noted, she would have done something a little more interesting with the collar, perhaps have added a belt. The woman was pushing a baby carriage, and once she maneuvered it through the door, a man followed her, a person with nearly black hair and a tall, slender frame, a pleasant-looking man like Tyler, Bec thought, studying him, then lifting her hand to cover her mouth, for it *was* Tyler, this man who was now leaning out the shop's door and kissing the woman in the tailored suit on the cheek, perfunctorily, a way of saying good-bye.

In the next moment, though, he wasn't saying good-bye but was on the sidewalk, lifting the baby from the carriage and kissing that small person, too. These kisses were hardly perfunctory but joyful, plentiful. Instead of laying the baby back down in the carriage, he continued holding the child as he said a few words to Irene. Then, baby in one arm, other arm linked with the woman's, he began to stroll down the street with them. When the woman momentarily unlinked her arm and turned, glancing back to call out something to Irene, Bec suddenly recognized her — Tyler's wife, a woman she hadn't seen in at least ten years.

Once they'd rounded a corner and were out of sight, Bec managed to cross the street and spent a moment inside the shop speaking to Irene, who was dumbfounded to see her.

"He was out of his mind without you," Irene explained. "I don't think he knew what he was doing. Truly, I don't. He thought you'd left him. But the baby is what's saved him." She paused, shaking her head. "Do you want to meet Mildred?" she then asked. "Mildred Butler? She's just in the back, sewing. She's not you, but she's very good."

"No. No time," Bec said. She glanced at the dresses neatly arranged on the racks and was dismayed to see everything in such good order.

"Shall I tell Tyler you were here?" Irene asked.

"No point in that. Please don't." Bec continued to take stock of the place, the cherished chairs at the back of the store, the pale blue walls, a color she'd chosen.

"I know what was between you two," Irene said. She shook her head and for a moment held a hand over her mouth. "How could I not know?"

Bec lowered her head and stared at the planks of the shop's wooden floor. "Not to worry," she told Irene at last. "I didn't come for anything."

Back in the car she did the math. March. It would have been sometime in March when the baby, now just a few weeks old, was conceived. She and Tyler weren't talking in March. They'd last talked and seen each other, briefly, toward the end of February. "Take your time," he'd said then about her eventual though clearly questionable return. "Bec, I'm here. I'm waiting."

That peculiar hell: waiting. He'd lost faith.

And, of course, she hadn't helped matters with her all too typical response: "Ada needs me."

She didn't want to see it then, how that last time they were together at the diner he'd seemed wounded at the words, had winced, and then he'd raised his eyes and given her a look she'd never seen before. He was nodding, confident of some assessment in his mind. "Yes," he'd told her. "Ada sure does."

She believed then what she'd said: Ada needed her, and she'd thought she was doing the right thing, the good thing. How easy it was, she realized in hindsight, to have convinced herself of her goodness. But now she could see it, that that the willingness with which she'd abandoned Tyler was cruel.

She left New Haven. As she approached the Wilbur Cross Parkway she thought for a moment she'd head farther south, past New Haven toward Milford, where she'd visit the Woodmont cottage. It was still only morning and Mort had lent her the Dodge for the entire day. But within moments she changed her mind. "Ada needs me," she told herself numbly, unable to think of anything else to say as she steered the car back where she'd come from, toward Middletown.

All that year, while my mother did indeed need Bec, at first in the most basic ways, and then as a supportive friend, my father needed Nelson. He needed Nelson to pick him up each morning to get to services on time, for though it was a duty to say Kaddish every day for Davy, and though he wouldn't think of not observing this sacred task, the truth was my father was having trouble getting himself together each morning and out the door on time. Howard was no help in these matters, for he was having the same trouble. Later, Mort struggled while opening the car door, then again while walking the short route on Broad Street from the car to the synagogue. He needed Nelson there in our driveway honking his horn again and again, and once the car was parked near the synagogue, he needed Nelson to take his arm as he shambled timidly toward the service. Nelson was a help, too, when, mid-service, holding his prayer book, Mort invariably lost his place, couldn't connect with even one Hebrew word. For my father, every day had become Yom Kippur and every prayer a litany of sins for which he desperately tried to atone. There was the sin of not praying well enough, of constantly losing his place; and the sin of enjoying his time — those crucial last months of Davy's life — without the family; there was the sin of not instilling in Howard a strong enough commitment to Judaism; and the sin, worse than it sounded, of stopping for hot dogs on Fridays as he made his way to Woodmont. Finally, there was the sin of not knowing his role in life anymore. "What am I?" he asked God in his prayers each day at the morning service, but he never heard an answer. "Come on," Nelson would say when the service ended. "Let's get a bite before work." And Mort came to rely on those quiet breakfasts — a bowl of oatmeal for him, a pile of eggs and toast for his ever-hungry brother and for his son — as at least some means of nourishment, sustenance that neither prayer nor work nor being home with the family was able to bring anymore.

There were moments when Bec and Nelson crossed paths, nodded at each other, occasionally said hello.

Gradually their conversations grew longer. They talked sometimes of Ada and of Mort, giving each other brief reports. They talked, like everybody, about the weather. They talked about business at Leibritsky's, its ups and downs. Once Nelson mentioned something personal to Bec: that he enjoyed music. Big bands, he said, were the best.

One evening in December of 1949 — almost fifteen months after the death and two weeks before her drive to New Haven — they had their first conversation about their mutual roles as caretakers. Nelson had driven Mort home from work rather late and had walked him inside.

"He's spent," Nelson explained to Bec, who held the door open for the men. Once Mort had disappeared, after handing Bec his hat and coat and then going straight upstairs to bed, Bec turned to Nelson, who had stood the whole time in the doorway.

"I know how much Mort leans on you," Bec told Nelson. "You're a good brother."

"And you're a good sister," he answered.

They stood for a moment without speaking. After a while Nelson said, his eyes cast to the kitchen floor, "You know, we should treat ourselves, take a break. It's been a long haul."

"I suppose you're right," Bec said, sigh-

271

ing. "Maybe I'll take a bath. You know, a long soaking bath."

Nelson nodded. Then he said, "Regina's has a nice lunch. Very nice."

"Lunch?"

"If you'd like. You know, for a break."

She said okay, and the two went to lunch together that Saturday when Nelson was through with Shabbos services. And they went to lunch together again, the first Saturday of the following month, just a week after her journey to New Haven, a time when she could barely touch her food, when she sat there, across from Nelson, sipping tea and nodding as he rattled on, best he could, just to keep the meal a pleasant one. They lunched again the first Saturday of the next month. By March of 1950 they were going to Regina's two Saturdays a month, and were beginning to talk more, Nelson about the store's history, or even more about Mort, or sometimes about the records he collected, and Bec about childhood with Ada and Vivie, and about her parents, Maks and Risel. She never mentioned the years of her adult life, her dresses, the time in New Haven. She hoped she seemed grateful enough for each meal. By May of that year they were lunching at Regina's every Saturday. The meal finished, the bill paid, Regina would lean over the table, tell them, "Listen, I'll make something special for you two next week. Veal cutlets and spaghetti. Chicken cacciatore. Something like that. See you then, right?" The two would nod, and the next week's engagement would be agreed upon without Nelson, who was awkward at such matters, having to ask Bec, and without Bec, who still loved Tyler, having to respond to an invitation from Nelson.

Late in May, almost five months since Bec had seen Tyler and his wife and baby, Bec decided to drive to New Haven once again but ended up driving to Woodmont, visiting the cottage there for the last time in her life.

She didn't know that would be the case when she set out. She intended to make her way to Tyler. Unlike her last attempt at seeing him, this time she knew that she couldn't change the past or repair the damage she'd done. But she could at least tell Tyler she loved him, had never intended to part ways with him forever, had gotten mixed up, confused, more than a little lost. And then she could say, her dignity intact, a proper good-bye.

But for all her bold intentions, when she

got to New Haven she didn't exit from the highway but kept driving south.

When she arrived at Woodmont it was still morning, overcast, the sun behind the clouds pushing its way through every so often in brief flashes of light. She would have liked to stop for a cup of coffee but Sloppy Joe's and the Villa Rosa hadn't yet opened for the season. The entire village, it seemed, was closed. She drove past the synagogue, the words *Hebrew Congregation of Woodmont* as distinct as ever over its entranceway but its windows nailed tight with winter shutters and its front doors sealed with a large lock. Minutes later, from the cottage's front porch, she glanced at the many other cottages in the cluster along the Bagel Beach shore. A wave of sadness struck her as she took in their emptiness: windows shut, doors locked, porches cleared of the summer clutter of outdoor furniture and towels and rafts and rubber tubes.

Inside the cottage silence settled around her like dust. She stood for a moment in the thick of it: the hush, the emptiness. Then, slowly, she took stock of the place, just as she and her sisters always had, roaming from room to room, unable to keep from touching the old family furnishings. Everything was still the same: the sofa bed, the corner chairs, the covered dining table, her cot and wicker chair. Upstairs, the claw-footed tub looked as freshly scrubbed as it had when she'd cleaned it the last day of the summer before.

In the back bedroom, the one Vivie and Leo had shared, Bec opened the closet only to find hanging there a lone remnant of the past, the strapless dress and matching jacket she'd made, with such hope in her heart, for Nina two summers ago. She pulled it from the closet, then sat on the bed holding the dress in her lap, her arms circling it, her body rocking back and forth. In its folds there wasn't even a hint of that hopefulness left — for Nina, for her, for anyone else. She could feel that as she sat there, clinging helplessly.

Minutes passed. Finally she rose, re-hung the dress, shut the closet door with a final click, and made her way downstairs. Standing once again on the porch, she turned to lock the front door.

Outside she felt different, surer. There was nothing here for her anymore, she knew. And in the salty shoreline breezes she could almost smell the new life, a landlocked one filled with, come a given Saturday after-noon, veal cutlets and spaghetti or chicken cacciatore or maybe, sometimes, just meat-balls.

The door locked, she reached for the mezuzah. She touched it then brought her hand to her lips. The gesture was the same one her father had made on his last day at the cottage in early September of 1939 when he was closing the place up, leaving for the season. The mezuzah was still new then. By the following January, Maks was dead from a heart attack that had overtaken him in his sleep.

Risel's last day at the cottage, a week before her death, came at the start of the next summer. Standing in for Maks, Bec had watched her mother touch the mezuzah before entering the cottage. But once inside the place, she was overwhelmed by the memories. "Where is he?" Risel kept asking of Maks. She walked through the living room, the dining room, into the kitchen, and back out again. Slowly, she made her way to the water's edge. "Where is he?" she called to the Sound, as if during the months of Maks's absence he'd not been under-ground in the Jewish cemetery in Middle-town but there in Woodmont, dunking, wait-ing for her to join him. "I'm tired," she finally said at day's end. But rather than go to bed she handed Mort the car keys. She begged him to take her away. "Done," she said, simply enough. Then, "Away."

PART TWO

8
SHNEL

Those weeks before Davy's death in 1948 we relaxed in Woodmont even more than in previous years. Indeed, our whole Jewish neighborhood was relaxed, the recent news of Israel's independence — life, as we saw it, birthed from the graves of six million — filling our lungs with an easier air. By summertime the conflict in the Middle East had lessened some, and the hopefulness that saturated Woodmont, that had brought so many Jewish families back to the shore after staying clear of the place during the war years, was undeniable. You could hear it in the optimistic tone of conversations. You could see it, too, in the amiable, untroubled way people walked each evening, back and forth, the length of Woodmont — from Hillside and Merwin avenues to the west end of Beach Avenue, and once there all the way to its east end — whistling, chatting, calling out hello.

By the end of our first month at the beach, Ada, Vivie, and Bec were practically care-free, or so it seemed by the way they let their duties slide, particularly the pre-Shabbos housecleaning that normally began first thing every Friday morning but that summer had incrementally been pushed back later and later. The last Friday in July, late afternoon, and the sisters were just beginning to get the house together before the men arrived from Middletown. Before that Bec had taken an especially long walk, her Friday claustrophobia setting in just after breakfast rather than after lunch. At the same time Ada and Vivie were on Mrs. Isaacson's porch, chatting and sipping coffee, Mrs. Isaacson especially talkative about her granddaughter Judy, who was upstairs, as she was most mornings, still in bed. "Bad hormones," Mrs. Isaacson, sighing, concluded about Judy. But then Judy appeared, looking unexpectedly chipper in a short red bathrobe and bare feet, and the women sat her down, fed her slices of peaches, combed and braided her hair, and generally fussed so much that Judy, for the first time that summer, smiled. "Do I look pretty?" she asked, touching her hair, and then she smiled again when the word "yes" came rushing at her from so many sources. She even agreed to come to the beach, at least for a spell, and, post-lunch, the women did just that, passing the time by playing rounds of bridge, reading magazines, and finally napping.

The afternoon peaked and ebbed without anyone taking notice. By four thirty, though, Ada was in the dining room, her hair unkempt, her cheeks red from either sunburn or adrenaline, and as she grabbed the better china from the dining room cabinet and practically threw it at me to set on the dining table she muttered, *"Shnel, shnel,"* reverting in her haste to the Yiddish of her mother. She was saying *quick, quick,* but even these words, normally of warning, were spoken with a playful edge as if our last-minute preparations were a kind of fun prank, something, if we timed it just right, we'd in fact get away with. In the kitchen, Vivie, Bec, and Nina were rinsing and chopping away, while upstairs Howard, once he'd arrived home from Treat's, was hastily vacuuming a week's worth of sand. Davy, who was not participating in the preparations but rather watching them, transfixed, as he sat at the head of the dining table, was finally summoned to race to the nearby bakery for the loaves of challah that nobody that morning had been in the mood to bake.

Davy had just returned and handed the bread to my mother when the familiar clank of our Dodge coming to a stop caused all of us to stop abruptly as well. But the pause was fleeting. In the next seconds the challahs were set down and covered on the table, the vacuum cleaner was shoved into an upstairs closet where it didn't belong, and the four burners of the gas stove were cranked up until small bursts of flames emerged from each one.

When Mort walked through the back door of the cottage and into the kitchen, he had no idea how quickly it had emptied of us just a moment before. Instead he saw the usual worn pots of this and that going on the burners, and the smell of dinner cooking was a familiar one. And he found the empty dining room, its table neatly enough set, looking as it always did. He might very well have found everything to be in order had Davy not called from upstairs, where we were all frantically changing clothes, "We almost forgot!"

"Forgot what?" Mort yelled back.

"Shabbos," Davy answered, laughing.

A skirmish in the boys' room sounded through the walls, and from Davy's muffled squeals it appeared plain that Howard was smothering his face with a pillow.

My father, his steps heavy, began to climb the stairs.

"What's going on?" he asked from the hallway. From behind shut doors no one answered. In the back bedroom Nina and I had already managed to change into the summer dresses we wore each Sabbath, and we were passing a hairbrush back and forth. Through the wall I could hear Howard once again muffling Davy, who was trying to tell Howard to cut it out. "You cut it out," was Howard's clearer reply.

Mort knocked on a door and in the next moment Ada was in the hallway explaining that everyone had taken a long nap that afternoon, the whole clan had fallen right to sleep — "Poof! Out just like that!" she claimed — but we'd wakened and now everything was as usual, she insisted, just a tiny bit late. She laughed, and then laughed again more determinedly. With that she must have convinced my father that nothing odd was up because I could hear him trail her down the stairs, and within seconds a familiar clanking from the kitchen meant that she was at it — checking the food, busying herself — and that Mort, satisfied that all was as it should be, had already landed in the living room, where, until dinner was served, he'd claimed a corner chair.

■ ■ ■ ■

An hour or so later we ate our Shabbos meal. After the blessings, my father read to us his most recent letter from our cousin Reuben Leibritsky, who was living in Israel but was not particularly happy there. *Israel! Reuben had written. I hear it, cousin. I hear the word and how it's spoken. Israel! But I have to tell you, no matter how much I hear it, I still don't know where I am.* Everybody expected my father to follow the reading of the letter with a lecture about our Jewish obligations, or our luck, but Mort was silenced by his cousin's anguished sense of displacement. "Let's keep Reuben in our hearts tonight," was all Mort said.

The next morning the men and boys went off to shul while we women and girls had a Saturday morning ritual of our own, sipping coffee and cocoa on the porch. That morning there was an especially deep tranquility among us, as if the arrival of the men the evening before and the rushed preparations for Shabbos and the long dinner that followed had been some kind of storm we'd managed to survive and we were now in the calm of an aftermath. Not that the men had done anything alarming. They'd merely arrived. But their very presence shifted the way of things so much it was as if we didn't see each other while they were there. And so our gathering on the porch that Saturday morning was a time of reconnection. We didn't talk. But even the silent gesture of looking at each other was a means of communication, and essential, it seemed, to our regaining a sense of presence. Even Nina and Vivie, whose relationship with Leo was more balanced than my mother's and mine with Mort, required this composed time, this all-female Sabbath breather.

We were doing just that — breathing on the porch, our hot drinks long ago consumed — when we heard the men's voices only yards away.

My mother jumped up first. "Tuna salad," she said, before she rushed inside and, as instantly as if by magic, disappeared.

Our parents were going out that night, Saturday, post-Shabbos, to a fund-raiser for Israel at the Hebrew Congregation of Woodmont's new social hall. They were going dancing, and the cost of the event's tickets was their donation. Vivie and Leo were going too. The Isaacsons were going, as were the Radnicks and Weinsteins, though according to Mrs. Weinstein, Mr. Weinstein would have preferred to work on his latest radio like it was any old night. In fact, all the Jews of Woodmont of a certain age were going — all the grownups, it seemed, except Mrs. Isaacson's granddaughter Judy, who preferred to stay home alone, and Bec, who preferred to stay with us kids, she said. So that evening she stood on the porch just like Nina, Davy, and I did, waving to the departing couples, the women bejeweled and perfumed and wobbling in heels they hadn't worn all summer. But as soon as the couples were gone, Bec told us she really did feel like going out. Just not to the dance. Instead she felt like taking a walk. But first she had to make a phone call. "Yes . . . yes . . . now," she whispered into the phone. After that she brushed her hair and restyled it, slathered on some lipstick, and then told me and Nina to watch Davy and to be good girls. "I might be a while," she said.

Howard had already gone out for the evening, with Mark Fishbaum, we assumed. But it turned out we were wrong. After Bec left, Nina, Davy, and I took our own walk, to Anchor Beach, where we each bought a treat from Sal. Though the crowd at Anchor Beach was mixed, as Jews we could feel good there, safe, and we stayed, as we so often did, climbing atop a massive spread of rock to eat our treats. For a time we watched Arthur Weinstein race his twin, Jimmy, to Sal's truck, but soon Davy drew our attention away from the antics of the Weinstein brothers. Pointing in the opposite direction, Davy had his eye on Howard, walking at some distance with his hands in his pockets, away from the Anchor crowd, until he finally stopped, settling on the sand behind a smaller patch of rock. To our surprise Megan O'Donnell followed him, lagging by ten yards or so, but once seated she leaned back on the same shale boulder that Howard was sitting against. They were clearly trying to hide, and for the most part their shared rock concealed them, but from our elevated position we could see them well enough. They were looking straight ahead, at the ocean or perhaps at the horizon line, which grew fuzzy in the distance as the day's light dimmed.

"Shush," Nina told Davy, yanking his arm down and then wrapping her arm around his shoulders. "Let's spy on them," she whispered.

For a time we watched as Howard and Megan did absolutely nothing. They stared ahead. Howard crossed his arms over his chest at one point then uncrossed them.

Megan swatted at what must have been a bug. He finally said something to her, we saw, because she nodded, turning to him at last.

"They're talking," Nina reported, stating the obvious but voicing it with curiosity, as if the two were from such foreign worlds you'd think they didn't share a common language.

"Who is she?" Davy asked.

"She's the girl from Treat's checkout stand," I told him, having recalled seeing her — those frizzy strawberry-blond bangs — from our trip to Treat's the other week.

"Name's Megan," Nina asserted. "We had a good talk that day. Remember?" She looked at me briefly, only to nod and see me nod back, and then she continued to stare at Howard and Megan.

Howard began gesturing in a way that suggested he was telling Megan a story. He also turned more her way, which put his back to us. The gestures continued for some time while Megan O'Donnell sat with her legs pressed to her chest, her body still except when she raised a hand to cover her mouth in what was apparently a laugh.

"How in the world could she think he's funny?" Nina remarked.

"Howard's *very* funny," Davy said, surprised.

Nina leaned Davy's way, gently bumping her shoulder against his. "Yeah, what funny thing has he done to you lately?" Her tone was consciously gentle, a way to keep Davy invested in the scene before them.

"I don't know." Davy swallowed a final bite of his ice cream. "Just is."

"Molly, has Howard done anything funny lately?" Nina asked.

"He wakes up every morning with his hair sticking straight up. That's funny," I offered.

"*Very* funny," Davy agreed.

Howard was still gesturing. Nina was running out of things to say to keep Davy still — Howard's looks in the morning, it turned out, weren't all that funny — but she clearly wanted to keep us there on the rocks.

Nina once again wrapped her arm over Davy's shoulder and he leaned her way, allowing himself to be snuggled. I was no longer watching the two against the boulder but rather was watching Nina, who, despite the warmth she projected toward Davy, was otherwise sitting with her back straight, alarmed. When Howard leaned Megan's way and put his arm around her, Nina groaned, as if in pain.

"What's he think he's doing?" she said,

291

more to herself than to us. She turned away from Howard and Megan, toward the fading horizon line.

"He kissed her!" I said. "Nina, look!"

Though Nina snapped her head back, the kiss was over. And in the second that passed there wasn't even a trace of its occurrence. Howard and Megan were sitting back, not touching, speaking, or even looking at each other. They simply faced the water. It seemed to me they might as well have been strangers. Or two people who simply couldn't stand each other but were somehow stuck together, backs glued to that particular mound of shale.

"That's pretty daring," Nina declared, despite missing the moment. I knew she referred not so much to Howard kissing a girl — he'd already kissed lots of them — as to Howard's kissing *that* girl, one he wasn't supposed to kiss.

"It's a free country," I said, though not with complete conviction.

"Not that free, Molly," Nina countered, a response that affirmed my doubts.

"Can we go now?" Davy asked, as uninterested in Howard as I'd ever seen him. Davy rose and began nimbly hopping, not rock to rock so much as ledge to ledge, rushing, it seemed, to leave Howard, Megan, and that kiss behind.

Nina and I slowly followed Davy's lead, off the rocks and back to Beach Avenue, and finally back to our cottage.

The sun had fully set. We were sitting on the porch steps, watching for the occasional lightning bug to flicker before our eyes, and waiting for our parents to return from the dance, or for Bec to return from her walk, or even for Howard to return from his not-so-secret rendezvous, when Nina whispered into the darkness, "It isn't fair. He always gets the girl, *always.*"

"He's charming," I explained, my answer matter-of-fact. "He got it from our mother."

"Damn Aunt Ada," Nina said, sighing. "Did you ever hear the story of what she did to my mother?"

Of course I had. The story even had a name: "Poor Vivie." I'd heard it more than once — but never from my mother.

Several lightning bugs lit up simultaneously and we three cried out, momentarily startled. Davy grabbed at the air but didn't catch any.

Soon enough we were back to darkness.

"I think you're charming," I said, speaking into the night.

"Oh, Molly. You really think that helps?" Nina said.

■ ■ ■ ■

The next morning at breakfast all the news was that my parents and aunt and uncle had danced like mad. Had Leo, so frail and cerebral, really danced? we asked. Even Nina couldn't see it, but Vivie assured us that indeed he had. Vivie, clearly uplifted by the fun of the night before, had made oatmeal, which she urged us to garnish not just with sugar but with a mix of cinnamon and sugar, and we could add raisins and dried apricots too if we liked. "Try something new," she said. She'd also made cinnamon-spiced muffins. "Get 'em while they're hot," she told us, in the charged voice of a saleslady, an odd tone for her. She uttered the phrase again as she set another platter of the muffins on the table in the dining room where my father and Leo ate, our "kids' table" too crowded for them.

Howard finally came downstairs. Oddly, this Sunday he split his time between the kitchen table, where he ate a bowl of oatmeal, and the men's table, where he devoured three muffins. Upon leaving us for the dining room he announced, "I'm a wandering Jew," and then he wandered from one room to the next.

"Don't go too far," Nina called, "or you'll find yourself in trouble."

"What's that supposed to mean?" Howard asked. He'd returned to the doorway between the rooms.

"Just that you'd better watch it," Nina said. She smirked as she stirred her oatmeal. "We know something, Howard."

Howard laughed. When the sisters weren't looking, he pursed his lips as if to kiss. "All that reading, Nina," he taunted, "and you don't know a thing."

"Howard, I heard that," Vivie interjected sternly.

"Doesn't matter," Nina said. She smiled at her mother then glared at Howard. "I really do know something," she told him. "Don't push me, Howard. I know something big," she said.

That weekend, my father had brought to Woodmont the next installment of the picture Davy and Lucinda Rossetti were drawing together. Rather than mail it again, Mrs. Rossetti had dropped the drawing off at the store. But by then the picture was a mere chore to Davy, and just as he would have done had school been in session, he waited until the last minutes of that Sunday afternoon to open the envelope. He looked at the page from every angle before shrugging in surrender. "Here goes nothing," he mumbled, and then lengthened and fattened each of the tubes of brown, gray, and blue emerging from the picture's red base.

"Want me to ask Mrs. Rossetti for a hint?" Mort said, his palm affectionately encasing the top of Davy's head. Before he left, Mort bent low for a kiss, which Davy delivered on his cheek.

"I can do it myself," Davy answered with a weariness that suggested otherwise.

Davy's heaviness of heart must have touched our father, for he whisked Davy up. "It can't be that bad," he told him.

"Homework," Davy complained into Mort's chest.

"Homework," Mort repeated, his voice as grave as Davy's. "That's the end of the world. No question. The very end of it."

He lifted Davy's face and smiled. "You're a father's joy," he said, which left Davy, once he was back on his feet, silent and nodding — his way of telling Mort that he loved him, too.

The men's departure began the start of our fifth week in Woodmont, a time when Howard went back to Middletown, as he had the summer before, to help with the store's semiannual inventory check.

Bec, who hadn't sewn anything since she'd successfully delivered Mrs. Coventry's dress, was anxious to begin another project, though this time she planned to sew something for each of us. In years past she'd been the one to decide what she'd make, but Monday night over supper she asked Vivie and Ada to tell her what they wanted. "I'll make you anything. You name it. I'll make you the dress of your dreams," she announced to her sisters, turning from one to the other, then rushing at both of them, pulling each into a strange, desperate hug. Only she knew that with her decision to go to New York she was preparing to leave them. "You've both done so much for me," she said, by way of explanation.

"It's not like you haven't done a thing or two for us," Ada responded, taken aback by the emotional outburst but clearly flattered by it also. Or perhaps it was the idea of the dress of her dreams that pleased my mother so, because the next moment she was patting her pinned-up hair, a gesture that signaled she was feeling the full extent of her beauty, and she told Bec, "Let me just put up a fresh pot of coffee and we'll get at it. Burgundy, Bec. I just can't get that burgundy of Mrs. Coventry's fabric out of

297

my mind."

Bec was willing to make me the dress of my dreams as well, but I didn't dream of dresses and had no response for her for several days. It was already Thursday of that fifth week when I told my friends Melissa Bornstein and Anna Weiss about Bec's offer, and then I described for them the dress that Bec had made for Nina. What did they think about that kind of thing for me? I asked. By way of answering we decided to find the dress, which meant leaving the beach and wandering up our cottage's front steps, where we walked past Nina, who was on the porch finishing the last chapters of that Lincoln biography. "Hey," we each called to Nina, who waved to us and murmured a responsive "hey" without even looking up.

We filed into the upstairs bedroom and I pulled from the closet the strapless dress and matching jacket. Holding the dress before my friends, I explained to them that the upper half had fallen down when I'd tried it on earlier that summer, but that didn't stop them from wanting to see it on me anyway.

This time I knew to hold the dress up, but it fell down again when Melissa grabbed the jacket from my grip and I let go of the dress to grab the jacket back. But before I could, she'd wriggled into it. The yellow background with cream-colored flowers looked ridiculous over her striped bathing suit with its little skirt, but she didn't seem to notice as she stared in the mirror. "Can I?" she asked, pointing to the dress at my feet, and I assented by stepping out of the way.

"My turn," Anna soon said. She was on the chunky side, which made for a struggle with the zipper, but as long as she sucked everything in and didn't breathe, we could pull it up. Pleased with how she looked, she paced across the room, modeling.

"What are you doing?" Nina asked. She was suddenly standing in front of Anna. Startled by Nina's presence, Anna jumped back as if this upstairs Nina were a ghost of the one we'd passed on the porch.

"But you won't wear it," I told Nina.

"It's mine. She made it for me," Nina insisted with a possessiveness that didn't square with the neglect she'd shown all summer toward the dress. To my surprise she grabbed Anna's shoulders, forcibly turned her, and yanked the back zipper down. Anna's body, already squeezed tight inside the dress, burst from it, and she stood there, shocked, nearly naked. Nina pointed to the puddle of the dress that circled

299

Anna's bare feet. "Mine," she said.

After that I didn't want a dress and told Bec so. This was the next day, Friday, and Bec was just readying herself for her weekly solitary walk. I didn't know the dress had meant that much to Nina, I explained to Bec, but it clearly did.

"Can I walk with you?" I asked Bec, feeling low about the incident with my friends and even lower that I'd disappointed Nina.

"Not today," Bec said, and then she pulled me into a hug, as urgent as the embraces she'd offered Ada and Vivie earlier that week. "I really think the world of you, Molly," she told me, though I had no idea why. "I just want you to know that."

It turned out Bec wasn't the only one acting odd that day. Davy was back to playing with our puppets, but instead of Samson Bagel's usual heroic exploits, Davy had him beside Vivie in the kitchen, narrating in a voice very much like our mother's as Vivie mixed eggs in a bowl, preparing to make her first soufflé. And, as if she and Davy had exchanged roles, my mother was on the beach, playing — not cards with the adult women but hopscotch with my friends Melissa and Anna, who clapped as my mother made a series of wobbly but successful one-legged leaps. Nina's behavior was the most out of character: she was in the back bedroom rather than at her usual reading spot on the porch. Seated at her mother's vanity, she had her hair twisted and pinned in a style I'd never seen her wear before. For a while I sat on the bed, watching.

"You know what Howard would say about this?" she asked me. Her hair was styled like Bec's, pinned high and worked into an interesting, complicated twist. "He'd say, 'You think you know something? Something about *fun*?' Then he'd laugh. I hate his laugh." She laughed then, in just the way she hated. "Molly," she asked, "why does he always laugh?"

"He's not here," I reminded her, though her imitation of him, especially of his laugh, was so true that I could practically see him in the doorway.

But any sense of him disappeared when Nina said, "Right, Molly. So simple. He isn't here."

She secured the new hair twist with several more pins and then smiled widely, beautifully. She turned to me. "He isn't here!" she said.

But it was Friday and the men, including Howard, returned. This was at about five or so, and when Mort entered the house this time no pots were going on the stove, no dishes were set on the table, nor were there challah loaves placed there, because the very idea of them hadn't yet crossed anyone's mind that day. Nor had anyone thought to dust or vacuum, and in the living room Nina's and my sofa bed was still unfolded. All of us, in our way, had had a grand day.

"What difference does it make?" Ada argued to Mort once he'd pulled her from the beach. "We can always light the candles and say the blessings. We don't need a meal to do that. Can't we have an easy summer, Mort? Can't we all have a little fun?"

"What are you asking for, Ada — a whole summer of seventh days?" Mort paced between the kitchen and the dining room, staring stupefied into each. "Look," he added, "I don't make the rules. God does."

"Well, sir," Ada said as she thrust her balled hands into the pockets of her house-dress. "You're going to have to bargain with *me* one of these days. This is *my* cottage. *My* home."

"Ada, come on now. We can't break the rules," Mort argued, his voice stern. "We live by the law. That's our job as Jews. That's what *makes* us Jews."

By this time everyone had gathered in the

dining room.

"Law?" Ada said. Her tone was piqued, her voice quavering. "Here's your law," she asserted. Without looking into a mirror she yanked her mass of hair into a tidy knot. Then she grabbed her black pocketbook, which sat on the table with the telephone on it, pulled a tube of lipstick from it, and smeared the red coloring on her face so that she looked more like a clown than anything else. She stood tall in her wedge sandals as she turned to face Mort. She smiled at him. "Like your law?" she asked, crossing her arms over her loose housedress. Then she pulled the kiddush cup from a cabinet, along with wine, and filled the cup. "Good Shabbos," she told my father, holding the cup high before she tipped it, pouring the wine down her throat in one long sip. "Good law," she said, before she smacked her lips. She was shouting when she reached for the bottle again. "Hell, more law! More law!" she said.

Mort left.

He walked through the living room, making his way around the open sofa bed, and stood on the porch, staring at the ocean and at the back of the Isaacsons' cottage.

Ada stood in the dining room with her hand over her mouth. When she finally dropped it she said to Nina and me, her words repentant, anxious, "Come, girls, let's clean this house. Come on. *Shnel, shnel.*"

9

THE REASON FOR TOOTSIE ROLLS

That summer, like all the years before, Nelson stayed in Middletown on weekends. Friday afternoons Mort and Leo would head off to Woodmont, but Nelson knew, even if the others were too polite to say it, that there was no room for him there. "You're always invited," Ada had told him years ago and had reiterated any number of times, but the truth was that should he ever have taken her up on the offer the entire configuration in the cottage would have been upset. He knew perfectly well there wasn't a bed to spare, that Bec, single like him, was put out to pasture on the screened porch. Where would they put him? On the roof? Moreover, what would he do there? He'd grown too fat to be anything but embarrassed at the thought of sitting in bathing trunks in the sun. And, apart from Howard, he rarely engaged with the children; he knew we took notice of him only for his ready supply of Tootsie Rolls. His brother and Leo would be involved with their wives, their children. And the women — Ada, Vivie, and Bec — who, for their high spirits and easy laughter, he would have liked to talk to the most, well, God only knew how to spend a weekend talking to women.

So the summer was a little quiet, a little lonely, but the first week in August — the week preceding my parents' Shabbos fight — Mort had brought Howard back to Middletown for a week to help out with end-of-summer inventory, and Nelson felt a surprising sense of relief at the sight of his nephew. "Hey, hey, hey," Nelson had called out when Howard first walked through the store's front doors. "Who's this big guy? Joe DiMaggio?" he asked, swinging his arms as if holding a bat. "Uncle!" Howard had cried in surprise as if he were as thrilled to see Nelson as Nelson was to see him.

Though Howard was full-grown it seemed to Nelson he'd gained substantial height in the weeks since he'd last seen him. Certainly he'd grown tan, and there he was, taller than ever, extraordinarily handsome, flashing a brilliant smile, with skin a golden brown that matched the stripes in his tie. The boy threw his arms around Nelson's shoulders.

"How are you, Uncle?" he asked.

"Fine, fine," Nelson said. "You looking good there," he added, nodding.

The rest of the men in the store gathered round.

"It's the sailing," Howard said.

"Sailing. Sure, sure. Wind's been your friend," Nelson muttered, admiring his nephew's vitality. "Sun's been your friend, too."

"But this week you stay the hell *inside*," Mort said, leaning to slap Howard's back affectionately. Nelson and Kurt Hanson, the new employee, rocked with a quick burst of laughter. Even Leo, typically dour, smiled. Yes, Nelson thought, that's what work was: not a week in the sun but a week inside the store, and didn't they know it. He found himself hoping that a week of inventory wouldn't cost Howard too much of his tan. The kid had a right to his good looks. He was young.

Inventory was a dogged, tiring business, and that's why Howard had been dragged back from the rocky shores of Woodmont to Main Street in Middletown to help. They had to negotiate the creaky steps leading to the basement to open any remaining boxes there, checking and counting their contents, deciding if anything was worth the schlep upstairs: pairs of socks and stacks of men's ties, boxes of stationery and greeting cards, a few women's hats; they sold it all at Leibritsky's Department Store. They had to go through every item on the floor and compare it to their records. They had to pull item after item off the main racks or shelves and place them onto sales racks or shelves, or into the basement for another season. To be prepared for fall, they had to reorganize the menswear, the women's wear, and the children's wear. Out with the old; in with the new. They had to reconfigure the kitchen appliances and stack the newest gems — more of the Waring blenders and Sunbeam's Mixmaster — where they couldn't be missed. Thanks to a soft spot Mort had for selling shoes, Leibritsky's had developed a reputation in this department, especially for its practical, all-purpose shoes, the kind with thick soles and heavy laces, the kind that stretched a dollar, and this required going up and down every row of shoe boxes, accounting for each box's contents. They had more than a few pair of men's shoes from 1940 that had never sold, several women's from 1942, '43, and '44. The wartime rationing of those later years had something to do with the unsold stock, Nelson knew.

It was late in the day on Tuesday by the time they got to those and Howard looked up, astonished.

"This is nuts. We're well into nineteen forty-eight," Howard pleaded to Nelson.

"Keep them," Nelson answered, briefly glancing around to see that neither Mort nor Leo had heard him. They, too, would think having such old inventory nuts. Then again, Nelson realized, what did it matter what they thought? After all, Nelson was the one with the MBA, and from Harvard no less, *Harvard.* They wouldn't dare contradict him even when his advice was so stupid a teenager's instincts immediately told him so.

"Not so nuts," Nelson stubbornly insisted to Howard. "There are people who like what they already know. They'll sell eventually. Trust me." And of course Howard did. Indeed, Howard nodded with appreciation as if he'd just been taught a wise lesson, not from uncle to nephew but from master to apprentice, professor to student. Absentminded nut, Nelson then admitted to himself, patting the box from 1940.

Yet a pair of the dated shoes did sell, the next day, a Wednesday. Midafternoon, the heat from the street wafting in, causing them all to slow down, to drop themselves into any one of the chairs strewn about the store, and Giorgio D'Almato trundled in, looking like he might fall down from fatigue or imbalance — he was eighty-seven and refused a cane. Nelson and Howard were still at the wall of shoes, the Wailing Wall, they had taken to calling it just that morning, and they had each written a favorite joke on a scrap of paper, folded the scrap tightly, then slipped it in a space between the boxes of shoes the way printed prayers were tucked around the stones of the sacred wall in Old Jerusalem. Howard, laughing, had davened for good measure.

"Let's not get crazy, you know?" Nelson had urged. "It's a tough business over there. Tough going. A little fun, that's all. A little fun."

But so far that week every moment around Howard had seemed exceptionally fun, whether they were overtly joking or simply engaged in everyday tasks. And that's why, perhaps, as Giorgio D'Almato slowly approached, Nelson found himself opening his arms wide and calling out in a welcoming tone he didn't even know he had, "Mr. D'Almato, sir. What do you say, young man, what do you say?"

When what the old man said was "Something practical, size nine, why ask, don't you know?" Nelson, winking Howard's way, turned toward the wall and pulled from it the unsold shoes from 1940. Old man D'Almato leaned his face toward the open box, scrutinized the contents, sniffed the leather, and gave a quick nod of assent. Nelson held Mr. D'Almato's arm as he lowered himself to sit in a nearby chair. With a nod toward Howard, Nelson watched as Howard helped relieve the man of his worn shoes, the soles cracked, the laces nearly gone. He had bought them here, Nelson knew, probably some ten years ago. Indeed, everyone in the D'Almato family bought at Leibritsky's Department Store and the Leibritsky men, in turn, got their hair cut at the D'Almato barbershop. If you were good to people, Nelson knew, the people of those people were good to you. This was the first rule of business, absolutely, and do you think even one knucklehead at Harvard had ever heard of it? A shoehorn at one heel, then the other, Howard eased the man's feet into the new shoes. Howard practically lifted the man upright so he could take a turn in the new pair. Old man D'Almato liked them. He rubbed his palms together and mumbled to himself. Nelson smiled.

Once the shoes were purchased — at a spontaneous and decent discount — Nelson told his customer, "Let me get Mort. He'll be sorry not to have said hello."

The man nodded. This, too, was a rule of business, the greeting from the eldest brother. And Giorgio D'Almato, like everybody else, knew the rules. He waited.

Thursday morning, the inventory still under way, Nelson felt sorry that the time with Howard, a particularly congenial thing, would soon end. But the weekend was coming. He'd be staying; they'd be going. As if reading his thoughts, Mort patted Nelson's shoulder, telling him, "Look, you're doing a nice job here. Nice job. Howard's enjoying it. He likes your company. Always has."

A little boost was what his brother's remarks gave him, a boost of energy, a boost of confidence, and when he found his nephew a few minutes later sitting by the new display of kitchen appliances, clearly bored, fingering the Sunbeam Mixmaster, Nelson motioned to him. Howard rose and followed Nelson into the basement.

"Look, there's some old things in the back, see, and nobody will be the wiser if we just let them go. Maybe we can find you something. You never know, maybe you need a new shirt, something like that. A boy heading off to college like you are. A new tie, maybe," Nelson urged.

"A new tie, circa what, Uncle — nineteen twenty-eight?" Howard smiled. " 'Twenty-eight. Was it a good year, Uncle?"

Nelson glanced at Howard, who was laughing, and the two walked toward the several large boxes pushed against a back wall which Nelson had discovered earlier that summer and, to save face, had kept out of the inventory.

"Some wisecracker," Nelson said, opening one of the boxes. Inside were the men's shirts from the summer before, short-sleeved, cotton. Though the box was covered with dust, the shirts inside were pristine, still wrapped in their original packaging. "Forgot about these one year and they've been hiding here ever since. But the time has come," Nelson announced, pulling out several and handing them to Howard. "Yes?"

"This store is a crazy mess!" Howard kicked the box as he grabbed the packages and studied them. Like Giorgio D'Almato the day before, Howard soon began happily mumbling.

Now was no time to play a record, but it was a good time for a sit, and Nelson dragged his rocker toward Howard and watched as the boy continued to fish through the box. "Five too many?" Howard asked.

"Whatever you need." Nelson pulled a Tootsie Roll from his pocket. He threw one to Howard and the two silently chewed under the weak glow of the basement's lights. It was warm down here, Nelson reflected, rocking forward and back, but not so bad. Relaxing, he heaved a tired sigh. "Long week," he said.

Howard nodded and continued chewing. He held his new shirts in one hand as he might notebooks for school. Upon swallowing, he cleared his throat.

"Uncle?" His voice was quieter than before, tentative.

Nelson stopped rocking. He waited for Howard to go on, but the boy said nothing, his posture suddenly tense. Nelson reached to pull another chocolate from his pocket for Howard, but Howard shook his head no. A silent moment followed, at least between the two of them. Above, the floors persistently creaked.

"I really can't tell anyone," Howard began. "You know, anyone down there."

Nelson realized soon enough that the boy was speaking of Woodmont.

Down there. The place he never went.

"There's this girl," Howard finally began,

and because his tone of voice was unusually earnest, it took Nelson back to a collage of moments sitting beside a much younger Howard at Middletown's Palace Theater. Before each movie Howard would stare entranced at the blank screen, curtain still down, as if the show were already under way. Finally he'd turn to Nelson and beseech him in a voice not so different from the one he'd just heard, "Will it start soon?" "Soon, soon," Nelson would answer, and then he'd pass Howard a candy, and, feeling good, like a father, he'd cup the top of Howard's head then give the kid a pat.

Yes, there was a girl, Howard repeated, and he was pretty sure she was the one.

Green eyes, a lot of freckles, a big smile, though she was often serious, and with each detail Nelson nodded, until Howard paused, suddenly somber, and then said, "I don't know why I'm telling you this. Forget it, Uncle."

The words made Nelson self-conscious, as if they implied that a man like him knew nothing about love. *But Howard,* he longed to say in response, *I wasn't always this fat.*

He'd been a handsome kid himself, shorter than Howard, but good-looking in his own way, a wide face, a soft smile, a little shyness that wore off once people got to know him. Back then, when he was Howard's age, people did take the time to know him. Before Harvard he'd gone to Boston University — his father insisted that he and Mort get their college educations, this was America after all, this was what it was all about, what all the saving and scrimping was for. But Mort had been pulled from college after only a year and a half — the store was too much for just the old man — and it was consequently left to Nelson to do the learning for them all. He'd studied history, just like Mort did before he left, just like his father told him to, and in the course of things he'd met Mimmie Klein, up in Boston from New London, Connecticut. *Mimmie Klein,* Nelson almost said out loud to Howard.

"Tell you what," he said instead when he finally did interrupt his nephew. "We can't stay in this basement forever. Time to get back to it. But let's have dinner tonight, me and you. Then you can tell me the whole story. I do want to hear. The one? Is that what you said, Howard?"

Howard's expression remained grim. He nodded.

Nelson had risen from his rocker and had begun to climb the basement stairs when he turned back to Howard, behind him. "What'd you say her name was?" Nelson asked.

"Didn't say."

"No name? Howard, the girl for you has no name?"

Howard said, "Uncle, come on now. This is private business. We'll talk about that later."

They were seated in a booth at the Garden Restaurant, on the corner of Main and Washington, he and Howard waiting for their orders of hamburgers to arrive, Howard somewhat agitated, picking at his napkin, glancing about the place as if he'd never been there before, and Nelson felt it again, the old urge to pat the kid on the head, tell him, "Soon, soon." Instead he broached the subject of the girl again, the as yet unnamed girl, and Howard sighed. "Let's eat first," he suggested, and Nelson, though curious, nodded.

Mimmie Klein, he again almost blurted to Howard. *Isn't that some name?*

The first time he'd met Mimmie he'd treated her to a meal, though unlike the present one with Howard, that meal of long ago was an inadvertent gift. He was at a deli on Commonwealth Avenue the winter

317

of his sophomore year at college and she, a stranger then, was there too. It was nearly seven in the evening and Nelson, hungry, already had his sandwich wrapped to go and was in line to pay. Even as the sandwich was being made he'd begun to sweat inside his winter coat, but waiting in line he started rapidly to overheat. Someone ahead was taking a long time to pay. Nelson, like the person before him, unbuttoned his coat and pulled his hat off. Mimmie stood two people ahead of him in line. And ahead of her was an elderly man, dressed like the rest of them in heavy winter gear, who also had a sandwich wrapped to go. He was trying to pay but no matter which pocket he dug into, the change didn't add up. The young clerk behind the counter became angry. Nelson noticed how he was as red-faced as the flustered man. "Can't you see there's a line?" the clerk scolded as the old man reached into one more pocket. "I don't understand," the man said, glancing behind him at Nelson and the others, and the clerk answered, "It's simple. Pay up or give up. We can't be running a charity."

Nelson stepped past the customer ahead of him and then past Mimmie. Standing beside the elderly man, he told the clerk he would pay for the man's sandwich.

"What?" the clerk said, still glaring at the man. "You're doing what?"

Nelson paused. He'd already pulled out a dollar but he fished in his pocket for another. "In fact, I'm paying for everybody," Nelson added.

A fifth customer joined the line.

"Paying for everybody," the clerk said, loudly and mockingly, as if Nelson were attempting to show off. But that wasn't his intent. He just didn't like the clerk. Not at all.

Nelson glanced behind him, then back at the clerk. Even though a sixth person, hearing the news, joined the line, Nelson nodded, then searched his pocket for more dollar bills, but there were none, just some change. As he pulled out everything he had, the elderly man beside him held a weathered hand to his shoulder.

Nelson was eleven cents short and the clerk let him and everybody else know it. "Paying for everybody," the clerk gibed.

"Here you go," someone, a woman, said from behind Nelson, and in the next moment Mimmie was standing next to him, looking not at him but at the clerk. She handed him the extra change. She glanced Nelson's way then leaned around him to catch the eye of the older man. "Generosity," she said, her eyes back on the clerk. "Ever hear of it?"

The clerk took the money — two dollars and seventy cents from Nelson and eleven cents from Mimmie — and without further conversation, five sandwiches and a tub of potato salad were purchased.

The last person in line was a father holding his child's hand, and with the exchange of money the child unwrapped her sandwich and bit into it despite the father telling her, "Slow down, Clara. Don't want to get a stomachache." As Nelson passed him, the man reached into his pocket and threw a penny Tootsie Roll Nelson's way. Nelson caught it, instinctively, and the man nodded a silent thanks. Mimmie clapped.

Nelson was back outside, a block away, feeling all the chillier after sweating inside with his coat on, when Mimmie caught up to him.

She offered him two quarters but he shook his head. Snow had begun to fall and the traffic, what little there was on Commonwealth Avenue, had slowed.

"People don't always stick up for what's right," she told him.

"I don't know," Nelson said. "It was just a matter of some change." In fact it was a matter of all the money he had for the rest of the week — three more days — and re-alizing that, he began to grow anxious. He'd eat just half the sandwich that night and save the rest for the next day.

"Some change, as you say, can sometimes mean life and death," Mimmie asserted.

"Not today, thank God," Nelson an-swered, though he wasn't so sure about the days to come.

"No, not today," Mimmie agreed. She was tiny and had curly hair. Those were the only details he noted in the darkness.

Nelson was shivering and he could see that Mimmie was too. He was about to nod and turn to go when Mimmie said, "Come on, let's get some coffee." She pointed to a shop across the street. But for lack of any money, even pennies, Nelson shook his head.

He changed his mind, though, when Mim-mie insisted, "My treat. Least I can do." She showed him the quarters again. "Name's Mimmie Klein," she said.

They met for dinner the next week at the same coffee shop on Commonwealth. He already knew that she was up in Boston from New London — that first meeting they'd shared their backgrounds, their Con-necticut stories — but he hadn't yet learned that she was studying math.

"Surprised?" she asked him. He couldn't decide if she expected the reaction or wanted it.

Either way he was surprised, but only because he found mathematics so difficult. That anybody could be good at it surprised him.

"People often can't believe it," she said, telling him next that her being female was what threw people at first. After all, Boston University was among only a handful of places that even allowed a girl a higher education. So simply being female was quite the thing, quite the mystery, but being a *cutie* — she articulated the word with a seriousness it didn't often connote — was the kicker. She shook her head, causing her curls to bounce, and Nelson found the gesture appealing. She was cute. And she was serious and surprisingly direct. If she'd been ugly, Mimmie explained next, leaning with some urgency across the table toward Nelson, of course the matter would be a little easier to understand.

"But I'm not that bad," she concluded, frowning.

"No, no," Nelson agreed, blushing, then feeling an unusual stirring in his heart.

He stank at math, he confessed — he was

a word guy, not so much out loud, of course, everyone knew that, but he had words going in his head left and right, he was very busy with words in there, he told her — and for the rest of the semester as he and Mimmie grew close he discovered that he'd been right: he couldn't have passed introductory calculus but for the big mathematical brain inside the otherwise tiny Mimmie Klein.

But in the end he'd lost her. If he had told Howard about her, if he had put his burger down and asked Howard to do the same, and if, folding his napkin and shaking his head in seriousness, he had begun speaking, he would have said, *I lost her. I lost my love, Mimmie Klein.* But instead he said, "Pretty good, huh?" holding up his burger. And Howard said, "Someday I'd really like to try a cheeseburger."

"Hey, hey, hey," Nelson responded, his tone a warning to Howard about the rule banning meat with dairy.

"Just dreaming," Howard said.

Howard's girl in Woodmont played piano, he noted at long last, pushing his plate aside. She'd been taking lessons since she was six.

"You've heard her play?" Nelson was

genuinely interested. But Howard shook his head. She'd just told him all about it, he answered, suddenly embarrassed.

Nelson stopped asking after that. He would listen, merely listen. And soon enough Howard offered a bit more. She was good with numbers, he said. "She's the best checkout girl at Treat's," he boasted, and with his napkin and an imaginary pencil he did a quick imitation of a person adding numbers.

"Numbers," Nelson repeated, surprised to find Howard's girl having something in common with his own. The likeness caused a quickening in his heart, and he pulled two Tootsie Rolls from his pocket. He threw one Howard's way and waited for Howard to say more, but he didn't. Finally Howard began describing the walks he and his girl took along Beach Avenue, part of the many evenings they'd spent "just talking," Howard said. Then he corrected himself. "Mostly talking."

"Talking's good," Nelson responded. "She sounds like a catch, Howard. You're a lucky man."

"Uncle, there's more."

Howard shifted on his side of the booth. A moment ago, engrossed in unwrapping the candy, Howard had looked like the nephew Nelson had always known. Years had passed, but nothing, really, had changed. He could see the little boy right then inside the big kid. But a second later Howard looked so much older, so much more serious. Nelson blinked, surprised, when Howard buried his face in his hands and groaned — something Nelson had never seen him do before.

"Hey, hey, hey. She sounds like a nice girl. A good girl. Howard, you telling me you're in some kind of —" Nelson paused. Never had he had this kind of talk with his nephew. "Trouble?" he whispered. "Howard, you in trouble?"

"Not the kind you're thinking of," Howard answered, his voice resigned.

Embarrassed, Nelson turned away. He swallowed his chocolate. "Hell, Howard. I wasn't thinking of any particular kind of trouble. No, no. I wasn't."

"Want to know her name?" Howard asked.

"Of course."

"Megan."

"Megan," Nelson repeated, nodding.

"Megan O'Donnell."

There was a moment of silence and then Nelson said, "Dear God, Howard."

"I know."

"God almighty, boy."

"I *know*."

"Holy mackerel, Howard."

"Uncle, can't you stop? I thought I could tell you. I thought you'd be the only one who wouldn't jump down my throat. Uncle, what do I do?"

"Oh boy, Howard. If only all you wanted was a cheeseburger. That'd be easy. I'd say, for crying out loud, in my presence alone, have a goddamned cheeseburger. Just once and it'll be over with." Nelson paused, fingering the small pile of candy wrappers beside his plate. "But about that girl," he added at last. "I'm just your uncle. I can't be the one to tell you what to do."

Within weeks of meeting Mimmie, Nelson knew what to do: he made seeing her a regular thing. By spring of his sophomore year he and Mimmie were planning their days around each other, studying together at the university library in the evenings, taking walks along Commonwealth Avenue most afternoons, going to the movies on Saturday nights, eventually holding hands inside the darkened theater, turning to each other sometimes to laugh or smile.

She was the one, he soon concluded, no doubt about it. But he was too shy to even kiss her much less tell her so. Then, a week before they were to part for the summer, he finally made his move. They were in a theater and the movie — Buster Keaton's *Seven Chances* — was coming to a close. The music was swelling, the credits rolling. And if they rolled any faster, Nelson figured, the moment would be gone. He pulled Mimmie close and pressed his lips, quickly, to hers. When they parted she called his name, quietly, lovingly. He kissed her again.

A long summer came after that, and Nelson went home to work in the store while Mimmie stayed in Boston with an aunt, but when they returned to school the next year the affection flowed freely. Something had happened over the summer — a lot of letters back and forth, and, for Nelson at least, a lot of dreaming — and they couldn't keep themselves from sneaking kisses every chance they got. His third year of college passed in what felt like a flash: days as full and happy as Nelson had ever known. He was reading for classes and getting good grades; he was working part-time in a stationery store, easy enough tasks compared to the convoluted ordering for all the departments he did back home at Leibritsky's; and he was in love with Mimmie who, every time he kissed her — whether on the banks of the Charles River or in the doorway to her student house — kissed him back. "Nelson," she would so often murmur, just as she had that first time, whispering his name for no reason other than to say it.

For two and a half years they kissed, only kissed. Then, late in the fall of their senior year, they did more than kissing. They did — as he would have quietly told Howard, if he could have opened up and told him everything — they did the other thing: the act of love.

Thanksgiving break his senior year, Nelson traveled back to Middletown to be with the family and to work at the store. Moreover, he planned to broach the subject of marriage to Mimmie with his father. The year before she'd met the family, briefly, as she'd detoured through Middletown on her way home to New London. Everything had gone well. She had walked each aisle of Leibritsky's Department Store. She'd shaken Mort's hand and then Zelik's. Nelson and Mimmie had then ambled along Middletown's Main Street, Nelson pointing out each business to her as if it were an old friend. "I see. I see," Mimmie noted as Nelson told her the history of the enterprises along Main Street.

For two years already Nelson had saved every cent he could for an engagement ring.

By that Thanksgiving of 1927 he had forty-six dollars. It would have to do, he figured, as he hurried into Pinsker's Jewelers, at the corner of Main and College streets, several blocks south of Leibritsky's. A half hour later, and exactly forty-six dollars poorer, he returned to work.

"We have this idea," his father told him upon his return from the jewelers. Zelik, along with Mort, was sitting on a crate in what was then the back room, a storage room. The store was a smaller place then, just a hole in the wall, filled with odds and ends. For so many years before this Zelik had been a peddler, running goods first by horse and cart between Middletown and Hartford, following the routes along the Connecticut River, until one day, just outside Hartford, his horse's knees buckled, a trunk of women's clothes fell to the ground, opened, and spilled, muddying the lot of them, and that was it: Zelik Leibritsky was determined to open a shop. For some reason Zelik, once he'd urged Nelson to sit, repeated this personal history. Then he told Nelson to eat; for lunch they were nibbling sardines from small tins and drinking cream soda. Zelik's beard was already fully gray. He'd been forty by the time Nelson was born in 1906 and now he was closing in on sixty-two. Sometimes, it seemed to Nelson, listening to Zelik as he rattled on about how they could continue to build the business, all those years between them were as wide as a world. The old man still had one foot in age-old Europe, in Russia, where all his ideas came from. Nelson, on the other hand, was modern. He had a few ideas that came straight from Boston, USA.

"Yes, we have an idea. In the next years you'll get an MBA," Zelik said, his words a pronouncement. He nodded at Mort, who in turn nodded at Nelson. Nelson was stunned by the remark, which didn't sound old-fashioned at all. How did his father even know what an MBA was? he wondered. "Try for Harvard," the old man continued, astonishing Nelson further. "You're up there anyway. Why not? Knock on their door, see if they let you in. Let's get fancy is what I say. God knows, it's going to be good for the store. And good for the family." Zelik took his now empty soda bottle and blew over its lip until it whistled.

Until that moment Nelson had considered teaching, a notion that resurfaced just then as a whisper in his mind. He opened his mouth. "But —"

"But nothing," Mort told him, suddenly rising and looking down at Nelson. "We've all put in our time. Now it's time for you to put in yours."

Nelson nodded, though the thought in his mind still rustled for attention. When he nodded some more, its calling ceased.

Later that day, when Nelson spoke of Mimmie to his father, Zelik asked only one question. "Jewish?"

"Of course."

"Okay."

A week after Thanksgiving, and for a second time he and Mimmie made love. Like before, he snuck her up to his room, a rental on Beacon Street, a boardinghouse for male students only, a risky enough venture even if all they'd planned was a serious study session. He locked his door and pushed a wooden chair against it for good measure. He smoothed the sheets on his bed.

Mimmie was wearing a green wool coat and a matching green cap. She had auburn-colored hair, and the outfit, coupled with her petite figure, gave her the appearance almost of a leprechaun. Her cheeks and nose were red from the cold outside. Just as he lunged toward her she collapsed into a helpless shudder.

Their lovemaking, quiet, delicate, and cautious, nevertheless left them insatiably hungry. "Isn't that interesting?" Mimmie remarked of their sudden voraciousness, and Nelson, nodding, mumbled an embarrassed "Well, there's been a lot of . . ." He couldn't put words to what they'd just done. But the act had changed everything. Outside on Beacon Street the lamps on the sidewalk were glowing especially bright, and the whistling of the coastal winds, so often a hostile sound, seemed to blend into a kind of music. Every store they passed — a pharmacy, a shoe repair shop, another pharmacy — seemed exotic, compelling. It was as if they'd never walked on Beacon before. But how was that possible? Nelson wondered as they hopped a trolley and headed to nearby Brookline, where they could readily find the Jewish food they most craved.

Once they'd been seated at their favorite delicatessen, Mimmie laughed and held her hands to her face, smothering what would otherwise have been a near outburst. She continued laughing as she ordered pastrami on rye, chicken soup, and black coffee.

When the food arrived they ate rapaciously and in silence, except for Mimmie's occasional "Almost like my mother's."

"You know, Nelson," she said, finally pushing her plate back. She'd consumed all the soup and most of her sandwich. He'd had half as much. "I had a talk with my father last week when I was home."

"My father talked to me, too."

"Busy fathers, yes? Well, look. We're graduating soon. Our fathers are concerned. Mine asked me something surprising. He asked if I wanted to be a doctor like him, a medical doctor. Me, an M.D. Can you imagine? I told him I didn't know, I'd never thought about it."

She looked at Nelson for some kind of agreement, and he nodded. She'd never spoken about being a doctor, just a mathematician, which he still found remarkable enough.

"I mean, I've taken the biology and chemistry," Mimmie continued, "so maybe I *was* thinking about it all along, in the back of my mind. I don't know. Maybe. But you know what?" She stirred sugar into her coffee. "I've been thinking about it ever since, and I do. It's come to me. I really do." She raised her hands in front of her, palm to palm, as if to pray. "It's like a dream and I can't shake it," she told him. "Some things are meant to be."

For a week he'd carried in his coat pocket the engagement ring he'd purchased in Middletown. Each day that week he'd wondered if the moment to present it would arise, and as the days passed he began to worry that he'd not recognize the moment even if someone were to hold up a sign: *This is it.* But Mimmie had just said, "Some things are meant to be," and even though the delicatessen wasn't the setting of his dreams, he pulled the velvety jeweler's box from his pocket.

"Some things are meant to be," he said as he placed the box between them. "That's what I think too." He paused for some time, staring at the box, too anxious to look at Mimmie. He finally continued. "You're the reason for everything. That's what I've been thinking."

He inched the box toward her but still didn't look at her face. "Life will be good, Mimmie, so long as you're with me."

She smiled at him then reached toward the box. But before she opened it she looked up. "With you where?" she asked. Seeing his surprise, she added quickly, "Nelson, we have to be sure of things."

He grabbed a napkin to swipe his brow. "Middletown," he began. "First I'll get an MBA. Then I'll go back to the store. We had a family meeting. It's been decided."

"By whom?"

"My father. Mort. Me. We discussed it."

"That's what you talked about with your father?"

He nodded.

"And me?" she said.

"I talked with him about you too." From her questioning look he knew that wasn't what she meant. He added, "There are doctors in Middletown. God knows, there are plenty of sick people. You could be a doctor in Middletown just as well as anywhere else. I won't hold you back. Mimmie, I'd never do that."

She paused, considering, then plucked up the little box, springing it open. She gasped. "Nelson, what did you do?" she whispered.

"It's for you," he blurted, then felt stupid for saying something so obvious.

But she didn't mind. She nodded more vigorously as if coming to an understanding, as if his words had actually helped. She looked at the ring for a long while without trying it on or remarking further. She turned the open box one way and then the other. Finally she put the box down and took a bite of what remained of her pastrami sandwich. She chewed, then sipped her coffee. Nelson watched in disbelief. All the after-sex euphoria had drained from her face. She looked serious, almost grim. She swallowed and said, "But you love history.

You're good at it. You write beautiful papers. All your professors say so. You could study history and become, I don't know, a professor or a teacher or something, and I could study medicine, and we could stay right here. *Right here.*"

For a moment he imagined them spending years together nowhere else but at this Brookline delicatessen.

"I have to get the MBA. I promised. I agreed."

"The MBA," she said with disgust. "That's not you."

Unable to think of a reply, he shrugged. He didn't know where to begin to explain why he'd agreed. "*You're* doing what your father asked," he said defensively.

"My father opened up a world. He made it a thousand times bigger. He gave me *permission.* But your father. What did your father do?"

"Everything he does, he does for us," Nelson answered, still defensive. "How many people get an education like this? It's not like he has one. Mort couldn't even finish college. You talk as if this is a bad thing. Mimmie, it's a chance for me."

"And then you're indebted. Then he wants you to do what he wants you to do. And you and your brother," she snapped her fingers, "you just do it, like that."

"Mimmie, we *want* to do it. We're *family.*" His voice had almost left him. For reasons that baffled him, he was losing what was always the most persuasive argument in the world. Her people were German Jews and his were Russian, so much poorer, so much more religious. Perhaps that explained the gulf that now emerged between them. In a near whisper he said, "It's a *family* business. Don't you know about *family*?"

"Of course. That's what I'm saying." She lifted her coffee cup, then lowered it without taking a sip. Holding the engagement ring up to the light she said, "So pretty, Nelson. And thoughtful. Just like you."

He waited for more but there wasn't more. She hadn't said yes. But she hadn't said no, either.

"Nelson, I'm thinking," Mimmie explained. When she reached for his hand across the table he felt an intense relief. They loved each other; everything had to work out.

A few minutes later she pulled her hand back and began speaking, her words deliberately paced, her tone firm. "Nelson, I don't want you to get an MBA because it isn't you. And I don't want to go back with you to Middletown because it's not where I should be. Your family, it's going to swallow me up and I'm going to choke, Nelson. I can tell from everything you've said, from everything I've seen. But even more than that it's not where *you* should be. You're no businessman. You and I both know this is true. What I'm saying is, it's not a good fit, that life in Middletown. And neither you nor I deserve to be unhappy." She placed the ring back into the box. When she snapped the cover shut, causing a loud clap, Nelson's shoulders jumped.

He stared at Mimmie. He loved her.

"You're going to have to choose," she continued, calmly as before.

"Uncle, you've got to tell me what to do," Howard repeated. But before Nelson could explain to Howard why he was the last person to ask such a question of they were interrupted by a waitress who took Nelson's and Howard's plates and then brought them coffee. "Everything good?" she asked. She chatted with them for a minute as Nelson stirred his coffee then slipped another Tootsie Roll into his mouth. He'd eaten five since they'd finished their burgers and Howard had announced that Megan O'Donnell was the one for him.

"Uncle, please," Howard said once the

waitress left.

Nelson shook his head. He stared into his coffee. He glanced at Howard — still so young — then turned back to his drink. His hands on the cup were fat, ugly, old.

His next thought was not a new one but it nevertheless came to him with urgency: how right Mimmie had been all those years ago. He'd had a choice, but at the time he couldn't see it. All he could see then was an inevitable unfolding of something he called, simply enough, the way of things. And by the time he saw that the way of things was like a river, fierce with current, but something you didn't have to fall into, get dragged along by, by the time he'd had that revelation, he'd graduated from Harvard, had been working at Leibritsky's Department Store a long time, had settled into something he'd never imagined, a bachelor's life, a life the others, respectful as they were, pitied.

"Uncle?"

"Soon, soon."

He was still thinking, still taking in Howard's youthfulness, contrasting it with his own age, his own regrets.

On most days he felt like a fool. That was another thought, equally urgent. So often at family dinners, Erev Rosh Hashanah, for example, or Passover seder, he felt like a fool, sitting there without a wife, without children, except for a few friendly enough banalities talking to no one, having a life no one else in the family could even imagine, so many dinners alone at diners on either end of Main Street, so much solitude on the weekend. Everything about life, Jewish life, *their* life, was about having a family, and so many times he'd wondered what kind of Jew he was if he'd missed out on this most basic thing. The answer wasn't so hard to find, really. He was an idiot Jew. An outcast Jew. All three of them, Mort, Leo, and Howard, would be heading to Woodmont the next day and he'd be left behind, as he'd been left behind for years and years. "You're always welcome," Ada had insisted because she had to, because he was her husband's brother, because it was the respectful thing to do. But there wasn't any room for him there. He knew that. And they did too.

"Am I crazy, Uncle? Am I out of my mind?"

Nelson didn't know. It could go either way, he figured, crazy to say yes, crazy to say no.

He motioned to the waitress, asked that she clear the table of the used napkins and candy wrappers. They reminded him of his life, and the depth of disgust that he felt for it just then was overwhelming.

Crazier to say no. That was the truth of it. His truth. A little morsel of life experience he could unwrap, offer to Howard.

"Okay, so," he began, slowly, once the table had been cleaned. Howard, who'd been silent and sulking, looked up. "Consider it a theory is what I was thinking," Nelson told him. "Consider your feelings for this Megan O'Donnell a theory, something you have to test to be sure."

"We've talked for *hours,* Uncle."

"So you talk for some hours more. You take some more walks. I recommend you take in a picture or two. Just the way we used to back in the old days. Two people can get to know each other quite well by going to the pictures."

Howard nodded.

"And if in the end you still feel she's the one, then what I say is it's okay to do in life what you really, really want to do. You just can't be stupid about knowing you really, really want it. You can't be a jerk on that one. Of course that's just my opinion. Someone else —" Mort came to mind. "Someone else may have something different to say. That's how life is, Howard. A bundle of opinions. But maybe you should know of mine."

Howard's eyes were wide. "I won't be a stupid jerk," he said gravely.

"I didn't think you would be. I was just saying."

Howard grinned and Nelson nodded. He reached into a pocket but there were no more candies. "Some night out," Nelson said, shrugging, wondering already — as he would the rest of the evening — if he'd said too much.

"Some night!" Howard agreed, slapping the tabletop as if it were a drum. "Now how about that?"

The next morning, Friday, Nelson woke with a mild headache. He hadn't slept well. But some news in the morning paper got him just a little bit charged up: at the London Olympics an American named Bob Mathias, a kid just Howard's age, had surprised the world by pulling ahead in the decathlon. Nelson brought the sports section in to work to show Howard, who perhaps hadn't slept well either. But Howard, not the least tired, had already read about it. "I know, I know," he said confidently when Nelson passed him the paper.

All morning Howard seemed that way:

confident, knowing. By noon he'd made an easy seven sales, a good number, but not so unusual for a talented salesman like him. After lunch, though, and in just an hour, he made seven more. "Call me Bob!" Howard quipped at one point, passing Nelson, who was standing near the register, doing nothing but gazing at Main Street. Crazy to say yes, he was telling himself anxiously.

A few hours later Nelson stood in the office as Mort and Leo, their weekend suitcases nearby, prepared to go to Woodmont. Seeing those suitcases, Nelson dropped down into the basement. Soon the drums of "Sing, Sing, Sing" had his feet tapping despite the melancholy — a regular piece of Friday — that he felt creeping up on him.

Crazier, he realized anew, to say no.

When he emerged from the basement it was time for them to leave, and Howard was suddenly at Nelson's side. "Thanks again for everything," Howard said. Through the office doorway Nelson could see Mort speaking on the phone and jotting something down as he did. Nelson cleared his throat. "Sure, sure," he said.

Then he and Howard walked into the back office together.

"What's that?" Mort asked Howard, noticing the packages of shirts in his hands, the ones he'd chosen the day before.

"I thought he could use a few things for college," Nelson explained, stepping in front of Howard protectively. But Howard didn't need his help. Not just then. He was back on the sales floor, whistling. A few minutes later Mort, Leo, Howard, and Nelson walked to the front doorway and Howard practically ran from the dim interior of Leibritsky's Department Store past his father and uncle and into the brightness of the afternoon. "Let's go," he said. He had his suitcase in one hand and the car key in the other.

Mort took a few steps outside then turned back to speak to Nelson.

"Happy kid. He really enjoyed this week, Nelson. You're what he enjoyed the most." He patted Nelson's shoulder several times. "You're a good brother. A good uncle."

Out on the sidewalk again, Mort turned Nelson's way and waved.

"Good Shabbos, my brother."

"Sure, sure. Good Shabbos," he said.

10
OTHER WAYS, OTHER POSSIBILITIES

But in Woodmont, Shabbos that evening wasn't good. The men arrived and my mother, in her oddly matched housedress and wedge sandals, had challenged the rules. After that — and throughout what felt like the longest meal ever — my parents didn't speak, and the next morning, after the men returned from services, Mort packed his bag, told Leo to pack his, and they were off. "See you in two weeks," Mort announced, stunning us. He wasn't coming back the next week. That hadn't happened before.

Hearing the news, my mother hung her head. He might as well have punched her in the stomach. His absence, we all knew, was her punishment, her humiliation.

But then the car revved, they were gone, and suddenly Ada's mood shifted. She raised her head. She crossed her arms over her chest. She kicked a clamshell that had made its way onto our front porch. "Good riddance," she told the thing. Then she breathed deeply. Then she smiled.

Vivie was less content. "It's not just about you," she told Ada once the men had left. She was standing on the porch beside Ada.

"Leo can drive right back once he gets to Middletown. He has a car," Ada countered.

"He'd never. You know that. He can barely drive himself from home to work without getting queasy." Vivie turned to go inside. "Two weeks!" she said as the screen door slammed behind her.

Two weeks was a long time away from Leo, but once Vivie had her say with Ada, she didn't raise the matter again. Instead, whatever discontent lingered she channeled into her cooking, or so it seemed, for that week and the next Vivie spent largely in the kitchen, experimenting with an array of new recipes, only to cook by the end of that first week entirely recipe free. She was inventing meals of a kind we'd not had before. One night she served us a noodle casserole filled with tomatoes, zucchini, onions, and peas — all from Treat's — simmered in a mushroom sauce. On another night she made a cold noodle salad, also filled with the season's vegetables and lightly flavored with a garlic mayonnaise. These were new tastes for us — so different from the meatloaf and potatoes, the roasts of beef and chicken, or the franks and beans we were used to — and we couldn't heave enough spoonfuls of her concoctions onto our plates. Nearly every day she needed fresh vegetables from Treat's, and by Thursday of the first week without Leo she took to bicycling there herself, borrowing one of the Weinsteins' bikes to do so. She looked hilarious, Nina and I thought, pedaling off in her skirt and hose that she'd changed into just for the shopping, the kerchief she'd wrapped around her head flapping as she gained speed.

That week, the second one of August, while Vivie expanded her range in the kitchen, Ada expanded her dunking to a second time daily, in the late afternoon. This she did with Davy and me jumping in delight beside her. "Don't splash or I'll turn myself right around," she'd warn, and then she'd stand still for a moment before she'd turn and splash each of us, and then lower herself until we couldn't see her anymore. A moment later she'd pop up, the water streaming off her rubber cap, her eyes shut tight as if she were still beneath the sea. The sight of her this way, drenched and happy, teasing us, taking time out for us like this, was exhilarating. In we'd dive, following her, and just as we'd catch up to her, our arms outstretched, ready to grab her — for that became the instant point of this new game: to touch her, grab her, be grabbed by her — down she'd go again, only to pop up a few feet away. And so the chase continued until, exhausted, we'd just float, the gentle waves of the Long Island Sound undulating softly beneath our backs, the wispy clouds in the sky above as interesting to gaze at as any face, the murmur of water in our ears a kind of song.

Those afternoons while we swam and Vivie cooked, Bec sewed with renewed vigor. Before taking off for New York with Tyler, she was determined to leave her mark on each of us, a specially designed new dress, the dresses of our dreams. She was even making another one for Nina, this time in a less flashy style, a dress she'd be more apt to actually wear. "Too bad I'm not a girl," Davy remarked one afternoon, leaning on Bec's shoulder as he watched her run a seam under her Singer. That's when Bec decided she'd make Davy a fall jacket. "I just have to get myself back to New Haven for some fabric," she said, and then she called Tyler from the phone in our dining room, for the first time suggesting he come get her on a Thursday rather than Friday. She'd stay Thursday night in her apartment in New Haven, she told us, then she'd be there for a fitting she had to attend anyway on Friday while she also shopped for Davy's fabric. She needed a little more time in town, she noted. "Don't want to be late again for Shabbos," she added, winking and smiling as if she'd just made a great joke.

"Shabbos?" my mother quipped, as if she'd never heard the word before.

"Oh, Ada," Vivie said. But by this time even she grinned. "Just don't push your luck too far," she warned her sister. "Remember, it's our luck too."

That week Davy and his drawing partner Lucinda Rossetti weren't getting along, at least as far as he was concerned. She kept mailing him that confounding picture, making the lines of brown, gray, and blue, on top of the red foundation, taller and thicker, like stalks of an unidentifiable species. Even Sal Luccino, to whom Davy showed the picture in something like desperation, couldn't figure it out. "You got me," Sal said, handing the drawing back to Davy and then handing him an ice cream. "But why not ask Lenny Bagel?" Sal said. "He knows everything."

This idea pleased Davy, and though Lenny Bagel was home, in his box with the other puppets, Davy instantly adopted his persona. "What the goddamn hell? You call that a *picture*?" Davy said, and as he turned from Sal he didn't walk home so much as shuffle, for it was old news already that Lenny Bagel was exhausted from his life of work, work, and more work.

For a whole three days that week Nina didn't read a book. She'd finished the Lincoln biography. I happened to be reading a pile of *Archie* comic books I'd borrowed from my friend Anna Weiss, which I suggested Nina might like to share. To my delight she agreed. And so on Monday, Tuesday, and Wednesday we read those comics on the porch after breakfast, at the beach at midday while deepening our tans, and just before sleep while side by side in the sofa bed. Something about the comics, though they weren't exactly hilarious, loosened her up, made her laugh. And the more she did, I did too, in a kind of helpless, hysterical simpatico.

By Thursday of that week we were done with the pile of comics, and before I knew it Nina had abandoned me for another serious book that her father had left with her. This one was called *Coming of Age in Samoa*. Of the author, anthropologist Margaret Mead, Leo had written, *Bravery: all by herself, only twenty-four years old, a mind as sharp as yours, Nina, and Mead goes halfway around the world to live the primitive life. What does she find there? Who does she come to know? Girls, just your age, Nina. But are they just like you?*

By bedtime Thursday night Nina had nearly finished the book. The focus on girls compelled her, and she'd not stopped reading, except to eat, the entire day.

"Are they?" I asked that night from my side of the sofa bed. "Are the Samoan girls just like you?"

"Reading my father's notes?" Nina answered, mildly irked. She held the book, her father's note tucked into its pages, close to her chest.

"Maybe."

"Maybe, Molly? Maybe?"

"Maybe, yes. Maybe, yes, I saw it on the bed. I'm sorry."

She nodded, accepting the apology.

"Well, are they?" I repeated.

"You want to read it yourself?"

"I'd rather hear it from you. Are the Samoan girls just like you?"

She stared at the living room ceiling. The floor creaked upstairs; my mother was getting ready for bed. So was Vivie. Bec had already left that day for New Haven and the sunporch off the far end of the living room seemed not only dark but sadly so.

Finally Nina answered. "I'd say they're more like *you.* They're easy. Relaxed. They're a bunch of Linda Bagels, those happy Samoan girls."

"I'm not so relaxed," I said, suddenly defensive of my personality, the same as my alter ego puppet, who was in fact relatively untroubled.

"Molly, it's a good thing," Nina said. "I wish I were more like you."

This was news. Hopeful, I asked, "You want to go to Sloppy Joe's tomorrow, get a ras-lime soda?" Just recently, Howard and Mark Fishbaum had gotten into the habit of going there with a gang of friends after dinner. They'd abandoned all the childishness of Sal Baby and his Good Humor truck. I was hoping to follow their lead.

"Oh, Molly," Nina answered, almost exasperated. She kicked her legs under the sheet and threw the book in the air then caught it. "I'd rather go to Samoa," she said. "I really would."

We were quiet then, Nina staring up at

the ceiling, and me staring at the book in her hands. There was a photograph of young Margaret Mead on the cover, dressed in native Samoan attire — a headband, a tiered skirt, a long beaded necklace — and standing between two smiling Samoan girls. "Are they always smiling?" I asked after a time. "Is that what you mean?"

"Let's put it this way, Molly. If we were in Samoa we'd probably lose our virginity about now — at my age I would, at least — and with an older man. A grown man. But not someone who wanted to marry me. The whole thing would be a kind of fling, and not a particularly big deal. The culture is relaxed about it." She paused then repeated the word *relaxed.* "And if we were Samoan," she continued, her voice suddenly but a whisper, "we might even have a special girl our own age to play around with — you know, to *sexually* play around with." Nina's eyebrows were raised as she turned my way. "It's not common, but it's possible. Can you imagine *that,* Molly?"

But she was way ahead of me. I couldn't imagine any of it. I answered by turning from the Samoan girls on the book's cover and slipping my head under my pillow. "They're not like me," I called into the pillow.

"Molly, I didn't mean they're like you sexually. I just meant they have a certain comfort with their lives, like you."

I lifted the pillow and blinked up at Nina. No one had ever used the word *sexually* in a sentence directed at me before.

Nina pressed on. "When the time comes, it's going to be easy," she assured me. She put the book on the floor by her side of the sofa bed and then slipped under the covers. We were face to face. "I didn't mean to upset you," she said quietly.

"That's a scary book," I told her. "Did your father really read it?"

"It's a wonderful book. And no, he got this one just for me. Other worlds," she then said, her voice soft, as if she were about to tell me a child's story. "Other ways, other possibilities."

And with that Nina's breath deepened, and I sensed soon enough that though she typically fell asleep after me, she was already pleasantly dreaming.

Since arriving back at Woodmont, Howard had taken Nelson's advice. He and Megan had talked each day, for a half hour or so, at the close of their shifts at Treat's. He'd begun to see her in the evenings too. On Tuesday he'd walked with her after their respective dinners from a mutual meeting point on Hillside Avenue the short distance to Sloppy Joe's. When they arrived he didn't see Mark and his other friends milling about outside the place as they often were, and so he suggested that they head inside. "Let's get something cold," he suggested.

He and Megan were just inside the door when he spotted Mark sitting in a booth with two other friends, Steve Gutterman and Jack Epstein. Jack had a sailboat too, a Lightning, and just the day before he and Steve had sailed alongside Mark and Howard in the direction of Long Island and back. The sail had the charged edge of a race, though no one acknowledged as much. Still, Howard was glad that Mark's Sailfish, with some careful tacking by Howard, had come ashore first. At that moment, noticing the three turn toward then quickly away from him and Megan, whom he knew they didn't think he should be with, the memory of winning that unofficial race gave him at least some confidence.

A hand on the small of Megan's back, Howard steered her toward the booth, where he introduced her to his friends. Mark was the only one to speak to her, offering a tentative "hey," before he, like Steve and Jack, took to sipping his drink with unnecessary focus. A crushing silence followed. Ordinarily Howard would have squeezed himself in on one side of the booth and suggested Megan take the other side, but none of the three signaled in any way that they join them.

"Looks good," Megan said, obviously speaking about the drinks.

Again, no one responded.

"Mark?" Howard said. "Mark?" He didn't know what he meant to ask him, but Mark's acquiescence to the silence surprised Howard. Mark wasn't just a friend, he was a best friend, and that meant they'd never betray each other. "Mark?" Howard repeated.

"It's okay," Megan said, and when Howard turned her way he saw that she was embarrassed, blushing. Her arms were crossed tightly over her white blouse and tiny drops of perspiration had formed over her top lip. When she nodded toward the door Howard returned his hand to the small of her back, ready to walk with her out of Sloppy Joe's.

But before he did he appealed once more to Mark. "For crying out loud, Mark," he said. "It's me. *Me.*"

"I know it's you," Mark answered, finally looking at Howard, but only at Howard. Megan, Howard sensed, must have felt she was shrinking away.

Howard threw his arm over Megan's shoulders, pulled her close, gave her a grin. "See you 'round," he told the three at the table. He continued holding Megan close as he walked out the door.

"I wasn't really thirsty," he told her when they stepped outside, beyond Sloppy Joe's.

"Me neither," she said with such sadness he was sorry he'd thought to bring her there.

They began walking, toward no place in particular.

"Where should we go?" Megan finally asked.

Together they looked behind them at the all-Jewish crowd still gathered at Sloppy Joe's. If they turned away from the water they'd end up in the Irish community of Woodmont's hills and their situation would be reversed — she'd be in, he'd be out — but not any better. Even the mixed crowd at Anchor Beach didn't offer a haven; they could be recognized there too easily and word could reach their respective homes.

"Where should we go?" Megan repeated, and this time when he put his hand on the small of her back, as if to steer her, he admitted to himself that he had no idea where they were going.

"I think we're going to have to leave

Woodmont," he finally said.

On Wednesday they planned to meet up at the eastern border of Woodmont, where they figured they'd be unlikely to encounter anyone they knew. During Howard's solitary trek toward the border, he sensed with each step that his life was changing. Inexplicably, he didn't miss his friends but only longed for the sight of Megan, her quick and open smile. When he finally joined Megan just past the little sign that read *Entering Woodmont on the Sound,* technically on West Haven soil but only inches from Woodmont, the two of them settled against a seawall that separated the shore from the road. For a time they sat quiet and exhausted, as if they'd walked a full day rather than just a small portion of the evening, and they stared at the water before them and then at the moon, a slender crescent set loose in the sky. Howard told her about Mark, what a good guy he really was — once you got to know him, he added, taking her hand — and her response was to nod but then say, "I don't know. I just don't know about that."

They grew quiet again for a time, though he still had her hand in his. They stared at the stars, which to Howard seemed as abundant and scattered as the freckles across Megan's face. As night settled around them, Howard felt a keen desire to kiss Megan, just as he'd done, several times in fact, the week before last. But he didn't give in to the feeling, didn't grab her waist and pull her close as in years past he'd done with other girls, the Francine Cohens and Cookie Susteins of yesteryear. Instead, he listened to Nelson's voice lodged in a competing compartment of his mind: "Don't be a stupid jerk." He heard his father's voice, too, a voice that bubbled up in his mind at moments throughout almost any day, a voice that was telling him right then, "Judaism is all about responsibility." And so he rose quickly, purportedly to grab a loose piece of shale and skim it over the water, but in reality to put some space between him and Megan. But he quickly tripped and fell in the sand. "Whoa!" he said, laughing, "I'm all out of whack," which caused Megan to reach out to him, grab his arm, pull him back beside her. When he toppled down they both laughed, and when the keen desire to kiss her returned, only seconds after he'd talked himself out of it, the voices began again, the uncle in his head, then the father in his head, until finally, his head actually aching, the desire to kiss Megan ebbed and he resumed with her a normal conversation.

By the time he got to Treat's the next day, at noon, the throbbing in his head had returned. I'm heartsick, he told himself sadly, as he lifted ears of corn to shuck, finally understanding as he ripped the leaves from the husks the full meaning of that term. Indeed, he was *dying* to see Megan. That's what was going on with all that pain. Something about her was actually killing him, he understood. He knew, too, the discomfort was connected to the battle that would surely ensue between himself and his parents should he tell them his girl, the one he was crazy for, was not Jewish. He'd be fighting not only his parents but everyone, each person in the entire universe of Woodmont, in the whole of Connecticut as well, even in the entire world.

Except, of course, for Nelson. He'd always seen his uncle as simply a quiet man, wonderful to him but otherwise quiet. But a man doesn't arm himself with a lifetime of Tootsie Rolls for no reason, was the beginning of a new thought for Howard, and he suddenly wished Nelson were there and he could ask him a thing or two about his past, something Nelson never went into, as if he had something to hide. This understanding and others had come to Howard since his

360

return that week from Middletown to Woodmont, since he was expected to show the judiciousness of an adult ("Don't be a stupid jerk"), and especially since he'd stood by Megan the other night at Sloppy Joe's. Yes, especially since then, something in him was awakening, which was a good thing, he knew, though it also made him sorry for the corollary understanding of how soundly he'd been asleep.

"Honey, honey," a customer, Mrs. Delmire, was now saying to him. "I'm going to need some fruit as well as that corn. Some peaches, some cherries. Maybe a pound each. When you're done with the corn, honey. Okay?"

Howard nodded. He rose from the crate he was sitting on and entered the maze of fruit, arranged in a multitude of cardboard baskets. Once he'd collected the fruit he placed it, bag by bag, on the scales beside the checkout counter where Megan was stationed. She looked pretty in her yellow cotton blouse with short sleeves and tiny buttons down the front. She nodded his way then did some quick figuring on a lined pad. Watching her, Howard smiled. This was what he'd been telling Nelson about: her good nature, her quick mind.

Once Mrs. Delmire had paid, Megan

turned to him. "Got a minute?" she asked brightly.

He nodded and she took his arm, leading him to the back of the produce stand where they could be alone. They stood beside a stack of empty wooden crates. She leaned her back against the wall of the shed and stood still for a moment, squinting as she looked at him. He stood before her, his arms crossed, his brow furrowed in a sudden bout of anxiety. Was he about to be a stupid jerk? Feeling a desire to reach for her he asked himself this, as if the answer were beyond his powers to determine. No, no, he then assured himself. He wasn't. He took a tiny step backward, away from Megan.

"I was wondering," she said, "if maybe tonight we could go even farther into West Haven. Get away from all this." She looked around her as if speaking of the fruit and vegetables, but he knew she was thinking of the way they couldn't be a couple in Woodmont. In all probability West Haven was no different from Woodmont, at least when you got to know it, he figured, but he decided not to say as much. Instead he watched as Megan bent her right leg, placing her foot on the wall behind her. Her yellow blouse opened slightly at the neck.

"Sounds good," he answered, his arms still

crossed, his head now throbbing insistently. "But we have a family dinner tonight," he then added, remembering that in lieu of his father, who was still away, he'd be at the head of the table. "It's Friday," he explained to Megan. "So I'll be a little later than usual. Eight thirty okay?"

She nodded. She dropped her foot and stood upright, her back no longer on the wall. For some reason she looked down. His eyes followed her gaze. As she gradually raised her head he raised his, and the next thing he knew they were standing but a foot apart, looking directly into each other's eyes. His stomach felt empty and a sharp pang of hunger startled him. He almost felt woozy from it. She took a tiny step his way, so tiny it was something he sensed more than saw. His arms fell to his sides. When he next looked her way her arms were lifting, like birds, up and off of her body; they were reaching toward him and his arms rose as well and met hers. Their hands locked first, but soon they were embracing. He couldn't figure out how, exactly, this had happened, but there he was, against what he knew was his better judgment, engaged in his first long kiss with Megan — so different from the short, tentative ones they'd shared before. When the hunger he'd just felt returned, almost knocking him sideways, he pulled her closer to him, then closer again, as if she were ballast against this stunning force. Briefly he opened his eyes, curious if he could actually see himself kissing Megan O'Donnell. A part of him wanted the confirmation of knowing that this moment was, in an objective sense, real, and not a piece of the many fantasies he'd been so unsuccessfully suppressing. But her freckled forehead was all he could take in, that and the brightness of the sun glaring from behind her, and soon enough he closed his eyes, returned to the dark.

A few minutes later he was running, back to his neighborhood, his cottage, running, around corners, over curbs, fueled by the pleasure of that kiss. Bob Mathias, he dared to call himself, imagining as his the Olympic gold the young American had ultimately won. Racing straight for the beach, he collapsed when he reached its sands. The day was clear, the sky an extraordinary blue. No one was around. Friday, late afternoon, and the world of Bagel Beach had packed up, gone inside to prepare for Shabbos. But there Howard was. Singular. On his own.

I can do this, he told himself.

Then he looked around again, eager to

find at least one other person with him.

A moment later he heard his name being called, and when he looked behind him he saw Davy approaching, throwing a rubber ball and swinging a miniature bat. Wouldn't Howard come play with him? Davy yelled. "Hey, hey hey," he called insistently.

What a squirt he was, Howard thought, lifting himself upright and sauntering down to where the sand was hard from the water but not so wet a person would sink. Davy caught up to him and threw the ball his way, then stood some distance from him, bent forward, at bat. Howard gave a toss and Davy whacked the thing soundly. The ball traveled high into the blue of the day and the two stood nearly side by side, heads tilted upward, feet turning to follow the ball's trajectory.

"Got it," Howard called, only to be surprised when Davy countered, "Nope, I got it." The two of them were in a battle then to make the catch, and they rushed forward into the water, where the ball was now falling. Just as Davy jumped high, Howard jumped higher and clenched the ball with one hand. At the same time he pushed down on Davy's head, causing him to go under, and when Davy recovered, shaking the water from his face and still calling, absurdly, "I got it, I got it," the two lunged at each other and Howard released the ball so he could reach for Davy. As Howard grabbed him, he was thinking of Megan, of how smooth her skin had felt. Howard was still wearing his work pants, which didn't make sense, but he didn't care; he stayed where he was, teasing Davy, lifting him over his head, telling him he'd better watch it, he was going to throw him well past the horizon, and with those words Bob Mathias came to mind again, his strength, his endurance, his age, exactly Howard's, just two months out of high school and life for them both — at least right then — something golden, golden.

The brothers raced out of the water and began chasing each other along the shore, Davy in pursuit until Howard stopped in his tracks, turned, and charged at Davy, who then jumped and screamed before setting off as if for his life.

Mark Fishbaum then arrived, clad in bathing trunks and carrying several towels. "Come on," he said to Howard, cutting off the chase. "Let's get a quick one in before it's too late."

They hadn't seen each other since the night at Sloppy Joe's. Howard stood still, his arms crossed, his breathing heavy.

"You coming?" Mark asked.

"I don't know," Howard told him. "We have to talk."

"Talk?"

"I thought you were my friend, Mark."

The two stared at the ground rather than at each other. Howard dug his toes deep into the sand.

"I *am* your friend," Mark said. "I just don't want you to do something that gets your head chopped off."

Howard stared past Mark at the cottages behind him, then at the hills rising beyond. "You know me," he said, his gaze back on Mark. "I'll just grow another one."

But then Davy ran to them and Howard didn't want to say anything more. He nodded Mark's way, the gesture an assent to go with him.

They carried the Sailfish to the water and within minutes had the boat rigged and ready to launch. Davy had stood by them the whole while, holding a loose line when necessary, offering a hand as the sail went up.

As Howard and Mark walked the boat out a ways, Davy began following them.

"Where you going?" Howard asked, turning back to Davy.

"Can't I come?" Davy asked.

"Not today, buddy. Got some things to talk to Mark about." Howard looked at Mark, who shrugged. "Besides, Davy, this is going to take a while," he said. "I'll take you on a better ride tomorrow."

"I can't come?"

"Not today."

"How come I can't come?"

"Come on, now. I just told you. Now get going. I think I see Mommy. There she is. She's waving."

Davy turned and in just that moment Howard and Mark set off. Of course Ada wasn't there. When Davy turned back he jumped up and down in the water. "Liar!" he called, and then, more desperately, "I wanted to come too! I helped!"

In a moment, though, Davy had stopped the pleading and jumping and had begun a slow retreat out of the water. As the youngest kid he was used to being picked up and put down; that's what was always happening to him, or so it seemed to Howard as he looked shoreward, toward the little brother who now turned back toward the boat to offer one more wave good-bye.

"Listen," Howard yelled toward him. "I'm going to take you for a ride tomorrow. A long one. You hear?"

Seated beside him, Mark said, "Two heads. That's like having two lives, Howard. You ready for two lives?"

But Mark was wrong, he knew. It was one life. His life. He was about to tell Mark that when he turned shoreward once again and there was Davy, standing where the waves hit the sand, picking up stones and skimming them across the water's surface, and weirdly enough Howard saw in Davy something of himself, the kid self that in just those last days was feeling about a million years away. Two lives: then and now. Maybe Mark was right. "Ready enough," Howard told his friend, his voice heavy, his hand unsteady on the tiller. "Hey!" he then called behind him to the ever-shrinking image of Davy, but just as he did the Sailfish caught a breeze, the movement of the boat picked up, and the little boy on the shore, bending now to gather more stones, could no longer hear him.

11
ANYTHING LEFT TO GIVE

A year after Davy died Howard began classes at Wesleyan University. And he continued, by choice, working at the store. It was clear to us all that he was willfully exhausting himself. Sometimes I would come into the store at six in the evening and there he'd be, helping his umpteenth customer of the day, bending low as he measured a foot for a shoe size, or reaching for some obscure appliance, or selecting yet another pair of women's gloves for a fussy customer. He had a kind of walk when he was tired, a kind of shuffle, just like our grandfather Zelik Leibritsky, who'd acquired his signature gait when he was young, peddling still from a cart, and could barely stand up after a long day of sharpening knives, selling pots and pans, and enduring the weather. When I saw Howard like that I could see him the day Davy was hit by Sal's truck, after Howard had fallen from the Sailfish into the water. Hearing our mother's screams he chose not to get back on the boat after he had fallen overboard, believing that swimming the eighty yards to shore would be faster. Then he ran another thirty yards up the beach and to us, on the street. When he got to the accident scene he fell to his knees with anguish and fatigue; still, he reached under Sal's truck to touch our brother's head. He always felt that if he'd arrived two or three minutes earlier things would have been different. As it was he stayed there, prone, sobbing though he didn't realize it, all the while straining to comfort Davy, until a policeman dragged him away.

He didn't date Megan O'Donnell for long. He dropped her as soon as Davy died. Howard and Megan were young, of course, and the duration of their relationship might very well have been circumscribed regardless of the summer's tragic events. Then again, they might have persevered inasmuch as Howard's connection to Megan was drawing forth qualities from within him he didn't know he had: a will of his own, greater sensitivity. As it turned out, though, he saw her only once after Davy's death, on a day trip to Woodmont from Middletown a week or so after Davy's funeral, a trip to gather some odds and ends left behind, and he was as cold to her, as rejecting, as Mark Fishbaum, Steve Gutterman, and Jack Epstein had been at Sloppy Joe's.

"Howard?" she said. "Howard?" She'd come to the cottage and stood on the porch, holding a filled cookie tin, which, because he wouldn't take it from her hands, she'd finally thrust his way, forcing him to reflexively grab it. The moment before she'd told him how very sorry she was about the loss of his little brother. She'd said the words carefully, as if she'd rehearsed them, but her voice trembled with the gravity of the message nonetheless. She'd bitten her lower lip upon their utterance but otherwise stood there, more or less composed, staring at him with a concerned, compassionate expression. But in the face of his silence — a thick fog of silence that encased him, held him captive — her words became anxious, even frantic. "Howard? Howard, it's me," she pleaded at last, the same thing, though she didn't realize it, that Howard had said to Mark Fishbaum.

If he could have he would have said to her, "That was self-indulgent, wasn't it?" speaking of their time together, the walks, the talking, the many kisses. "I was a stupid jerk," he would have said, not meaning to hurt her, but rather to inform her of what had become to him in the last week such an obvious, even glaring truth. But he was too choked up to speak. Cookie tin in hand, he nodded, went back inside.

She wrote him several letters that fall from her home in Cheshire to his in Middletown. Because of the Cheshire return address I knew they were from Megan, though she didn't write her name on the envelopes. She must have known that our parents would have disapproved of her presence, even by mail, in our home. Howard opened the letters, read them, and stacked them neatly on his bedroom dresser. Once, a silent evening in early October, I spotted him in his room, sitting on his bed, a pad and pencil on his lap, the pile of letters beside him. But he wasn't writing anything down. He was simply staring ahead at his bedroom wall, his gaze unfocused as if he were dreaming. Then he blinked awake. Upon doing so he ripped free the top page of the pad — apparently he'd begun a letter — crumpled the paper, and hurled it into the wastebasket.

"Take them, Molly," he called to me, rising. From his doorway he handed me the letters.

"What for?" I asked. I didn't dare take

them; they seemed too personal.

"Hide them from me," he said.

"You mean throw them out?" I still wouldn't reach for them.

"No. I mean hide them. But don't throw them out, okay?" He thrust them at me and reluctantly I took them, placing them in a corner of my closet. When I asked him some months later if he wanted them back he looked at me surprised, as if he'd entirely forgotten them. Megan hadn't written another one. He hadn't heard from her in five months.

He sighed. The five months had changed him; he was quieter, more considerate in some ways — he rarely barked at me, for example — but he was also more tense, his forehead almost always furrowed in worry. He was older, it seemed, by a whole five years. "Just throw them out," he said.

"Shouldn't you?" I asked.

"Look, it's just better if I don't see them again," he said, and I nodded, though secretly I wished he would take them back, as if in doing so he'd return in some small way to the person he'd refused to be since Davy's death: sarcastic, bossy, but so much more alive. But Howard was resolute, and that night after dinner I pulled the letters from my closet and dropped them into our kitchen garbage, which got taken out each night. I thought it was best that, if this was the way Howard wanted it, the letters go quickly into oblivion rather than linger in some upstairs wastebasket. And in this way I was just a tiny bit complicit in how Howard freed himself of Megan O'Donnell for all time, except, of course, what he managed to carry with him in his memory. Whatever that was, though, he chose never to speak of it.

The first year following Davy's death there was a long period in which Howard, Nina, and I stayed apart: Nina (when not at school) in her Middletown home five miles from ours, Howard (with his deferral from entering college) at work with my father at the store, and me (when not at school) at home, standing alongside either my mother or Bec in the kitchen, or sitting next to one or both of them in what was mostly in those days a darkened living room.

But something changed that second year when Howard returned to his studies. We three had each stayed so close to our respective parents in the wake of things, had practically attached ourselves to them like we'd been when we were so much younger, only this new attachment, at least Howard's and mine, was less for our sake than for them. But with the start of college, Howard was the first of us to gain just a little of his own life back.

It was the beginning of his sophomore year in the fall of 1950, which coincided with Nina's last year of high school, when the three of us began to meet together, about once weekly, on the Wesleyan campus. Nina, who could drive by then and was encouraged to do so by Leo, who gave her access to his car, a more rickety Dodge than ours, would initiate these meetings by driving to my home to get me. From there we'd leave the Dodge behind and leisurely walk the remaining distance toward High Street, past a lineup of houses, to where the open green of the campus began. We'd climb the hill of the green toward a series of imposing brownstone buildings at the heart of the campus, where we'd settle ourselves next to Judd Hall, where science classes were held. "I'd like to go here," Nina said on more than one of those afternoons, leaning her back against the brownstone wall as she did, but of course that was impossible. The place was for boys only.

Howard would have gotten the message that we'd be coming from me. Nina would have telephoned me the night before, not to talk in a general way, but to set the time and to have the message passed on to Howard the next morning at breakfast that we'd meet him, if he wanted to meet us. The tension between Howard and Nina was still there, an alive thing, and all the more so with its key place in the unfolding of events the day of Davy's accident, and it was easier if I served as a go-between. But in fact they wanted, even needed, to see each other — to try to mend what had finally broken between them. The whole matter, then, was an attempt at healing, I suppose, all that near-silent sitting we did on the grass beside Judd Hall, or sometimes when it snowed on the worn, iced-over steps of the place. When Nina asked to see him, Howard never said no.

Sometime during the course of that year Howard took up smoking cigarettes. And sometime during that year he began passing his lit cigarette — always a Lucky Strike — to Nina, who would take it, hold it between her fingers, watch the smoke rise from its lit end and curl into the air, and finally take a hasty drag on it before handing it over to Howard. Back and forth the cigarette went between them, and it seemed to me they were communicating with each other through the plumes of smoke they blew from that same burning stick. One day midwinter, shivering from the cold and from our inactivity, I asked if I could please have a smoke too.

"Oh, no, Molly," they both replied in near unison, their voices carrying the same protective concern for me, the same nearly parental sense of caution. Then, still in an unplanned coordination with each other, they reached for me, Howard to punch me lightly and affectionately on the shoulder, Nina to quickly wrap her arm around me. But it wasn't me they were protecting, I knew, it was Davy, or the idea of Davy. They both felt entirely responsible for his death.

Weeks passed. Spring was just breaking through, tulips and irises had blossomed, grass was being mowed, when one day, our backs against Judd Hall, Howard mentioned that this semester he'd spent most of his time right there, inside the very building we were leaning against.

"What do you mean?" Nina asked, provoked by the idea that Howard had taken up an interest in the sciences, which were more or less her exclusive terrain.

"Premed," Howard said, looking straight ahead of him rather than at either Nina or me.

Nina smirked and I knew it was at the

thought of Howard actually having academic ambitions. I was surprised, too, as Howard was by far the store's best salesman. In the year when he was working there full-time, sales had gone up by some measure, and everyone knew this was Howard's doing, despite his grief. It seemed inevitable that one day he'd run the store.

Howard saw Nina's skepticism. "What's it to you, pimple face?" he responded, his voice reverting in an instant to the cutting one from before Davy's death.

Nina's complexion was a clear one, skin to be admired, but she raised her hand to hide her face anyway. Then she rose to her feet, crossed her arms over her chest, and loped away from Judd Hall. And, as if out of nowhere, there it was again, the old rivalry between them, the one that had lain dormant, as if snowed over, for so many months.

But Nina stopped, paused, turned slowly around, and a moment later sat down once again on the grass. "Premed," she said, calmly enough.

When Howard explained that as a doctor he just might save a kid's life, Nina nodded encouragingly. With an honesty I wasn't prepared for, Howard added, "Premed. It's not like I'm good at it or anything" — which was the same thing he'd say in many a letter to Nina in the years that followed.

At first, once Nina left for college, she and Howard communicated rarely — a birthday card perfunctorily sent every other year or so. But fifteen years later, in May of 1966, Howard attended a meeting of the American Academy of Pediatrics, which that year was being held in San Francisco, a stone's throw from Berkeley, where Nina then lived. Howard had, after much struggling, become a doctor.

"I was a fool. You don't know how many letters I've written over the years wanting to apologize for how I treated you," he told Nina. Earlier in the evening they'd eaten dinner at the conference hotel and then decided to drive to the nearest beach. They were standing beside Nina's car, looking at the Pacific. It would be another hour, at least, before dark.

"That sounds like a dying man's confession, Howard," Nina responded.

"Not dying. I've matured. That's all." He leaned her way and for the first time ever put an arm over her shoulders, a gesture that made them both, at first, quietly laugh. After that visit they corresponded at an unfailing rate of a letter a week.

At Wesleyan that day, after Nina had

rejoined us, she turned to Howard and reached for the Lucky Strike. Howard inhaled one more time, with deliberate slowness, forcing her to wait, but soon enough passed it on, and with that gesture — a kind of offering — the competition between them ended.

By the time he entered medical school in Boston, Howard looked like a different man: slightly overweight, tired, his dark hair already threaded with gray. But our parents were proud of the fact that he was making something of himself, something surprisingly grand, as they saw it.

Marjorie Blumfield was the girl they picked for him. Consumed with the studies that remained so difficult for him, Howard hadn't dated seriously, or even much at all, during college or medical school, and finally his last year there my mother put her foot down. "We don't want a son who's a lousy monk," she said, by way of introducing the subject of his getting married.

Marjorie was the daughter of a friend of a friend, someone my father had heard about at morning minyan. She was a senior at Wellesley College, Jewish, and very much wanting to settle down just as soon as she graduated. "By all accounts she's a good girl," my father told Howard, who nodded and then agreed to the Shabbos dinner my parents suggested as a means of bringing the two together.

The night of her arrival, in early April of 1957, I helped my mother prepare the meal. I then washed my hair before dinner and quickly set it, as if I too had something at stake in meeting Marjorie Blumfield. There was a feeling of desperation about this meal, as if it were a make-or-break moment; I had gotten that sense from my mother, who called Vivie several times during the week prior to it to get ideas for more elegant food to prepare than she'd normally make. Like my mother, I didn't want to provide any reason to put Marjorie off, or her parents. It occurred to me that Howard, who was clearly punishing himself with his ill-suited studies and his unnatural social austerity, had suffered enough; I wished him well.

Marjorie Blumfield was not pretty, though not unattractive either. She was short, slight, and wore a significant amount of jewelry, bracelets that rattled whenever she lifted her arms, delicate pearls around her neck. Her nails were painted the precise shade of red of her lipstick, and her hair was styled into a smooth, brushed-under bob. When asked by Howard what she'd studied at college she answered, giggling, "Oh, every-thing." That night she giggled often through-out the meal, particularly so when, later in the evening, as my mother and I cleared dishes, Howard described his plans to return from Boston to set up a pediatric practice. He answered her laughter with a befuddled glance. But I understood. "She thinks she's won the lottery," I told my mother, angrily, in the kitchen.

The meal was winding down, our dessert and coffee had been consumed, when Mar-jorie's giggles ceased at last. For a moment she looked worried, glancing at her parents, signaling them to do something, and her father began questioning Howard about his more immediate plans, such as those for next week's Shabbos. "I wonder what's up?" was how Marjorie's father put it as he adjusted the knot of his tie.

Howard turned to Marjorie and, to our surprise, asked her if she'd like to join us next week, even though this meant another two-hour drive for him from Boston to Mid-dletown and then back again. Oddly, he didn't look at her when he spoke but rather stared past her, at our father, who sat silently at the end of the table, nodding at the question, as if Mort were the one Howard had just asked to Shabbos dinner and the answer was a resounding, happy yes.

The last time I saw Howard, two months before his death at forty-one of a heart attack, a loss that left my parents for a second time without a son, it was at a family dinner at my parents'. Howard had seemed so much older than he was — his hair, what was left of it, a solid gray, his back slouched, his stomach protruding in a way that took me by surprise, reminding me of our uncle Nelson. Howard had been married to Marjorie for nearly fourteen years, and they had two girls. Though I didn't see Howard often — in our adult lives we stayed as separate as in that first year following Davy's death — I'd heard plenty about his medical practice; he was known for his extraordinary care with children, his gentleness, and the time he gave to both the kids and their parents.

That evening, as we quietly ate our mother's food, Howard looked worn out, his eyes heavy, his face drawn, and I was worried for him. But then I got busy again with my own life, my bland career at G. Fox & Co., a department store in Hartford, where I was a buyer of women's clothing. Since my divorce from Mark Fishbaum five years before, the job was like a cave I'd come to live in. Off duty and I'd blink at the brightness of a world I barely knew. By the time I got the call two months later that Howard was dead, I was wholly preoccupied, as I so often was, with the minutiae of hose, bras, and underwear.

At Howard's burial, staring at my devastated parents and then at Howard's grave, all I could think of was how he'd been determined since Davy's death never to make another mistake, never to displease our parents.

"But you never made a mistake," I once told him. Howard was a senior in college then, still living at home, already committed to medical school though his natural talents lay so much in the business of the store. Almost five years had gone by since Davy's death. I was seventeen, still stupid about so many things, but this much I understood: "Howard, nothing that happened was your fault."

"It was all my fault," he answered, his voice steady, his conviction unshakable, his body, though seated, tense and pumped with adrenaline, as if it were still that day five years ago and he were in the water swimming toward us while Mark Fishbaum — sailing behind him, then beside him, and then ahead of him — brought the Sailfish onto shore.

For years Nina had nightmares about Davy's death, though she wasn't actually there at the accident scene. Nevertheless, she woke in the night screaming, seeing the events — the particular stretch of Beach Avenue, the ice cream truck, the blue sky, Davy's body up and running then down and broken — as if the whole thing had unfolded right before her. That was why she couldn't imagine coming back to Woodmont the summer following the death when Bec called, asking Vivie, along with Nina, to join me, Bec, and my mother there. "It isn't possible," Vivie had said simply enough, speaking for Nina. Vivie had taken to speaking for Nina often that year, as Nina had no words for what ailed her, left her bedridden on many a weekend, left her spacey and languid at school. For the first time her grades weren't stellar, but they were good enough for her to pass each class.

To put distance between herself and the nightmares, she chose to attend the University of California at Berkeley. For a time she was content, her engagement with academics bringing her back to life. Her second semester there she had a romance, too, her first, with a boy from Santa Monica named Rick. But Connecticut and the summer of 1948 were always there in her mind, and before long she broke it off with him. Happiness, Nina felt, was not hers to have.

But then she met Estelle Casey. Nina had just begun a Ph.D. program to focus on biological anthropology (which according to Leo was like putting the minds of her two long-held heroes Charles Darwin and Margaret Mead into a Waring blender and pushing "go"). Estelle Casey was one of Nina's professors and Nina was Estelle's prodigy, her best student, the one with pressing questions for Estelle after class, the one who quickly became her research assistant. Throughout the autumn of 1954, shocked by her attraction, Nina wished it wasn't so. Her sexual inclination, the true one that, since she was fifteen and just gaining an awareness of, she'd barely allowed herself to feel, shamed her. She tried to hold her feelings at bay, but in Estelle's presence, staring at her bright eyes and intelligent face, she could hold them back no better than a sky filled with ever-darkening clouds could hold back the inevitability of rain. For some months Nina found a twisted reconciliation with her feelings by calling Estelle "Eddie," at least in her mind. Once she even mentioned "Eddie" in a call home to Vivie, who she knew so desperately wanted her to feel loved. "I love Eddie," she told her mother. "But the thing is, I don't know if Eddie loves me."

She knew the neighborhood in which Estelle lived, and on weekends during those first months of working for her she began to go there, stopping at a bakery for some bread she didn't need, drinking cup after cup of coffee at a small café. But in over a dozen such trips she never bumped into Estelle, and it occurred to Nina upon her return from each journey that if she actually met Estelle by chance, as she dreamed of, she'd not live through the encounter. The mere sight of Estelle Casey — her tall frame, her colorful fringed scarves draping over her shoulders, her nearly pitch-black hair — would surely knock Nina dead.

It would be a feat, therefore, to survive an entire dinner with Estelle, but upon Estelle's insisting that she and Nina eat together to celebrate the publication of Estelle's first book, Nina did just that. Nina had contributed to the last year of work on that book, one for which Estelle held out hopes of becoming notable in the field. In it she'd synthesized the latest research, including her own, on the physiological changes in primates once they became bipedal. The foot, for example, had gone from a grasping agent, more like a hand, to something that supported a body's weight. "Enjoy every walk," Estelle often told Nina over the long months of editing and fact-checking, of hours spent side by side in Estelle's office, and she said it again, almost giddily, that night at dinner as they talked in Estelle's kitchen, a small room with an oak table pushed against one of its walls and a single lit candle at the table's center. Estelle sat at one end of the table and Nina catty-corner to her. They'd touched knees already, though only by accident. Still, Nina couldn't lift her glass of wine for fear of its trembling in her hands. "Enjoy every walk," Estelle breezily said, to which Nina nodded and replied, the follow-up by then rote, "because it was long in the making."

Everything in human evolution was long in the making — the opposable thumb, the human brain, the dual curvature of the human spine. Dinner with Estelle Casey, too, was long in the making, Nina thought to herself as she sat, watching Estelle butter a second slice of bread, hoping she wouldn't notice that Nina couldn't manage more than a few bites of food.

But Estelle did notice. "Not so hungry?"

she asked.

Nina had been in love with Estelle for eight months. Before that she'd been purposefully alone, avoiding happiness, for close to five years. "Starved," Nina answered.

They touched knees again, this time on purpose, this time Estelle tapping Nina in a way that signaled she knew what she meant. They held hands. They gazed at each other, a protracted look, and Estelle smiled gently, kindly, when Nina began to blink back tears.

"It's okay," Estelle said. "Really, it is." She leaned toward Nina and kissed her cheek. Then Estelle stroked Nina's face: her chin, hair, lips. She kissed her again, more intimately. After several minutes, Nina dared to kiss back.

Estelle pulled away and took a sip of wine. "Ready?" she said, looking at Nina.

"For what?" Nina asked, her hand pressed to her mouth where her lips felt new to her.

"A walk," Estelle told her, gently, whispering the words, "to bed. Upstairs."

There were detriments to the bipedal physiological structure as well as benefits. Arthritis, for example, was a sorry cost, one that, depending on the weather, affected Estelle Casey, caused her back and hips to throb, though she was only thirty-two. "I try to take the long view when it comes to my aches and pains," she explained to Nina one morning, three months into their love affair. Just the week before, Nina had moved in with Estelle. "I try to take the long view — we've been upright for only what, four million years? But then a day like this rolls around," Estelle said, glancing out a window. A rainstorm had begun overnight and the day was determinedly gray. "My damn back," she groaned at last, giving in to it.

They spent that day, a Sunday, in bed, not making love as they'd done the evening before, but simply lying next to each other, Nina rubbing Estelle's back from time to time. They read. Eventually they napped. By midday they were restless, though, and, finally dressed, they grabbed a pair of umbrellas and hit the sidewalks of Berkeley. They walked miles, barely talking, but Nina understood that this silence, comfortable between them, was not to be feared. Because of the rain, the university campus, which they eventually arrived at, was less populated than usual. Over several minutes only a few students entered the library's door. Something about the emptiness touched Nina. "The whole place looks beautiful today. Like a beautiful world," she said, taking Estelle's hand, briefly, as they paused to look around. A moment later Estelle pulled her hand back out of a sense of caution that Nina knew wasn't personal. "Beautiful, yes. But even here, almost a home, not our world," Estelle said.

From Vivie Nina had learned a thing or two about cooking, and that night Nina made minestrone and Vivie's beloved cinnamon muffins. Estelle and Nina ate in the living room, where Nina kept a small but steady fire going. If Estelle's back still ached she didn't complain. Nor did she complain over the following weeks and months as the two settled into a routine of living together. In one of her weekly calls home Nina told Vivie, "Eddie loves your food." Responding to Vivie's question about the state of Nina's happiness, she answered, simply enough, "Very."

She was so very happy, in fact, that when she first met the pair of brothers who delivered the morning paper — one eight and the other ten, they'd told her — she didn't make any connection between them and Davy. They were just two determined little boys and she took to tipping them generously, twenty-five percent, when they came by on Tuesday afternoons to collect payment for the week's papers. But two weeks after describing her joy to her mother, Nina answered the doorbell to find that it was just the one brother, suddenly, collecting the week's payment. She asked about the missing one, the older brother, and was told he was sick. "What's your name?" she asked the eight-year-old. "Teddie," he said, and then he thanked her when she tipped him, this time thirty percent. The next week and the week after Teddie came collecting by himself. "How's your brother?" she asked the third Tuesday that Teddie appeared solo. Her tip this time was fifty percent. The boy only looked at his feet.

For some weeks after that no one came to collect money for the newspaper, though the paper itself was delivered on time each morning. During those weeks Nina began to worry about Teddie and his ill brother, and she'd spend late Tuesday afternoons at the living room window looking for the boy, longing for him and planning, should he arrive, to tip him sixty percent. By then her dreams of Woodmont had resurfaced. When Vivie called and asked if she was as happy as always, Nina answered, "I shouldn't be. I know I shouldn't be."

She thought that way even after the doorbell rang the following Tuesday and there was Teddie along with Alfred, his older brother. Apart from being paler than before, Alfred looked well. Teddie made sure to introduce him. "She likes us," Teddie told Alfred while smiling at Nina. "You have no idea how much you mean to me," Nina almost responded. But she didn't. She simply sent them off after tipping them one hundred percent.

That night Estelle complained that she was having one of her bad days. At dinner she spun her spaghetti rather than ate it, and moaned as she shifted in her chair, searching for comfort. "I need to lie down," she finally said, offering Nina an apology by way of a weak smile. Before she left the kitchen she paused to kiss Nina, her long scarf unraveling onto Nina as she did. Holding the ends of the scarf, Nina kept Estelle close for a moment beyond the kiss. Then, Estelle gone, Nina began slamming pots and pans, an imitation of anger. She'd seen her mother do this on more than one occasion as a way to get her father's attention when his head was too long in a book. But Nina saw too that Vivie would quickly regret doing so and stop.

"What's the matter?" Estelle asked, having risen from bed and returned downstairs.

"You think it's fun living with a goddamned invalid?" Nina almost asked Estelle.

Goddamned invalid. Her uncle Mort had called her father that the very day of Davy's accident. But Nina knew that even though the words, ones she'd practiced, would do the trick — smash the love she didn't deserve — she couldn't bring herself to use them. Instead she said, "This isn't working."

"Really?" Estelle asked, startled. She took a step toward Nina, who, backing away, knocked over a chair.

"Why don't you go back to bed?" she told Estelle, her tone of voice deliberately piqued and hostile. That she was good at this level of deception amazed her. She glanced dramatically at the ceiling as if seeing through it to the bedroom. "Why don't you?" she repeated.

But Estelle was too stunned to move. She finally righted the chair that Nina had knocked over and dropped into it. Eventually Nina sat down too. They were silent, elbows on the table, for nearly an hour.

"Really?" Estelle said at last, her eyes hurt, her upper body slumped over the table.

"Really," Nina answered, though this time she said the word quietly, even gently, her body aching and slumped, exactly like Estelle's.

■ ■ ■ ■

Three months after her breakup with Estelle, Nina went back to Connecticut. Her father was ill. Her mother had been trying to hide it from her but Nina had finally overheard him in the background of one of her weekly calls home. "Tell her I'm fine," Leo had said to Vivie. "I'm coming home," Nina responded into the phone.

It was during the second week of her stay in Middletown, when her father, recovered, was back at work, that Nina went to the Jewish cemetery to visit Davy's grave. Early August, and three days of rain had given way at last to bouts of sunshine. Nina wore sunglasses and a silk scarf that Estelle had given her.

For a time she knelt by the grave, staring not so much at it as at the patch of grass at its base. Finally she reached for a stone and placed it on top of the grave, where several stones already lay. "I remember you," she said as she released the stone.

She rose and walked several paces, but before she'd reached her car she stopped and returned to the grave, dropping again to her knees and staring again at the ground, then finally reaching for another stone to place atop the grave.

Four times Nina rose and returned, knelt, and found a stone, until finally she managed to leave the graveyard.

Five months later, her life in Berkeley busy but lonely, Nina forced herself to marry. The man's name was Ed, which meant she didn't have to explain to her mother anything about her change of circumstances during any of her weekly calls leading up to her marriage. The ceremony was a simple one before a local justice of the peace. Her parents, who had taken their first plane ride to be there, were better dressed than Nina and Ed. Vivie wore a blue suit that Bec had made for the occasion and a new pair of white gloves. Around Leo's thin neck was a tie he'd acquired for the wedding, something just in at Leibritsky's. But she and Ed just wore trousers and sweaters. "Is that what you're wearing?" her mother asked, questioning her attire minutes before they left their apartment for the court. Nina nodded. "Good enough," she said. This was January of 1957, a sunny weekday afternoon, but unusually cold.

She finished her dissertation the first year of her marriage, and by the next year she was an assistant professor at Berkeley.

Estelle Casey had left to take a position in New York. Nina's husband, Ed Glass, a mathematician, was also hired at Berkeley that same year. And so the two were busy — too busy, to Nina's mind, to get bogged down in anything like the absence of true happiness, something she couldn't feel with Ed, though he was a good man, just a little remote and as confounding to her as his theoretical work, which, despite the range of her learning and curiosity, she couldn't bring herself to understand.

In the next years she and Ed had two children, Max and Russell, the first named in honor of her maternal grandfather, the second for her maternal grandmother, though naming a boy after a woman, she knew, was, in a traditional family like hers, risky stuff. Motherhood, though, was risky business altogether, a whole life suddenly and literally in her hands, and it was something Nina had never imagined until the babies were right there, one after the other, two chubby lumps of love who burped and spat and slept on her shoulder.

"It isn't fair," she once told Ed. They were standing in the doorway of their children's bedroom, watching the boys sleep. Ed, whose life before Nina had been a bubble of pure mathematics, seemed as amazed as she was to have become a parent. He hadn't so much pursued Nina as merely stood there while she'd hurled herself at him.

"What's not fair?" he asked.

"This much luck," she said, shaking her head.

But in fact the luck was tempered by many dreams of Estelle Casey and the less frequent but so much more violent Woodmont nightmare. For a time, then, she accepted it, this luck: motherhood, her fascinating growing boys, cooking and grocery shopping and cleaning for four, teaching and researching while all the rest was happening, Ed's occasional suggestion that she lie on top of him, rather than the other way around, in an attempt at more satisfying sex — all that and the private anguish that caught up to her in her sleep.

The boys were four and six when, on a walk to their favorite park one June day, Nina saw the tall, slender figure of a woman approaching, one who, with her dark hair and colorful scarf, looked so very much like Estelle Casey. Nina gripped each boy's hand and signaled to them to stop. She needed a rest, she explained, straining her eyes to better see the woman. It had been almost ten years since Nina had smashed her life with Estelle, and there were many times during those years that she considered attending one of the professional conferences at which she knew Estelle had become a favorite speaker. There, sitting anonymously in a crowded auditorium, she could look at her. That's all she wanted to do, she told herself: look and look and look.

Max tugged at her arm. "Mommy, what's wrong?" he asked.

"Mommy's seeing ghosts," she answered, still scanning the distance. Then she bent toward Max's questioning face. "Just kidding," she said. She loosened her tight grip and the three commenced walking.

She sat on a park bench while the boys took to the swings. Nervously, she nibbled a cookie from the bag she'd brought for the boys' treat. The woman was sitting not so far away on another park bench. Still, Nina couldn't be sure if it was Estelle or not. It certainly looked like her, but did she really know what Estelle looked like anymore? she wondered. She wanted to approach, but she was afraid. "Really?" Estelle might say to Nina, her voice as shocked and pain-ridden as it had been that day when Nina broke up with her out of the blue.

The boys had joined some other children and a group of five was now running together in jagged spurts, like a school of fish.

Only when one fell did the group stop, waiting until the child had successfully risen. Her younger boy, Russell, was the pack's slowest.

What she would do, she decided, was make a slow circle around the park's perimeter. At the closest corner this would bring her toward Estelle — if in fact it was Estelle — but not so close as to force an interaction. She could safely check the woman out.

It only took several steps to see that, yes, the woman was indeed Estelle Casey. Nina could identify her, despite the eyeglasses that Estelle had not worn before. She was reading. The children's squeals, increasingly rambunctious, didn't disturb her. Nina froze. Then she turned and began to retreat back to her bench. Then she froze again, torn between directions, the one toward Estelle and the one away from her, both of which she wanted to traverse at a run. In the middle of the playground Russell began to cry. And so it was in his direction that she finally rushed.

Nina was holding Russell in her arms, carrying him to the bench where she'd left the bag of cookies, when another woman approached Estelle. Nina watched as Estelle rose, opened her arms, and the two embraced. They did so just long enough and in such a way that Nina knew in an instant that this person was a lover, not a friend. Instinctively, Nina scanned the park, wondering if the other adults had noticed, but no one seemed to. Sensing that indifference, Nina shook her head. Never had she and Estelle dared to be as affectionate in public. Ten years, Nina told herself, and the world had changed in ways she had never dreamed of.

Oddly, she'd never imagined Estelle loving again. Instead she preferred to think she'd gone on to live a purely professional existence, as if in leaving her Nina had stolen Estelle's very capacity for love.

Stupid, she saw now. And self-serving. For they go on, the betrayed do. She was witnessing it right then as the women pulled apart, laughed, kicked their legs out like kids, laughed some more.

They go on to better people.

Just the sight of Estelle Casey, all those years later, marked Nina. In the weeks that followed something came to the surface, a repressed feeling, the dread of not loving the best she could, of not being who she really was. She loved her children with all her heart, but she loved her partner in life, Ed Glass, like she would anything that familiar, a couch, a favorite movie, a vista she would be happy enough to see though she wouldn't go out of her way to visit it.

I could die, Nina told herself at last. Then she concluded, just as Bec had so many years before: *No, no. Am already dead.*

That revelation came in July 1965, and in April of 1971 I saw Nina for the first time in fifteen years at Howard's funeral. Not since her trip to Davy's grave had she come back home. Nor had I, unlike Howard, ventured west. At thirty-eight she was still so pretty, but she looked pale and was ravaged with sorrow over Howard's death. I was too. That he and I weren't close in the last years didn't make any difference. The grief was as raw and overwhelming as when Davy had died, and in a way the pain seemed to be about Davy all over again, as much as about Howard. When I told Nina that she nodded. "I see a connection between their deaths too," she said. Then she took my hands in hers. "Come visit me, won't you, Molly?" she asked.

A month later I traveled to Berkeley. There Nina lived in a small stucco house with her two boys, scientists in the making. By this time she'd been divorced for five years and she had a new lover, a woman named

Sandra Pierce.

We were in her kitchen, painted the same pale green as the outside of her house. At the kitchen table we sipped coffee as Nina cautiously laid out the truth of her life for me. Staring more at the tabletop than at me, she blushed almost scarlet as she determinedly revealed herself, telling me first about Estelle, then Ed, and finally Sandra. She seemed compelled to do this telling, however uncomfortable it made her, or me. Other ways, other possibilities — I hadn't really thought about that in terms of Nina's sexuality, but there it was, made plain at last.

For a variety of reasons — maintaining custody of the kids being primary — she and Sandra didn't live together, Nina explained. Besides, she added, that would be too much happiness. "Can't have that," she said. "Makes me crazy."

"Too much happiness?" I asked, referring to the distance she purposefully kept from her lover, who lived only blocks away. "Would Davy really want you to be deprived?"

"You're not telling me anything my analyst hasn't told me for the last six years, Molly," she said.

My marriage to Mark Fishbaum had gone

south just when Nina's had with Ed, and we talked about that, too. My situation was easy enough to explain. I hadn't really loved Mark, I told Nina. Over time I realized that he'd just filled a hole in my life, the one created not only by Davy's death but also by everyone scattering in its aftermath. I wanted more from a relationship than just that. Being an only child, Mark had always wanted children, but I kept delaying, and in our fifth year I lied to him, telling him that I didn't want children and had never wanted children, thinking he might take that and leave. "Bingo," I said, and sighed.

Nina placed a hand on my shoulder. "I'm sorry it didn't work out, Molly," she said.

That was how our visit began — the catching up, the confessions of our confused adult lives — but we got busy soon enough. Each day Nina had a class to prepare for and teach, and meetings with students beyond that. Max and Russell, then eleven and nine, needed to be taken care of too. She was glad, she told me, for the extra help, and the third day of my visit, while I made toast and eggs for breakfast, there was a moment when Nina and I looked at each other, recognized our mothers in ourselves, and suddenly whooped with a kind of laughter reminiscent of theirs.

"I *get* it," Nina said, speaking of my mother's mood, which invariably lifted each summer in the company of her sisters.

"I get it too," I told Nina, speaking of Vivie, spatula held high, delighting, as I was just then, in feeding a whole clan. And a moment later, when Russell hopped onto my lap, I got it even more, though this time it was Bec's journey I'd segued into, the piece of it about not becoming a mother, and of how lovely it was — a holy moment — sitting there and holding a child.

Because of Nina's unyielding schedule I had toured the Bay Area largely on my own for the first days of my weeklong visit, but on Thursday I went with Nina to the Berkeley campus. The class she taught that day wowed her students. If the entire evolution of life — Big Bang to now — was likened to a single year, she explained to a packed auditorium, then mankind's appearance comes at about one thirty p.m. on December 31. At 11:59:59, the Renaissance begins. And with less than a second to go, everything else — the Enlightenment, modernity, life as we actually know it. "Feeling insignificant yet?" Nina quipped, and the class howled. I got the shivers.

When we left the auditorium a group of

five students followed us, each one pushing past the next, seeking an appointment with Nina. She had no openings that week, she explained, but then she met with two of them on the spot anyway. I waited over an hour in the hallway.

"Dr. Cohen?" yet another student asked just as we were about to leave. This student was a young woman, clearly distraught, her eyes dark with fatigue.

"Give me a few minutes, Molly, okay?" Nina asked, and back I went to the worn chair outside her office door, where I overheard Nina gently tell the student, "You'll survive this. You really will."

That evening after the boys were in bed, the house was silent. Nina was in her study, grading papers or preparing yet another class; I couldn't be sure. As I'd done before, I wandered through the house, looking at photos. Just outside Nina's study was a shot of her and Howard that day when they met for dinner after Howard's meeting with the Academy of Pediatrics. As they'd stood together, Howard's arm over Nina's shoulder for the first time, Nina had said, "Howard, I always felt that if I hadn't lied the day of the accident Davy would be alive. I can't shake it. The feeling's at the core of my being."

"Nina, that's just not true," Howard urged.

"You're not telling me anything my analyst hasn't told me for the last year," Nina said, and then they stood there, not talking further, for another five minutes.

Nina spotted me staring at the photo and called me in. Her study was crammed with books and papers. On one wall she'd hung up her various diplomas and I took to gawking at them — there were so many. But when I peered closer at an honorary doctorate from Georgetown University in Washington, D.C., I was confused to read that it was made out to Leo Cohen rather than to Nina.

"Oh, it's mine," Nina said. "But I thought he deserved it more than me so I had his name put on it. When I gave it to him he said he hadn't earned it and wouldn't take it." She paused to wipe a smudge from its glass frame. "It's pretty much what I'm most proud of, Molly."

She got back to work and I went to bed. At three in the morning I woke and rose to get some water. The light in Nina's study was on and she was talking on the phone. I'd been in Berkeley just shy of a week by then and I wasn't surprised to see that Nina was still up, still working, counseling someone — "You'll survive," I heard her say — giving of herself though it was late and the day had been long and there couldn't have been anything left to give.

12
NOT CHOCOLATE, NOT STRAWBERRY

Bec's kitchen contains a utility closet, a place to hide the ironing board, brooms, and mops, and yesterday, inspired by the pristine quality of the season's first snowfall, I found myself compelled to give the floors inside a good cleaning. To do that I opened the closet — for the first time ever. Quickly, though, I shut it. But a moment later I opened it again, more slowly, preparing myself as I did, for framed and hanging on the inside of the door was Davy's picture, the one he'd drawn with Lucinda Rossetti that summer of 1948. The pair had almost managed to finish it: a crayon-based lineup of vases containing flowers. That so many years ago Bec had taken it from our home was a new fact, a new moment to consider, and the thought of her forcing herself to face the drawing and all its associated memories each time she swept her floors or ironed a shirt gave me a chill. Then a rush of admiration. Then a chill. Then a rush of love.

It was still the second week in August 1948 — a week before the week we wished had never begun — when Davy understood at last what Lucinda Rossetti was getting at. The red on the bottom of the picture was a tabletop, or perhaps a counter, and the tubes emerging from it — one gray, one brown, and the other blue — were vases. Davy had finally grasped the idea when she began to draw stems and leaves where the vases would end, just about where Davy had colored the page a lighter sky blue. Holding the picture, he began a fit of ecstatic jumping.

"She had you worried there, huh?" Ada remarked, holding his chin in her palm as if this would calm him. It didn't. He squirmed from her grip and began jumping again. All of us were in the kitchen, unable to eat lunch with this eruption beside us.

"Take it outside," Ada warned, and when Davy only jumped more, she snapped, "Now!"

For a moment he looked stricken but then he dashed through the cottage and out the front door, where he took to prancing on the porch. "I get it!" he called over and over.

By this time Bec had planned the jacket she'd promised Davy and she'd made progress on dresses for the start of the school year for Nina and me. Long-sleeved and belted, mine was of checkered rayon and easily would be the best school dress I ever had. Nina liked hers, in a solid dusty rose, just as much. For Vivie and Ada — the two people Bec would miss the most — she'd embarked on more elaborate wear: the dresses they'd asked for were for the upcoming High Holidays. In recent days there were fittings, and after that seams were taken in and seams were ripped out. Half-made, one of the dresses hung over the body of the mannequin Eleanor Roosevelt, and the other hung from a hanger Bec had secured over the top of one of her porch's glass doors. My mother's dress was made of burgundy wool, the same color as the fancier dress Bec had made for Mrs. Coventry. The likeness pleased Ada no end. "I'm going to look fine," she whispered to herself every time she passed by Bec's sunporch. Vivie's dress was the same light wool, in dark green. She didn't say anything as she walked past the sunporch, but she often glanced at Eleanor, wearing that forest green, and then she'd purse her lips to form a silent, delighted "Oh!"

Because of rain and high winds, Howard and Mark Fishbaum sailed only once the second week of August, but by the third week — *the* week — they were back to their daily journeys. Out they'd go, in the direction of Long Island, or perhaps over toward West Haven, now a familiar run. And in they'd finally come again, a good hour and a half later, sometimes longer, pulling the Sailfish out of the shallow waters onto the shore, lowering its sail, lifting its mast, pulling free its rudder board and tiller, then finally lifting the naked hull of the boat and hauling it up the beach, well past where the waters rose at high tide. They'd often sit there in the hot sand beside the boat's hull, their bottoms atop the orange life preservers they'd carried on board, and they wouldn't talk so much as stare out at the waters they'd just navigated, as if that long ride hadn't been quite extensive enough to ponder the world that was unfolding, so nicely, before them. Their tans were remarkable by this time. Perhaps it was their futures, free of war, as open as the sea before them, that gave them such an endless sense of wonder. Perhaps it was the social life sure to unfold those evenings. By this time Howard had persuaded Mark to be, if not altogether accepting, than at least kind toward Megan O'Donnell.

"There was a bit of me that was jealous of you," Mark had even recently confessed.

"You were snubbing her and me because you were a jealous ass?"

"That's only ten percent of it. The rest was about the mess between Jews and Catholics. Howard, think about it. You really want that mess?"

Wednesday evening of that third week in August, and just before supper Nina yelled for me from her parents' bedroom. I was in the kitchen snapping beans, but dropped them in an instant to heed her call. Since Nina had finished *Coming of Age in Samoa* she'd resumed hanging around with me. The book had had a good effect, it seemed. On the heels of reading it she'd been more willing to do things: swim with Ada, Davy, and me, talk in the sun, and walk after dinner from our cottage to Anchor Beach to hang out there, chatting a bit with the other girls our ages.

When I reached her parents' bedroom, Nina was standing beside her mother's vanity, her back both twisted and arched as she struggled to zip the strapless sundress that Bec had sewn for her. That Nina had finally put the thing on surprised me. But here it was, that pale yellow cotton with a white floral print that so far that summer had caused such turmoil each time it had been pulled out of the closet. Even though she hadn't yet gotten it fully on, I could already see how good it looked. The dress's coloring contrasted beautifully with her newly bronzed skin. Though she wasn't the kind to flaunt her figure, in fact it was a lovely one, lean and curvy.

"What took you so long?" she asked, giving up on the zipper, exasperated. Her hair, which was usually pulled back, was loose and flowing down her back in curly ringlets.

"Excuse me?" I said. I was as surprised by her rebuke as I was by the sight of the dress and her cascading curls. "I rushed, fast as I could."

Laughter erupted then from next door — boy laughter: loud, sarcastic. Howard would be changing clothes after sailing and showering, and we could hear that Mark was there too, which meant he was staying for supper.

"Shut the door, Molly," Nina, alarmed, commanded, and I lunged at the door just in case the boys should emerge in the next second and see Nina — perfectly covered but somehow more naked than ever in this new outfit, this sea change of style.

"Can you help me zip it?" Nina then asked, more relaxed. "I think it's stuck."

I stood behind her and gripped the tab of the zipper. "Hold your hair up," I said, and Nina thrust a hand behind her head, lifting her mass of curls.

We were standing like that, my hands at the small of her back, her hand holding up her hair, the strapless sundress draped precariously over her body, soon to slip off as I jiggled the pull tab to get the zipper going, when we heard the bedroom door creaking open. I hadn't shut it properly.

Howard and Mark stepped into the hallway. Howard didn't notice us and simply walked to the stairs, away from us. Mark, though, lagging behind Howard, head bent toward his chest as he finished buttoning his shirt, turned our way.

"Zip it, Molly," Nina whispered, her tone frantic. "Zip it *now.*" As I struggled to do so, Mark remained standing in the hallway before the open door, his head gradually raised until his eyes were fixed on Nina.

"You wearing that tonight?" he asked, breaking into a bit of a smile.

"Just trying it on," Nina replied, her voice flat. But she wasn't calm, I knew. My hands still on her back, I felt her body rapidly warming. The instant I pulled the zipper up and released her, she leaped forward to shut the door again.

Beyond the doorway Mark was still there, staring.

"Looks good!" we heard next through the newly shut door. Then we heard clomping down the stairs and then nothing except the bedroom door creaking open again.

"It doesn't stay shut," I noted.

"Apparently not," Nina replied, slamming it this time, then latching it with a hook so it wouldn't open again. When she turned from the door to me she softened. "Does it really look good?" she asked. "Did you hear him?"

In fact she looked stunning, transformed. I wondered why in all the times I'd seen Nina change clothes I'd never noticed her square shoulders or long neck. More than that, she had hips and breasts and a solid bump of a behind. Her loose hair looked dramatic rather than merely frizzy. She had come of age — clearly — and not in Samoa but right here, in Woodmont, in front of our very eyes. But when had this happened?

"Do I know you?" I asked, amazed.

Nina didn't wear the dress out that night. Instead, she chose rolled dungarees. But the next night, just minutes before she and I were to head out for what had become our regular evening walk, Nina called to me. She was once again in her parents' bedroom, once again slipping on the dress Bec had made. This time she'd had no problem with the zipper and by the time I arrived, she was already in the dress and had the matching jacket slung over one of her arms. Her hair wasn't loose as it had been the night before but pulled back with her usual ribbon. Yet the simple hairdo suddenly looked as stylish as the dress. On her feet she wore sandals and she had even polished her toenails pink sometime during the day. I was in a favorite playsuit of lavender pedal pushers and a matching crop top.

"Can you dress better than that?" she asked me. "I don't want to stick out so much."

But this outfit was about as good as it got for me. I told her as much.

"Please, Molly," Nina implored, lifting one foot and almost stamping it down.

"All right already," I said. "Don't go crazy, Nina."

After I'd slipped on a skirt, she gratefully nodded. Together we emerged from the back bedroom, and as we made our way down the hallway toward the stairs Nina pulled me into the bathroom. She walked straight to a row of shelves by the sink, where she grabbed a tube of lipstick. Even though we'd never done this before it seemed natural enough to round our lips in tomato red then press them together as we'd seen our mothers do.

Our mothers and Bec were in the kitchen having their after-dinner coffee. We could see them as we scrambled down the stairs, but instead of turning their way we turned in the other direction. As we did, Nina let them know that we were on our way out. We'd already stepped onto the porch and into the evening air when I heard my mother calling.

"Molly, let me see you," she said, and I stopped, mid-porch, annoyed at the delay. Lately she'd been doing this every night: asking to see me before I headed out into the world without her. I didn't understand what she was looking for. She knew I dressed well enough. And I always remembered to comb my hair. If I'd realized that by giving me a discerning once-over all she was really doing was claiming me as hers for a moment, that this tiresome ritual was actually a part of her love, I might not have minded as much. But I didn't understand, and the new habit seemed intrusive, ridiculous.

"Here I am," I said, dashing back, almost scolding her. But when I caught her eye I could see that she was already peering at Nina, standing off to the left, in the dining room, behind me.

"Nina?" Ada said. She shot a look at Vivie and Bec, who then leaned over the kitchen table to better see into the dining room. All three put down their coffee cups.

"Nina," Vivie called, alarmed by Ada's tone. "Nina, come here."

When Nina entered the kitchen a surprised silence took hold. With all eyes on her, Nina stared at the floor as if entranced suddenly by the random flecks of color in the linoleum.

"Honey, look up," Bec said, her voice calm, encouraging.

Nina slowly raised her head and looked at Bec, who I knew she felt was the least likely of the three to pick faults with her. As she waited for a reaction, she lifted her hand to her hair and needlessly smoothed it.

"That's quite a fit. Turn, turn. Let me see," Bec said, gesturing in a circling motion. She was beaming at Nina.

As Nina turned, the others joined in.

"Honestly, I never thought I'd see the day," Ada said.

"You're telling me," Vivie answered, raising her hands and clapping.

"Why so surprised?" Bec asked.

"Why? *Why?*" said Vivie, turning from Nina to Bec in disbelief.

"The girl has spent the whole summer on the goddamned porch is why," Ada answered, settling it. "I don't know about you two," she added, "but I was beginning to —" My mother paused, fishing for the right word. "Wonder," she finally said, gravely. She raised her eyebrows and glanced at Vivie, then Bec. Though I had no idea what she'd begun to wonder about, I could see the matter was obvious to them. Catching Bec's eye, Ada quickly lowered her own. She'd been wondering about Bec, too, the dubious eye movement indicated.

Its implication was not lost on Bec. "Oh, come on," she snapped. "A girl can like to read and still be a *girl*. Ada, you just think everyone should be like you were, that's all. Boy crazy, insane, baking cakes, trying on shoes, *you.*"

My mother shut up, crossing her arms defensively over her chest, but Vivie suddenly rose, the coffee cups on the table tottering as she did, her chair almost falling backward, and she rushed to the door just off the kitchen, pushing it open while she let loose a quiet but anguished cry. It

421

seemed like a cry she'd held inside for a long time. I wondered if it was the past, referred to in Bec's comment, or the present that she was wailing over. A minute later she returned, holding a tissue she'd pulled from the pocket of the apron she still wore. She dabbed at her eyes.

"I'm your mother," she said to Nina, balling the tissue in her hand. "And the truth is, I *have* been a little worried. Not about, you know —" She glanced Ada's way, then lowered her eyes just as my mother had before. "Just about you. You getting out a little. Not being, you know, always so inside a book, always so afraid."

Nina nodded. The conversation had suddenly become an intimate one between just the two of them.

"So?" Nina asked.

"Oh, sweetheart, but it's *good*!" Vivie answered, pronouncing the last word just the way her mother, Risel, always had.

Nina broke into a relieved, delighted smile, and she spun around, her arms out wide, her hair lifting off her bare back.

"Now get the hell out of here," Ada said, yelping as she did and laughing, and pretty soon Vivie and Bec yelped and laughed as well, forming that particular high-spirited chorus of three that I'd heard a million times at least, and it was to this familiar clamor that we took off, out the back this time, past Davy playing jacks by himself on the steps.

Nina and I were still on Merwin Avenue, having only just left the cottage minutes before, when a car, passing us, honked. Then another did. Each of the cars was driven by a teenage boy, someone Howard's age or close to it. With both honks Nina and I turned to each other, surprised.

We were just rounding the corner to Beach Avenue and nearing Anchor Beach when we were not only honked at but also approached. The car slowed, swerved toward us, and the front-seat passenger leaned his head out the window. "Hey, gorgeous. What's up?" he called to Nina. This time Nina didn't turn to me but simply walked on, her head held high. I reached out, instinctively, for Nina's hand, alarmed by the car's proximity and by the man — so much older than Howard — leering from the open window. But to my consternation Nina wanted nothing to do with me. She shook herself free of my grip, then put distance between us, at least two strides. "Wait up!" I wailed, and because of my dismay Nina finally stopped and glared at the man in the car, and strangely enough that was all it took to get the driver to gun the engine and drive off.

"Come on, Molly," she said, laughing and motioning for me to catch up.

As we approached the crowd at Anchor Beach, Nina uncharacteristically strode forward, right into the thick of it. She homed in on Sal's Good Humor truck, which was drawing its usual profitable after-dinner business. The evening temperature was comfortable, almost cool. The sea breezes, common enough, were noteworthy only for the strange smell they carried, a combination of the salty sea scent and the sweetness of any number of perfumes rising from the bodies of so many girls and young women. When we stopped several yards from Sal's truck, Nina began scanning the crowd, searching.

"Look!" she said after a moment, pointing to a foursome in the distance that included Howard and Mark Fishbaum. They were standing some distance from us, on the rock outcropping there. Two girls were with them: Megan O'Donnell and another I couldn't identify.

"So?" I couldn't see what was so remarkable. Of course Howard would be talking to a girl. And we'd already seen him kiss

Megan O'Donnell.

"Oh, nothing," Nina said. "Just thought you might want to know where Howard was." But she wasn't looking at Howard, I saw; she was obviously more interested in Mark.

When my friends Melissa Bornstein and Anna Weiss approached us, we chatted with them until Sal, calling from several yards away, interrupted.

"Jiminy Cricket. Nina Cohen. Is that really you?"

Nina darted toward Sal. Craving an ice cream, I left Melissa and Anna behind too.

"Sweethearts," Sal said to us, though in fact he pointed only at Nina, who already stood directly in front of him, first in line, aggressively beating out the Weinstein twins. "Hey, hey," Sal said to calm us all, and then he winked at Nina. She doubled over at the waist, collapsing in an embarrassed but happy fit of laughter. Amused, Sal asked, "What'll it be tonight, sweet potato?" He puffed his cigar while looking at Nina with a kind of fatherly approval, and it wasn't lost on me that this far into summer he knew us better than our fathers, in a way that was more like our mothers and Bec. Soon he began to beam, much like Bec had earlier. Finally he said proudly, "You're some lady, Nina Cohen. I always knew it. Yes, I did." She collapsed a second time. Once upright, she spun around.

"What'll it be? Something special? Strawberry?" Sal said this because he knew she always ordered chocolate.

But Nina shook her head; she wasn't going to eat tonight, she explained, not when the ice cream could melt and drip onto her dress.

I, on the other hand, *was* eating, and I practically threw my change at Sal.

"Here you go, sweet potato," he sang, handing me my usual toasted almond. Then he warned, "Don't drip on her. She's a real beauty tonight. Molly Leibritsky, you keep your ice cream to yourself."

From behind us, the Weinstein twins were pushing forward. "Bye-bye, apple pie," Sal said, winking once more as he waved us off to keep the line moving.

"Bye-bye, apple pie," we called back, and I added, laughing, *"Sal Baby."*

After we'd parted from Sal, Nina was the one to note that Howard and Mark were still talking to Megan and the other girl. From the look on Nina's face I could see that she was trying to figure how to work her way over toward them. Her arms were crossed, like those of the girl beside Megan, who, even from this distance, looked angry, her arms twisted over her chest, her head turned not toward Howard or Mark but resolutely toward the horizon line. It wasn't often that someone Irish like Megan spent time at Anchor Beach with someone Jewish like Howard, and I wondered if the girl beside Megan was also Irish.

But my thoughts were interrupted when I suddenly jerked forward, losing the grip on my ice cream. When I spun around to see who had bumped me — it felt deliberate — there was Arthur Weinstein, smirking.

"Hey, sorry," he said. He glanced from me to my ice cream, melting on the sidewalk.

"Look where you're going," I complained.

"Hey, *sorry,*" he repeated, growing irritated.

"And I said look where you're going."

"Well, who are *you?*" he asked, nearly as hostile now as I was. As he began a mocking imitation of me, empty-handed and upset, his brother Jimmy tried to pull him away.

But Nina stepped in first. "Who the hell are *you?*" she said, her voice a bark.

Shocked by the sharpness, the twins took off.

Watching them, Nina muttered a contemptuous "Idiots," then wrapped an arm around my shoulder. But a moment later, her mood brightening, she said, "I know! Let's go tell Howard."

It seemed a risky strategy, telling Howard something he was likely to care little about — something about me — but I nevertheless followed Nina. As we approached the foursome I could see that the angry girl, in dungarees and a loose blouse, had unfolded her arms, but her face was still stern. Megan, wearing a floral print skirt, was dressed more specially, almost as nicely as Nina. She wasn't angry in the least but laughed as she pointed to a majestic sailboat skimming along the horizon.

"Like that?" she was asking as we approached.

"A little smaller," Howard answered. "Our boat's a touch smaller."

The Sailfish was in fact puny.

"Come on," the girl in pants said to Megan. "We should go home."

"Already?" Howard asked, his voice anxious.

Nina and I had fully approached them and now stood just outside their circle.

Spotting us, Howard looked surprisingly relieved. "This is my little sister," he told the girls, pointing at me, grinning. For once my presence was useful to Howard; he could delay Megan's departure by introducing me. "This is Molly. And this —" He looked at Nina. For a moment he almost lost his footing. "This is my cousin Nina."

Nina forced a smile, said hello, and glanced at each of the girls. Her gaze, so confident just minutes before, had become more or less focused on the ground, then Mark Fishbaum's knees, and then his face. "Hi, Mark," she added coolly, though I knew she felt anything but cool.

"Hey, Nina. Watcha reading?" Mark answered, and both he and Howard chuckled at that.

When Nina dropped her head again, Mark said gently, "Only kidding. Nice dress. Really."

I could see Nina's relief. The evening still held promise. She raised her head and gave Mark a flash of a smile. Howard then introduced Megan to us, formally, as if we'd never seen her before, and then he introduced her sister Sheila, the angry one beside her. "This one," Howard noted, nodding toward Megan, "works with me at Treat's. She's the checkout girl."

Nina and I glanced at each other, clearly wondering why Howard couldn't remember that we'd all met before.

"We *know,*" Nina said. She turned to Megan briefly.

"How soon he forgets," Megan remarked, grinning back at Nina.

"I remember," Howard snapped, glancing Megan's way, reddening.

"Did you see what happened to Molly?" The question asked, Nina glanced again at Mark, then at no one in particular.

"What happened?" Howard said, clearly annoyed. He'd never meant for us to actually get involved in the conversation.

Nina caught Howard's eye and they shared a short, hostile stare-down, the kind they were so prone to at the cottage.

"You didn't see Arthur Weinstein knock Molly?" Nina finally added.

Before anyone answered, Sheila suddenly turned to Megan, glaring at her. "We should *go.* Megan, I feel *weird,*" she said, imploring her sister.

"*You* go," Megan said.

"I *am,*" Sheila answered. She took a few steps but then turned back to say "Bye," raising her hand in an impulse of manners she apparently couldn't resist.

"Good riddance," I heard Megan mutter. To Howard she said, "Sorry about that. I

know you worked hard to bring us all together."

Nina then told them about my ice cream.

"So?" Howard asked. He couldn't have
sounded more indifferent.

But Megan was sympathetic. "That's a
letdown," she said to me. "Nice dress," she
then told Nina, turning her way.

Nina smiled and Megan smiled back. In a
shy voice Nina said, "My aunt made it for
me. Can you believe it?"

"Oh, for God's sake," Howard mumbled,
but Nina ignored him.

"She's a dressmaker," Nina determinedly
explained to Megan. "A very good one. She
probably made this in about three days."

"I made my skirt," Megan responded.
"But it took three weeks, not three days."

"Nice," Nina said, more relaxed, even
animated. "Hey, you should come over and
meet my aunt Bec. She's working on dresses
now. One for my mother, the other for Molly's."

"That would be *my* mother too," Howard
noted with impatience. "And I'll be the one
inviting Megan over." He looked at her then
quickly away. "When the time is right," he
added quietly.

Nina reached out and put a hand on
Megan's arm. "I can be her buddy too," she

said, staring at Howard.

"Are you kidding me?" Howard's eyes narrowed.

"Girlfriends!" Megan said, willing enough to tease Howard further.

"Exactly," Nina agreed. "Girlfriends!" With that she took a step closer toward Megan then carefully placed her arm over Megan's shoulder.

Scowling, Howard looked from Megan to Mark to me and then to Nina.

"Dyke," he finally muttered her way.

The word was spoken quietly, but we all heard it clearly enough.

Nina froze. As she lifted her arm off Megan, so much faster than she'd placed it there, she turned pink, first in the face, then along her neck and exposed chest.

"Howard," Megan said. "That's disgusting!"

"Yeah, Howard. Low blow," Mark added.

I remained quiet, uncertain what the word meant.

When Nina spoke, her voice was tense and shrill. "You don't deserve her. What you deserve, Howard, is a paper doll!" Her voice cracked on "doll" and her eyes began to tear.

"Oh, come on," Howard said, still annoyed but trying, too, to calm her. He approached Nina, touching her flaming cheeks, and said sweetly, "Laugh, Nina, laugh. I know you want to." He repeated into her ear, "Laugh, Nina, laugh," many times over until she was both crying and hiccupping with unwanted laughter. This was one of Howard's tricks: he could make you crack up just when you wanted to kill him. Obviously if you laughed you weren't feeling bad anymore, he seemed to figure. But what he didn't grasp, I knew from my own experience, was that the forced and unwanted laughter made you feel completely out of control.

I stepped toward Nina and touched her arm to comfort her. Unlike earlier in the evening, she didn't mind my touch this time; she even stepped toward me.

She was laughing and crying, though she didn't want to be doing either. All she wanted, I thought, was a response from Mark like she'd gotten from everyone else that night: Sal, the men who'd passed us by as we walked to Anchor Beach, our mothers and Bec.

But then, as if they had a will of their own, Nina's eyes turned curiously away from Mark and toward Megan.

"Come on!" she called, her face burning

even more intensely. Whatever her eyes were seeking, she clearly wasn't ready for it. She grabbed my arm as she turned herself around.

I followed her as she walked, slowly at first, as controlled as she could be, away from Mark, Howard, and Megan, and then, picking up the pace, toward home. When Nina finally caught sight of our cottage, she broke into a full-fledged bawl and began to run.

"Nina!" I called, chasing her. "Nina!"

But she didn't turn and wait. Rather, she ran full speed, past and around a series of neighbors' cottages, up our front steps, and, just as she was about to open the screen door, she ran right into it when my mother happened to open it a second before. In the time we'd been away the three women had moved from the kitchen table to the front porch, and Ada was bringing her sisters a freshly made pot of coffee.

When Nina hit the door, her forehead banging into it right along its edge, her dark hair rising from the back of her head, my mother let loose the pot of coffee, which landed just off the porch in the bushes. Her hands free, my mother caught in them a spiraling, screaming Nina.

By the time I caught up and climbed the

stairs, the others were on their feet, all of them surrounding Nina, holding her up, lifting her chin in their hands.

"Dear God," Ada said. "Dear God."

There was blood trickling down Nina's forehead, then down her face, and finally splattering on the collar of the jacket and the front of her dress.

"Let me see," Vivie called. Then she too said, "Dear God."

Bec was the one to suggest they go immediately to the house four doors away where a doctor was renting for the week with his family.

One of them could have run and gotten the doctor to come to us, but in their haste and confusion they simply began to drag Nina along with them, Ada repeating, "Dear God," and Vivie whispering in Nina's ear, "Hold on, sweetheart. You're going to be just fine. Just fine." Bec raced ahead to tell the doctor they were coming.

As they helped Nina down the steps, my mother called to me, standing in shock on the porch, "Molly, watch your little brother."

I nodded. I was sure she'd turn around as she headed off just to note my presence, as always. For once I wanted her to give me that stare. But she didn't turn. She didn't even call back to see if I'd heard. Instead, she held Nina by one arm while Vivie held her by the other, and they proceeded to guide her toward the doctor's cottage.

Soon they were out of sight. Even so, I could still hear Nina's horrifying scream, as if it hadn't stopped yet, and I could still see her head smacking against the door's edge, and the bruise on her forehead that had formed almost instantly, a large bump, and most of all the spill of blood trickling down her face, soiling the delicate flowers and pale yellow of her dress.

Though queasy, I managed to open the door, which had long since slammed shut, and stumbled into the living room. Something had happened to me too, it seemed: my head was spinning, my legs buckling.

I lay on the sofa a long time, alternating between closing my eyes and keeping them open. Either way, though, I kept seeing the blood, and the sickening spinning in my head and the roiling in my stomach didn't cease.

It seemed like ages had passed when Davy wandered into the living room. He found me lying there and wormed his way onto the couch by lifting my feet and sliding under them.

"Hey," I said weakly. My feet were in his lap and I tried to kick him, a friendly hello, but didn't have the strength. "Where you been?"

"Out back," he said, too calm to have been aware of what had happened. He was speaking in puppet talk, in the voice of Samson Bagel, whom he was wearing on one hand. "What's wrong?" he asked when, after he jiggled my legs, I only lay there, unmoving.

"Nina got hurt," I answered and then began to cry.

When I'd recovered some, Davy asked, still through the persona of Samson Bagel, "Is she dead?"

"Maybe." At that my eyes welled again. "Maybe not," I finally added. "I think she's not, but maybe she is. She got really, really hurt."

Davy didn't say anything for a moment. "What do we do now?" he asked. This time he used his real voice.

"We're supposed to stay here and wait," I told him, and that's what we did. For two hours, Davy and I stayed on the couch. The waning evening light grew gradually dimmer and finally we waited in silence and in the dark. I lay there the whole time, my head slowly regaining its equilibrium, my feet nicely raised by Davy when he'd slid under them. Davy sat patiently, moving only occasionally to lift his left hand and glance at Samson Bagel. Even when we sat in complete darkness, just the moonlight through the windows lending a touch of illumination, he didn't squirm or ask me for anything.

At long last Nina returned, her head successfully stitched and bandaged. Vivie and Bec helped her out of her bloodstained dress and into her summer nightgown while Ada warmed a glass of milk, which Nina was urged to drink while lying in bed. All three of them sat on the edges of our sofa bed as Nina and I settled under the blanket. Both of us, but especially Nina, were blanketed as well by consoling touches from everyone surrounding us.

That's when I sensed something I hadn't before: that I needed them, that I couldn't be me, the person only I spoke to, a quiet patter in my head, a near vision when in the dry upstairs tub — I couldn't be me, *her,* without them. Just then, as I stared at all of them and then at Nina, that steady sense I had of myself disappeared, the voice I knew so well quieted, and I didn't know anymore where I began or ended. For the moment it seemed I'd lost my boundaries, that I extended all the way into each of them, that Nina's felling had been my felling and that Ada, Vivie, and Bec's words and soothing pats were my words and pats.

Even Davy's gestures seemed as much my own as his. With Samson Bagel raised high on his hand he had him doing a kind of dance, waving him back and forth, like a hypnotist's pendulum, in front of Nina's face. "All better now," a comforting Samson Bagel chanted with each move. "All better now, you sleepyhead."

PART THREE

13
BOTTOM OF THE EIGHTH

In Middletown the next morning, Friday —
the day of Davy's accident — my father was
up early, as usual. By seven thirty he was
sipping his Nescafé and searching through
the newspaper for the latest on Babe Ruth,
just as he'd been doing all summer. Only
now there was no living Ruth to read about.
Rather the news was of the Babe's death,
just that past Monday, August 16. For the
next two days he'd been lying in state at
Yankee Stadium, where his fans, a whole
world of them, filed past. His funeral had
followed, at St. Patrick's Cathedral in New
York City. Mort sighed to read that even
the weather, hot and rainy, had seemed
mournful.

Five miles away, Leo Cohen was also sipping Nescafé, but he was not reading the
newspaper. Instead he was reading an
article that the librarian he knew best at
Middletown's Russell Library had pulled

for him. A scientist named George Gamow had written the article, which explained that the universe, estimated at fourteen billion years old, was created in a gigantic explosion of the earliest atom, and that the chemical elements observed now, hydrogen and helium in particular, were produced within minutes after the Big Bang. The universe had been in continual expansion ever since. Leo wanted to pass on this astonishing news, what little he could take in of it, to Nina, if he could just figure out how to put it to her. Fourteen billion years, he said to himself, shaking his head, unable to wrap his mind around the number. He reached for a nearby notepad. *My dear Nina,* he wrote, but then, stumped, he pushed the pad aside.

When the two men met at the synagogue twenty minutes later they nodded at each other, signaling a silent hello. By the mourner's Kaddish at the end of the service both men wore perplexed expressions and heavy hearts. During the service each man had made his own ruminative journey toward the truth of it: a human life's sad insignificance. They said the Kaddish, though for both the prayer was rote.

Then Mort suggested they say it again, this time exclusively honoring the memory of Babe Ruth. Leo didn't see the point — even as remarkable a life as Ruth's was, in the grand scheme of things, a mere speck beyond nothing — but he wasn't in the mood for objecting. It's not that our lives don't mean anything, he told himself, attempting to reconcile the chasm of time — fourteen billion years — between a single human life and that of the universe. Just that our lives are so small, so very, very small.

But looking to the group of men, he was heartened to see that it did matter — a single life, however small it was — for no one objected to Mort's idea. In fact, all it took was the sound of Ruth's name and the men dropped their heads and began chanting the prayer all over again.

In Woodmont the sisters also rose early, as usual, for their dunk. Nina and I slept in, extra late, and by the time we got up, after ten, the sisters had finished off the day's first pot of coffee and had long ago had their morning toast. Davy, too, had risen and eaten. Howard, who hadn't arrived home the night before until well after we'd gone to bed, was still asleep. This fact, his increasingly lax weekday sleeping schedule, which correlated precisely with his increasingly late nights out, was a secret my mother was willing to keep from my father, who still expected Howard up, at least some days, in time to join the daily minyan at the Woodmont synagogue. But only on weekends did Howard rise in time for services. As Nina and I entered the kitchen, Ada was discussing this very fact. "He's eighteen," she was explaining to Vivie and Bec. "He's too old for me to be telling him what to do." Shaking her head, she added, "I was *married* at eighteen, for God's sake. You see what I'm saying?"

When the sisters noticed Nina and me at the kitchen entrance they instantly began fussing over Nina's injury, which overnight had turned into an ominously protruding dark purple mass. The bandaging she wore could barely hide it.

"I'm glad you didn't die," Davy told her, sliding his glass of orange juice her way, offering it to her.

Bec, leaning on a counter, quickly veered toward Davy. "Of course she didn't die," she said. "Davy, where'd you get that idea?"

"I was never going to die," Nina insisted. "Sometimes things look worse than they really are. That's what the doctor said. I didn't even need but four stitches." She touched her forehead then quickly pulled her hand back. "Ouch," she said.

"You're going to take it easy today, is what I say," Ada told her, pulling out a chair from the kitchen table and pointing to it. Nina dutifully dropped into it. My mother sat down beside her and threw her arm over Nina's shoulder.

"French toast?" Vivie asked. She stood by the stove, apron wrapped at her waist, spatula clutched in her hand.

"French toast?" Nina answered, excited. We loved French toast, but the sisters, even Vivie, rarely mustered the energy for it on a weekday.

"Me too," Davy called, and I joined in as well.

"We're going to have a nice breakfast this morning," Vivie declared, stirring her egg batter, "and then we're going to get the house ready for Shabbos. A little morning cleaning before anyone goes to the beach. Let's get it done early today, for a change. Your fathers are coming, don't forget, and we've been cutting it close. Except, Nina, you can just sit outside, honey, and read if you like." She made reading sound as if it might be a rare pleasure for Nina.

"It isn't that big a deal," Nina said, as if she really preferred to clean and was being left out. She touched her forehead again.

"Ouch," she squealed.

"Honey, don't touch," Ada warned, pulling her arm. "You've got to keep your hands away."

"Can I touch?" Davy asked.

"Dear God," Bec answered, dropping into a chair and pulling Davy onto her lap. "You may not touch. Don't even think about it." She wrapped her arms around Davy and kissed his cheek.

"I'll have some French toast," I repeated, in case no one had heard before.

"Of course you will, Molly," Vivie answered from her station at the stove. "It's not just for Nina. It's for everybody," she added, though she directed a wide smile exclusively Nina's way. At that, Nina broke into a warm smile of her own.

But then Howard walked in, a bit earlier than usual, pajama-clad, hair tousled from bed, and Nina's joy vanished.

"Hey," he said, taking notice of her bump and bandage. He leaned over her with his hand extended as if he were about to feel it. "Got beaten up again?" he teased.

"Don't touch me!" Nina said.

It was Ada who came to Nina's rescue. "What is it with you boys and touching?" she said, slapping Howard's arm down. She looked woefully at Nina then scornfully at

Howard. "Can't you see she's hurting?"

"Sorry," he said, lifting his hand. "I was only pointing, not touching. Didn't mean to scare you."

"Oh, hell, honey," Ada offered, relaxing. "Have some French toast."

From a plate that Vivie had just placed on a counter Howard grabbed several of the first slices of French toast, not noticing that no one else had been served yet, and then he joined us at the kitchen table. He landed in between Nina and me, which caused Nina to readjust her chair away from him, almost backing into Ada.

Nina and I had just bitten into our first slices when Ada started divvying up the morning's chores: Davy and I would go to the Jewish bakery for challah, then next door to the kosher butcher's for two whole chickens. Before he set off for Treat's, Howard was to clean his and Davy's room then vacuum the downstairs. At the mention of vacuuming Howard threw his head back and groaned, but with a tired "Come on, you always do this" from Vivie and Bec, he assented soon enough. Bec would dust the house then iron the tablecloth for the evening dinner. She was also going to wash the blood from Nina's dress, she noted, assuring Nina she could get it back to new in no time. Vivie would mop the kitchen floor and wipe the counters. My mother had the honor, as she put it, of cleaning the bathrooms. And if everyone did as they were told, Ada, the sudden organizer, urged, we'd be done in no time and could head to the beach.

"Then again," Nina added, "we could head to the hills. The *Irish* hills." She lifted her head and glanced at Howard. He smirked and filled his mouth with more French toast.

"So what's in the Irish hills?" Ada asked, turning to Howard, a worried edge to her words. Immediately we all sighed in resignation and sorrow, readying for one of my mother's rants. She'd start with the Irish of Woodmont, then quickly move on to the Italians of nearby Bayview Beach, and then she might even get going on the tiny pockets of Greeks and Poles scattered here and there along the shore. Inevitably she'd arrive at the Negroes, utterly absent from the Milford coastline, people she hadn't had one direct thing to do with in her entire life.

"Oh, God," Bec muttered.

"Let's take it easy, Ada," Vivie urged. "This is supposed to be a *nice* breakfast." She hurried to bring the remaining slices of

French toast to the table, a kind a peace offering.

"Nice!" Ada exclaimed. Her expression
was already tense. I glanced at Nina, who
understood as much as anyone the nature
of this button she'd so willingly pushed to
get back at Howard.

But Howard sabotaged Nina's attack with
kindness.

"No one's going to the Irish hills," Howard told Ada gently. He squeezed our mother's arm and stared into her eyes, forcing
her to focus not on the idea of the Irish but
on the idea of him, her beloved firstborn, a
boy no less, and one as charming and good-
looking as she was. "No one's going anywhere," he assured her. In what I considered
a brilliant move, he leaned over and kissed
her cheek. "Except Molly and Davy, who
are going to get the challah and chickens,
just like you said."

"Yeah, okay," she answered, a little flustered, as if she didn't know anymore what
had overcome her, as if with Howard's kiss
she'd been released from a bad spell.

I watched Nina shoot Howard an angry
look; in freeing Ada he'd freed himself.

"That's right," Vivie added. "No one's going anywhere." She too was angry, though
not with Howard, having no idea he had af-

fronted Nina the night before. She was irked at Nina for being so foolish as to get Ada on that malicious track. "Nina," she continued, "I think you're well enough to sweep the porch." She stood behind Nina and pulled her chair back so Nina couldn't help but stand. "Up, up," she said.

Though sweeping the porch was hardly hard labor, Vivie's stripping Nina of her special status as the injured party cut her. She rose from the table and stormed out, by way of stomping and slamming the door, to the front porch. For the next hour she did not sweep. She read.

Davy and I set off with a basket for the chickens. After that was done we went to the bakery, and just inside the door was Mark Fishbaum, standing beside his father. Though Judge Fishbaum waved to us, Mark offered no greeting, which made me wonder if, like me, he was still grappling with uncomfortable thoughts about the events that had taken place the evening before. After a minute, though, Mark leaned toward me, stretching to hand me a numbered ticket from the dispenser I still couldn't reach, and as I took the ticket I offered him a bit of a smile.

Davy busied himself by watching the bakers kneading and slicing and wrapping, as carefully as he would juggling clowns. I focused on the smells: the baking bread, the sweet pastries. But then I saw Mark fascinated by something happening outside, and when I looked there was Howard, with Megan, rushing past the bakery. When they were beyond our view I turned back to Mark. Catching my eye, he raised his finger to his lips as if shushing me. Then he gave me the same bit of a smile I'd given him, a look of pensive acceptance, a look that, so many years later, during our marriage, and especially close to its end, I'd come to know all too well.

"Challah, please," I finally ordered. "Two loaves."

"And two of those," I heard Mark say. He was pointing at a platter of large cookies frosted in chocolate and vanilla. "Add those to her order."

Their generosity had Mark and his father beaming. "Friday's a good day for a treat," Judge Fishbaum announced, pulling out a quarter to pay for the cookies. With some more change he paid for our bread, too.

Davy and I might as well have witnessed a miracle. I looked at Mark, surprised, as if I'd never seen him before. His hair was its usual curly mess and his face was the same, but away from Howard he was different, I remember thinking, which was the first time I'd ever considered Mark Fishbaum as someone to know just for himself, separate from his connection to Howard.

Davy and I didn't go straight home. Instead, we walked to Anchor Beach, where we sat on a wooden bench while we ate the cookies. We nibbled in silence, entranced by the gray-blue mass of water before us, and by the movement of a sailboat in the distance, its open sails a series of tiny triangles that looked no bigger than the wings of the gulls flying some distance above. When we finally returned to the cottage Bec was taking off, the Friday claustrophobia having hit her once again. She walked, and then, out of our sight, approaching a certain corner of New Haven Avenue, she ran.

She and Tyler weren't in a rush to get to Bec's apartment in New Haven. After all, they had their entire lives ahead of them now that they'd decided to take a stand for their love, to be in the world together, a couple for all to see. And so they took the time to stop for hot dogs in West Haven at Jimmies at Savin Rock. Seated at a picnic table, they stared at each other, which every so often caused them to erupt into laughter.

To calm themselves they turned toward the ocean, or sometimes toward the Savin Rock roller coaster, its intricate trestle a sight, its curvy tracks rising high into the blue of the day, its chain of cars climbing those tracks slowly, creeping upward toward the peak. As they ate they could hear shrieks in the distance, of gulls and of the people on the roller coaster, past the peak, accelerating forward and heading straight down.

"I could never do that," Bec said, turning from the roller coaster to Tyler. Just watching had taken her breath away. "Looks like they're falling to their deaths."

"They're having fun. Come on, let's dare," Tyler urged. "It'll give you a thrill."

Bec shook her head but then smiled, catching Tyler's eye. "I can think of other thrills," she said.

That afternoon, after they'd made love in Bec's New Haven apartment, Tyler fell asleep, and for the next hour Bec lay beside him, her body turned his way. Thrilling, she thought, just to look.

"What do you think?" Tyler asked upon waking. "Time to head back?"

Bec swept her hand across his forehead. "Ten more minutes," she said. "Then ten more after that."

■ ■ ■ ■

At about the same time, midafternoon, at Woodmont, behind Treat's fruit and vegetable stand, my brother Howard was kissing Megan O'Donnell. This was old hat by now, this afternoon kissing, a time when the smell of peaches and berries and cucumbers and zucchini mixed with the smell of Megan O'Donnell, her rose-scented shampoo, her salty skin.

"Sheila told me this morning she's going to tell our parents about you and me," Megan said, pulling away suddenly.

"What'll they do?" Howard asked, leaning in, hoping the kissing wouldn't cease.

"Have a conniption. What else?"

"Is that all?"

"Is that *all*?"

"My parents would kill me." Howard nodded, sure of it.

"That's just a figure of speech."

"Not really. I'd be dead in their eyes. At least eventually I would. If this thing between us really took off. That's the rule."

"Whose rule?" Megan said blithely, as if the old way were but a game. But the look in her eyes was serious.

He reached for her hand.

For a minute they didn't speak.

Then she said, "Meet you at Bagel Beach tonight, dead man?"

He tried to answer her joking tone. *"Pow, pow,"* he said, a fake pistol to his chest, but he regretted the move as soon as he saw her horrified look. He kissed her cheek quickly. "Wouldn't miss it for the world," he said.

Four o'clock that afternoon and Mort and Leo were on the road from Middletown to Woodmont, listening to a ball game. After so many trips like this it seemed to Leo that the car was fueled as much by games as by gasoline. As always, Mort drove impatiently, swerving to pass nearly every car he could.

Leo, his eyes half-closed, felt only mildly queasy. If he opened his eyes fully, the queasiness expanded, which was interesting to think about given that other expansion, the universe's, already on his mind.

He turned his thoughts back to his reading, to the past that was with us now, according to Gamow, if in fact he'd read him correctly. Such ruminations could keep the queasiness at bay. But Mort, speaking to him, interrupted his thinking. "You okay?" Mort asked. "Looking peaked. Very peaked. You okay?" he repeated.

Leo nodded.

Mort cleared his throat as if to say more but then quieted. "She's a hothead, that Ada," he finally muttered.

Leo turned to find Mort glancing his way. He seemed intent on talking, his eyes serious, his face grim. "Yes, let's face it," Mort continued, "I married the family hothead."

Leo swallowed. He couldn't disagree.

"And you married the family chef," Mort added, his tone a little brighter.

Two weeks. They hadn't seen Vivie and Ada in two weeks. Leo couldn't tell which was the truth: that his brother-in-law missed his wife or that he dreaded the reunion. Yet because the human heart was its own inexplicable and expansive universe, it was possible, he knew, for both to be true.

The two weeks had seemed to Leo like two months. He sighed with relief when he realized they were approaching Savin Rock.

"A hothead and a chef," he managed to say. "Then why are you so calm and me so nervous? And so thin?"

Mort liked that. He laughed. He reached for the radio dial, turning up the volume. Leo watched him, grinning suddenly and feeling hopeful as he heard the report: bottom of the eighth, score tied, man on first, man on second, one out, DiMaggio at bat.

14
A MOB OF RULES

As Mort and Leo pulled into Savin Rock for their weekly hot dogs at Jimmies — two hours after Tyler and Bec had pulled out — in Middletown Nelson was breathing in the dank air of the store's basement, listening to Benny Goodman playing Mozart's clarinet concerto. The piece was quiet compared to the buoyancy of something like "Sing, Sing, Sing," and Nelson was particularly taken with the concerto's dolorous second movement, which suited his mood. Come Friday afternoons he could get a little low, a little tired; often, he found himself wrestling with a bit of a headache. It was maybe the worst time of the week, he acknowledged, rocking in his chair to the adagio rhythm of the second movement. Then again, he thought, the hours ahead would also be pretty lousy, Friday night, when he'd light Shabbos candles by himself, pull off a hunk of challah, then another, then finally eat the whole damn loaf in what felt like one breath.

While my uncle rocked in his chair, and while my father and Leo finished their hot dogs, my brother Howard arrived home from Treat's and headed off on his usual afternoon sail with Mark Fishbaum. As they rigged the boat, Davy hung around them, as he so often did lately, but he'd had a ride just the day before. Howard could argue without guilt that he'd take the squirt again the next day, or the next, but not that day. Once aboard the Sailfish, Mark sat starboard, tiller in hand, sail line in the other, while Howard sat beside him, hands free, body relaxed, as he let Mark manage the mechanics of sailing so that he, dreaming of Megan O'Donnell, could simply be taken for a ride.

On land, at the corner of New Haven Avenue and Warner, near the eastern border of Woodmont, Tyler McMannus pulled his Roadmaster to the curb to let Bec out. She'd asked to get off there, farther from the cottage than usual. Before she saw her sisters again she felt the need for some time alone. A good walk, she figured, would be just the thing. She turned to Tyler before opening the car door and smiled, taking in his face, the gray eyes, the sad mouth. She knew that her smile and his frown were but different takes on the same mixed emotions: love, fear, hope, worry. They'd been quiet the whole ride from New Haven back to Woodmont; during the afternoon they'd further cemented the decision to move together to New York, and all they'd been able to do since then was to sit together in silence. *Once the holidays are over,* Bec had finally said, speaking of Rosh Hashanah and Yom Kippur. That's when they'd make their move. One hand on the door handle, she released her grip when he pulled her toward him, kissed her, and then held her. Once separated, they both laughed nervously. "Look what we've done" was what she thought to say to him, and to her surprise, when he spoke it was to that very idea: "Look what we're doing." They nodded, smiled this time with more ease, even some excitement, and then she turned from him and opened the door.

A mile away, at the Bagel Beach cottage, my aunt Vivie flipped through a cookbook wondering if she could do something else besides simply roasting the two chickens that lay side by side on the kitchen table, already greased with butter and seasoned with salt and pepper. When she spotted a recipe that called for garlic in, on, and around the bird, she realized that was enough of a stretch for her. "Garlic-y Chicken," the recipe was called. She folded down the corner of the page, reached for the peeled garlic, and began, slowly, carefully, to slice.

In the dining room Ada set the table. She placed the kiddush cup, sterling silver, near Mort's seat, then set a platter for the challahs to its right. She counted the place settings: two husbands, three sisters, four kids. Flushed and warm, she sat for a moment at the head of the table, Mort's place, sinking into his chair, larger than those that flanked the table's two sides and even the one she typically sat in at the opposite end. Sitting like a king, she thought to herself, and feeling suddenly regal she raised her hand and smoothed her mass of hair, carelessly twisted and pinned. She considered for a moment her decision the night before not to call the husbands about Nina's injury. The women could handle it, she'd convinced her sisters. By the time the husbands arrived the matter would be no bigger than a few stitches and a Band-Aid. Good choice, she told herself as she rose from Mort's chair, a kind of throne.

In the kitchen, Nina and I stood by the sink, each of us holding a thick brass candlestick that we were polishing. I couldn't help but stare at the deep purple bruise on Nina's forehead, over her left eye, and at the bandage and tape covering it. Nina, on the other hand, already seemed to have forgotten about the incident and its imprint; wholly in the present moment, she attacked a spot on her candlestick with fierce concentration as if shining that candlestick were all that could possibly matter.

Davy wandered in then, through the back door off the kitchen, his wavy hair wind-blown, his bathing trunks wet, his feet sandy.

"Young man?" Vivie said, pointing.

Of the rules in this house, spoken and unspoken, ancient and new, religious and secular, visible and invisible — of the mob of rules that controlled a given moment — the one about sandy feet was perhaps the one most strictly enforced.

"Sorry," he answered, and he did so with such earnest regret that Vivie rushed toward him to hug him.

"And where's your brother?" asked Ada, who stood now in the doorway between the kitchen and dining room, her hands on her hips.

"Sailing," Davy answered, still standing sandy-footed in the middle of the kitchen. If he didn't move soon, I thought, I'd whisk him up myself and carry him outdoors to the shower. I placed my candlestick, still smeared with polish, in the sink just in case.

"Sailing toward Megan O'Donnell is more like it," Nina interjected, her face unchanged, as focused as ever on her polishing.

"Megan O'Donnell? Who's that?" Ada said.

There were moments when Sal Luccino hardly knew his name anymore, and that third Friday in August was one. Sitting in his truck, calmly making his late-afternoon rounds, he was only Sal Baby, known as much for his whistling as for his ice cream. Just then, whistling straight into the winds of Milford yet still sounding loud and clear, he grasped anew that his was a rare operatic capacity. Should his truck's bells ever give out, he could compensate, he knew, with the work of his own breath. Considering his two talents, the one for Good Humor, the other for Art, he got such a feeling in his gut, such a deep love for life, and he knew himself to be as lucky as any man could be. Add to that the day's blue sky and lovely temperature, not to mention the energetic boost of low humidity, and all he could think to do was to take a private moment off the beaten path, hop down from his truck, and drink it all in: the ocean, the clear sky, the shrubs beside him of wild roses, a few still in bloom, and the familiar hum of his truck's engine, which was something like his own heart, a murmur of comforting steadiness.

While Sal took a moment for himself in Woodmont, Nelson Leibritsky finally rose from his rocking chair in the corner of the store's basement to lift the phonograph needle, bobbing now at the record's end. The third movement of the Mozart concerto, marked allegro, had finally got him going, out of his chair, up those stairs. He could do it, he figured. He could rejoin the world, put on a grin, work until day's end. He was at the top step, about to walk onto the creaky planks of Leibritsky's sales floor, when he stopped, gasped, needed in a way that was just plain embarrassing to rest.

By this time, four fifty that afternoon, at the Savin Rock amusement park, near Jimmies hot dog stand, Leo Cohen had upchucked. For a time, while in the throes of celebrating Joe DiMaggio's triple, then in swallowing the first bites of his dog, he'd felt better. And the two men had been having an unusually friendly conversation. The anticipation of seeing the women was making Mort, at least, especially chatty. He kept

465

repeating the phrase "a hothead and a chef." He'd also asserted, multiple times, "She'll have the place ready. I know she will." Mort had finally turned to DiMaggio as a subject for conversation, recalling the best moment, the fifty-six-game hitting streak of '41. But as Mort talked, the sickness — motion sickness, Leo had always thought of it — returned. This time, though, there was no motion to induce the sudden clammy feeling. Leo had risen, scoured the grounds of Savin Rock for the nearest trash can, rushed over to it, and stood there, bent over, feeling — because he knew Mort was staring at him — like one of the world's biggest fools.

Minutes later, Mort, waiting in the car for Leo, was watching his brother-in-law's protracted, stumbling approach. Leo was pale, rail thin, about to pass out, or so it seemed. There were so many responsibilities in a given day, so damn many, and one of them, for Vivie's sake, was to keep Leo Cohen alive. Mort owed her that much, he reminded himself as he opened the car door. "Hey, buddy, feeling better?" he asked as Leo settled himself in the passenger seat. When Leo nodded, Mort said with a tenderness that rose from a place he didn't even know he had, "Rest now, buddy. Everything's going to be okay. We'll be there soon."

Everything's going to be okay is what Bec was telling herself, too, as she ambled slowly away from Tyler's Roadmaster and headed toward the cottage, toward us. She was walking along New Haven Avenue, which was a busy street, and not nearly as scenic as even Hawley Avenue, just a block away. But she wasn't thinking about scenery. She was thinking about her sisters, her life soon to ensue without them, the dresses she would no longer be making for them, the summers she would no longer be spending with them at the cottage. The thing about family, she knew, was that you were either in or you were out. She only wished she understood why that was so. When a dog began yapping at her from a nearby front porch, she stopped, startled. She stood still while the dog, an unleashed hound, still barking, approached. But once beside her the hound ceased barking and merely sniffed the hem of her skirt then glanced at her longingly. "You're just lonely," she told the thing, relaxing, bending to pet it, thinking as she did of her sisters once again. "You and me."

In the kitchen Vivie swiped her brow with the back of her hand. *Oh for crying out loud,*

467

she thought, watching Ada's eyes grow wide as she took in the meaning of the name that Nina had just uttered: Megan O'Donnell. Why was Nina raising a matter sure to rile Ada? Vivie wondered. She was about to go over to Nina, to tap her shoulder, take her calmly to the front porch where the two would seat themselves in the cool metal chairs and talk, just them, mother and daughter. No one was on Nina's side more than Vivie, she would tell her daughter. No one loved her like she did. She realized Nina might not know that, what with a father she was so close to, but Vivie was in the picture too. She was about to make her move toward Nina when Ada charged at the girl, said again, "Who? Megan who?"

"Megan O'Donnell," Nina repeated, her hands on the candlestick moving rapidly back and forth but her face, as she turned to look directly at Ada, resolutely calm. "Howard's Irish girl."

"Howard's *what*?" my mother asked, her voice low.

Vivie tensed.

"Howard's Irish girl," Nina repeated. "Doesn't everybody know that?"

For a moment my mother stood still, her hands in midair, her head held high. As she considered the meaning of Nina's remark, her coloring changed from her neck up and by the time she spoke again she looked blanched. "Which direction did Howard sail?" she demanded, her voice heavy, full of foreboding.

Nina shrugged, but Davy said, "That way," and he pointed east. His answer was matter-of-fact, as if he didn't seem to notice our mother's growing anger. He started moving, finally, toward the back door, toward the shower, as oblivious to his wake of sandy footprints as he'd been to Ada's rapid change of mood.

"Damn Irish," she muttered.

Though strapped to her feet were her favorite summer wedges, the faded house-dress that covered her body was one I knew she'd never be caught wearing in public. Moreover, her hair needed re-pinning. And she was vain about her good looks. That's why I was so surprised when she dashed past Davy, flew out the door, and headed for Hillside Avenue, where the largest segment of the Woodmont population could see her. But this was the best route to Anchor Beach, where I knew she was determined to catch up with Howard.

"Howard!" she called, as if he could already hear her. But she was nowhere near the water yet. "Howard!"

She took two long steps, then ran a pace or two, then returned to the long steps. "Not under my roof!" she muttered in time with her strides. Though our feet were bare, Davy and I followed her. Within moments we three were at the intersection of Hillside and Merwin avenues, and we quickly swerved in the direction of Anchor Beach. As we passed the Villa Rosa and Sloppy Joe's, Ada called more vigorously, "Not under my roof!"

At Anchor Beach we hopped onto its mass of rocks to get a view of the Sound. Any number of sailboats could be seen in the distance, but closer to the shore we easily spotted the Sailfish, its crew of two eighteen-year-old boys sitting high while their boat heeled at what appeared to be a dangerous angle. They were sailing parallel to the coastline of Woodmont and were past Anchor Beach. In a moment we'd lose sight of them. With even more urgency Ada called out, "Howard! Howard!" If only to stop her imminent fit, the one I could predict had only barely begun, I called out as well and Davy joined me. "Howard!" we yelled. But to no avail. The boat sailed on.

Beach Avenue was the road to take next, and my mother, wobbling occasionally in her wedges as she rushed forth, scurried off the rocks and onto the road. Soon we arrived at the point at which Beach Avenue turned, running behind a row of beachfront cottages rather than in front of them as it had thus far, and there we got off the road. By walking instead along a cement seawall we managed to maintain our seaward view. By the time the seawall ended and we rejoined Beach Avenue where it emerged from behind that batch of cottages, we were abreast of the Sailfish, though out on the water it remained a considerable distance from us. We stood, breathing hard, just where Beach Avenue intersected with Clinton Street. Across the pavement of Beach Avenue the cottages behind us formed a neat line of white clapboard and broad porches that gave way to tiny green lawns. Several sprinklers were set on the lawns, and as I noticed them I was tempted to dash across the street and run under one or another of them to cool off, especially my bare feet, which burned from the heat of the sidewalks and roads. But Ada, almost doubled over as she worked to catch her breath, was an even more compelling sight, her hair now fallen free of any pins and hanging completely loose in a way we'd never seen.

"Howard!" she yelled again. "What the hell do you think you're doing? Come back!"

"Howard!" Davy and I echoed. Davy jumped up and down. "Hey, Howard!" he added, waving his arms, and I turned to him, telling him sternly, "This isn't a game, you know."

"What is it?" he asked.

"Not sure," I warily said.

The Sailfish traveled on but the boys in it turned their heads our way. My mother called again and again and finally in the distance a hand shot up, Howard's, and he was waving. He yelled something but his words didn't reach us with any clarity. In a moment he'd gone past us and in frustration Ada began to jump, not unlike the way Davy just had. Davy mimicked her, calling out to Howard for reasons he didn't understand, and between the two of them the racket was substantial. Several people on the beach below us turned to stare. A woman emerged from a cottage behind us, the second one in from the corner of Clinton Street and Beach Avenue, and she stood on her porch, wearing a housecoat similar to my mother's, and glared in our direction. She looked so much like my mother, with dark hair and a similar face and build, and for a moment I thought this was our cottage, our life, moved in a flash from Bagel Beach to this other, better section of Woodmont, where the homes lined Beach Avenue in a trim, neat row and even had little lawns of mowed grass on which to play badminton, say, or to sit when you tired of the sand. Life here wouldn't be a bad thing, I sensed, and I turned to this stranger, compelled to give her a wave.

Five twenty p.m. and Nelson was thinking about closing early. Mort and Leo would never know. A late Friday afternoon, especially one as sunny and bright as this one, was a lousy time for shopping. But just as Nelson was about to tell Kurt Hanson, the new hire, to pack it up and have a good one, Giorgio D'Almato came wandering in. "These new shoes are like heaven," he said once he'd reached Nelson and shaken his hand. Nelson nodded, wishing Howard was there to hear this. Nelson then accompanied him to the front door and for some minutes they stood outside on the sidewalk, talking in the afternoon sunshine. The old man was now a grandfather of five, he told Nelson, the newest child born just in the last week. "Lucky man. You've got it all," Nelson told his customer, a prick of envy in his voice.

But Giorgio D'Almato didn't hear the bitterness. He simply turned and began, in those shoes as good as heaven, his slow march north on Main Street.

In the kitchen at the Woodmont cottage Vivie pulled out a chair and dropped herself into it. She dragged out another chair, pointed, said in her firmest voice, "Nina, sit down." Nina finished wiping the candlestick in her hands then came to the table carrying it, setting it on the kitchen table beside the two chickens that were now sitting in roasting pans, surrounded, in a way that made Vivie a little uncomfortable but a little giddy, too, by a profusion of garlic cloves. "You've got to drop this thing with Howard," Vivie began, her voice still firm. "I know you're out to get him. I see it," she added. She was not yelling at Nina, or even scolding, but rather talking with concerned seriousness. "I know a thing or two about quarreling siblings, or in your case almost-siblings," Vivie confessed. The girl was tearing up. "Honey, tell me — what's wrong?" She leaned toward Nina. "What's wrong with you?" At that Nina burst out. "Something," she wailed, "I *know* something's wrong with me. Something's *terribly* wrong with me. But I can't tell you *what.*"

A full heart is like a packed suitcase, Bec

realized as she headed downhill toward the glinting ocean water and Beach Avenue. Feeling heavy with it all — the aching loneliness of a Friday afternoon — she forced herself to pick up her pace. In the next moment she could almost see it: the Shabbos table, set with candlesticks and wine cups, the extended family seated around it, and there she was at the table too, she and Tyler, and they were accepted by the family for what they were, a unit of their own design, a tight little package of love. Not so hard, really, she argued to herself, to set one extra place, to open a clearing for the unexpected, certainly it was possible, and when she turned onto Beach Avenue and to her surprise spotted Ada standing on the other side of the road facing seaward only yards away, and then saw Davy and then me, she rushed forward, calling to us in a voice filled with hope. Davy heard her first, turned, and upon seeing her across the street he offered a surprised, delighted smile, which led her to instantly drop to her knees and throw her arms wide. "Davy!" she called.

From Howard's perch on the heeling Sailfish it looked like everybody was waving — his mother, his siblings, even the lady behind them, a stranger standing on her cottage porch. So he joined in, waved back. As loudly as possible he yelled, "What's up? What's going on?" but there was no way to hear what they were trying to tell him, nor could they hear him, he knew. He told Mark they should come about, and as Mark released the sail's line Howard yanked the tiller toward him. The boat turned and a moment later the sail, which had gone fluttery with the loss of the wind, suddenly swung to the other side, gradually filling as it caught the breeze. As the boat came about, Mark, in the nick of time, ducked underneath the boom, but Howard, his attention on his family on the shore, forgot to duck, and as the boom shifted it slammed against Howard's shoulder, causing him to lose balance and tumble backward off the boat. He splashed, went under, surfaced, spat. Treading frantically, he looked shoreward, toward Ada. Then he shouted to Mark, who'd already caught the loose tiller and was turning about again, heading his way, "Can *you* hear what they're yelling?"

"Not under *my* roof!" is what Ada called over and over again, wondering as she yelled why she'd not known about the Irish girl and Howard. And if she didn't put an end to it now, she figured, Mort would find out, and that *would* be the end of it — not only for Howard, whom Mort would surely punish to the hilt, but for her too, it would be the end of something beautiful, untouched, the end of something she didn't even know the name of besides calling it *summer,* calling it *the cottage,* calling it *my time with my sisters,* which she needed, she realized, couldn't possibly live without, or the other three seasons of the year would simply sink her.

As he rounded the corner from Clinton Street to Beach Avenue, Sal Luccino was imagining the roses, a solid dozen, he'd bring home that evening for his wife, Marie. Inspired by the wild roses he'd spotted along the shore, he'd come up with the idea of the gift just moments ago. By this point in summer, the busiest time of year, he and his wife hardly saw each other. The roses, he'd concluded, would let her know she wasn't forgotten. He was just picturing Marie's bemused smile and the roses in her arms when, having made the turn, he saw Ada Leibritsky on the sidewalk of Beach Avenue, screaming and jumping as she faced the sea. As if by rote, because for ten years already he'd always done so at this turn, he rang the truck's bells. But then he did something atypical: he turned his gaze momentarily from the road, following the direction of Ada's cries, until he spotted the boy, Howard, flapping in the water while his boat sailed on without him.

Eyes locked on Howard, Sal inhaled deeply, took his forefinger and thumb to his mouth, and gave the loudest whistle he could summon, a sound that soared across the water and rose in the air with the ease of a flying gull. Help, the whistle surely told Howard, was close at hand.

It was confusing then when Ada, alarmed by Sal's sharp call, turned away from the water and toward the road, toward him, her eyes popping anew as she did, her mouth dropping open, her throat tightening as she struggled to yell, "Stop! Stop!"

So he did.

He hit the brake. But in the second before he heard an undeniable and awful thud and his head snapped back.

In the next moment he was crouched beside the truck, his mouth open as he examined the small body, back to the ground, head askew, beneath it.

Sal couldn't help himself, the way he pursed his lips, began to whistle — this time a single, barely audible note of bewilderment — as he grasped Davy's closest hand, open and outstretched toward him.

15
SOMETHING TO DO

That day, but moments after the accident, before I could fully understand what had happened, I felt a hand on my shoulder and heard an unfamiliar voice telling me to leave the scene. "Come away, come away," this person urged, gripping my arm and tugging me forward. It turned out she was the lady on the porch to whom I'd waved the minute before.

For a good part of that afternoon I sat in her living room on her scratchy gold couch staring at either the old braided rug covering the floor, a faded watercolor of a pot of daisies on her wall, a photograph hung on the wall of her surrounded by her large and smiling family, or at the woman herself, a person who upon closer inspection looked less like my mother than I'd previously thought, older by some degree, and who, from her post at the doorway between her living room and front porch, kept a near-constant vigil over the events outside. In the midst of the commotion the woman never introduced herself, but I subsequently learned that she was Ida Rankoff, and in the summers to come I would bring Mrs. Rankoff several tokens of thanks for her help that day: once an actual pot of daisies and another time a blueberry cobbler that Vivie and I made after buying the blueberries at Treat's. During these visits Mrs. Rankoff and I always sat on her porch, and though I'd be talking to her, nodding my head and smiling her way, simultaneously I'd be searching the accident scene, scanning the roadway's black tar as if Davy had melted right into it and was still there, intact, just waiting for one of us to look hard enough to finally find him.

That day the only words I said to Ida Rankoff were the occasional "What's happening now?" And though it was clear from the sounds of the outside world that much was going on — an ambulance had arrived, as had the police, as had, in time, my father — Mrs. Rankoff always answered, her voice a near whisper, "There's no need for you to see this, sweetie. Just hold still."

Davy was taken to the nearest hospital, in Milford, and his condition that night, following surgery to stop internal bleeding, was poor but stable. He'd been crushed by one of Sal's tires and was broken all over — ribs, shoulders, pelvis, his left arm — but the internal bleeding was the worst of it. He was lucky to be alive at all, my parents were told. For the remainder of the afternoon and evening my parents hadn't left his side, nor had Howard or Bec. Leo and Vivie stayed at the cottage with Nina and me. The hours there were long and quiet, and I spent most of them cradling Samson Bagel in my lap. Finally, Vivie told Nina and me that we might as well try to sleep, and we pulled out the sofa bed, crawled under a sheet, and lay there, wide awake. Nina didn't laugh at me when I asked her if we could keep Samson Bagel there in the bed between us.

When the group from the hospital finally arrived home at midnight — since Davy was stable they'd been directed to get some sleep and return in the morning — they plodded through the back entrance and kitchen and then dropped themselves into their respective dining room chairs. In the next instant Nina and I were up and joined them, and a moment later Vivie and Leo did as well.

We had no idea what to do except sit in silence.

Davy was hanging in there, Mort said at last. We should pray, we should hope, he added.

And so we did, or at least I thought that's what we were trying to do, each of us in our way, during the next long minutes of silence. But the silence felt complicated, troubled. When my mother finally broke it, her head raised, her eyes fixed on Nina, it was obvious that she'd been neither praying nor hoping. "He wasn't sailing to the Irish girl like you said. He was sailing to West Haven, as usual. As usual, you damn liar. As *usual.*"

With that Vivie threw her arm around Nina and leaned forward, her body protecting Nina from the bullets of her sister's words.

"She's a child, Ada, please. A child," Vivie implored.

"A child?" Ada asked, her eyes popping, her words menacing. "I'll tell you who's a child. *Davy's* a child." And with that she made a fist and shook it threateningly Nina's way.

"But you've seen it yourself, Ada, the way Howard torments my girl. How could she not want to get back at him? How could she not, Ada?" Vivie's voice had modulated from a pleading tone to one of indignation. She tightened the belt of her bathrobe.

"Nothing justifies a lie," my mother declared.

Vivie responded by pushing her chair, which was catty-corner to Ada's, away from her, the few inches she could, and there it was again, that old space, reemerged, between them. "That's pretty funny, Ada. Coming from you," Vivie said.

"That's enough," Mort snapped, cutting off the sisters and causing both women to turn, surprised, from each other to him. Then he asked, "What happened to her?" He was looking at Nina, at the bruise and bandage on her forehead.

When no one spoke, he asked again.

"An accident," my mother said, her voice anxious. "Last night."

"She's fine," Vivie added, still holding Nina close.

"Two children, two accidents," Leo said, his voice so hushed he seemed to speak only to himself.

Mort drummed his fingers on the tabletop. "Two accidents," he finally repeated, his gaze so completely focused on Ada it seemed to cause the rest of us to disappear. But we were there, listening, as he said, "Ada. Howard has something going with an Irish girl, and you don't call me? Last night Nina needs stitches over her eye, and you

483

don't call me?" He pointed past her, to the phone on the little table. Quickly, he shot a glance from it to her. After a long pause, he asked, "What am I, Ada?"

As he continued to drum his fingers, I stared at the center of my empty dinner plate, which, because I was too scared to blink, began to blur.

"Do I not deserve to know what's happening in my own family?" Mort finally thundered. He pounded the table, and the wine cups at his end, including the silver kiddush cup, toppled over. Red wine, poured into the cup hours before, spilled onto the white tablecloth.

"Look at you, Ada," he continued, ignoring the spreading stain. At that we all looked; his words seemed like a command. But what I saw was a moment of such deep anguish, such a private moment, I instantly regretted turning my mother's way. She was tear-streaked, rocking back and forth in her chair, her crossed arms squeezing her middle and wrinkling her housedress, her hair utterly disheveled and falling over her face.

"You're a mess," Mort said, nodding. Then, gesturing at the dining table, which was perfectly set only minutes ago but was now in disarray, he declared, "This place is a mess." He darted from his chair and rushed to the kitchen, where dinner preparations had been cut short and the chickens still sat uncooked in their pans on the kitchen table, the loaves of challah still sat in the bakery bags, used cooking utensils were strewn about the table and counters, and dishes were piled at the sink. "A mess!" he sniped, pointing into the kitchen.

As my father re-seated himself my mother rose. She stood for a moment as she'd done the day of our arrival: perfectly still, her eyes closed. But she was a shadow of that self. She held her body with such rigidity it looked contorted. And her grimacing mouth told only of pain.

Finally she opened her eyes.

"How dare you call my house a mess," she told Mort, surprising all of us with her response. But she went on to surprise us further. Pointing to the spilled wine she said, "Morton Leibritsky, son of Zelik Leibritsky, father of Howard, Molly, and our darling Davy Leibritsky: that's *your* mess."

Furious, my father stood, while Ada, finished, dropped into her seat. Her tears began again.

Mort waited before glancing once more at Nina. "Look at this child. Look at that bruise. A *mess,*" he said.

"And there's another child," he added, his voice hushed, his eyes locked on Ada's. "A worse mess," he hissed her way.

While my father condemned my mother, and while the rest of us sat as if frozen, Bec stared dumbly in front of her, her eyes red, her gaze unfocused, her body not stiff, like ours, but slumped. Every so often she buried her head in her hands. "It's my fault," she muttered at long last. "I motioned for him to cross the street. But there was no truck then. I swear. No truck."

At that Mort turned to her, glowered, opened his mouth as if to ask her a question, then closed it as if unable to find the words to speak. He dropped his head again, silenced by Bec's confession. But by the way he'd looked at Bec the instant before, like she'd actually intended to harm Davy, he'd said plenty.

It's hard to know how much time passed after that. Maybe another minute. Maybe an hour. It seemed we were deep into an endless span of night. My mother continued to rock back and forth in her chair. Quietly, she moaned. Bec continued to sit with her head buried in her hands. Vivie continued to console Nina, as did Leo. I continued to stare at the center of my plate. Howard, who'd seemed dazed this whole time, finally got up.

"You're leaving?" Mort asked.

"Toilet," Howard said as he walked away from us, toward the kitchen.

"Let's not blame each other," Leo offered some minutes later, breaking another tense silence. "Clearly it's no one's fault. We all love Davy, yes?"

I glanced up from my dinner plate. *Yes, yes, yes,* I wanted to cry.

But no one spoke; we were silent again, though this time the silence didn't seem so fraught with hostility.

"Where were *you?*" Ada then asked Mort, changing the mood yet again. We were back to blaming. "You usually arrive by then. Why weren't you here?"

At that my father turned to Leo, taking him in fully for the first time that night. "I wasn't here because this man's a god-damned *invalid,*" he snapped. "I was taking care of *him.*"

The words caused Nina and Vivie to jump up, defiantly. "He's a better man than you," I heard Nina whisper. I thought I was the only one. But Vivie repeated Nina's words verbatim. "Yes, he's a better man than you," she told Mort, her voice quavering. She and Nina then looked at each other, surprised.

All the while Leo stared into his lap, sadly.

As Vivie sat back down, careful still to place herself at some distance from Ada, she said, "Nobody's an invalid. Let's not get carried away."

"A little late for that," Mort answered, clearly insulted. After a moment he said, "Where's Howard? Why's he not back yet?" He looked around and then asked about Howard a second time. By the third time his wrath was full-blown, his voice the loudest that night. "Goddamnit. Where the hell's Howard?" he cried again and again.

In fact Howard had not gone to the bathroom but had left the cottage, snuck out the back door, and gone down to the beach. He spent a long night there, exhausting himself by hammering his fists into the sand, by racing a jagged to-and-fro in the dark, and by calling out to Davy, over and over.

Bec, too, went down to the beach, eventually. Her journey was at dawn. Making her way to the shore's edge, she passed Howard, asleep by then on the sand. She was still in her New Haven clothes: pleated skirt, paisley print blouse, new hose. Once at the water, she felt its coolness on her ankles and shins. After a time she dropped down, first to her knees, and then she sat, letting the water rush into her lap, up to her waist, splashing as high as her chest. At some point she ripped her blouse at its collar then ripped her pleated skirt, many times, at its hem. When she returned to the cottage to finally try to sleep, I sat up, momentarily, to see her pass by me on her way to the sunporch. I almost didn't know her, this woman in wet shreds.

Upstairs in the cottage my father spent the night alone, in the boys' room, on Davy's bed.

Nina slept upstairs too that night, on blankets laid on the floor beside her parents.

And that left me alone on the sofa bed for the first time that summer.

"What's happening now?" I so often uttered as I tossed and turned that night. At one point I actually dreamed myself asking the question. I was in Mrs. Rankoff's living room, still staring at her braided rug, her faded still life of daisies, and that happy photograph of her family on the wall. She was on guard at the door, as before, but in the dream she was bigger, filling the room as she did my mind, like a kind of omnipresence, a kind of god. "There's no need for you to see this, sweetie," she said in the dream. Then she commanded, "Now just hold still."

To obey her I hauled in a deep breath and held it. I began to see stars. I began to feel like I was exploding. I understood, even in my dream state, that this deprivation was not what Mrs. Rankoff meant. But still I refused to breathe. To do so would have been to move one tiny speck past the moment of Davy's accident. To do so would have been to leave him behind. That was the dream's logic, and it was bigger, even more commanding, than the reenvisioned Mrs. Rankoff.

And so I didn't breathe, didn't move, and continued in my dream to see stars, then after a time to see myself weeping as I floated along with millions of stars in an otherwise dark and endless expanse.

Though Davy would live for the next week, he died on the eighth day after the accident. Between that first Saturday and the next my parents stood vigil at the hospital, with Howard driving them to the center of Milford, dropping them off, then returning late each evening to drive them back to us at Woodmont so they could get a little sleep. There were days when Howard would drive back again, to see Davy himself or to take one or another of us in for a visit. During a crisis like that it was good to have a thing to do, one useful thing, and that's what the driving that week gave him.

Vivie also had one useful thing: she prepared our food, except when Mrs. Isaacson's granddaughter Judy came by to take over that task. To everyone's surprise, Judy, by then five months pregnant, was as unstoppable that week as she'd been lethargic all summer. But our crisis became Judy's cause. She cooked for us, cleaned for us, shopped for us. In our kitchen, she and Vivie even argued once, gently, over who would sit for a much-needed rest, the pregnant one with the sore feet or the one who didn't know minute by minute if her nephew would live or die. That's how Judy with her newfound purpose put it, and Vivie, hand to her heart, sat.

Bec, who in ordinary times had many useful things to do, all connected to her sewing and designing, stopped her work, and most of the week she stayed by herself, sitting for hours in the wicker chair in her sunporch and smoking more than usual, or going off in bare feet for long, solitary walks along the water's edge. At supper Vivie nearly had to force her to eat. "Come on, Bec," Vivie urged over and over. "We can't afford another disaster in the form of you starving."

Nina and Leo were inseparable, sitting side by side on the front porch, his arm over her shoulders, her face often pressed into his chest as she cried yet again. They didn't read. They simply sat there, looking seaward.

Sometimes I sat with them. Other times I wandered into the kitchen to watch as Vivie or Judy prepared the next meal.

Occasionally one of them would ask me to set the table and I'd rush forward, a little too eager to finally have something clear and useful to do.

Mark Fishbaum, who had also been at the accident scene, came by each day that week, always with a fresh bouquet of flowers. "For your family," he told me each time he arrived, knocking on our cottage door, and I'd nod and take the bouquet from him. "See you tomorrow," he'd then say. He didn't even ask for Howard, who he seemed to know wouldn't have the heart yet to say hello. I didn't say anything to him the entire week either, but each afternoon from Wednesday on I found myself peeking out a side window to see if Mark was on his way again.

That was another thing to do.

The first Wednesday following the accident,

early in the evening, Howard drove us all in together to see Davy. This was the first time we'd be there en masse. Our parents were already there. Howard knew that later that evening he'd have to take us home in two trips.

"I don't mind," Howard said. "Really, I don't."

Upon our arrival Ada was sitting by Davy's bed, holding his hand, rubbing it between hers. Mort was behind Ada, pacing the length of the room.

Davy had tubes stuck into him, and his head, partially wound with white bandages, looked larger than it should have, out of proportion with his small, thin body. His left arm was in a cast, and most of his torso was wound with white bandaging as well. He looked like a mummy, a wrapped-up little mummy with a blanket thrown over his legs and tubes coming out of his nose and wrist.

He was asleep. Ada told us he'd been that way the whole day, which wasn't surprising. He'd been out nearly nonstop since the accident, and in the few moments when he'd awakened he'd not said a word.

"He needs his rest," she said, reaching over his body to rub his hand. "He's hungry, he needs nourishment, but he needs his rest most of all."

Then she admonished us to whisper because to talk would risk waking Davy and
risk the hospital staff finding out, against
their rules, that so many of us were there.
Our whispers were ridiculous in their banality. "Hi, Davy," most of us offered, for lack
of anything better to say. Bec said more.
"Get better. You get better now," she urged,
leaning over his face, kissing his nose, which
was one of the only unwrapped pieces of
him.

My father stopped pacing and made a
point of standing by Bec, looking at her
coldly while she spoke to Davy. When Bec
finished, she stood off to the side, a step or
so away from the rest of us. Though days
had passed since the accident and we were
no longer hurling blame at each other, Mort
was still looking at everyone with a stunned
expression, as if only then seeing us for who
we were: Ada, Bec, Howard, Nina, Leo,
everyone, as he saw it, who'd had a direct
role in the unfolding of the events leading
to the accident. He was no longer yelling at
everyone, just glaring now and again. He
was even angry with Vivie, just for being
Nina's mother. And, it seemed, with me too,
for my role, innocent as it was, as witness to
the whole thing. Then there were other

times when he seemed more irate at himself than anyone else for his absence when his family was in need.

"He knows to get better," Mort said in response to Bec's words, his tone agitated but controlled.

"Shoosh," Ada scolded. "Mort, *whisper.*"

We'd fallen into another one of our collective wordless trances, all of us mute as we stared and stared at the sleeping Davy, when footsteps outside the door grew louder and the faint smell of something smoky and familiar — cigars — wafted into the room. I turned and there was Sal, standing meekly in the doorway. He was dressed not in his usual Good Humor whites but in a dark suit and tie, and at first I didn't recognize him. He wasn't smoking a cigar, but his clothes reeked nonetheless. In one hand he held his fedora while in the other he carried a large bouquet of late-summer flowers, mums and daisies.

"I hope you don't mind I've come," Sal said, taking the smallest step toward us. Everyone had turned his way by then. When no one answered, Sal didn't proceed farther.

Just seeing Sal caused a relief I couldn't explain. I rushed over to him and wrapped my arms around him, and when I felt his arms around me I began to wail as if it were last Friday again and the accident and ordeal to ensue had just begun. I'd been wanting to do that — bury my head in someone's chest — for the longest time, though I hadn't known it until that moment.

"Molly, darling," Sal said quietly as he patted my head and back. "Ah, darling . . . It's a terrible thing. I'm so sorry. So very sorry."

When I recovered some and lifted my head I stayed where I was, beside Sal in the doorway. The rest of the family silently faced us. Nina's eyes were almost as tearful as mine, and Leo had his arm wrapped tightly around her. She seemed to want to join me and Sal but something kept her from moving. Then Howard took a step Sal's way, but only a step. Still, Sal moved his hat to the same hand that was holding the bouquet and reached out to Howard, but Howard didn't come closer.

"Oh, you kids," Sal said, dropping his hand and looking at each of us. "So terribly sad . . ."

"Of course they're sad," my mother said, still trying to keep her voice to a whisper. "And why do you think they're sad? Why is that, Sal?"

Instinctively, I froze. Though I let go of

Sal, I remained at his side.

Sal was about to speak again, but before he could Vivie spoke on his behalf. "Ada, come on, we're past that now," she urged, her voice no louder than my mother's.

"Careful now," Howard said, speaking particularly gently, as he did whenever he wanted to win our mother over. "You don't need to get wound up."

"Wound up?" Ada said, her voice, against her own advice, rising in volume. "How can I not get wound up when the man who hit my son is here?"

Bec said, "Ada, we all know it's not his fault. We've been through this so many times already."

Ada was nevertheless adamant. "Get him out of here," she said, her voice even louder than before. "Get him away from my son."

But Sal had already stepped backward, just out of the room, when Davy rolled a bit to one side and then, blinking first, opened his eyes.

Our mother had wakened him.

He blinked several times more before focusing his gaze on the doorway, directly in his line of vision.

He lifted a finger as if waving Sal's way. He even mouthed something, though no sound came forth. Then his eyelids dropped closed again.

"See you later, Davy boy," Sal whispered. The flowers in his hand shook from his trembling.

He backed fully out of the room, turned, and raced down the hospital hallway. I followed him, calling to him. When he stopped, I caught up and he held me again. It was an accident, I assured him, crying as I told him so. Even if we didn't act like it, I said, we all knew that.

He hung his head; he nodded.

Two days later Sal had a fruit basket delivered to the hospital. Then, the following Tuesday, he ordered flowers to be delivered to our home in Middletown, a late-afternoon drop-off following Davy's funeral. He didn't risk any cards, any identification of himself, but we knew who'd sent the flowers. My mother wanted them thrown in the wastebasket, but Vivie took them. "Something to console Nina," she said. The third delivery was of money, fifty dollars, as much as Sal could spare that month. Ada wanted to throw that out too, but Mort took the bills from her before she could tear them up. By the next month, when Sal sent another fifty dollars, Ada had calmed down just enough to hand over the envelope to

Mort without comment. And so it began: fifty-dollar payments every month, always the first Monday, for the next decade, and always, once received, forwarded promptly to Reuben Leibritsky in Israel, who needed it the most, Mort insisted, even in the years after Reuben's small department store, opened in Haifa, finally began to thrive.

For weeks after the accident Sal's Good Humor truck, which he refused to drive, remained parked in front of his house. During this time there were moments when he wondered about the children on his route, and sometimes he approached his truck, leaned his back against it, and rattled off their names — Edna Muldoon, Kevin Amato, Binnie Rosenstein, Amanda Pratt, Tommy Monroe — one after the other until his feet ached and he had to go inside to sit down.

One night nearly a month after the accident, after his own children were asleep in bed, he walked outside, climbed into the truck, and stared at the night sky. He hadn't dared sit in the driver's seat since the accident. But having finally returned, he leaned forward to grip the steering wheel as if acknowledging an old friend. Then he pulled at it, attempted to rip it out. When he couldn't he sat back, exhausted. Through the windshield he observed the full moon, emitting a radiance that obliterated the light of most of the stars. The glowing moon looked like a distant spotlight aimed absolutely and singularly at him. He knew he couldn't duck the light. He knew that his life, the one he'd lived for so long, had already become a thing of the past.

Eventually he got out of the truck, stepped onto the tar of his driveway, and, as if he were suddenly on the moon, he watched himself walk away.

He interviewed weeks later for the position of janitor at the hospital in Milford and told his boss-to-be that he knew a lot about cleaning up messes. He used to be a plumber, after all, he explained, but the family business had recently closed, his father had gotten old, and neither he nor his brothers had the heart to carry the business on into the future.

This was the truth — though not nearly the whole, nor central, truth.

When he was asked his name he spoke it in full for the first time in a long time. It didn't even sound like his. "Salvatore Giuseppe Luccino," he said.

16
A Pair of Leibritskys

There was a long-held rumor in the family: Bec didn't ever sleep with her husband, Nelson, not even once. Three years after Davy's death she married him, all right, but no one was convinced that she'd done so with even a modicum of passion for Nelson. Add to that how odd they looked together, she such an attractive, stylish woman and he such a sluggish, squat man, and it was hard to see them as a couple. Or at least a couple with any physical life.

And yet the marriage lasted.

Yesterday when I visited Bec's house I was consumed by those dual mysteries, the way the marriage held and the question of any shared sexual passion between them. Once they'd built their Middletown home in 1953, two years into the marriage, Bec never allowed anyone upstairs. This boundary was similar to the one they'd had from the get-go: they'd never had anyone over to

501

the apartment they shared before that. They were hiding something, we all felt, and what could be more obvious to hide, we figured, than their highly suspected roommate status. Bec reinforced this idea in the way she described the upstairs rooms: a study, a guest bedroom (though they never had guests who stayed over), and "the bedroom." Not once did she say "our bedroom," or even "his" or "my" bedroom.

Last night — New Year's Eve — I climbed the stairs with trepidation, as if finally entering that private realm would bring to it, or myself, some kind of bad luck. Yet how could I make this place my home if half of it was closed off to me? I argued, climbing farther.

Earlier in the day I'd e-mailed Nina the weekly note I sent her. We'd begun exchanging updates after that first visit I made to Berkeley following Howard's death. I sent mine even before hers arrived. There was so much talk of doom this particular New Year's Eve, I wasn't taking chances. *Happy New Millennium,* I wrote. *Fingers crossed,* I added, *We're good to go in the a.m.* And because it was Friday I closed the usual way: *Shabbat Shalom, dearest Nina.*

Hours later I went upstairs. What I saw there was a bedroom, attractive enough and comfortable. A double bed covered with a gray bedspread. A matching gray carpet with a complementary border design of dusty-mauve-colored roses. Straightforward enough furnishings that said nothing of how Bec and Nelson had lived their lives. The guest bedroom offered no clues either. So this is it, I told myself, realizing I wasn't ever going to know any more than I already did, that all the mysteries of the inheritance were coming along with it.

Yet it always seemed that Bec lived here well, or well enough. She did the best she could. After Davy's accident she became what we all became, a survivor of one sort or another, though her guilt — those open arms she held out to Davy — was overwhelming. She had as much reason to blame herself as everyone else involved, and for a long while, she did just that.

But then she took a turn the others didn't take. On the long, tortuous road away from herself, she somehow reversed the process, came back.

Her marriage to Nelson was a first step, though at the time she wouldn't have thought of it that way. Back then the bond between the two was all about their shared grief and shared guilt. Nelson was the first to confess his culpability. He knew about Megan O'Donnell before anyone else did, he told Bec. He could have discouraged Howard, told him he was nuts. And if he had . . . He shook his head. He stared not at Bec, who sat across from him at Regina's restaurant, where they were out for lunch. Early April of 1951, and they'd been coming there for lunch every Saturday for over a year, yet for the first time ever Bec gave Nelson what felt to him like her whole attention. Then she told him her part of it.

"I don't feel so alone," she said once she'd finished, turning to Nelson as they rose to fetch their coats at the meal's end. "Thank you for that. I don't feel good. Just not so alone."

"Me too," Nelson had said.

Once she married Nelson, some five months later, she had more reason than before to stop in every so often at Leibritsky's Department Store, and the work there — which gradually became central to Bec's life — was another step bringing her closer to her lost self, the person she was the moment before she opened her arms to Davy from the other side of Beach Avenue.

At first her trips to the store were only occasional, and mostly to get away from Ada, whom Bec still cared for. By the fall of 1951 my mother was functioning well enough, but she'd turned her loss of Davy into many unappealing things: a reason to hate the largely Italian community of Middletown, a reason to hate especially clear and sunny days, a reason to hate her present life in favor of an ever more nostalgically perfected past.

Bec, like the rest of us, didn't have the patience she'd once had for Ada, despite her lingering anguish. And so Bec occasionally gave herself a day off, spending the morning quietly at home, sipping coffee at the table, staring out the window, then flipping on the radio and listening to whatever program she happened upon. But sometimes she spent those rare mornings cooking something up for Nelson for lunch. "Hot lunch," she'd then announce, marching into Leibritsky's Department Store, the paper bag in her arms filled with containers of roasted chicken, mashed potatoes, and boiled peas.

Early April of 1952 Bec had done just that, brought Nelson a hot lunch, when she made her first foray into business, suggesting before she even set down the bag of food a minor rearrangement of the sales floor. Some women's hats had come in, perfect for Easter. "Perhaps if you put that hat rack where more women see it," Bec said, turning to Mort, "more would sell." She smiled, as glad to stretch some old, unused muscle in her mind as she was to be away from Ada. Though her sister had shed her initial anger at Nina for fibbing about Howard, for setting her in motion that day out the door and on the chase, she continued to hold on to her blame of Sal Luccino. If Ada had been ugly with her prejudice before the accident, after it she was worse, more hateful, more irrationally so. But it was easier for Ada to blame Sal, Bec knew, than herself. And the strategy, however unfair, may very well have been the only way her sister could survive. The ugliness was choking, though, and on that day Bec had fled, leaving Ada with her bitterness.

At Leibritsky's, Bec glanced from Mort to the hat rack, motioning that the rack should be moved from the rear of the store, where the women's apparel was, to the entrance.

Mort thought not. "I think we know what we're doing by now," he told her.

Bec opened her mouth to disagree, but the way Mort looked, the tightness in his neck and jaw, the slight rise of his chest, suggested to her that she had best be quiet. "Just a thought," she managed at long last to mutter.

A month later, once Bec and Nelson finished lunch — salami grinders which they ate in the basement while listening to a new Sinatra album — Bec attempted again to make a change in the way the store did business.

She and Nelson had just emerged from below when a female customer walked in. She looked around then turned to Leo, and then to Nelson.

"I'm looking for a dress for my daughter's graduation," the woman explained. "I've been to two other places but the folks there were so pushy. And they just don't seem to have what I want."

"Leibritsky's never pushes," Bec said, scooting past Leo and Nelson, then taking the woman's gloved hand in her own. And even though Bec did push, urging the woman, by way of compliments, to purchase both an afternoon and an evening dress, the woman said at the end, speaking to Mort, who rang up the purchase, "She was right. She knew exactly what I wanted."

Only Howard, now at Wesleyan, had been so slick at sales. Once the woman left, Leo pointed that out to Mort. But Mort said nothing, just looked stone-faced as he held the door open for Bec even before she was gloved, buttoned, and ready to go.

That night Bec asked Nelson if she'd gone too far. "I really do think I see what the store could use," she told him, recalling the hat rack they should have moved. "I've got an itch to participate. But maybe the thing to do is to set up my own dressmaking shop," she said.

"Mort's a bully," Nelson remarked, surprising Bec. "The more you fade away with each punch, the stronger Mort gets."

Emboldened by Nelson's words, the next time Bec went to Leibritsky's she insisted the hat rack be moved. As a matter of fact, she added, she had ideas about rearranging the departments, changing their locations so that "one thing, naturally enough, leads to the next." First in that process, she declared, was women's clothes and accessories, which should be moved from the back to the front, where the men's clothes were now. "Let's face it. *Far* more of your customers are women," she told Mort, who with his bristling was clinging, she saw, to what little control he had left in the world. "But everything she's said makes sense," Leo pointed out as Mort stood, arms crossed, his chin tucked in, slowly shaking his head.

Despite Mort's resistance, Leo's comment pushed the debate in Bec's direction. After a stretch of silence, Mort relented. "We'll try it for a month," he said before turning from them and shutting himself in his office for the rest of the afternoon.

That month was a good one for profits, and another boom month led to the next until finally, come the new year, even Mort agreed the change should be permanent. Bec's next idea came readily enough and included that the very items Leibritsky's Department Store sold were problematic. "You're out of date," she told the men on a cloudy afternoon in February 1953. She straightened Nelson's ten-year-old tie. She brushed the dusty shoulders of Mort's ancient suit jacket. For Leo, drowning in his oversized pants and jacket, she offered only a sad smile. "Just look at you," she said to the three, shaking her head. "Not even a whiff of fashion sense."

The next morning my father woke from a troubling dream. He and his father were standing on the Leibritsky's Department Store sales floor, though the place, oddly, was clean of any merchandise. Zelik Leibritsky, facing him, wore a business suit, stylishly double-breasted. On his feet were gleaming wing tips, which was also strange. Mort wanted to ask his father, "What happened to you?" but before he did his father asked him that very question.

"What do you mean?" Mort's forehead was beaded with sweat.

"I started this store in nineteen nineteen," his father told him. "Back then Jews weren't always welcome in the stores of goyim, or in the doctors' offices of goyim, or in the universities of goyim, or even in their towns. But it's a different day now."

Zelik was already leaving. As he opened the front door and a gust of cold February air blew in, he asked, "How's Mrs. Leibritsky?"

"What's Ada got to do with this?" Mort was chilled by the air and confused by the question.

"That's just it," Zelik said. "My son, times have changed. There's more than one Mrs. Leibritsky now."

As Zelik left, walking down Main Street, he became smaller, then smaller still, until finally the man looked to be the size of a boy, someone eight years old, say, and then he was nothing, just the palpable absence of someone disappeared.

Mort shot up, awake, and reviewed the sequence of events that had led to Davy's accident. He could see Nina polishing the candlestick just as she was telling Ada about the Irish girl. And he could see Ada running out of the house, and even hear her sandals clomp as she rushed out onto Beach Avenue. He could see Howard tumble from the Sailfish and shoot forward, swimming to shore. *And if he had not indulged himself in a hot dog.* He could see Bec across Beach Avenue, surprised and delighted at the sight of Ada and the children. And he could see Sal Luccino in his driver's seat, leaning out the side window of his truck. *And if he had not been late.*

My father pushed himself to his feet, attempting to rise from his bed. But he couldn't.

He fell back. He fainted.

In 1972 I began to work at Leibritsky's Department Store. Bec was fully in charge of the store by then. My father, who ever since that dream had come to the store not five days a week but three days, or sometimes two, had finally fully retired. Leo retired as well. Nelson, at sixty-six years old, still hung about the place, but mainly in the mornings. For so many years already Nelson's role was mainly as Bec's helping hand, a function for which he was so much better suited than that of the store's so-called business executive. He had ample time, then, in the afternoons to sit at the booth in his kitchen, flipping through cookbooks, planning what to make Bec that night. She didn't love him, she merely liked him, but that didn't mean he couldn't love her. In his married life Nelson gave himself that much freedom and in doing so he became, to everyone's astonishment, an accomplished chef.

The year I came to Leibritsky's, Bec would begin the third and final step in her largely accidental process of self-reclamation: she would start to sew again, make dresses to order. One quiet Saturday night in May she had Nelson help her lug her old Singer up from the basement and move it to a corner of the living room. Carefully, she greased the treadle. Minutes later, her foot pumping, she revved the ancient thing back to life.

By the end of that evening she knew she'd buy an electric; of course she would. No one would take her seriously with that primitive clunker. Swiping her brow, she knew she wouldn't have to work as hard either. But she grew unnerved by the thought that she'd lose the physical give and take between herself and the machine if it were powered by some foreign, outside source. Electricity would take her body out of it, the body that was the conduit for the language she and the Singer had come to speak, were speaking again.

"How's it going?" Nelson asked as he looked in on her later that night.

"Lost in talk," Bec answered, nodding. "Lost in talk."

Lost in talk was how I often felt with Bec, who by then had become one of my closest friends as well as a kind of second mother. Since my divorce in 1966 we'd met every other week or so for dinner out, just us two. "I don't like that you're so alone, Molly," Bec had told me when we'd begun sharing meals.

A month after Bec had revived her dormant Singer we met at a small Greek restaurant in Hartford, close enough to G. Fox's that I could walk there when I got off that night from work. Lost in talk that night meant that Bec listened and nodded as I complained about the man I was then dating, Bob Neddlestein, who had a job at Aetna Insurance. He was at the top of Aetna's corporate ladder, had plenty of money, and once we began our relationship he liked to treat me to lavish vacations. I'd never been on lavish vacations before and they were certainly easy to take, even if I sometimes yawned at the dinner table conversation. That night with Bec, Bob and I had just returned from a week at a Swiss spa, where I'd done as much yawning as lying around.

"An entire week of lying around?" Bec looked skeptical.

"Pretty much," I answered. "The whole point of a spa is to relax. We read. Talked. Ate. Bob took long swims and I took mineral baths. In the afternoons we both couldn't help it: we napped." I nodded, recalling the pleasant enough bed I'd so easily dropped off on. "We went to bed early, too," I added.

"Oh, Molly," Bec said, clearly disappointed. "You sound like you're eighty years old. I just don't believe that two people who love each other, healthy and young enough like you two, rest and nap and go to bed early for an *entire* vacation."

I was eating a salad, but I stopped. I'd never heard Bec talk about the nuts and bolts of romance, but here she was, doing so with surprising authority.

"You're not even close to being in love," she continued. "What are you doing with that man? Is this Mark Fishbaum all over again? Are you just filling a hole? Is that what this is?"

When I dropped my fork, flummoxed, a

waiter came rushing over to hand me a new one.

"I think there was something a little more genuine with Mark," I told Bec after a time. My words, measured, were also sad.

She nodded. "Of course there was." Her tone was gentler. "All that history. That's very real stuff, Molly. You can't say he didn't know where you were coming from."

"No. Can't say that."

I went silent. Bec ate some of her food but I only stared at my salad.

"Penny for your thoughts," Bec said after some minutes had passed.

I shrugged but otherwise didn't answer.

She waited another minute. "Two pennies."

"I was just remembering how I woke up this morning at seven fifteen," I told Bec, my voice hesitant. "I sat on the side of the bed and all I could do was look down at my bare feet. When I looked at the clock again it was nine twelve. Bec, I don't know where the time went." I paused. "Which is kind of what I'd say about my whole life."

Bec sighed. "Molly, maybe a change of scenery would be good," she then suggested. Soon enough she rolled out her plan: she and I would co-own the family store. We'd rename Leibritsky's Department

Store, simply enough, Leibritsky's. The new place would be just for women's wear, much of it specially made by her. She wanted it to look like a parlor, with plush upholstered chairs strewn throughout and an openness that would replace the cramped aisles. She also wanted a back room for her sewing machines, the old Singer that she couldn't part with and the new one she'd just bought. "Eleanor Roosevelt," she said, speaking of her aged mannequin, "is dusted off and ready to go too."

I listened, ate some salad, listened some more.

A moment later, when I still hadn't spoken, she grew even more intent. "I'm throwing you a lifeline. Grab it, Molly. Grab it."

"I'm not drowning," I insisted.

"No? Seems to me you've been under water since you were twelve years old," she said.

And with that — a smack of truth — I agreed to become part of Leibritsky's.

And with that — Bec's and my co-ownership — Leibritsky's stopped having anything at all to do with men.

We worked well together, Bec and I, and when I think of those years, which were the years of my late thirties and forties, I can't help but feel the relief that the change was meant to bring, as big a relief as breaking it off, finally, with Bob Neddlestein. Bec's and my joint venture worked straightforwardly: as the store's buyer I sometimes traveled, but more often I was in town, in the store, generally managing things. Bec was pretty much always in the back room, making something. Her reputation spread quickly throughout the Connecticut River Valley.

Though busy, we made time for each other, lunching together at least three times a week. All those years, then, we were lost in talk. And all those words and lunches and dresses and customers added up to something profound. She showed me that, in the end, with the gift of her house.

In 1986, when Bec was seventy-five, she began to consider retiring. Nelson had already died, as had Leo and my father — the deaths of age and illness, which were deeply sad but not shocking, bruising, unacceptable deaths. But Bec seemed to flourish with time rather than wither. How often did I see her, a woman in her seventies, bending over one of her worktables, her forehead wrinkled in concentration, scissors in hand, slicing through a sheet of fabric, only to look up suddenly and break into a wide smile and an effortless wave? How pretty she was, I often thought, waving back, apologizing if I'd interrupted her. Her short hair curled around her face, her glasses hung over her chest, her typical plain turtleneck fit snugly about her upper body, her slacks bagged around her bottom, and her shoes — "old lady" shoes, I used to call them, thick with rubber soles — lifted her nearly an inch from the floor. Though fashion was her work, she was hardly a beacon of style anymore herself. She was simply somebody who made things — dresses, it turned out — and as long as she was concentrating on her craft she was satisfied. That absorption was her beauty, and it was a gift to witness.

We were, as they say, ladies of a certain age, both of whom had been married and not, both of whom had had careers that were unexpected and unexpectedly long, both of whom had never had children and therefore wouldn't have grandchildren, both of whom had extra time during the evenings which were often spent alone. Late winter of 1986, though Bec could certainly justify retiring, she still wasn't sure. She had her health. She was a little stiff, maybe, but otherwise, she said, she couldn't complain. What would she do with her days? We talked about this one evening. She had a dress in one hand at the time, a bat mitzvah dress, a green velvet mini, and the steamer in the other, giving it the final touch. Once it was done, she held it up for me to see.

"Wasn't so long ago when a girl wouldn't even dream of having a bat mitzvah, much less having one in a minidress," she said.

She nodded thoughtfully. But after a minute it seemed to me her mind was less on the dress than on some private memory. She smiled to herself.

I mentioned how lovely I thought the dress was and she refocused, hanging it on a nearby rack. Then she sat. For a time, while I fussed with paperwork, she was quiet.

I'm not sure how much time passed, but eventually I turned her way. "So?" I said.

"So?"

"So what do we do now?" I closed the accounts book I had opened and scooped up my paperwork.

Bec laughed, and when I turned her way she said, "Molly, you sound just like you did as a child. 'What do we do now?' How many times did I hear that? The three of you never seemed to know quite how to fill a day. But Nina could. She was in the driver's seat, even then. Am I right?"

"Nina didn't always know," I suggested,

but without much conviction. "She had her moments too."

Again we were silent, and as Bec reached for some peanuts her quiet munching was the only sound that filled the room. "I can hear myself asking that question," she said after a time. "We were little girls once, me and Ada and Vivie, and we asked it over and over. Our father would get exasperated sometimes. He'd turn to our mother and say, 'What are you waiting for? Tell them what to do!' 'Be good,' she'd say to us. 'Be *good* girls.' " Bec laughed. "But that wasn't anything to *do.*"

Bec walked over to the dress and tugged at it, though it didn't need adjusting.

"I was supposed to marry Milton Goldberg," she continued. I knew as much. I nodded. "And when he broke it off, I had to ask myself, 'What do I do now?' I was sewing at the time, so it seemed a pretty good idea, to keep on sewing."

"But would you have been happy as Mrs. Goldberg?" I asked. I was thinking less of the past than of the present, of our contented time running the store. Nothing about marrying Milton Goldberg would have gotten her to this place, I suspected, and told her as much.

"Maybe. But there would have been children," she said. "That part of it, at least, I know I would have liked."

She turned to me, and recognizing that it was loss, too, that had clouded my life during my childbearing years, she pulled me close. "We're a pair," she whispered. "You and me, Molly."

"A pair of Leibritskys," I said, and for some reason that made us laugh.

When we ate lunch together the next day Bec told me the story of her and Tyler Mc-Mannus. Our talk the night before — its "what ifs" — had clearly stirred her up. That she'd withheld such a tale amazed me. I thought I knew her completely. "Not such a pair of Leibritskys," I suggested at one point.

"Why didn't you go back?" I asked some minutes later, after she told me about that doomed trip to New Haven in those months after Davy's death. "Why'd you marry Nelson?"

"I made Tyler wait too long," she said. "In fact, for a while I actually gave up on him. He knew it better than me."

She stared into her teacup for several minutes. When she looked up, her smile was deliberate. "Well, as it turned out I wasn't alone. I had Nelson. And what we shared

521

between us, about Davy, was quite a bond, really. And then we grew to know each other. Nelson, you know, was a pretty dear fellow. He told me over and over again that he'd never hold me back."

I'd heard Nelson say that very thing.

"But he wasn't Tyler," I remarked.

"God, no," was all she said to that.

We finally paid the bill, then walked arm in arm up Main Street. Bare dogwoods, still decorated with holiday lights, lined the street. "Did you ever speak to Tyler after that?" I asked. By *that* I meant the day she saw Tyler with his newborn and his wife. We'd gotten that far in her recollections.

"No, never."

"You didn't try to get in touch even once?"

"Oh, I tried," she said. "You've no idea how I tried." She almost stumbled and I grabbed her arm. When she turned to thank me her expression was strained.

"Too late to try again?" I asked, gently, as we moved forward once more.

"Much too late. He's dead. Gone six years now."

We'd approached the store but she didn't seem in a hurry to get back to work. As we lingered outside, I asked, "Did you go to his funeral?"

"No. I would have, but I found out too

late. He was buried by the time I knew. But I've taken a drive, visited his grave from time to time. I like to bring him flowers. Him and Sal Luccino. Found his grave, too, not far from Tyler's. Wasn't looking for it. Just found it. Amidst a whole crowd of Luccinos."

She nodded while I took a moment to take in the news of Sal.

"Maybe you and Tyler can be buried side by side," I finally offered, thinking — nonsensically — they'd at least have that.

"I'd rather be able to really talk to him, but I appreciate the thought. Anyway, it's a Catholic cemetery. I can visit, Molly, but I can't stay, not for the long haul. Besides," she added, "at this point I want to be buried near my sisters."

She opened the door of the store and I followed her to the back room, where we hung up our coats.

"Molly," she called as I left for the sales floor. Her tone had a touch of urgency. "It's *you* who can still go back," she said.

17
DISPLACED PERSONS

Bec's words turned out to be prescient. I could go back, and I did, first to Mark Fishbaum, and then to Woodmont itself.

As it happened, I ran into Mark the next week, in Hartford, where we were both visiting his father in the hospital. Judge Fishbaum, as everyone still called him, had broken his hip, and the news came my way fast, the way it always did, via the busy mouths of several Leibritsky's customers.

"I didn't know you'd be here," I told Mark when I stepped into the hospital room. In the twenty years since our divorce we'd seen each other only a few times, the last of which was at Howard's funeral. I stood with my hand over my heart.

"Sit down, Molly, this could take a while," Mark said. He lifted *War and Peace* from his lap. "See what I mean?" he quipped. But instead of reading he rose, and I was so pleased when he rushed over to embrace me.

His father, meanwhile, begged him not to joke; it hurt when he laughed, he complained. Judge Fishbaum — I was never able to call him anything less formal, though he'd wanted me to — reached for my hand. "Dear Molly," he said. "It's been too long. Where you been?"

We got our hellos and don't-you-look-goods out of the way quickly. Mark did look good, insofar as he looked remarkably unchanged, despite the fifteen years that had passed since I'd last seen him. I tried not to stare, but I couldn't help it, and Mark, I noticed, couldn't help but stare at me. We smiled, truly happy for the unexpected reunion.

Judge Fishbaum, unlike Mark, had certainly aged. Upon my arrival he struggled to sit up but, too tired, eased back against his stacked pillows. He was a widower now, I knew, just two years beyond the loss. Despite his happy greeting I saw sadness in his face, some lingering grief, and I apologized up front for missing my former mother-in-law's funeral; I'd been on a buying trip for the store, I explained. He nodded while Mark said for them both, "We loved your card and flowers. We understand,

Molly." Once I settled into a chair, Mark began to read, to both of us this time, an act I found comforting and so much wiser than pushing for an instant conversation between us. Yes, Mark looked the same — and he said as much about me — but in fact we were strangers.

"Going to drop off. Nothing personal, Molly," Judge Fishbaum, yawning, announced after a time, and indeed he did drop off, closing his eyes a moment later. Mark rose, kissed his father's forehead, pulled the blanket to his neck.

"Coffee?" he then asked me, his voice a whisper, and though I knew I should get back to the store, I was struck by how caring he'd just been. I remembered, suddenly, how many times during our courtship and short marriage he'd brought me a cup of tea, or a blanket, or simply held me close. I recalled, too, the summer bouquets he carried to our cottage each day following Davy's accident, the way he'd simply drop them off and know, with a wisdom beyond his years, to leave us be.

That afternoon, back at the store, when I told Bec about the hospital visit and that Mark and I had decided to meet for lunch the next week, she asked, "Filling a hole still, Molly?"

"Maybe I missed something back then," I answered. "But it doesn't matter. I'm pretty sure he's still married. He wasn't wearing a ring and I didn't ask, but I'm pretty sure."

"How could you not have asked *that*?"

"We kept to the present: his father's health, the hospital's bad coffee, traffic, weather. Simple stuff. It was like we were in a little bubble. Bec, I didn't want it to burst."

"I hope for your sake, then, he's not married. Take it from me, Molly," she said, "that'll burst it. Sure will."

"For old times' sake" is the rationale I offered Mark for the suggestion that he and I get together the next week at Jimmies of Savin Rock, the old hot dog stand in West Haven, now a full, and fully enclosed, restaurant. Mark lived in a suburb north of New York City and he figured we could meet in the vicinity of New Haven. We settled on the following Thursday, which turned out to be a chilly and windy March day. We were seated in a booth by one of the restaurant's large ocean-side windows, and because of how I felt — anxious with yearning — I peered out the window rather than at Mark while I offered him a series of banal opening remarks about the ocean's lively, frothy waves.

"Haven't seen that in a while," Mark said, nodding toward the water, then peering at it, and I could see him then on the shore's edge at Woodmont, a year after Davy died, the year of our coming together, upside down and walking on his hands, trying to make me smile. "Give it a try," he'd urged of the handstands, but I didn't. I'd hurled my sorrow into cartwheels instead.

For the next hour I poured out the news from the years of our separation. In the end I said everything I'd hoped to say to Mark except what I'd only just begun to grasp: that as long as I expected him to fill a hole that no one could fill, it wasn't that I didn't love him but that I couldn't love him. Or couldn't feel my love for him. I was too busy blaming him for not assuaging my grief.

But a confession like that was too much too soon. Instead I listened as he told me his story: the second marriage that was still on, the three children's ages, looks, and interests. I nodded, and though my heart sank further with each detail he imparted, I managed to smile agreeably throughout. By the time he'd finished we'd eaten most everything. Our waitress brought us coffee, and as we sipped it I began, as I had earlier, to glance anxiously out the window. The sea

seemed so suddenly and terribly lonely —
but that was just a projection, I knew, of
me.

"I was hoping," I told Mark when I looked
back at him. I pointed at him then at myself.
"But that would be too easy, right? Like
magic. Like a fairy tale."

Mark was kind, as usual. He reached for
my hands and I extended them, perhaps too
eagerly, his way. "I've got this family now.
But I've never stopped loving you." He
paused, then said gently, "Linda Bagel."

My eyes welled up at the sound of the old
puppet's name. What didn't Mark know
about me?

He continued, "But I love my family, too."

"Of course."

"It's just bad timing. That's all it is."

We both turned to the window again.

When we got outside we stood for a time
leaning against the hood of his car. The
gusts had calmed, enough to allow me to
feel the sun on my face more than the wind.
Mark's eyes gleamed in the brightness.

"Guess we won't be doing this again
anytime soon." I squinted up at him.

"No, guess not," he said.

We'd pulled apart and were about to get
going, in our separate cars, when Mark sug-

gested we take a drive to Woodmont together. He checked his watch; it was going
on four o'clock. But he'd recently gotten a
call from Arthur Weinstein, the pugnacious
one of the twins, who'd become a major
developer in the area. Arthur thought he
might have something for Mark and his
family.

"The brat's persuasive," Mark told me,
his eyebrows raised, as were mine. "And get
this, Molly. He's stinking rich. Why do the
goods always go to the undeserving?"

I shook my head. "My uncle Leo used to
ask that same thing," I said.

We drove first to Woodmont's west end,
where the cottages of Bagel Beach used to
be. But even before we'd parked we knew
that the homes there were long gone to
more developers than just Arthur Weinstein.
After all, it had been a while since Jews
needed to huddle so close together. In the
decades since our childhood the tight ethnic
worlds inside Milford had gradually opened
their borders. A newer wave of immigrants
were now telling their tales from whatever
pockets of America they inhabited about
huddling and separating and assimilating
and holding on. Our story, in that sense,
was over. And our cottage, too, was gone,
had been sold long ago, ten years after the

accident, when everyone finally realized they just didn't want to go back anymore. But rising from Mark's car, staring wide-eyed at the extensive condominium complex before me and seeing right through its concrete walls to the old mishmash of wooden cottages that used to be there, I felt the call of memory, which is a different kind of story, born of a separate need.

And remember we did. We stood on the sands of a beach no longer known as Bagel Beach and suddenly there was a younger Mark, sitting on a bright orange life preserver beside Howard and then rising to drag the Sailfish's shiny hull to the water's edge. And there I was, cross-legged on the porch steps of the cottage, dissatisfied with Linda Bagel on my hand, hoping that Nina, her head in a book, sitting right behind me, would finally take notice of me. Minutes later, Mark and I passed the synagogue, still known as Hebrew Congregation of Woodmont, but more than the building I saw my father, with Leo, Howard, and Davy in tow, walking briskly and confidently on their way to join the minyan.

Beyond the synagogue Mark and I soon passed Sloppy Joe's, now called Sloppy José's, and the Villa Rosa, and I felt some relief to see these businesses still intact, though empty and boarded up for the off season. Finally we came to Anchor Beach, where we dropped onto a bench. Yards away was another bench, the one Davy and I had sat on, or so it seemed, eating our chocolate-and-vanilla-frosted cookies only hours before his accident. I was sure that was the very bench, I told Mark, but when we rose and walked to it, I could see it was in fact relatively new.

From there we made our way to the corner of Clinton Street and Beach Avenue, where the accident took place. We stood for a time, our backs to the road, staring at the ocean before us, a vast and empty thing, no boats in sight. The intrepid March winds still stirred the waters, and the waves, tumbling forward, were as loud as any in my memory. *Hello, hello,* they seemed intent on calling. Or perhaps their song was more in the way of *good-bye, good-bye.* Across Beach Avenue, Mrs. Rankoff's modest cottage had gone to demolition, replaced by a towering new summer home, plain in the modern way. For a long time, while Mark waited at some distance, I stared into the road at the spot where Davy landed. In the end, I did what people do: grabbed a stone and marked the spot as one would a Jewish grave. Then Mark said gently, "We'd better get going," and so we returned to the car, then left Woodmont and drove off, first toward Jimmies, where I'd left my car, and then, separately, toward what turned out to be our vastly different lives, knowing they'd not intersect like this again.

Only you can go back, Bec had said, but this was years ago already, before she passed away, the last of the sisters to go, leaving her home to me. Now that I've moved in, there are days when I wander around in it and can hear her pumping the treadle of her Singer, expertly running a seam. Other days I sit at that cozy booth, staring out at a wondrous Japanese maple tree, its burgundy foliage — just out — so unlike the green of the other trees. It's not lost on me that what I've become — an experienced business-woman, unmarried, with no children, the final inheritor of the family business — is nothing I'd ever thought I'd be, and perhaps because of that, an oddness I often feel, a deep solitariness, I've come to identify with the singularity of that maple. I consider it a friend. Sometimes — because why not? — I even talk to it, tell it that I'm no more an Esther Bagel than a Linda Bagel, in that my less than conventional attributes have come my way only by default. This particular brand of turmoil is what Bec and I shared most deeply, perhaps, a constant need to figure it out — *what do I do now?* — when the plan, that predictable life we'd always imagined for ourselves, my mother's "right track," slipped, like a loose ring, off our fingers and out of our reach. We arrived at the unmarked territory of our adult female lives not as pioneers but, like our cousin Reuben and all the Jews pouring into Israel after the war — or like the rest of my family, forever unmoored by the events of 1948 — as displaced persons, as refugees.

That day after Sal visited Davy at the hospital, after my mother's rant, after Davy's miraculous near wave of one of his fingers and the way he opened his mouth, seemingly to speak to Sal, Howard drove the family back to the cottage in two shifts. I was taken in the second shift along with my silent parents, my father in the front beside Howard, my mother in the back with me, a seating arrangement we were used to except for the absence of Davy, who always took the hump between me and my mother. Except for Howard, who had to keep his eye on the road, each of us kept turning to that spot, as if seeing Davy there.

Once inside the cottage we walked directly to the dining table, where we'd been gathering each night of the ordeal. The fighting, at least for now, was over. For days we'd simply sat there in the evenings, eaten a bit, and sat some more. Even when my father had taken it upon himself the night before to address Howard's relationship with Megan O'Donnell, there wasn't the yelling we'd expected. He'd said, calmly enough, "You have responsibilities as a Jew. You can't just drop them. You can't just go out into the wide world of America and pick anybody. For you it's different." Howard nodded but then asked, "What about love?" My father laughed wearily. "Love is putting up with a whole lot. Putting up with it and feeling good about it. Howard, my son," he said, gripping his shoulder, "that's love."

Our refrigerator was filled with gifts of casseroles, and by the time our shift arrived at the cottage Bec and Vivie had already heated one and had made a salad to go with it. Nina had set the table and she'd placed one of the many flower bouquets from Mark Fishbaum in the center. And so we began almost instantly and in silence to eat the evening's meal. "Things are looking up," someone, at long last, said. Another added, "Did you see how he wanted to speak to Sal? Did you see Davy recognize him and wave?" Yes, we'd seen, and with all eyes on

Ada each one of us assured her that Davy was progressing nicely, that in fact he'd be fine. There was an upside to Sal's visit, Howard gently suggested, for it had gotten Davy to focus, just a bit, at long last. To our surprise, even my mother agreed that the visit was useful in this singular way. "He's improving, isn't he?" she asked, and a chorus of us rushed to answer, "Sure is. Sure is."

A bubble of hope floated invisibly in the air over our heads, and with it a sense of normalcy — the old life — momentarily returned. Several of us took second helpings. A little boy was injured but he'd soon enough heal. And our lives, too, weren't so deeply changed. There'd be time, still, to pick up where we'd left off. And so sometime during that meal Howard's thoughts drifted, quite helplessly, and despite my father's warnings, to Megan O'Donnell. And Bec spent a moment envisioning the new life that she and Tyler McMannus would soon share. Just before the table was cleared Ada gave a proprietary glance around the dining room, and there it was, just for a second, her old satisfaction with the place — *her* place — rising once again to the surface. And between Vivie and Nina those worries that had arisen in the last week, worries about something, unnameable as yet — a something that was wrong with Nina — were now but a fleeting thing. After dinner Leo could finally get back to his reading, to that article about universal chaos and motion. And Mort could tune in to a baseball game, catch up on the Yankees, whom, like God, he hadn't had any contact with in the last week and sorely missed.

As for myself, I could believe, as I had many times that summer while in the upstairs bathtub, that I was separate from them, wholly different from them. When I said *me,* I sensed anew, I didn't mean *them.*

But then my mother began sobbing and in response we snapped back to attention, dropped our dreams.

The table was almost cleared when the doorbell rang. That would be another neighbor delivering another casserole, some of us must have thought. Though that night Bec was the one to open the door, and to our surprise there was Nelson, making his first visit to Woodmont, asking in a worried voice if there was any news, lately in my dreams when I return to this moment it's me, rushing forward, beating out the others, opening the door, and hoping against hope that with my doing so a faint but unending scream —

which is mine, my mother's, and even my grandfather Maks's — will finally cease.

But when I do no one is there, no one is ever there, and each time this empty space is as much a shock as the last.

"I thought I should come," Nelson said next, his tone hesitant. He then thanked Bec, who he told us had phoned him the day before.

As Bec rose to make Nelson a plate of food, she handed me his hat, which I placed beside my father's on the little table in the dining room with the telephone on it. Earlier the day's mail had arrived and had been placed there too. That's when I saw that Lucinda Rossetti had sent Davy yet another installment of their picture. As Howard carried in an extra chair from the kitchen, and as Nelson sat himself in it, catty-corner between my father and Howard, and as everyone shifted a little, to the left, to the right, and as my father patted Nelson's back, saying, "Good of you to come, brother," I opened the envelope and unfolded its contents. What was remarkable was how clear and perfectly ordinary the scene had become: the original red panel at the bottom was now a red-and-white-checked tablecloth, the three vases on it were rounded and shaded, and the bouquets arising from each vase were fleshed out, one with daisies, one with tulips, and the third left blank for Davy to fill.

ACKNOWLEDGMENTS

I'm deeply grateful to Lee Boudreaux, for her spot-on insights, unstoppable enthusiasm, wise heart, and abundant joy — this process could not have been a happier one; Duvall Osteen, for her kindness, dedication, and skill in agenting this work; Nicole Aragi, for her expert helping hand; Amanda Heller, for the precision and thoroughness of her copyediting; Carina Guiterman, Carrie Neill, Betsy Uhrig, and the entire crew at Little, Brown, for their care and professionalism; my parents, Marian Katz and Myron Poliner, for sharing with me their knowledge and memories of Woodmont, Middletown, the 1940s, and absolutely everything else I asked about; Katherine Krauss Murphy, author of *Woodmont on the Sound* (Postcard History Series), for a book that so helped me envision Woodmont in 1948; Maryke Barber and Rebecca Seipp of the Wyndham Robertson Library at Hollins

University, for invaluable research assistance; the reference team at Russell Library in Middletown, Connecticut, for additional research assistance; Debbie Sessions and Katherine Kominis, for their special knowledge of period details; Rachel Poliner, Tina Daub, Julia Campbell Johnson, Lynne Bonde, and Melanie May, for their unflagging support and for the many helpful mini-consults; the creative writers of Hollins University, colleagues and students, for their fellowship; rabbis Daniel Zemel and Jean Eglinton, for answering my questions about Judaism; and rabbis Louis Witt and Chaim Stern, for the words of prayer from which the title and epigraph of this novel are derived. For three Januarys the Virginia Center for the Creative Arts was a peaceful and enriching environment in which to write, and over several summers Carol Ridker's home was too. I'm grateful to have worked on this book in both places. I'm especially thankful for the time and comments of those who read this work in progress: Marty Lopez, Dan Poliner, and Karen Osborn. I offer special thanks to Barbara Wiechmann, reader of my heart as much as my words. A final and most heartfelt thanks to Edward P. Jones, whose brilliance is boundless, and whose time, talent, generosity, and friendship have meant the world to me.

ABOUT THE AUTHOR

Elizabeth Poliner is the author of *Mutual Life & Casualty,* a novel-in-stories, and *What You Know in Your Hands,* a poetry collection. She teaches creative writing at Hollins University.

The employees of Thorndike Press hope you have enjoyed this Large Print book. All our Thorndike, Wheeler, and Kennebec Large Print titles are designed for easy reading, and all our books are made to last. Other Thorndike Press Large Print books are available at your library, through selected bookstores, or directly from us.

For information about titles, please call:
(800) 223-1244

or visit our Web site at:
http://gale.cengage.com/thorndike

To share your comments, please write:
Publisher
Thorndike Press
10 Water St., Suite 310
Waterville, ME 04901